CW00516959

Who's
Next :

BOOKS BY CHRIS MERRITT

Who's Next?

Chris Merritt

bookouture

Published by Bookouture in 2020

An imprint of Storyfire Ltd.
Carmelite House
50 Victoria Embankment
London EC4Y 0DZ

www.bookouture.com

ISBN: 978-1-83888-022-4
eBook ISBN: 978-1-83888-021-7

For DC, friends twenty years.

DAY ONE

CHAPTER ONE

For as long as I can remember, I wanted to know what it would be like to kill someone.

I'm not exactly sure when I was first aware of that desire to take life. I guess it goes way back, though. One of my earliest memories is of turning over a rock in the park to find a whole world of insects underneath, then squealing in delight as I stamped them all to death while they tried to flee. I hadn't learned that from anyone. I worked out for myself how much fun it was.

A few years later, I developed a fascination with murder in films. My dad owned a huge collection of those old video cassettes and, because he was always out, I watched them whenever I wanted. Whether it was an action flick with Schwarzenegger or Stallone gunning down hapless enemies, or a slasher movie with plenty of up-close blood and guts, killing seemed about the most exciting thing anyone could do. I knew I had to try it someday.

As a teenager, I considered joining the army – even the police – and becoming a sniper or whatever. A job where, if you shot the right person, they'd give you a medal. But I couldn't have dealt with the discipline, the endless orders, the early mornings. There were quicker and easier ways to get a kick out of life. And, the older I got, the more I found.

My lifestyle made the impulse to murder recede for a while. It never completely went away, though. It just lay dormant inside me until the day that everything fell apart. Until my other sources of pleasure and respect were destroyed. Then, nothing was holding me back any longer. More than that, I had a reason to kill. I knew it was time to give in to my fantasy.

Last night, I finally did. Now I've popped my cherry, I'm not going to stop. I've already gone past the point of no return. There are four more people who deserve to die, who need to take the blame for what happened. And, since I've found a new purpose in life, even that may not be the end of it.

It'll only end when they catch me.

If they catch me.

CHAPTER TWO

The older man squinted at the photograph, frowning with effort that turned his craggy face into a mass of lines like a dry riverbed. Then he handed the picture back.

'Nope. Haven't seen her.'

'You sure about that?' Detective Inspector Dan Lockhart held up the image of his wife, Jess. 'Have another look.'

The guy blew out his cheeks, shook his head. 'Sorry, mate. Can't help you.'

A dozen people had already said the same thing today.

'Thanks anyway.'

The older man nodded once, then turned back towards his boathouse.

Lockhart re-folded and pocketed Jess's picture. It was eleven years old now, and he imagined she'd have changed a lot in that time. But he'd bet her piercing blue eyes, wide smile and the dimples in her cheeks would be just the same.

The photo was taken only a few weeks before Jess had disappeared while he was on a six-month tour of duty with the British Army in Afghanistan. She'd simply vanished, and no one had a clue what had happened to her. There was talk of a mental health episode, of accidental drowning in the Thames, even abduction and trafficking, slavery. Lockhart didn't know what to believe. All he knew was that, one day, Jess hadn't answered his weekly scheduled telephone call from the camp. Lockhart's mum, Iris, had gone over to check their tiny flat in Hammersmith. The door was open, but Jess wasn't there.

Lockhart still lived in the cramped, noisy apartment they'd bought together. As far as he was concerned, the place was their home, preserved like a time capsule from the day Jess vanished, ready for when she returned. He was pretty much the only person who believed that would happen. The police had long since given up an active investigation and shelved her file. Even Jess's own family thought she was dead, now. But Lockhart wasn't ready to stop looking for her. Especially when he had a new lead.

This was the tenth time he'd visited the fishing port of Whitstable in Kent over the past three months. If his work in a murder squad didn't often mean seven-day weeks, he would've come here more. Late last year, a woman had replied to his post on a missing persons website, saying she thought she'd seen Jess in Whitstable, perhaps two years ago. Walking in the harbour, alone. There was no more detail than that. Yet, it was possible: Jess had spent a few summers here with her family as a child. She had a connection to the place. So far, though, Lockhart hadn't found anyone else who'd caught sight of her. But he had to keep trying. As his dear old mum liked to remind him whenever they got together, her son didn't know the meaning of the words 'give up'. Just like his old man, she'd say, right up until the day he died.

Lockhart walked away from East Quay, past the surfboard shacks, seafood restaurants and beach huts. He felt deflated at his lack of progress and wondered if he should fetch his wetsuit from the car and dunk himself in the sea for half an hour. Now, in mid-February, it'd be cold as ice. But he could deal with that. The mile he swam every week in the Thames – freezing, whatever the weather – always made him feel better.

Behind the buildings, he could hear waves breaking and spreading over the sand. Seagulls cried out, buffeted by the salt breeze as they circled the water. For a few seconds, he just listened. That was one thing Dr Lexi Green had told him during their therapy sessions last year: be in the moment.

Over a period of months, Lockhart had opened up to Green about his mental health in a way he hadn't done with anyone else – even his mum – since Jess had gone missing. Despite the short time he'd known her, Green had become one of the people he trusted most in his life. That was why, last autumn, he'd brought her in to help profile a serial killer whom the media liked to call the Throat Ripper.

The case had nearly cost the young psychologist her life, and he felt responsible for that. Since she wasn't his therapist anymore, they hadn't spoken in a while and Lockhart wondered how she was doing. No, that wasn't accurate. After what had happened, he needed to know. It'd been too long. Following the impulse, he took out his phone and called her.

Waiting for Green to pick up, he suddenly became unsure of himself. What would he say to her? *How's it going? Have you got Post-Traumatic Stress Disorder now, like me?* Then her voicemail cut in. He didn't leave a message.

Lockhart tried to bring himself back to the sound of the waves, but was still thinking about Green minutes later when his phone rang. It was Detective Sergeant Maxine Smith.

'Sorry to bother you, guv,' she said. 'I know you'd rostered a rest day.'

'Don't worry about it, Max.' He wasn't really resting, and she wouldn't call unless it was serious. 'What's going on?'

'Body's been found in Wimbledon. Looks like one for us. Boss wants to know if you can come.'

'*If* I can come?'

'Fair one, I'm putting it more politely than he did. You in town?'

'No.'

'How fast can you get here?'

'Couple of hours.' He checked his watch. 'Hour and a bit if I do a ton on the motorway.'

'I'll text you the location.'

Lockhart rang off and jogged to his car at the double march his old regiment used when tabbing.

It was a matter of when, not if, he'd be back here to look for Jess.

CHAPTER THREE

Dr Lexi Green stole a glance at the clock. Five minutes to go. It wasn't that she was bored, exactly, although the private client she was seeing during her lunch hour did repeat himself. A lot. Lexi's theory was that this repetition was part of the guy's problem: he was stuck in a trauma-related cycle of depression. She understood why he was ruminating about recent events, and it was her job to fix that. All fine. It was just the subject matter that bothered her.

The client, Oliver Soames, couldn't move on from the loss of his baby. More precisely, he was fixated on the fact that his ex-partner had aborted her – or, as he put it, 'my' – baby without telling him. The scenario wasn't exactly uncommon, but it was just too close to home for Lexi. In her senior year at Princeton, she'd terminated her own unplanned pregnancy. It was the hardest decision she'd ever taken. She had been too young; not ready to have a kid. She'd made the right call, though it'd ended her long-term relationship.

Those were the events which, seven years ago, had brought her back here from the States, where she'd spent the previous decade trailing round after her American dad as the US Air Force moved him from base to base. There was also the fact that her kid brother, Shep, had died ten months earlier of a drug overdose which Lexi blamed herself for not preventing. After that year, she didn't want to stay in the States anymore.

Fortunately for Lexi, she had a UK passport, thanks to her British mom. So, she'd moved here, to London, where she was born during the time her dad was stationed at the US embassy. A gigantic, anonymous city where no one knew her, and she could just start over. Like none of it had happened.

'I mean, sometimes, you know, I just feel so… angry.' Oliver was clenching his fist in the low armchair opposite her. 'Not one word of discussion and then just, like, by the way, your kid's dead.' He slapped the armrest. '*Dead.*'

'That sounds as if it was really tough to deal with. I'm wondering, though, what we can do?—'

'They give you special training in that, do they?'

'Uh, I'm sorry?'

'Understatements. How to make the understatement of the century with sincerity.'

Jeez. *Way to go, Lexi.* Not exactly what you'd call a textbook therapeutic alliance. She took a breath. 'I'm just trying to understand how you're feeling, Olly. So I can help. That's all.'

'You can help by telling me how to not be so bloody depressed all the time!'

Lexi's phone vibrated in her pocket. It kept going: a call. She ignored it.

'OK,' she said calmly. 'I can see that this is really bothering you, so why don't we just—'

'We should've got a surrogate mother,' he stated, his gaze shifting from Lexi to the hospital lawns outside her window. 'Just paid someone else to have it for us. Simple. Then none of this would've happened.'

Or maybe you should've talked to your partner about how she was feeling, Lexi thought, sensing her frustration tip into anger. *And what she wanted for her body.* Following the assessment a few weeks back, Lexi knew she never should've accepted Oliver Soames as a client. His problems were too much like those of her own past. She couldn't maintain the non-judgemental stance that was essential to therapy. But private clients paid well, and Lexi had bills. So…

A few minutes later, when Oliver had left, Lexi pulled out her phone. Her heart jumped a little when she saw who the missed call was from. Dan Lockhart. Her ex-patient, for whom she'd developed feelings that even she couldn't quite understand. A man to whom she owed her life. She was lucky to have escaped the so-called Throat Ripper. Several others hadn't, including someone very close to her. Since then, there'd been no contact between her and Dan for months. Why was he calling her now? He hadn't left a voicemail.

Lexi wanted to call him back but, after everything that'd happened last year, she didn't know how to begin the conversation. In any case, she had another client coming in a few minutes. There wouldn't be enough time to speak properly, she told herself. Putting her phone in a drawer, she selected the manila file of notes for her next patient.

But her mind was still on Dan.

CHAPTER FOUR

Lockhart parked his old Land Rover Defender by the cluster of police vehicles at the edge of the woods. The track between the trees was so narrow that the only way to reach the crime scene was on foot. In less than a minute's walk from the road, he could've forgotten that he was in London at all. It amazed him that these pockets of forest still existed in the city. On another day, he might've enjoyed a hike on Wimbledon Common.

As the twisting path straightened ahead of him, Lockhart saw the large white tent that would be covering the body. A perimeter had been established with blue-and-white tape, beyond which a couple of gazebos sheltered boxes of equipment from the drizzle. A few scene of crime officers in pale blue hooded suits moved between the structures, stepping on raised metal plates as they entered the red-and-white inner cordon around the tent.

Lockhart signed in with the Crime Scene Manager at the outer tape and suited up from one of the kit boxes. His colleagues from Major Investigation Team 8 were already here. And he knew where to find them. Approaching the tent, he spotted Sergeant Harry Wiseman, a handler from the local Dog Support Unit at Nine Elms. A German shepherd sat patiently beside the man.

'All right, Hazza,' nodded Lockhart, picking his way across the stepping plates.

'Sir.'

'Found anything yet?'

'Just a second body.'

Lockhart stopped. 'Eh?'

Wiseman shook his head ruefully. 'Looks like whoever done this murdered the bloke's dog 'n' all. Evil bastard.'

'Shit. You got a trail away from the scene?'

'Nope, not yet. Rain isn't helping.' Wiseman paused. 'Who'd kill a dog?'

'Good question.' Lockhart wondered whether Dr Green would have an answer to that.

He passed a SOCO who was taking a cast of a footprint in the mud, opened the tent flaps and stepped inside.

The first thing he saw was a middle-aged man's body supine on the bare ground, his limbs crooked and head turned to one side. His face was a mess. Battered, bloodied and smeared with dirt. A few damp leaves clung to his thick, grey beard. One eye was closed, enveloped by a swollen lump of livid, purple skin. Lockhart had a vague sense that, despite the disfigurement, he recognised the man, but couldn't place him. To the left of the victim stood DS Smith, to the right Detective Constable Mohammed Khan.

'Morning, guv,' said Smith.

'Max.' He turned to Khan. 'Mo.'

'How's it going, boss?' The young DC spoke, as usual, through a wad of chewing gum. Khan's protective suit was a size too small and strained against his chest and shoulders. Lockhart knew that Khan's parents, with whom he still lived, wished their son spent less time in the gym and more in the mosque. But that was never going to happen.

'Could be worse.' Lockhart returned his gaze to the body. 'Any idea who our man is?'

'None so far,' replied Smith. 'Jogger found him couple of hours ago. Berry's checking mispers reports for possible matches.'

Lockhart was pleased that Lucy Berry, MIT 8's civilian analyst, was already working on this. Berry was a mum to two young children, but between the hours of nine and five not even they could distract her from investigative data.

'Doesn't look like that happened to his face by accident,' he said.

'Yeah. Seems as though he's been whacked on the head, too. There's blood matted into his hair.'

Smith indicated the area with her left pinkie. Lockhart saw the index and middle fingers of the nitrile glove hanging limp where Smith was missing two digits. The cleft hand, which she'd had from birth, might've stopped others joining the police altogether. But, for Smith, the disability only seemed to fuel the grit that'd characterised her twenty-plus years in the Met. She was someone Lockhart knew he could rely on.

'What do you reckon to cause of death?' he asked.

Smith stood to take in the victim's whole body. 'We don't know what's under his clothing, but there's no obvious stab or gunshot wound. So, I'd say, most likely head trauma. Looks as though he's had a proper beating.'

Without warning, an image came into Lockhart's mind. A bleached mud-brick building, baking in the Afghan sun. A Taliban fighter inside who'd just shot dead one of Lockhart's men, a young private named Billy Ross. A gap in the window, wide enough for a stun grenade, and—

'Boss? You OK?' Khan's voice snapped him out of the flashback. Lockhart realised his pulse was racing and his hands felt clammy inside the gloves. It had been four months since he'd stopped his treatment at the trauma clinic with Dr Green. Evidently, he still needed her help.

'Yeah. I'm fine.' Lockhart composed himself again.

'And probably robbed, too,' added Khan, displaying a tan line beneath the man's left wrist. 'No watch.'

'No wallet either, guv.' Smith stooped and lifted the base of the jacket. The trouser pocket lining was half pulled out. 'Hence no ID.'

'Robbery gone wrong,' stated Khan.

'Maybe.' Lockhart squatted down to inspect the man. Beneath the mud and dried blood, his beard was well-groomed, his clothes expensive looking. The Arc'teryx jacket – Lockhart recognised the logo – would have been six hundred quid alone. A rope leash with metal clip poked out from beneath the body. 'Hazza said there was a dead dog, too?'

'That's right.' Khan jerked a thumb behind him. 'Lids found it just over there.' The uniformed officers – or 'lids' – would've been first on the scene after the jogger had reported the discovery, well before any detectives – the 'suits' – arrived.

'Collar?'

'Don't know.' Khan looked sheepish.

'What do you mean, you don't know? You didn't check?'

'I thought it was just—'

'Fuck's sake,' growled Lockhart. 'This is basic stuff, Mo.'

'Sorry, boss.'

'Find the dog and see if there's anything on its collar. Name, address, phone number. If there's a number, ring it. Now!'

Khan stood and left quickly. Lockhart heard him outside, calling to the SOCOs.

'He's still learning, guv,' said Smith.

'We could've already had an ID.'

'I didn't think of it, either,' she admitted. 'We've only been here half an hour.'

Lockhart sighed. 'Fair enough.' He returned to examining the body. 'Have you rolled him?'

'Not yet. We left him as we found him. Don't think he was killed right here, though. Looks from those marks in the mud like he was dragged off the path.'

Getting closer to the ground, Lockhart reached out and gently lifted the man's chin. That was when he saw it.

'Max, look at this.'

She stepped around and bent low. 'What is *that*?'

It was a crudely drawn symbol. A triangle, each side a black line about two inches long.

Then a ringtone chirped somewhere on the corpse and they both recoiled slightly. Lockhart exchanged a glance with Smith and lowered the man's head carefully back down. Following the sound, he unzipped the jacket, probed the pockets of the fleece beneath it and extracted a slim smartphone. Its battery had only a few per cent remaining. The ringing stopped as Khan burst back into the tent, clutching his own phone.

'It just says "Pickle", and there's a mobile number,' Khan exclaimed breathlessly. 'Went to voicemail when I called, though.'

'Whoever robbed him didn't take his phone,' observed Smith. 'Either they didn't find it…'

'Or they knew it could be tracked.' Lockhart pressed the home button and a lock screen appeared showing a couple. The older man with a grey beard was probably their victim. The woman was younger and more glamorous. 'I'd say at least one person's missing him.'

'Hang on,' blurted Khan. 'Lemme see that, boss.'

Lockhart hesitated, then stood and held the handset out to him. Khan tapped the button and brought up the photo once more. 'That's that woman off the telly, innit?' He clicked his fingers. 'The one from *Cobbled Streets*. The fit one, you know? The MILF.'

'Mo.' Smith glared at him.

'What?'

Lockhart was googling the cast list for *Cobbled Streets* on his phone. He didn't watch a lot of telly, but the face of one of the actors, Jemima Stott-Peters, was a good match for the woman on the victim's screen. His next search was on her name plus the word 'partner'. Seconds later, he had an image that was, unmistakably, the man lying in front of him – and the name that accompanied it. 'Charles Stott.'

Voices rose outside, and Lockhart became aware of one louder and deeper than the others.

'He's a film director,' Smith announced, scrolling on the screen of her own phone.

'Find out where he lives,' said Lockhart.

The tent flap flew open and the large frame of Detective Chief Inspector Marcus Porter entered. 'Afternoon, all,' he boomed.

Though in his mid-forties, Lockhart's boss had retained the intimidating physique of his previous career as a semi-pro rugby player. At six-three, he was only a fraction taller than Lockhart, but carried considerably more weight, and not just physically. Porter was one of the Met's rising stars. The only thing that could stop him taking one of the force's top jobs was if he decided to quit the police for politics. Office gossip said he was interested. One detective in their team was offering odds on Porter being the first Mayor of London with Afro-Caribbean heritage. Another reckoned he'd stand for parliament in Croydon, where he'd grown up. Lockhart wouldn't bet against either possibility. He felt that Porter was more politician than policeman, anyway. It was the opposite of his own approach to work and that difference had already led to several run-ins between them in the seven months since Lockhart had joined MIT 8.

'Sir,' they said as one.

'Murder?' queried Porter.

'Appears so,' Lockhart replied. 'Massive head wounds, evidence of blunt force trauma, and, just on his neck, there's—'

'OK.' Porter surveyed the corpse, his eyes darting from one detail to the next. 'Does the deceased have a name?'

'Charles Stott.'

'*The* Charles Stott?' Porter raised his eyebrows and bent to examine the dead man's face. 'The director?'

Smith angled her phone towards the DCI. 'Wikipedia says he's a resident of Wimbledon.'

'This is going to be very high profile,' said Porter, still staring at the body.

'Looks like a robbery turned violent,' chipped in Khan. 'He's out walking the dog, someone jumps him, he resists, there's a fight, then boom, he's dead, mugger runs off with his wallet and watch.'

'Sounds plausible. Next of kin?'

'I'll track down his partner, sir,' said Smith. 'Jemima Stott-Peters.'

'The actor?' Porter pursed his lips as Smith nodded. 'Right,' he said. 'I'm going to call our press office now. We need to stay ahead of the media. Dan, I'm delegating the suspect strategy to you. Start with local ex-cons known for violent muggings.' The boss was already reaching for his phone as he swept out of the tent. He was gone before Lockhart could reply or show him the 'triangle'.

Porter had clearly accepted the robbery theory, for now. But something about that nagged at Lockhart. He knew most robberies took place in areas of high footfall. Phone thieves on bikes used snatch-and-run tactics. Pickpockets liked train stations and tourist hotspots. And the lone, knife-wielding attackers looking for drug money favoured pedestrian underpasses and cut-throughs. The dense woods of Wimbledon Common didn't fit any robbery profile that Lockhart knew. Which left another possibility: Charles Stott had been targeted by his killer. And, if that was true, it meant they were probably looking for someone who knew him.

Someone who had a reason to mark him with a symbol.

*

After work, Lexi had gone to the CrossFit gym in Tooting to sweat out the stress of a day's therapy. Working out was the perfect antidote to sitting on her butt in a consulting room for eight or nine hours straight. Maybe it was the session with Soames, maybe the memories stirred by the missed call from Dan. Either way, she had needed distraction and the gym had delivered it. So much, in fact, that she hadn't even checked her phone until she got back home. That was when she saw Dan's text, sent a few hours ago. She tapped to open it right away, at once scolding herself for her excitement to see what he'd written. Like all his communication, it was short and direct:

Got a new murder. Bit weird. Need your help. Can we meet tomorrow?

Lexi thought back to the moment she'd agreed to assist him last year and everything that had followed. She considering ignoring the request. Maybe responding to say she was too busy, or that she didn't do forensic work anymore. She stared at the screen for about a minute, weighing her decision. She needed to look after herself. But she sure as hell owed it to others to help, too, if she could. And she'd by lying if she pretended that she didn't want to see Dan. She hit reply and typed:

I'm free after work. Drink?

CHAPTER FIVE

It was late by the time Smith arrived outside the victim's house. Though the residence was only half a mile from where the body had been found, she'd gone back to the MIT office in Putney to shower and change before meeting Charles Stott's widow. It may have just been in Smith's mind, but she didn't want to walk into Jemima Stott-Peters's home still smelling of her late husband's corpse.

The detour had also mercifully relieved Smith of perhaps the hardest task for any copper: the 'death knock'. Fortunately, their Family Liaison Officer – or FLO – had arrived an hour ago to break the news. Now, it was Smith's job to ask some questions, as diplomatically as she could, to help their inquiry. She was primed; Lockhart had already told her that he didn't think it was a simple robbery. The guvnor's instincts were usually sound. On this occasion, however, she wanted him to be wrong.

Most murders were solved within the first forty-eight hours of a body's discovery, and Smith hoped this one would be wrapped up that quickly. She'd been taken away from a case where she was helping Wandsworth CID: a serial sex offender operating in the local area, who was targeting lone women waiting at isolated bus stops.

Seven victims had all reported the same stocky man with dark eyes, slightly below average height, wearing a black jacket and balaclava, and usually chewing gum. His crimes were escalating rapidly. The first two times he was reported, he'd just been watching, staring from a distance. As his confidence grew, he approached the third and fourth women and demanded they expose themselves for him. Then, in incidents five and six, he'd sexually assaulted his victims by touching, before running away.

The most recent event was what had triggered the MIT's involvement: a rape threat at knife point. Luckily, the woman had escaped without physical harm. Now, they were mapping the crimes for geographical patterns. Smith thought there was something solid about a map. It wasn't the wishy-washy mind-reading of that psychologist Lockhart knew, Dr Lexi Green. OK, the shrink had contributed to the 'Throat Ripper' case last year but, ultimately, it'd been leg work by her, Khan and Lockhart that'd got the result. All the graft had paid off. It was even worth the occasional nightmare she still had about the killer.

Smith felt that she and her CID colleagues were making progress on the bus stop attacks – collectively known as Operation Braddock – and part of her resented being taken away from it by DCI Porter to work on this millionaire's death. *They all count the same*, she reminded herself, getting out of the car and approaching the enormous front door with its grand portico. The bell produced a deep, resonant sound suggesting a cavernous hallway and, momentarily, Smith had a flicker of the inferiority that wealth often caused her to feel.

The door was opened by a small, slight woman with elfin features who Smith guessed was about her own age: mid-forties, give or take. She wore heavy make-up but, as Smith looked closer, she could see the lines around her mouth and eyes. The woman had clearly been crying. She swayed very slightly on the threshold and Smith's attention was drawn to the glass of white wine in her hand. Were those bubbles rising in it?

'Jemima Stott-Peters?' she asked softly, holding up her warrant card before introducing herself.

'Yah, come in.' She sniffed and wiped her eyes with her sleeve, then turned and sashayed back down the hallway, leaving Smith to follow her. 'We're through here.'

The interior was luxuriously furnished with a combination of antique and modern pieces, polished woods and silver alongside modern artworks in bright primary colours. There were stuffed animals, richly upholstered chairs and even a neon sign proclaiming 'Vacancy'. Smith wondered if her host had considered switching that off, now, or indeed if it had just been switched on…

In the living room, she greeted PC Rhona MacLeod, their team's FLO. Although still in her twenties, MacLeod had a maturity and sensitivity beyond her years and would've delivered the terrible news with empathy.

'Do sit down,' said Stott-Peters. 'Drink?'

Smith half-raised a palm as she took an armchair. 'Oh, no thanks, I'm fine. Do you mind if I call you Jemima?'

'Mimi's fine.' The actor knocked back the rest of her drink as she crossed to a side table. Smith saw her refill the glass from a champagne bottle before returning and flopping down into a low sofa, her expression blank.

'I'm so sorry for your loss, Mimi.'

'He, just… Yesterday, Charles was here. Right here.' She touched the empty cushion next to her. 'And now…' She tailed off and took another large mouthful of alcohol, rinsing it round before swallowing.

'It must've been such a shock.'

Stott-Peters nodded quickly, and Smith could see she was welling up. She didn't want to push the newly bereaved woman but, with a suspected murder, there were questions that had to be asked as soon as possible.

'Will I have to identify him? I mean, officially or whatever.'

'That'll be up to you,' Smith replied.

'When they do Charles's post-mortem tomorrow, the patholo-gist will check his dental records just to be a hundred per cent sure. You can be there, of course,' added MacLeod soothingly. 'But if you don't want to attend, that's fine.'

'I'm not going.' Stott-Peters rubbed her eyes. 'I don't think I could cope, seeing him like that for real. Perhaps Charles's sister could do it…'

'We can ask her,' said MacLeod.

Smith was wondering how to open her questions when a well-spoken male voice rang out.

'Where shall I put the coats?'

'Just bring them in here,' Stott-Peters called out.

'Righto.'

A young man marched into the living room. He was early-twenties, Smith guessed, and handsome, with chiselled facial features and thick arms in which he held a stack of jackets. He was probably not much taller than Smith but possessed a kind of coiled energy that made his presence seem much larger.

'Oh, hello.' He flashed her a pearly grin. 'I'm Xander.'

'Detective Sergeant Maxine Smith.' She hadn't seen any mention of a son or other male relative.

'Nice to meet you.' He gestured to the clothes. 'Mimi, should I take this lot to the charity shop tomorrow, do you think? Probably be closed by now, won't it?'

Stott-Peters flapped a hand at him. 'Yah. Maybe in the morning.'

'I could drop some of Pickle's stuff there, too.'

'OK,' said Stott-Peters weakly.

Xander sighed. 'Poor old Pickle.' He dumped the jackets over an empty armchair before helping himself to a glass of champagne. Then he sat down next to Stott-Peters, manspreading just enough so that his leg touched hers. His body language didn't suggest they were mother and son.

'Are you a family member?' Smith asked him.

'Ah, no.' He was gawping at her cleft hand with the same mixture of fascination and revulsion that Smith had seen a thousand times. She noticed that he had a pair of prominent, dark moles close together on one cheekbone, but *she* knew better than to stare at an unusual part of someone's appearance.

'Xandy's a friend.' Stott-Peters forced a smile. 'And he's an actor. Aren't you, darling?'

'Well, I try.' He broke his gaze from Smith's hand and shrugged. 'The right jobs aren't coming up at the moment, though. It's bloody tough out there.'

Smith gestured to the pile of coats. 'Are those…?'

'Charles's jackets,' replied Xander. 'I've told Mimi there's not much point having them here anymore, right? Bad memories and all that. We can have most of it gone by the end of the week, I'd expect.'

'I realise it might seem as if I'm trying to get rid of him.' Stott-Peters stared into her glass. 'But I loved him deeply.'

'Not that he cared.'

'Xandy!' Stott-Peters tensed. Then she drank some more. 'Charles loved me, too, in his own way.'

The young man snorted his disagreement, but Smith ignored him.

'How long were the two of you together?' she asked.

'Ten years.'

'It's a long time.'

Stott-Peters nodded briefly, then wiped a hand over her face, her shoulders curving inwards.

Smith discreetly took out a small notebook and pen. 'Mimi, I'm sorry to have to do this, but could I ask you a few questions, please?'

'OK.'

'Do you know of anyone who would've wanted to hurt your husband?'

'It was a robbery, wasn't it?' exclaimed Xander.

'We're looking at all possibilities. Were you aware of any specific threats made against him, Mimi?'

'No.'

'Anyone with a grudge against him, then?'

'Grudge?' She drained her champagne glass. 'I don't know if, I mean—'

'Come on Mimi!' blurted Xander. 'Where do we start? Charles had a hundred enemies. Spurned lovers, jealous men, husbands he'd cuckolded.'

'Don't talk about him like that,' Stott-Peters said quietly.

'But it's true!'

Smith had to proceed gently. 'Mimi,' she began, 'I know this might be hard to talk about, but if your husband was being unfaithful, then that's something that might help us investigate what happened to him.' She didn't mention the triangle symbol, for now.

Stott-Peters shut her eyes, as if summoning the energy to speak. 'Charles did have a number of...' She cleared her throat. 'Little dalliances. But he always came back. He apologised.'

'Sorry to ask, but roughly how many of these, er, dalliances did he have?'

'A few,' replied Stott-Peters.

'Dozens. He didn't treat you how you deserved to be treated, Mimi.' Xander laid a hand on her leg.

Smith made a note to get any names from her later. Each would represent a possible motive. But she also had to acknowledge that this Xander guy was becoming a person of interest for her, too. 'Can I just check, Mimi, when was the last time you saw your husband?'

'Last night. He went out to walk Pickle, as usual, around nine p.m. Same place, same time, every night. Unless he had some function or other to attend.'

'And when he didn't come back, what did you do?'

'Nothing. It wasn't the first time he… I mean, I just assumed he'd stopped over with one of his, you know.'

'Other women?' asked Smith.

'Mm.'

'Was his car still here?'

'Yes, but he often took taxis to get around.'

'Did you try calling him?'

'No. Charles was old enough to look after himself. He always came back, sooner or later.'

'Did your husband wear a watch?' Smith asked.

Stott-Peters managed a thin smile. 'Bloody great big silver thing. He almost never took it off. His parents gave it to him on his birthday years ago. They'd engraved the back of it: "To our Charlie, happy fortieth". I used to think sometimes that he loved that watch more than—' She broke off, her eyes moistening.

Smith noted the detail, waiting a moment before following up. 'Now, I realise this might be difficult, but I need to ask you for any names of people that your husband might've been romantically involved with.'

'I can help,' said Xander.

Stott-Peters drained her glass. 'I need a refill.'

As she stood and crossed to the champagne bottle, Smith settled into her seat. She wasn't going anywhere for a while. And her hope that this case would be closed quickly had already gone out the window.

DAY TWO

CHAPTER SIX

As Lockhart drove south from the MIT 8 office in Putney to the hospital in Tooting where Charles Stott's post-mortem was taking place, he reflected on the day's investigative work. It didn't take him long, because they hadn't really got anywhere since the discovery of Stott's body yesterday afternoon.

Smith had passed on what Jemima Stott-Peters had said about her husband's infidelity. They had a list of more than thirty women he'd apparently used and ditched over the past five years, and many of them had male partners who might've wanted revenge on Stott, too. But, with no evidence of a specific threat towards the director, Lockhart knew they'd need to speak to everyone on that list and eliminate each one by alibi. And that was only half of their suspect strategy.

Despite now acknowledging that Stott's promiscuity could be a possible motive for his murder, DCI Porter hadn't allowed Lockhart to drop the robbery-gone-wrong theory. Porter wasn't attributing much significance to the symbol drawn on Stott's neck, either. The DCI dismissed it as a distraction, perhaps a joke by the killer or drawn before the attack. Lockhart didn't agree, but since Porter was in charge as Senior Investigating Officer – or SIO – he was calling the shots.

It meant Lockhart was overseeing one of the broadest suspect strategies he'd ever known on a murder investigation. They didn't have the personnel to follow everything up, and each hour's delay identifying a credible suspect gave the killer a further advantage. But they were doing everything they could.

Khan was obtaining as much CCTV footage as possible, though that wasn't a lot. Unsurprisingly, there weren't many cameras watching the woods. On their witness strategy, another DC called Andy Parsons was leading local house-to-house inquiries, hoping someone might've heard or seen something, but that'd drawn a blank so far.

For their victim strategy, Berry was trawling social media for any indication of Stott's activities prior to his death, again without success. His phone might offer some leads, but it was way down the Met Police queue for data exploitation.

As for Porter, he'd spent most of the day briefing top brass and journalists, even asking Lockhart to return to the crime scene and record a short appeal for witnesses. Not that there was much chance of anyone credible coming forward with information. Overall, it was a pretty bleak picture.

However, Lockhart did hope that the post-mortem might offer them something to go on. In the absence of more definitive leads, it was always worth attending. You never knew when the single clue would emerge that jump-started an investigation. And, with Dr Mary Volz conducting the examination, there was every chance of finding it. Volz was one of the best in the business, an experienced Home Office Registered Forensic Pathologist whose work on the Throat Ripper murders last year had contributed more to the case than she'd realised.

As he parked outside St George's Hospital and put the 'Met Police Business' sign on top of the Defender's dashboard, Lockhart was again reminded of Green. The South-West London Trauma Clinic, where she had given his therapy sessions, was only a stone's throw from here. They'd arranged to meet nearby after work. He was hoping she could shed some light on the symbol. He told himself that was the only reason he wanted to see her.

*

Inside, St George's mortuary looked much like the other London mortuaries Lockhart had visited during his five years in homicide, with its standard fittings of stainless-steel tables, side benches and trollies on a pale linoleum floor. But the routine set-up and procedure didn't mean a conveyer belt for the corpses. On the contrary, it allowed pathologists like Volz to apply maximum attention to the details of a person's death – however tiny – that could determine how their final hours of life were spent.

Volz saw him through the viewing window and gestured that he should enter.

'Mary,' he said, walking over to the slab where Stott's body lay, covered to the neck by a white sheet.

She pulled down her surgical mask and tucked some loose strands of grey hair back under her cap. 'Dan. Haven't seen you since…'

'November.' He didn't need to remind her what'd happened then. He wondered if Volz thought about it as often as he did.

'That's right.' She held his gaze a moment. The strength in her pale blue eyes was unnerving. 'I followed all the news coverage. You and your team did an incredible job. I don't think I've known another case like it in all my time doing this.'

'We stopped him. That's the main thing.' He wasn't going to list all the stuff he could've done differently. Done better.

The silence hung between them briefly.

'So,' began Volz, turning back to the body, 'first things first. I can tell you that X-ray comparison of dental records confirms this is Charles Stott.'

'OK.' That answered Lockhart's initial question, at least. Victim ID was never a given in murder cases.

'Now, you want to know how he died. I need to send some tissue samples for toxicology, just to check if there were any drugs in his system. But I expect those tests to come back clear. I'm confident this is what killed him. Have a look.'

She folded the sheet down to Stott's waist and, for a moment, Lockhart simply stared in silence. He'd encountered dozens of dead bodies as a soldier and a murder detective, but he'd never seen one in this state.

Aside from Volz's Y-shaped incision in Stott's torso, now stitched closed, his body was intact. But deep bruises covered most of his skin, the various shades of blue and purple vivid under the LED lighting rig. The contusions were so numerous that they merged with blotches of red, yellow and black, virtually eclipsing the original pale skin tone. The extent of Stott's injuries had been impossible to see when he had been lying fully clothed in the woods.

'His back and legs are much the same,' she added. 'There was a single, perhaps initial blow to his head, probably by a large blunt object like a mallet. That's the only area of external bleeding. It would've stunned him, perhaps even briefly rendered him unconscious, but it's not serious enough to have killed him. The rest of the impact sites on the body are much smaller. My guess would be they represent punches and kicks, perhaps some stamping. There's no penetrating trauma, it's all blunt force. And the lividity around where he's been struck indicates he was alive throughout.'

Lockhart swallowed.

'My guess is that his cause of death was internal haemorrhage from the assault. He lost— Dan, are you all right?'

'Yeah, sorry. Carry on.' Lockhart became aware he'd been holding his breath. He was picturing that scene from Afghanistan again. Except, this time, he was inside the building, face to face with the Taliban sniper. He forced himself to focus on Charles Stott.

'So,' resumed Volz, 'he would've lost so much blood internally that, eventually, his organs would've ceased functioning. His pulse would have sped up until his heart failed. It would've been an agonising, drawn out way to die. I've counted over eighty separate impact sites. I'm not sure I've ever seen such a sustained, vicious attack.'

Lockhart nodded his agreement. He was already imagining who could be capable of such violence.

'I can't say for certain if it was one assailant or more, though,' she added.

'We only found one set of footprints around the body.'

'A number of his smaller bones were fractured,' Volz continued. 'Multiple ribs, carpals and phalanges in both hands – perhaps as he tried to shield himself – plus his left clavicle and the radius of his right arm.'

'So, the attacker was strong.'

'Very.' She took a deep breath, gazing at the injuries. 'And there are perhaps ten or so wounds without as much lividity and inflammation.'

He understood what that meant. 'Those blows were delivered after he'd died?'

'I believe so.'

He needed to tell Green about this. The symbol wouldn't be the only thing he'd need her help to interpret.

'What about time of death? We know he was last seen at nine p.m. and found at approximately eleven a.m. the following day.'

Volz shook her head. 'Without having been at the scene when he was found, I'm afraid I can't say accurately. Was his body rigid when you got there?'

'Yeah. That was about two p.m.'

'So, he probably died closer to the start of your fourteen-hour window than the end of it.'

'Between nine and, say, midnight?'

'Something like that.'

'Makes sense, given he went out to walk his dog. Much more than an hour or two and he'd either have returned home or gone to see one of his girlfriends.' He was thinking out loud.

'Hm.'

'Any DNA we missed at the scene?' he asked hopefully.

'No obvious sources that I could find so far. The attacker was probably wearing gloves and a hat or mask. Sometimes there are skin samples under a victim's fingernails from their attempts to resist the attack. But, as you can observe,' she gently lifted one of Stott's hands, 'his nails were bitten to the quick. I couldn't find anything to harvest from there, unfortunately.'

Lockhart knew the SOCOs at the crime scene hadn't found any biological evidence, either. He couldn't hide his disappointment. A DNA sample from their killer would've been a great starting point. Even if the person wasn't on the national database, it'd give them a means of comparison with suspects down the line. He gestured to the symbol on Stott's neck.

'What did you make of this?'

Volz frowned. 'I don't really know. It's drawn directly onto the skin. The lines are relatively clean and barely smudged, which suggests to me that it was applied after the attack. Therefore, I'd be amazed if anyone other than the killer had done it.'

Lockhart had thought the same. He took some photos in the bright mortuary lighting to show Green. 'Nothing else drawn on his body?'

'No.' She turned to him. 'Have you considered testing the triangle? Forensic ink analysis, perhaps?'

'Not yet.' He rubbed his chin. 'Do you reckon that's worth a shot?'

Volz bent to inspect the symbol. 'Well, it's more commonly done with tattoos. But it would be possible here, if you scraped a few skin cells. The procedures are expensive and time-consuming, though. So, the question is whether it'd tell you anything about the perpetrator. I'm stepping out of my area of expertise, but to my eye, it just looks like a simple marker pen.'

'I agree.' He sighed. 'Hard to see that blowing the case wide open.'

Lockhart had to face it: they were in the dark. Without much else to go on, he was pinning his hopes on Green. It wouldn't be the first time he'd done that.

CHAPTER SEVEN

Having checked the windows and exits, Lockhart allowed himself to relax slightly and take in his surroundings as he waited for Green to arrive. He approved of her choice of pub. The Selkirk in Tooting had the kind of simple, no-frills interior that Lockhart liked. It served his favourite beer, Stella Artois. And, at six o'clock on a Wednesday evening, it was pretty quiet. That made it easier to discuss a murder case, but it also made being out less stressful.

Back in the day, Lockhart was a big pub-goer. But the more training he got in situational awareness from his old unit, the Special Reconnaissance Regiment, the harder he found it to enjoy being out in a crowd. People equalled danger. If you switched off or let yourself go, you could be in trouble. Then, after Jess had gone missing, he gradually found himself preferring to drink alone in their flat. Since police social life centred on boozing, he had no choice but to force himself into a crowded pub now and then. Several pints of Stella usually helped, though that, too, was something Green had been encouraging him to change last year. A *dysfunctional coping strategy*, she'd called it. Or something like that.

Out of habit, Lockhart had positioned himself facing the door. He saw Green as she passed the window and stood as she entered and walked across to him. She was dressed casually, with jeans, trainers and chunky roll-neck sweater under a slim down jacket, her long dark hair pulled back into a ponytail. She seemed to have aged a bit since the last time he'd seen her. Maybe it was the stress of what'd happened with the Throat Ripper. But she looked stronger than before, too, athletic and broad-shouldered. He knew she did CrossFit and wondered whether that'd been helping her overcome the trauma.

'Hey, Dan,' she said, not quite smiling but holding his gaze with sharp eyes.

'All right, Lexi.' He didn't know how to greet her. Suddenly, he was aware of the distance that'd grown between them since they last spoke. Awkwardly, he stuck out a hand for her to shake. She looked at it for a moment, then took it. They each made a step towards one another. And, before he knew it, they were in a tight embrace, Lockhart wrapping his arms around her and Green pulling him close, resting her head on his chest. They stayed like that for a moment. He realised it was the first hug he'd given a woman other than his mum since, well… since Jess had disappeared. It felt good. He immediately got a stab of guilt and let go of her.

'Been a while,' he said.

'Jeez, I know.'

There were a few seconds of silence before he spoke. 'Cheers for coming.'

'Sure.'

They took their seats at a small wooden table and Lockhart slid a bottle of pale ale towards her. 'Got you this. Thought it looked hoppy or whatever.'

She smiled. 'Thanks.'

'So, how's it going?' he asked, his eyes flicking to the roll-neck of her sweater. He knew there'd be a scar underneath.

'You know, OK, I guess.'

'Sorry about your flatmate,' said Lockhart.

Green closed her eyes and swigged the beer deeply. 'It was my fault,' she replied, eventually.

'No, it wasn't. You couldn't have known.'

She shook her head as if dismissing his words. 'Anyway, how are you?'

'Surviving.' He knew that wasn't what she was after. Green cared about him. She would want details: work, his mental health, the search for his wife, all of it. She'd even be interested in his recent flashbacks from Afghanistan. But that stuff could wait. Green wasn't his therapist anymore and he didn't like to burden her with his personal problems. She had enough of her own to deal with. 'Surviving,' he repeated.

'Yeah, me too,' she said quietly, taking another long pull on her beer bottle. Lockhart noticed that she'd drunk almost half of it in two gulps.

'Sometimes, that's all we can do.'

'Right.' She paused a beat. 'So, there's a case?'

*

Lexi listened carefully while Dan described the murder of Charles Stott and his post-mortem, showing her the photos on his phone. They weren't easy to look at, but she forced herself to take in the details. She'd seen a piece on the news about the murder today. Lexi recognised the director's name and thought maybe she'd even watched one of his movies. While Dan finished, she drained the rest of her IPA.

'So, what do you think?' he asked.

Lexi held up the bottle. 'I think I need another one of these.' She pointed at his pint. 'You want one?…'

'I'm all right, thanks.' He'd barely had a third of his beer. She was drinking faster than him. So what? There was a time when that might've bothered her, but not now.

'I'll be right back,' she said.

Returning a couple of minutes later with a fresh IPA, she sat down.

'OK,' she said. 'So, there's a couple things going on here. One is the ferocity of this attack. It's a total blitz. Charles Stott was taken by surprise and initially hit with a heavy, blunt object.'

'Yeah.'

'But, despite possessing that object, the killer chose not to use it again. Instead, they repeatedly punched, kicked and stamped the victim to death, what, eighty times?'

'That's what Volz reckons.'

Lexi knew the pathologist was one of the few people Dan trusted, which meant her judgement was probably on point.

'There was no let up,' she continued. 'They wanted him to suffer, but it's like they were so into it that they didn't even know to stop after he'd died. It was driven by hatred.'

Lexi watched as he glazed over a little, like he was someplace else.

'Dan?' She moved her head to make eye contact with him. 'Is everything?—'

'Yeah.'

She knew him well enough to recognise he was lying. It was like he'd dissociated, just for a second. It could be one of the PTSD symptoms he'd been experiencing last year. A flashback, maybe? But Lexi reminded herself that she'd left work; this wasn't a therapy session. Whatever it was, if he wanted to talk about it, he'd tell her.

'So, this kind of blitz attack is usually highly personal. It's the venting of a whole lot of anger that has built up over time and is finally unleashed.'

'You reckon the attacker knew Stott personally?'

'Either that,' she replied, 'or he was a stranger who represented someone of deep psychological significance to the murderer.'

'Don't tell me that. Our suspect list is long enough as it is.'

'I'm just saying it's a possibility.' Lexi drank some beer. 'And there's the dog, too. The victim is out walking it when the assault takes place. The dog is maybe barking or whatever, and the attacker wants it to stop. So, they just kill it. Instrumental violence.'

'Meaning?'

'You're probably dealing with a true psychopath. Someone pretty far down the spectrum, I'd say. Like, almost zero empathy. As if it's just been switched off. Chances are that someone like that has committed a crime before.'

Dan nodded slowly. 'What about the triangular symbol?'

She turned the bottle in her hands, thinking. 'We assume it was drawn by the killer, probably after they realised Stott was dead, right?'

'Yeah.'

'Show me again.'

He unlocked his phone once more and handed it to her, the image of Stott's neck filling the screen. She scrutinised it. The triangle was pointing left, its right-hand edge vertical. The other two lines were about the same length, making it equilateral.

'I don't have a damn clue,' she said.

'Bollocks,' he muttered. 'Sorry, Lexi. It's not you, it's just the—'

'Wait.' She turned her head so that, from her viewpoint, it was like Stott was standing up. Now, the triangle was pointing downwards, its flat edge horizontal. 'I mean, it could be nothing…'

'What?'

'Well, the triangle is a strong shape, right? Solid base.'

'If you say so.'

'But turn it upside-down and it's completely unstable. It represents change. The Greek letter delta is the symbol for change in math and science. It's a triangle.'

Dan just looked confused.

'It also represents one of the elements,' she went on, getting into her stride. 'Fire. No, water. That's like an alchemy thing. It's common to wicca, too.'

'What's that when it's at home?'

'You know, witchcraft.'

'*Witchcraft?*'

'Yeah. I'm not sure if any of that is relevant, it's just what I remembered.'

'How do you even know that?'

'I've read some pretty random stuff.' She was already on her own phone, googling the symbolism of triangles. 'Yes! I knew there was something else, too.'

His lips were curling into a playful smile. 'Let me guess, it's the sign for a magical beast, isn't it? Dragon? No, unicorn, right?'

'It's the symbol of woman.'

Dan didn't respond.

'You said the guy had had a number of affairs. It could be about a woman.' She slapped her phone on the table. 'Maybe it was even a rejected lover who did this.'

He laughed into his pint glass. 'Come on. The bloke was punched and kicked to death. Eighty times or more. By someone strong enough to break his bones.'

'What, you're saying a woman couldn't do that?' Lexi could hear herself getting louder.

He shrugged. Then he wagged a finger at her. 'Actually, you might be on to something. Stott's widow said that he'd sometimes go out to walk the dog and end up stopping over with one of "his women", as she put it. Maybe a woman set it up so her fella could ambush him. Like a team. There's an idea.' He reached for his beer and took a satisfied gulp.

'That wasn't what I was suggesting.' Lexi could feel her frustration mounting. She took a deep breath, calmed herself.

'Yeah, I know. I'm not dismissing the idea, I just… I wanted your opinion.' He laid his non-drinking hand flat on the table, perhaps by way of reassurance. 'Even if I don't agree with it.'

'OK.' She raised the bottle again, studying his hand. It was square and strong, with veins like tree roots on the back. Looking at it, Lexi got the same feeling she'd had the first day Dan had walked into her therapy room: safety. Even if she hadn't read Dan's referral notes, Lexi would've known immediately that he'd been in the army. The short, neat haircut, the straight back, the North

Face jacket. Like a young version of her dad. She'd believed from the moment she met Dan that he was a guy she could depend on. And that belief had turned out to be right. Without thinking, she reached out and laid her hand on top of his, giving it a squeeze. She could feel the wedding ring he still wore every day, solid and smooth.

'It's good to see you, Dan,' she said.

'Yeah, you too,' he replied. But Lexi could tell he wasn't totally comfortable and released her grip, thinking maybe she'd gone a little too far. She was attracted to Dan – she could admit that much to herself, at least – but she knew it was complicated. He'd told her in their therapy sessions about his wife vanishing from their apartment while he was in Afghanistan. There were several theories about what'd happened, and Lexi knew they were all unbearably painful for Dan. He genuinely believed she was still alive, though Lexi thought that belief could be a defence mechanism, protecting him against her loss. It might even be part of a condition called Prolonged Grief Disorder. Either way, Dan didn't seem to want to move on, but part of her wished that he would.

Lexi wanted to ask him more about how he was doing. But she didn't need to rush in. She noticed he was nearing the end of his beer, now.

'You want another one?' she asked.

He glanced from her to the glass and back. 'Go on, then.'

CHAPTER EIGHT

I was bored for most of the evening, just watching TV at home. Not my home – I don't have one – but my mate John's place. I say 'mate', but I don't particularly like John, and he isn't really a friend. He's just a guy I used to know from work who's got a flat with a spare room. John works in film, like I did, and being one of the behind-the-scenes production people, he thought I was pretty cool. So, since I don't speak to my family anymore, he was an obvious person to call when I came back to London from the States.

John was always one of the nice guys. Too kind to say no when I asked if I could stay for a couple of nights. That was two months ago, and we've still not even had a conversation about me paying rent, let alone getting my own apartment. I guess he feels guilty after what happened to me. But he's weak, too, I can sense it – which means I'll always get my own way.

Tonight, for example, I didn't feel like talking to him, so I just said I wanted to watch TV alone. He nodded like that was fine and took his plate of the lasagne he'd cooked for us off to his own room to eat while I inhaled mine on the sofa and finished off the rest for seconds. John's good like that, he knows his place.

I've been following the TV coverage of my murder. It only really started today, which makes me think it took them a while to identify Charles. Since I still have his wallet, there wouldn't have been any ID on him when they found his body. Then they'd have needed to tell his wife and maybe other people in his family before they put it on the news.

In some ways, I'm a bit disappointed that it hasn't been a bigger story. But that will make it easier next time. And I reckon I'll get my fifteen minutes of fame soon enough. Judging by the news, the police have nothing. Just as I intended. They appealed for witnesses, which usually shows they've got no idea who they're looking for. The only interesting thing was the guy who made the appeal.

Detective Inspector Dan Lockhart.

He popped up on screen standing near the woods at Wimbledon Common, where I did it, talking about help from the public to catch the person responsible. I recognised something about the way he spoke. A detachment, as if a part of him was somewhere else. I know what that's like. And I was intrigued by what could've caused that for him. Something screwed up in his past, maybe?

It didn't take me long to find out. Googling him produced a ton of hits, which seemed to divide into three main groups. The first was murder cases he'd worked in London over the past few years, which included catching a serial killer called the Throat Ripper. Cool name. I went down a rabbit hole with that for a while. The guy was weird as hell, but he was creative, I'll give him that. The second group of hits on Lockhart was all about his missing wife, the lovely Jess. I found myself playing the world's smallest violin for them. It was the third group of hits that made me sit up and pay attention.

Before joining the Met, Lockhart had been a sergeant in the Special Reconnaissance Regiment of the British Army, the SRR. They were one of the elite units that operated undercover, doing all kinds of interesting stuff. Surveillance, breaking and entering, tracking targets in war zones. To get in, Lockhart would've needed to complete the Survive, Evade, Resist, Extract, or SERE, course, which was pretty hardcore. You got hunted across Cornwall by men and dogs before spending thirty-six hours in detention with isolation and interrogation. Enough to make most people shit their pants or go crazy. It got me thinking that there was probably some overlap in our skill sets.

Then I found out there definitely was. A *Daily Telegraph* article from 2009 described how Lockhart fought his way into a house in Helmand, Afghanistan, where a Taliban sniper was hiding. The sniper had just shot dead a soldier from his unit. Lockhart was the only one to come out of that building alive. So, he knows exactly how it feels to kill.

Reading about his bravery and medals, I had the thought that it'd be fun to try evading him, since he's looking for me. Carrying on with my plan while being pursued by Lockhart would be a real test of my abilities. I'm up to it, obviously. The question is: is he?

Then I had another idea, an even better one. What if I set him the challenge of catching me, but with a time limit? He's got a couple of weeks to find me, during which I'm going to kill some more people who need to be punished. I've identified the next one, but I haven't planned much beyond that yet. All I know is that my fifth victim needs to be somebody in the police. And I reckon I've just found the perfect candidate.

So, if he doesn't catch me, Lockhart's going to get one hell of a surprise. He's going to become part of his own serial murder case.

Once I'd come up with that plan, suddenly I didn't feel so bored anymore.

DAY THREE

CHAPTER NINE

'So, how well did you know Charles Stott?'

Smith had to tread carefully. Polly Hayes had been named by Jemima Stott-Peters as one of thirty-two women with whom the director may have been romantically involved in the past decade. Between Smith, Lockhart and a couple of their MIT 8 colleagues, they'd been able to hold voluntary interviews with twelve of them so far. Seven women had spoken about having some level of sexual relationship with Stott during his marriage.

A similar story was emerging, whereby Stott used a combination of charm, promises of career-defining opportunities, alcohol and weekends away to seduce them, before dropping them and moving on. One woman whom Smith interviewed yesterday had, following careful elicitation, stated that after she refused Stott's advances, he had sexually assaulted her during a casting audition. She added that she hadn't told anyone that before. Smith reckoned that wasn't the only incident and it angered her that Stott would never be held accountable for the crime. On the other hand, he'd paid the ultimate price, perhaps because of his actions.

While the revenge motive against Stott was believable, all twelve alibis had checked out, as had those of the partners of the women who were in relationships. There was a possibility that Hayes or her large boyfriend, Jimmy, who was currently lurking in the next room of their flat, was responsible. But it was more likely that she'd simply been another victim of Charles Stott's manipulation, even coercion.

'We worked together for three years,' replied Hayes. 'I was his assistant. I looked after his diary, his meetings, travel, that sort of thing.'

'And how would you describe your relationship with Mr Stott?'

Hayes gave an ironic laugh. 'Up and down.'

Smith waited.

'He was lovely, don't get me wrong. The pay was good, I had a decent amount of holiday. Of course, he'd get stressed around big deadlines or when he was shooting, but he was always… fair. And he could be really funny.'

'OK.' Smith made a couple of notes, waiting for the 'but'.

'It's just, you know, he was very…' She wiggled her fingers. 'Tactile.'

'Tactile, how, exactly?'

'He used to touch me, a lot,' whispered Hayes. 'I didn't think that much of it at the time. I was only twenty-three when I started working for him. I supposed it was, kind of, normal.'

'It's not normal,' Smith said, lowering her voice to match the young woman's. 'And it's not OK. Thank you for telling me, Polly. Can I ask, did he make any other sexual advances towards you?'

Hayes didn't reply immediately, instead picking a loose feather from the sofa cushion. 'Um, well, there was one night at a party after a premiere. Charles was very drunk and tried to kiss me. But I held him back and he didn't do it again.'

It was starting to sound like another case of sexual assault by Stott, rather than the 'romantic involvement' described by Jemima Stott-Peters.

'Were you seeing your current partner at the time you were working for Mr Stott?' asked Smith.

'Yeah, we've been together since uni.'

'And did you tell him about any of Mr Stott's touching or sexual behaviour towards you?'

'No, never.' Hayes frowned. 'Why did you need to speak to me, again?'

'We're talking to everyone who knew Charles in the last few years,' replied Smith. She didn't want to say too much about their investigation. 'Trying to build up a picture of his life and of anyone who might've wanted to hurt him.'

Hayes folded her arms. 'Well, it wasn't me or Jimmy. We were in a club for a friend's birthday the night he died. And for what it's worth, I liked Charles. Maybe you should be talking to that gold-digging wife of his, Mimi. Or the actor who's always hanging out with her. Xander whatever-his-name-is.'

Smith had an hour until her next interview. Blackstone's Police Investigator's Manual would've recommended that she return to her office and write up her notes from the Polly Hayes meeting while her memory was fresh, documenting any risk issues for colleagues. Instead, Smith chose to drop into Lavender Hill police station to see how Operation Braddock was progressing.

Entering the Wandsworth CID room, she instantly spotted the huge frame of Detective Sergeant Eddie Stagg, known as Big Ed. Stagg was leaning back in his chair with both feet on his desk, phone clamped between ear and shoulder as he spun an American football in his hands, grunting occasionally. He noticed Smith and nodded at her, finishing the call with a few terse words of thanks before slamming the handset back into its base unit.

'All right, Max?' He lobbed the football to her and Smith half-caught, half-gathered it into her stomach with her free left hand. She knew it was a souvenir from his holiday in Florida last winter.

'Shit, sorry,' blurted Stagg. 'I forgot about…' he twirled his long, sausage-like fingers and gestured vaguely to the hand she liked to refer to as her 'different one'. It was irritating, but nothing Smith hadn't encountered a hundred times before. At Paddington

Green police station, where Smith had started her Met career, her nickname had been 'Claw' before political correctness became a buzzword. It remained 'Claw' for years after the new guidance on inclusive language was circulated. No one called her that now, but back then everyone had a nickname, most of which were derogatory or offensive, and unless you wanted to be ostracised, you just accepted it and played along. *Give as good as you get*, Smith always said.

'Don't worry. I can still catch.' She threw the football back hard enough to take Stagg by surprise. His chair tipped back and for a moment Smith thought he was going to topple over. Flailing, Stagg righted himself but couldn't hide the terror that'd flashed across his face. He tossed the football under his desk.

'How's it going?' asked Smith cheerily, pulling up the free chair beside him.

Stagg blew out his cheeks. 'Pissed off would be putting it politely,' he replied, sweeping the *Daily Mail* and a packet of cigarettes to the side of his desk and picking up the report underneath them. He slapped it with the back of his other hand. 'No new forensics off the last one. Sod all.'

'Maybe we should be grateful for that,' she said.

'Eh?'

'She got away, Eddie. Unharmed.'

'Yeah, true.'

Smith became aware of a presence at her shoulder, accompanied by the sound of gum being chewed loudly. She turned to see Detective Constable Roland Wilkins loitering behind her.

'Roland!' Stagg said cheerfully. 'What've you got?'

'Er, just to let you know, sir, Merton borough is going to put on extra patrols around the parks and other areas of interest we sent them.'

'Cheers.' Stagg waited. 'Best mark it on the map, then,' he added.

'Sir.'

As Wilkins shuffled over to the large map they'd been working on last week, which showed and labelled each attack, Stagg shook his head.

'Not a lot of initiative, that one,' he muttered.

Smith was reminded of how Lockhart had treated Khan at the crime scene on Tuesday. She didn't suffer fools, but she also understood that junior detectives needed mentoring. Passing the exams didn't qualify you for anything more than getting started. The real learning was on the job.

Stagg lowered his voice. 'You know what some people in this team call him?'

'Go on.'

'Virgin.'

Smith winced. 'That's unfortunate.'

'Course, it's one of those things these days, isn't it? A choice or whatever. "Self-partnered", I heard it's called.'

'Not quite the same thing, is it?'

Whether or not Wilkins really was a virgin had nothing to do with his policework. But Smith had to admit, the DC was an easy target for ridicule. He stood about five-feet-eight in his shoes, was already balding and carrying a belly, despite only being in his mid-twenties, and had an unfortunate crater right on the tip of his nose, which Smith guessed was a chickenpox scar. The icing on the cake was a high-pitched voice. Poor lad.

Stagg shrugged. 'I don't particularly care what he gets up to when he's not here,' he continued. 'I just wish he had a bit more… you know, nous.'

'Give him time,' she suggested. 'He's just a newby.'

'That's the problem. How are we going to catch this sick bastard if we haven't got experienced coppers working on it? That's why we need you here.' Smith appreciated Stagg's sentiment; when his boss requested input from the MIT as Op Braddock grew, he could easily have been territorial and petulant about the involvement of an outsider. Instead, it was clear he respected Smith and wanted her there.

'Guvnor's got me working on a new murder case,' she said. 'You're lucky I've got half an hour to call in here.'

'Fair one.' He sighed. 'How can any of us get inside the head of someone like that, eh?'

'DC Wilkins?'

Stagg barked a laugh. 'I mean, what's this guy thinking, attacking women like that? Can't bloody well understand it. Just get yourself a girlfriend.'

Smith briefly wondered what Dr Green would have to say about it; would she be able to *get inside the head* of the attacker? She dismissed the thought instantly. It was old-fashioned graft that was going to catch this guy, not psychobabble.

'What's the latest, then?' she asked.

'Actually, I've got an idea I wanted to run by you.' Stagg interlocked his fingers over his gut and leant back in his chair. 'Our perpetrator seems to know the CCTV blind spots, right? So, I was going to propose setting up hidden cameras at the bus stops where he's most likely to attack. Get our own surveillance on him. We monitor the feeds and react in real time. Best chance of catching him, I reckon.'

'Could work. Do you think the brass will sign it off?'

'They've just allocated us a bit of extra budget, so I don't see why not.'

'Give it a go, then,' urged Smith.

'I know it's not a conventional tactic. But the system's just not set up to catch this guy. We haven't got enough cameras.'

'Some people in London think we've got too many,' she countered.

'Yeah, but that lot don't get it like we do, do they? The bleeding-heart liberals. They don't know how many scumbags are out there.' He jabbed a finger. 'I swear, if that bus stop bloke laid a finger on my missus or our daughter, I'd personally rip his bollocks off.'

Smith raised her eyebrows.

'I mean, *you* know what I'm talking about, Max.' He nodded at her, a sly grin forming. 'You did the right thing letting that guy drop last year.'

'Wait a minute. I didn't *let* him drop. He fell.' The memory came to Smith of a suspect from the Throat Ripper case losing his grip on her and plummeting. Sometimes, in her dreams, she'd see the moment his fingers slipped. His body getting smaller, travelling away from her. A split second of eye contact between them. His scream before he hit the ground.

'That's what you had to say for the record, obviously.' He winked at her.

'It's the truth.'

'Fine.' Stagg held up his palms. 'All I'm saying is, you've got to do what you've got to do to stop these bastards sometimes. Especially when the rules ain't helping you.'

CHAPTER TEN

There was always a buzz about team meetings during an active murder investigation. It reminded Lockhart of his time in the military, planning and running long-term operations: what do we know now, how is it useful, and where does it take us next? The only problem was that, in the case of Charles Stott, he didn't think they knew all that much. There had been a ton of activity without much end product. A lot like the search for Lockhart's wife, in fact.

It was at times like these, with the new case taking up most of his waking life, that Jess seemed to get pushed aside. Lockhart hated that and his awareness of it always sparked a sense of guilt. What was it Green had told him during their therapy sessions? *You can't look for her twenty-four-seven.* She was right. He might be feeling bad, but he had a job to do here, too. Protecting the people of London – where he'd failed to protect Jess – was his main motivation for joining the Met.

'Do you want a brew, guv?' The voice broke his train of thought.

DC Parsons was proffering a tray of fifteen mugs which tremored with the effort of holding their collective weight. Despite being furthest away, Lockhart had been given his drink first; a small sign of the hierarchy which he loathed. He'd still not got used to being called 'guv' by his juniors, a title that came with his promotion to Detective Inspector last year.

'White, one, yeah?' Parsons grinned hopefully.

'Spot on. Cheers, Andy.' Lockhart took a mug of tea and watched as Parsons set the tray down on a nearby desk, the rest of the team descending on it like swooping gannets. They were hauling their chairs into position and distributing Jaffa Cakes when DCI Porter marched over, notebook tucked under his arm, and clapped his hands.

'Gather round, everyone,' he announced, his words filling the sprawling MIT open-plan office. Porter was revelling in the exposure this case was giving him; a celebrity death on his patch with corresponding media interest. Lockhart wondered how long his enthusiasm for being SIO would last. If they didn't catch the perpetrator within a week, he reckoned, the balance would tip, and Porter would probably delegate oversight of the whole investigation to him. Which meant letting him take the flak for its failure.

'Shall we start with suspect strategy?' said Porter, though it wasn't a question. 'Dan.'

'OK.' Lockhart stood and turned to face the group. Behind him were two large whiteboards with their list of suspects' names. He gestured to the left-hand one. 'Violent muggers at large in south-west London. We've identified eight individuals, of which we've been able to discount six. Three are tagged and were confirmed as being in their homes, on curfew. Two were signed in for the night at hostels, and one was in Accident & Emergency until four a.m. getting stitched up after a fight in a pub – which is on camera. We've still got to trace the other two, but my money's not on them.'

'We need to keep the robbery theory on the agenda, though,' Porter insisted. 'Don't forget, the wallet and watch were probably taken by the attacker.'

'True, but I think that was just a bonus, if you like, for the killer. If I was going to mug someone, I wouldn't do it in the woods, in the middle of the night.'

Porter snorted. 'No, you'd just sneak up on them, commando-style, right? Knife in the ribs before they even knew you were there.' The DCI mimed a stabbing action.

There were some laughs from the assembled team. Lockhart forced a smile, but he hadn't found it funny. He'd killed six people in combat operations and didn't think it was something to joke about. There were limits to the famous gallows humour of the police.

'Moving on to the second suspect group,' Lockhart resumed, scanning the right-hand board, 'thirty-two women we believe were romantically involved with Charles Stott during his ten-year marriage. None has a male relative or partner with any record of violence. Not that we're aware of, at least. Everyone we've spoken to so far has a decent alibi. Details are in the final column.'

Porter nodded, like he'd expected that outcome and thought this entire strand of their investigation was a waste of time.

'But a pattern of behaviour by Mr Stott has emerged, which feeds into our victim strategy,' Lockhart continued. 'Max, do you want to take over?'

'Sure.' Smith stood and confidently informed the group about the disclosures of sexual assault by Stott, and how none had been reported until now. She concluded by mentioning that they'd never be taken forward because Stott was dead. The words were professional, but her voice indicated the anger she obviously felt. Lockhart shared her sentiment.

'This all needs to be kept very tightly under wraps,' said Porter coolly, when Smith had finished. Lockhart doubted his boss would have the same level of concern for a victim who wasn't a celebrity.

'I hope everyone understands that loud and clear,' Porter added. 'We need to keep the family's wellbeing front and centre.'

'We are,' said Lockhart. 'But we're also considering Stott's widow, Jemima, and her friend, Xander O'Neill, as persons of interest, too.'

Porter narrowed his eyes. 'Not suspects, I'm assuming. I'm not aware of any specific evidence to suggest their involvement. Are you?'

'No, sir,' replied Lockhart. 'But we have to remember that Stott-Peters had been repeatedly cheated on by her husband and will gain financially from his death. Those are potential motives. And there's also been a credible suggestion from a former colleague of Mr Stott that his wife was having an affair of her own, with Xander O'Neill.'

'Do we believe this?' Porter wrinkled his nose as if Lockhart's theory smelled bad.

'No reason to discount it, yet. In fact, Lucy's found something about Mr O'Neill just this afternoon. Right, Luce?'

'Um, yeah.' Lucy Berry, MIT 8's civilian analyst, picked up her notebook and held it almost completely in front of her face. Lockhart knew she could easily recall the relevant information without it, but it acted as a kind of buffer against being the centre of attention.

'Xander O'Neill has two juvenile convictions for violence,' she went on, summarising their dates and details. 'And there's an article online about how he was thrown out of a stage play for brawling with another cast member. No charges were pressed on that occasion, though.'

'Form, motive and opportunity,' Lockhart stated.

Porter shook his head. 'We all got into fights when we were that age. Didn't we?'

Lockhart couldn't disagree with that. But he pitied anyone who'd ever got into a fight with Porter.

'OK, so, don't put him on the suspect list just yet, eh?' The DCI extended a flat hand towards the whiteboards.

'The other thing to say about suspects is the psychological profile,' Lockhart resumed.

'We don't need a psychologist on this.' Porter crossed his arms.

'It's just that the post-mortem showed over eighty separate blows from the killer, several delivered after the point of death. And there's the dog, too. We're probably looking for someone on the psychopathic spectrum.'

'*Spectrum?*' Porter pulled a face. 'Have you been talking to that psychologist friend of yours?'

'No, sir.'

Lockhart knew that Porter wouldn't want him briefing Green on details of the murder which hadn't been made public, particularly on a case regarded as 'sensitive' because of the well-known victim. Porter thought Green was too expensive and hadn't approved of her approach to the Throat Ripper case. He seemed to be ignoring the fact that Green had worked for free, and that her personal investigation had made a significant contribution to them finding the killer last year.

'Good.'

'I think there's something about it, though. The symbol drawn on the neck, the level of violence. One possibility is that it's a man-woman team.'

Porter grunted, clearly unconvinced. 'What about forensics from the scene?'

'Nothing much yet, sir, I'm afraid. We got a couple of partial shoeprints from near the body that didn't belong to Stott. The distinctive honeycomb tread has been identified as a Nike Flex trainer, size eight, we believe. But until we find a credible suspect, we don't have anything to match them to. And we can probably assume the shoes have been ditched by now, anyway, along with other clothing from the murder.'

Porter swore under his breath, staring at the whiteboards with hands on hips, as if some new evidence might materialise. 'OK,' he said. 'Witness strategy?'

DC Andy Parsons stood. He didn't need his notebook, and Lockhart knew why. 'No witnesses, sir,' he stated. 'We went house to house along the roads on two sides of the Common. No one heard or saw anything.'

'Only two sides?'

'Yes, sir.'

'Why not four?'

'Um.' Parsons looked unsure of himself. 'It's, er, the park kind of tapers at that point, so two sides cover the north and east of—'

'Yes, I can see that from the map, Andy.' Porter was getting impatient. Things weren't going his way. 'What I want to know is why you haven't canvassed houses on the south and west sides.'

'There was only the two of us, sir, me and Priya. We prioritised the closest roads. The dog didn't pick anything up, so we didn't think our guy left the park west or south.'

'Do the other two sides.' Porter's tone left no room for argument.

Khan raised his hand briefly. 'Actually, sir, I think we've got a possible suspect on CCTV from inside a bus walking north away from the Common at ten twenty-one p.m.' The young detective was chewing hard, his arms now folded defiantly. 'Fits with time of death,' he added confidently, gesturing to another board where a grainy, distorted wide-angle image had been printed. Lockhart knew it was next to useless.

'And what happens to this so-called suspect after that?'

There was a moment's silence before Khan answered. 'We lose him, sir. But—'

'Well I suggest you find him again, then!' Porter had raised his voice. 'Christ. This is not good enough.'

Khan didn't reply. He just stared at the carpet, his jaw working furiously at the gum. He looked pissed off, for at least the second time since this case started.

Porter scanned the room. 'What about the appeal for witnesses?'

'Sod all, sir,' said Smith. 'There was one highlight worth sharing, though. A voice message from a woman saying she was happy someone had manned up and done it.'

'Any details on the caller, Max?' asked Lockhart. 'Could it be significant? One of our thirty-two, maybe? Or a victim of Stott's we don't know about yet.'

'No idea, guv. She didn't give a name or any other information. Withheld number, too.'

As Berry ran through the victim strategy – which also amounted to very little actionable detail from Stott's telephone or social media – Lockhart realised that they had almost nothing concrete. He sensed morale was low and some of the team were ambivalent about catching Stott's killer, given the accusations of sexual assault made against the victim. But whatever crimes Stott had committed, he didn't deserve to die for them.

Lockhart wasn't a believer in eye-for-an-eye justice. He subscribed to the rule of law, and the judicial process – flawed as it was. If the revenge theory for Stott's death was right, then someone had taken justice into their own hands. And right now, they had no idea who that person might be. Worst-case scenario, it was a stranger. The lack of result was demoralising, Lockhart thought. But it could be worse.

At least they weren't dealing with a serial murderer.

CHAPTER ELEVEN

'I mean, I like the *idea* of kids.' Lexi's flatmate Sarah stirred the wok. 'It's just the whole pregnancy, throwing up every morning, nearly dying while you give birth and then breastfeeding for six months or whatever that I'm not sure about. You know?' She kept a straight face for a few seconds before breaking into a massive grin.

'Sure.' Lexi lifted the chopping board and used the knife to guide the carrots she'd diced into the wok. 'Apart from all that stuff, it's easy, right?'

Sarah cackled; a loud, infectious laugh. 'Exactly. No biggie. Just a tiny lickle person growing inside you.' Her eyes widened. 'Nothing weird about that.'

Lexi knew she could always rely on Sarah to lift her mood when she was a little low or stressed. The two had met a few years back when Lexi was working in a Child and Adolescent Mental Health Services team, during her clinical psychology training. Sarah was the team's dedicated social worker. Despite dealing with heart-breaking situations every day, she somehow managed to stay cheerful. Having met Sarah's reserved, white, English father, Lexi knew she'd inherited this sunny disposition from her Jamaican mom, as well as her love of music. If a song Sarah liked came on, she'd be dancing. And, if Lexi was there, Sarah would always rope her into it. Resistance was useless. When it turned out they were both looking for somewhere to live, moving in together was a no-brainer. They'd become even better friends since sharing a house. Sarah knew about Lexi's brother Shep dying from a drug overdose. But, for some reason, Lexi hadn't told her about the abortion. Maybe even our closest friendships have their boundaries.

Lexi picked up her wine glass and took a gulp. 'I have a client right now whose partner terminated her pregnancy without telling him. He says they should've gotten a surrogate mom.'

Sarah turned to her. 'What did the partner say about that?'

'I don't think they even talked about it.'

'Huh.' Sarah paused. 'One of my uni mates works for a big tech company, right, and there's a bit in her contract where they'll give her twenty grand towards expenses for a surrogate mum.'

'So that she won't have to miss work, right?'

'Exactly. Twenty grand! That works out at pretty much the same wages as I get in the NHS. I told her to come to me first…' Sarah laughed and threw some more spice into the wok.

'Would you do it, though?' asked Lexi.

'What, be a surrogate mum, or have one for my baby?'

'Have one, I guess.'

'Need a man first, don't I?' Sarah winked at her.

'Not necessarily.'

'Talking of which, how's the dating going?' Sarah pointed an accusing finger at her. 'You signed up to that website, didn't you? Like *we* decided you would.'

Lexi didn't really want to discuss her romantic life, or lack of it, even with Sarah. 'Yeah, a little while back,' she mumbled, trying to recall the last time she'd even logged in.

'Come on, then. Any new guys on the scene? Wait.' She held up both hands. 'What about that detective you worked with? You asked him out yet?'

'Oh, you mean Dan?' Lexi knew exactly who she meant.

'Er, yeah.' Sarah pulled a face of mock confusion. 'Unless there are any other ones you wanna tell me about?'

'No. Um, it's complicated. He was my patient, and he's, uh…'

Lexi was spared having to elaborate by the arrival of their new flatmate, Rhys Barker. He shuffled into the kitchen wearing a dressing gown and slippers. Lexi glanced at the clock. It was quarter after seven in the evening. Rhys didn't seem to have much of a life; he came in from his work as some kind of IT manager at the hospital, got out of his office clothes and into his nightwear, then hung out in his room till bedtime. She wasn't going to lie: Rhys was not a natural fit for their house. But after their original flatmate, Liam, had been killed, the brutal fact was that she and Sarah couldn't afford the rent between just the two of them.

They needed someone to take Liam's room, otherwise they'd lose the house. Of course, they'd talked about moving out, bad memories and so on, but they loved the place and the area of Tooting. So, they'd decided to stay. Rhys wasn't their first-choice flatmate, but when the easy-going junior doctor they'd wanted had taken the offer of another apartment elsewhere, Rhys had been ready with his deposit and first month's rent. They couldn't say no.

'Hey, Rhys,' said Lexi.

'All right,' he grunted, taking a plate from the cupboard.

'What you up to?' asked Sarah, her tone light and friendly.

'Nothing much.' That probably meant gaming.

'Cool.' Sarah flicked her eyes to Lexi as she returned to the wok.

Rhys went to the fridge and extracted a grease-spotted pizza box. He slid the cold, hard slices from it onto his plate and leant the empty box against the wall.

'Oh, hey,' said Lexi. 'That can go in here.' She opened the cupboard door where they kept the recycling.

'Can you recycle that?' asked Rhys, nodding at the box.

'Sure.'

He offered her the box. Lexi felt a little stab of rage – she'd gotten a lot of those, recently – and forced herself to be nice. It wasn't her job to deal with his trash. 'That's OK. You can just put it in there yourself.'

Rhys seemed to live on pizza. Lexi and Sarah had invited him to join them for dinner enough times, but he clearly preferred his own company.

Lexi knew from adding him to their lease that he was thirty-one, a couple years older than her, but the poor guy looked forty. He was overweight and had deep purple bags under his dark eyes, as if he didn't sleep. His receding hairline appeared to have retreated further just in the time he'd lived with them, exposing a blotchy purple birthmark high on his domed forehead. She guessed it would've been covered when he had all his hair. It was hard not to stare at it while talking to him.

The only times Lexi had ever seen Rhys get excited were when he was gaming, or when he talked about buses. He seemed to know every route in London and where they all connected, almost like a map in his head. Lexi thought maybe he was a little farther right on the autism spectrum than most people.

He picked up the plate of cold pizza and left without another word. They listened to him trudging up the stairs, and when they heard his door shut Lexi and Sarah looked at one another. Sarah was biting her lower lip.

'Bless him,' she said.

'I'd feel a little more sympathetic if he knew how to recycle his shit.' Lexi took a slug of wine.

'He's probably lovely when you get to know him.'

'And how long is that gonna take? He's been here two months already.'

'OK…' Sarah held up her hands. 'I admit, it's a slow-burn thing. You should tell him about the dating website, Lex. Get him on there…'

'Piss off.' That was one of her go-to British expressions. 'Must be hard dating if you're short.'

Sarah squeezed a lime into the wok. 'I'm five-foot-one and it's never caused me any problems.'

'Yeah, but, you're hot. Anyway, I mean for a guy. Rhys is what, five-seven, five-eight?'

'If that.'

'Hm.' Lexi found herself thinking about Dan. She guessed he was about six-two. Without further consideration, she took out her phone and tapped him a text:

How's it going with the case?

CHAPTER TWELVE

It's incredible how alone it's possible to feel in London. I'm not talking about myself, obviously. I don't give a shit if I'm on my own. I actually prefer it. Having other human beings around is just something which serves a purpose. Whether it's their money, their food, their bodies or whatever else they can offer, people are either useful to me, or they're not. That's the way I've lived my entire life.

What I mean by alone is how, in a densely packed city of nearly nine million inhabitants, you can find yourself completely unprotected. It could be because the richer someone gets in London, the more secluded they become. They buy a larger, detached place to live in, that they don't have to share with neighbours. They pay for the privilege of space, greenery and exclusivity. And that isolation makes them vulnerable.

Like the man I'm looking at right now, for example. He has no idea he's going to die tomorrow. I don't think anyone will miss him. Sitting on his own in a massive house full of rooms he doesn't need. He made his money through law. Compensation claims, specifically. That's important to me. It means he can take some of the blame for what happened. He's brought that on himself with his choice of specialism. It's one reason I've chosen him.

The other is that I can get to him. He plays a solo round of golf every Friday evening, booking the last available tee time at Wimbledon Park course when it's nice and quiet. No one will be playing behind him. There's a spot by the fifteenth hole where I can wait, hidden in the trees. He'll come past, alone, around 7 p.m., just as the light is fading. No one will see or hear a thing.

The thought of attacking him gives me a flutter of anticipation at the pleasure I'll get from doing it. But, once it's over, I don't expect to feel much else. I certainly won't lose any sleep over it.

They should connect it to the last murder pretty quickly. Then Dan Lockhart will investigate. He'll understand that he's dealing with somebody serious.

But he won't know that he's also a step closer to his own death.

DAY FOUR

CHAPTER THIRTEEN

No one could predict where the three murders that London averaged per week would take place. Though MITs under the Met's Homicide and Major Crime Command were based in specific geographical areas, in practice they took cases from all over the city, as and when they were available. That could mean travelling for an hour or two by car just to visit a scene or speak to a person of interest. It was rare that Lockhart got the chance to interview someone within walking distance, so he was trying to appreciate it this morning. Notice the sunshine. Be in the moment, as Green had told him.

As he crossed the Thames at Putney Bridge, heading towards Parsons Green, he thought of her, recalling their text exchange from the previous night. She'd asked how the investigation was going, and whether he'd given any more thought to the meaning of the triangle. He still didn't have a clue. But it had made him think about the relationship between Stott's widow, Jemima, and her young friend, Xander O'Neill.

Lockhart remembered a famous murder case in London from the 1920s. A woman had taken a younger man as her lover and, together, they had concocted a plot to kill her husband and start a new life together. The deed was done by the lover, who stabbed the husband to death while the wife watched. Both were found guilty of murder after the discovery of letters they'd exchanged. It wasn't beyond the realms of possibility that a similar thing had happened here.

Green had suggested they meet again to talk over the case. Lockhart was visiting his mum later this evening, but they agreed to grab a coffee straight after work. Spending time with Green like this gave him a small, nagging sense of unease, but he reminded himself it was business, nothing more.

The Climbing Hangar was tucked away among a narrow strip of industrial units that housed furniture workshops, stone masons and, incongruously, a bridge club. Inside the gym, a few people were on the walls, bouldering to some funk beats that Lockhart had to admit he quite liked. He made a mental note to come here for a climb in the future.

He flashed his warrant card to the guy behind the desk and gestured towards the man he guessed was Xander O'Neill. The actor was mid-climb, grunting his way through a long, punchy overhang route that Lockhart guessed was about a V6 in difficulty: harder than anything he could do. Approaching the wall, he watched as O'Neill progressed higher, his muscles flexing and limbs contorting. Finally, he slapped the top hold with two chalky hands and unleashed a triumphant cry, before dropping to the crash mat, grinning.

Lockhart waited for O'Neill to register his presence before introducing himself and showing his ID. 'Do you mind if we have a quick chat?'

'What about?'

'Charles Stott.'

The young man's smile evaporated. 'I'm on my break.'

'It won't take long,' Lockhart said pleasantly. He needed to keep O'Neill on side, at least for now. 'Just some extra background to help us out.'

A moment later, they were seated opposite each other at one of the small tables next to the reception desk. There was nobody else around them. O'Neill had taken off his climbing shoes and was leaning back in the chair, relaxed.

'How did you know I was here?' he asked, the corner of his mouth twisted in mild amusement.

'I called Jemima Stott-Peters first thing this morning. She said you usually work here on Fridays.'

'Yeah. I do a few shifts in the week. The guys are pretty flexible about me dashing out for auditions. I always keep half a wardrobe in my locker here, so I can do smart, casual, whatever the casting director needs. Hop on the bike and I'm in Soho in twenty minutes.'

'Very handy.'

The actor nodded. 'All right, then. What do you need to know?'

'What was your relationship with Charles Stott like?'

'Well…' O'Neill shrugged. 'To be honest, I didn't really like him all that much.'

'Why was that?'

'As I told your colleague, Charles didn't treat Mimi well. Cheated on her all the bloody time. She was too good for him, and too nice as well. He abused that.'

'How long have you known Mimi?'

'Oh, about… three years. We did a stage show together.'

'Right.'

'We became close friends,' O'Neill said. 'She's wonderful. I care a lot about her.'

Enough to kill for her? Lockhart wondered. 'Did you ever work with Charles?'

'No, but I—' O'Neill cut himself off.

'But what?'

'I… well, this is going to sound strange, but I think he was jealous of me. I probably had a better relationship with Mimi than he did. I mean, she and I actually *talked* about things, you know? Charles didn't like it. Despite sleeping around, he still wanted to possess her exclusively.'

'So, are you saying that he wouldn't have wanted to work with you, because of those personal feelings?'

'Yeah. But I think it went beyond that.' O'Neill flexed his hands. Lockhart could see through the climbing chalk that they were grazed, the knuckles red. 'He never admitted it, but he didn't have to. I reckon it's his fault I haven't been getting work. People in film and theatre talk. And they'd listen to him.'

The *motive* rating had just gone up a notch. 'And what was your relationship with Mimi like?'

The actor met Lockhart's gaze, his expression defiant. 'What do you mean?'

'Were the two of you romantically involved?'

'No!'

'Are you sure?'

'Look, what is this?' O'Neill glanced around before returning his stare to Lockhart. 'Am I a suspect or something? Because if I am, I want a bloody lawyer.'

'No, Mr O'Neill, you're not a suspect.' Lockhart wasn't about to explain to him how reduced custody facilities and higher arrest thresholds meant suspects often had to be interviewed voluntarily now. 'That said, it would be useful if you could tell us where you were on the night that Charles died, just for our records.'

'This is bullshit. You're not pinning this on me.'

'We're not trying to pin anything on anyone. It's just a simple matter of—'

'I was out for a while, OK?' The actor was indignant. 'I was at home, then I went out, then I came home again.'

'What time did you get home?'

'I don't know, ten or so. Nine, maybe. I didn't check my watch.'

'Do you live with anyone else?'

'Yes. There are five of us in the house.'

'So, perhaps one of them would've heard you come in?'

'Perhaps.'

Lockhart nodded. 'And where did you go, when you were out?'

'Just around. Up by the river. Walking. I like to clear my head, you know?'

'Mm.' Lockhart did the same, sometimes. But he wasn't a person of interest in a murder investigation. 'Can anyone confirm your location?'

'No.' O'Neill crossed his bulky arms, a confident look on his face. 'But if you think I'm involved in this, you're the ones that have to prove it.' He winked and Lockhart felt like punching the arrogant prick. Instead, he forced himself to smile.

'Well, that's all for the moment, I think. Thanks for your time, Mr O'Neill.'

'My pleasure,' he said, without a trace of sincerity.

'I'll let you get back to your bouldering.'

The young man reached for his climbing shoes and, as they both stood, Lockhart pointed to them. 'I was thinking of getting a pair of those,' he said. 'They any good?'

'You climb?' O'Neill looked surprised.

'Yeah, a bit. Can I?' He reached out for one of the shoes.

'Scarpa Vapor. They're pretty decent,' said O'Neill. 'Not cheap. They were a present from Mimi.'

'Nice,' observed Lockhart, turning the shoe over. He glanced inside at the label. It was a size 7.5. He knew climbing shoes ran half a size smaller than regular footwear. That made O'Neill a size eight.

CHAPTER FOURTEEN

Returning to Jubilee House, Lockhart went straight to see Porter. Through the window of the DCI's corner office, he could see that Porter was absorbed in paperwork. He knocked, waited for the invitation, and entered.

'Dan.' Porter put down his pen. 'I've just got off the phone to Jemima Stott-Peters. She's very upset that you've been harassing her and Mr O'Neill about her husband's murder.'

Lockhart tensed. 'I wasn't harassing anyone, sir. I spoke to him for background detail, and he happened to mention that—'

'She's grieving,' interjected Porter. 'Relatives of murder victims are to be treated with the utmost respect at all times.'

'Of course, but I believe that O'Neill and Stott-Peters could be in a relationship, and might have planned to get rid of Stott. We both know the stats, sir. In cases like this, killer and victim are usually close. It's often domestic.'

Porter frowned. 'You think O'Neill killed Stott?'

'Either that, or Stott-Peters might've hired someone.'

'And is there any evidence to support this speculation?'

'Xander O'Neill has no checkable alibi for the night of Charles Stott's murder, a personal grudge against the victim, and the same size shoes as the prints from the crime scene. I think he's more than a person of interest, I reckon he's a suspect.'

Porter shook his head. 'I'm not hearing anything definitive, Dan.' He sighed. 'Look, if he turns up on CCTV footage, a witness puts him at the scene, or we get better forensics than his shoe size, that's a different matter. Then, you could question him under caution.'

'But—'

'Until then, tread very carefully around O'Neill and Stott-Peters, OK? Work through that list of women Stott was involved with. Make sure you chase down all those men with form for violent robbery in the area and look wider if you need to. But do not insult our victims' loved ones.'

'Does that apply to all victims, sir, or just the famous ones?' As soon as the words were out, Lockhart regretted them.

Porter's eyes widened and he stood, raising himself up to his full height. 'Don't forget who's in charge here.'

Lockhart knew he'd overstepped the mark. If he wanted to work on his own theory, he needed to be smarter. He had to get evidence that Porter couldn't ignore.

'Sorry, sir,' he said, lowering his gaze to the desk. Now he could see the documents his boss had been reading. One bore an image of the iconic 'New Scotland Yard' sign and was entitled *Superintendent Selection Process*.

'You're going for Super?' asked Lockhart.

Porter glanced down, a flash of irritation crossing his features. He exhaled slowly. 'This is strictly for these four walls, Dan,' he said quietly, dropping back into his chair. 'I've passed the interview. Assessment centre is in three weeks. Scenarios, reports, tabletop exercises, law. God knows how I'm going to find time to prepare.'

'Result on this could really help, though, I'm sure,' offered Lockhart.

'True.' Porter pushed the document to one side. 'What I need you to remember, Dan, is that when there's a celebrity death, not only is the media scrutiny higher, but the deceased also has… influential friends. Powerful people.'

'You're worried this could damage your promotion chances?' Lockhart felt he was starting to understand Porter's approach to the case. He wondered if that same power and influence had led Stott to think he could make advances towards any woman, perhaps even sexually assaulting some, and get away with it.

'All I'm saying is, people are watching,' replied Porter. 'And that goes for you too. If I get the promotion, I'll be moving on to a DSI post somewhere else. That'll leave an acting DCI position open here.'

The implication was obvious. *Play your cards right, don't rock the boat, and it could be you in this seat.*

'I don't have the experience for DCI yet.'

'No? You may be relatively new as DI, but you've been SIO on a large case already. You know this team and it's clear they respect you. No reason why you couldn't take on the temporary duty. You'd get the extra pay plus responsibility. And, in my experience, if that goes well, these things tend to become permanent. I just need to know I can trust you.'

The message was clear.

'Sir,' was all Lockhart replied.

CHAPTER FIFTEEN

'So, in your own words, Emma, can you tell me what happened to you last night, please?' Smith already had a good sense what the woman opposite her would say; the profile fitted the Op Braddock attacks. But she needed to hear it from the victim herself.

Emma Harrison sat hunched over on the large sofa, cradling a mug of tea in both hands. She had just completed a medical examination to attempt retrieval of forensic evidence from her body, though the time elapsed since the assault, as well as the fact that she'd showered, made it less likely that the procedures would successfully detect material from her attacker. Understandably, Emma had gone home after the attack – terrified and traumatised – and only come here this morning.

The Havens in Camberwell, where they were meeting, was one of three specialist sexual assault referral centres in London, and covered the city's southern boroughs. The centres were a joint venture between the NHS and the Met Police, aimed at providing medical, law enforcement, legal and psychological support to victims of sexual crimes. Smith knew that visiting took a lot of courage, and she was determined to help Emma as much as she could.

'I'd been on a night out in Balham, at the pub.' Emma spoke without looking up at Smith. 'Had a bottle of wine with a friend. I was taking the bus home and I got off on Bedford Hill, to change buses. There's another one you can get there that goes a bit closer to my house, but…' She tailed off, her voice cracking. 'I should've just stayed on it. I'm so stupid.'

'No, you're not. This wasn't your fault, Emma.' Smith gave those words a moment to sink in. 'Go on,' she urged gently.

'It was about half eleven. I was sitting at the bus stop, waiting. Had my earbuds in, listening to some music on my phone. I was on Instagram, just, kind of, scrolling. And then he was there, next to me. I hadn't heard him at all.'

Smith had studied the map before meeting Emma. The bus stop where she had been assaulted backed onto a wooded area that was part of Tooting Commons. Smith already knew there were no cameras covering the road.

'What happened next?'

Emma took a sip of tea. 'He had a knife, and he just said, "If you scream, I'll fucking kill you." I couldn't react, I didn't know what to do. Don't know if it was the wine, or what…'

'You probably did what you needed to do to keep yourself safe. If someone with a knife is threatening to kill you, the smart thing is to do what they say.' This kind of reassurance was crucial; Smith had seen many victims of sexual assault blaming themselves afterwards.

Emma didn't reply. She was trembling slightly.

'And then what happened?'

'He grabbed me by the arm and pulled me away from the bus stop into the trees. I could feel the knife sticking in my ribs the whole time, and I just kept thinking, what if he stabs me, what if I end up bleeding to death and no one even knows I'm here?' She sniffed and wiped her eyes with the back of her hand.

'You're doing really well.' There was a brief silence and Smith waited for her to continue.

'Then he told me to open my jeans and pull them down. So, I did it. And then he put his fingers inside me.'

As Emma proceeded to give more details of the attack, Smith found herself becoming angrier and angrier. She wanted to find this bastard herself, and personally make him pay for what he'd done. Empathy for a victim was crucial motivation, but the level of emotion Smith was currently experiencing probably wasn't helpful. If you're too fired up, you miss stuff and your decision-making can get skewed. She needed to find the balance between personal connection and objective distance.

When Emma had finished recounting the man's distinctive appearance – short, stocky, balaclava and black anorak – Smith was certain it was their Op Braddock suspect. Even the gum-chewing detail matched. But she knew that his sexual assault by digital penetration, wearing gloves, would've left little evidence, and she didn't expect the forensic examination to yield any DNA. This guy was careful. He knew how not to leave traces. And that enraged her even more.

As Smith crossed the Wandsworth CID office towards Stagg's desk, the detective stood.

'How is she?' he asked.

'Not good, understandably,' replied Smith. 'But they're looking after her at The Havens. And at least she doesn't have a stab wound to deal with as well as everything else. Small mercies, eh?'

'And it's our guy again, yeah?'

'Yup. New location, but same physical description as the other attacks. Only now he's threatening to kill with his knife, and this sexual assault involved actually penetrating the victim. Digital,' she added.

Stagg had balled his fists and clenched his jaw. 'Bastard.'

'I know. He's expanding his area and escalating the level of violence. It's going to be out of control soon.'

'If I thought it'd make any difference, I'd grab a weapon and go sit at a bus stop myself all night.'

'Well, apart from you carrying a "weapon", Batman, he's targeting different locations anyway.'

'Exactly.' Stagg planted his hands on his hips. 'He's in front of us, Max. We've got to find a way to get ahead of him.'

'What about your cameras idea?'

'Rejected.' Stagg slumped into his desk chair and slapped his palms on his thighs. 'Can you believe it?'

'What did they say?'

'Not *proportionate*.' The big DS almost spat the word out. Then he rolled his eyes and shook his head in despair. 'We've got the technology to help us catch this scumbag and some lawyers are worried about infringing other people's so-called human rights by filming them without their knowledge. It's bollocks, that's what it is.'

'Makes you wonder what it'd take for them to sign it off.'

'Probably a murder.'

'I bloody well hope it doesn't come to that.' Smith looked out across the office at the CID team she knew were stretched to breaking point trying to work dozens of cases without enough staff. Since the Met's Sapphire teams – set up to specialise in sexual assault investigations – had folded two years back, they were covering that now, too. She spotted an empty desk in the next row.

'Where's DC Wilkins today?' she asked.

'He called in sick. Didn't say why.' Stagg arched his eyebrows. 'Gotta be careful these days, can't ask too many questions, you know?'

'Hm.'

'All right.' He snatched an empty mug off his desk. 'I'm making a brew. Want one?'

Smith checked her watch. 'Cheers, Eddie. But I'd better head back to Putney. I was lucky to get a couple of hours away from the murder case to speak to Emma. I'll write it up over there. Keep me updated, OK?'

'Course.' He leant back in his chair. 'So, you working on that director's murder this afternoon then?'

'Yeah.' She grimaced briefly. 'We've still got about fifteen potential suspects to interview who probably aren't suspects at all. If anything, they're more likely to be victims in their own right.'

'Serious? Your guy was a sex pest?'

'Worse than that. He assaulted at least two of the women we've spoken to so far.'

Stagg considered this a moment. 'I shouldn't say this but, between us, sometimes these guys have got it coming to them. Part of me hopes whoever killed your bloke finds our man too, before he scars anyone else for life. Or before he decides that killing someone is a good idea.'

Several members of their MIT had expressed similar feelings towards Charles Stott. Smith agreed with the underlying sentiment, though not the vigilante approach to justice.

'No reason to think our Wimbledon murderer is a serial offender,' she said.

'Unfortunately.' Stagg gave a lopsided grin. 'All right, see you later, Max. Hopefully we'll get a bit of luck on this; otherwise I might end up needing to do something about it myself.'

He turned back to his computer screen. Smith decided it was best not to ask what he meant by that last comment.

CHAPTER SIXTEEN

Martin Johnson closed his large paper file, pushed it to one side of his desk, and picked up the folder for his next case. He flipped the cover and immediately recalled the initial inquiry: a man who lost his footing on a loose paving slab that was supposed to have been fixed. The man had torn his ankle ligaments and was currently unable to work as a long-distance lorry driver. Johnson smelled a big fat pay-out for this one.

Work in compensation claims law was never ending. His firm didn't even need to advertise on TV or in newspapers like some of their rivals. Such was their record of success, they had more people coming to them than they had capacity to take on as clients. The stories varied in terms of physical injury, psychological distress or damage to property, but the bottom line was always the same: someone else was responsible. And that someone needed to pay up.

Councils, employers, leisure centre operators, the NHS, schools, supermarkets, police; it didn't matter. They'd all been dragged to court by Johnson and his firm. And they'd all been taken to the cleaners. Some didn't even make it that far, crying off at the prospect of their public image being destroyed and begging to settle out of court. Business was booming. There was only one thing that wasn't going according to plan: Eva.

Eva was a secretary in his firm. He'd personally hired her, over better qualified and more experienced applicants. Why? Because she was young, and she was bloody gorgeous, that was why. It was the part of Johnson's hiring strategy that he could never put down in writing. The extra mark he added or subtracted from candidates for such positions. And Eva had blown him away at the interview. He'd made it clear that the firm expected a certain level of appearance from its employees, to maintain the high standards that clients expected, of course. For women, this meant wearing make-up and heels every day in the office. Eva had enthusiastically said this wouldn't be a problem. There'd been a twinkle in her eye when she'd replied, he'd felt sure of it. A signal that she was interested.

Everything had gone swimmingly for the first few months. But, when he'd made his move, at the end of a long evening of celebratory drinks following another huge win for a client, she'd rebuffed him. He was certain that after copious champagne and cocktails, Eva would be delighted when he'd started stroking her leg. He'd even booked a hotel room, expecting that she'd drop her knickers that night. But all she'd given him was a firm 'no thanks, Martin' as she got up and left. Now the atmosphere in the office was frosty to say the least.

Johnson worried that Eva might try to file some sort of claim against him. It wouldn't be the first time that'd happened. His hit rate was about two in three, he guessed. Not bad, given that he only went for women half his age. You had to take the rough with the smooth. Usually he could squash the odd complaint before it became official. It was just a question of how much trouble this one would stir up.

Chin up, he told himself. It could be a lot worse. He knew the law on this sort of thing much better than Eva – she wasn't even a lawyer – and was confident he could scare her off long before he was ever called to defend his actions. And, six months from now, there'd be a new young filly in her place, ripe for a ride.

Besides, it was Friday, which didn't just mean the end of the week. It also meant he had a solo round of golf to look forward to this evening.

CHAPTER SEVENTEEN

It was nearly closing time and Monmouth Coffee was winding down for the day, but Lexi could see why Dan had asked to meet here. It wasn't just for the incredible aroma wafting from open crates of roasted coffee beans. Despite being in the middle of Borough Market, right by one of the capital's biggest transport hubs – London Bridge – at rush hour, this café was a chilled oasis. She knew Dan got a little stressed being out in crowded places; they'd been working on that last year in his therapy sessions. Lexi could've happily had a beer to celebrate the end of the week but, at almost six p.m. on a Friday, the pubs around here would be insanely busy.

In any case, she was going out later with Sarah and guessed they'd end up partying pretty hard. They'd always done that; it was just the number of nights out that Lexi had noticed rising in recent months, while her bank balance dropped accordingly. And the amount she was drinking… Before she was forced to interrogate that in more detail, Dan walked in.

She watched him checking the interior – the mental 'threat assessment' she knew he always did in a new place – before he spotted her. He pointed to the counter then to her, and she raised her own cup with the other hand over it to say *I'm good*. Dan got a coffee and brought it up to the mini-balcony where she was sitting, out of earshot from the handful of other customers. There was no hug this time. He took the stool next to her, repositioning it slightly so that he could observe the door.

'Thanks for coming up, Lexi. I know it's a bit out of your way, but this is perfect for me. I can walk to Bermondsey from here.'

Dan had told her he was going to see his mom at her apartment after this. It was cute that he called in on her so much; he obviously cared about her a lot. That old dating advice – *choose a man who's kind to his mother* – popped into her head from nowhere. *Come on, Lexi.*

'No problem,' she replied quickly. 'It's, like, a few tube stops up from work. And I'm meeting Sarah in Soho later on, so…' She didn't need to tell him her evening plans, but for some reason Lexi wanted him to know she wasn't spending Friday night alone. She realised that they could've had this conversation by phone, but neither of them had suggested that.

'You all right?' He took a sip of his coffee and made an appreciative noise.

'Oh, yeah,' she said. 'You know, tired. Long week.'

'Same here.'

'Hey, you ever think about jacking it in, just going and living by the beach or something? I sure as hell do.'

'Definitely.' He paused, lips twisted in amusement. 'But I don't think either of us is the sort of person to actually do that.'

'No?'

'We care too much.'

She considered this. 'You're probably right. Nice idea, though, huh?'

'The beach can always wait till we retire in, what, thirty years?'

'More like forty for me.' Lexi grinned. She was eight years younger than Dan and had occasionally enjoyed reminding him of that.

'Shit. Anyway, you said you had some ideas?'

'Uh-huh.' She shuffled on her stool. 'So, after we talked about the case a couple days ago, it got me thinking. About killers who leave symbols.'

'Right,' said Dan slowly. He already sounded a little sceptical.

'Yeah,' she continued. 'A bunch of psychologists have written about that. I just thought it might be relevant here, what with the triangle and all.'

'OK.'

'The main point they make is that a symbol – whether it's on the body, elsewhere at the crime scene, or in written communication from the killer – is not necessary for the act of violence.'

'Why do it, then?'

'It's about the perpetrator's fantasy. It has personal significance to them. So, if you can interpret the symbol, you can understand something about their state of mind, maybe even their motive.'

'Really?'

'Sure. Look at the Night Stalker, for example. Richard Ramirez. He drew pentagrams at the scenes of his murders, because he believed he was acting on behalf of the Devil.'

Dan drank some coffee. 'I mean, it's interesting… but how is that going to help us catch Charles Stott's killer?'

Lexi had struggled to answer that herself. 'I don't know. If the triangle's a witchcraft thing, could you look at anyone with a record who's expressed both violent fantasies and an interest in the occult? Or anything in the victim's personal life that might link to that? Like, was he a member of any groups?…'

He exhaled slowly, shook his head. 'We don't even know it is about witchcraft. It's a bloody triangle. You said yourself, it could mean a whole load of different things.'

'Right, but it's sure as hell not random.' There was a trace of hostility in her voice. 'Trust me.'

'Maybe.'

'Maybe?' She could feel her irritation rising. 'Come on, Dan. At least a half-dozen sexually motivated serial killers have left symbols on or around their victims' bodies, or signed messages with them. BTK, Zodiac, the Happy Face killer.'

'Happy face?' He snorted a laugh. 'That's not a real person.'

'Yes, it is,' she snapped. 'Keith Hunter Jesperson. Google him.'

He held up his palms. 'OK, I believe you.'

Lexi spent a few minutes explaining how the murderers she'd mentioned had used their symbols. When she'd finished, she sat back.

'Fine.' Dan spread his hands on the table. 'But even if that's accurate about symbols, we're not dealing with a sexually motivated killer, are we?'

'Not directly, perhaps—'

'And it's not a serial crime, either.'

'But the use of a symbol suggests it could be. Maybe this was just the first one.'

Dan took his time over a few sips of coffee. She waited, letting her point sink in, her anger simmering just below the surface.

'Look, I appreciate this, Lexi,' he said eventually. 'But the fact is, we've got to focus our efforts on the most likely suspect. Our victim had a wife who knew he'd cheated on her a lot. If he dies, she gets his multi-million-pound estate. And she's alleged to be having an affair with a young man who has no decent alibi for the time of death. This guy's strong, has a record of violent behaviour, hated Stott, and has the same shoe size as the footprints found near the body.'

'So why haven't you arrested him?'

He sighed heavily. 'DCI Porter doesn't buy it. He won't listen to me.'

'Frustrating, isn't it?'

If Dan had noticed her barb, he ignored it. 'Because they were a celebrity couple, Porter's mega-sensitive about the blowback of any decisions like that. Mainly on his chances of promotion.' He shook his head. 'We need better evidence. And, as of this moment, we haven't got it.'

'Well, maybe you're looking in the wrong place.'

Dan checked his watch. 'I need to go.'

'Sure. Let me leave you with one more fun fact.'

He stood. 'OK. Let's hear your fact, doctor.'

'If a white, heterosexual, middle-aged, middle-class man is murdered, his killer is most likely a *woman* whom he knows intimately. How 'bout that?'

He cocked his head. 'It's not incompatible with my theory. She just had a guy do it for her.'

'Whatever.'

Dan drained his coffee and jerked a thumb towards the street. 'You walking?'

'Yeah.'

As they went their separate ways at Borough High Street, Lexi wondered why the encounter had made her so mad. She felt there was something more to Charles Stott's murder, but she couldn't convince Dan, because she had nothing solid. Kind of like the case last fall...

Thinking back to it reminded Lexi of her old housemate Liam. Normally, he would've been with Lexi and Sarah on a night out, like tonight. Now, he wasn't around anymore. She felt tears prickle at her eyes and decided that she'd drink a little extra this evening to make up for him not being there. And to help her forget.

CHAPTER EIGHTEEN

It's nearly time for action. Almost, but not yet. My problem is that I'm no good at waiting, never have been. Whatever I've wanted, I always needed it right there and then. Some people would call that impulsive. I just call it getting my way. *Patience*, they'd always tell me at school. *Good things come to those who wait.* Or, to those who take what they want.

There's a freedom to letting yourself go, not giving a damn about anyone or anything else and giving in to your desires. How many people can say they live life like that? Almost nobody. Most people don't have the balls to do it. A lot of the ones who try just end up in prison; the dumb ones, anyway. That's where following your *desires* without thinking gets you. But, trust me, those desires are there in all of us.

Scratch the surface of a human being and we're all just chimpanzees with a bit less hair standing on two legs. There's a reason why getting violent is called *going ape shit*. Deep down, we're programmed to fight and fuck and eat and sleep. I mean, that sounds like a great existence to me. Waiting, on the other hand, is no fun. Ever seen a chimp *waiting*? Of course not.

But, in order to get what I want tonight, I need to wait. Until the lawyer comes through with his little trolley of clubs and his stupid plaid trousers. I've passed some of the time next door at the athletics track, where I can train and stretch and watch the golf course through the trees for his arrival. Working out on the track this evening reminded me how much pain there still is in my body after the accident. I have a high tolerance for it, but I still feel it, everywhere, every day. Worse when I do something physical. It's the kind of pain that a compensation lawyer should be able to turn into money. Unless they're corrupt, that is, or shit scared of the powerful people. That's why this guy has to pay. Because the job wasn't done.

I'm ready for it. I've got that low-level simmering excitement, like the anticipation I used to get before filming. But no nerves; I don't really get them. If you asked me to describe what nervous feels like, I couldn't really tell you. It's probably one of the main things that allowed me to be so good at my job. Before it all went sideways permanently. Thinking about that just makes the anger rise up, closer to the surface. It barely even needs a scratch to uncover the raging chimp beneath.

There's a mallet in my coat pocket, ready to get things started. And, when it's done, I'll be sure to leave my mark on this piece of shit. Just to keep them guessing. And to make sure that Dan Lockhart knows about it.

CHAPTER NINETEEN

As Lockhart marched south-east down Jamaica Road and the swish new-build flats gave way to old housing blocks, he replayed his conversation with Green from the café. He'd asked for her help on Stott's murder because of the weird symbol drawn on his neck. But, when she'd given him her theory, he'd pretty much tossed it out.

And, yet, what had happened last time he'd asked Green to profile a killer? He'd dismissed her opinion then, too, and it'd turned out she was right. But this was different, he reassured himself. Then, there'd been evidence that he'd ignored. This time, there was nothing concrete beyond Green's dubious reading of three lines drawn on skin. He wasn't changing his entire suspect strategy because of that. His instincts told him he needed to look more closely at Xander O'Neill. Something wasn't quite right about the cocky young actor.

Turning into the street where his mum, Iris, lived, Lockhart's attention was immediately drawn by raised voices. Two men were shouting at each other on a balcony three floors up, the one outside an open door arrowing his fingers and demanding to know why the man inside hadn't been answering his calls. Lockhart paused, briefly wondering if it was going to escalate and whether he'd need to intervene. But the man inside simply returned a barrage of expletives and slammed the door, leaving his visitor kicking it impotently a few times before giving up and walking off.

As Lockhart started up the stairs towards his mum's flat – he didn't even bother checking if the lift had been fixed – the man passed him, glaring with the wild-eyed look of an addict. He shouldered his way through, muttering to himself. Lockhart had no beef with him, but the whole business was symptomatic of how volatile the estate where his mum lived had become. When Lockhart was growing up here, there were rivalries and fights, but people knew one another and, basically, it was safe. The most dangerous thing you'd encounter was some rowdy lads who'd drunk too much.

These days, there were drugs on the estate, and that changed everything. There were the dealers he'd spot and tip off his Operation Trident colleagues about. Kids cycling around on BMX bikes with little bags across their shoulders when they should be in school. The occasional flat with covered windows whose tell-tale extractor fans couldn't eliminate the thick odour of cannabis plants growing inside. Late-night flying visits from blacked-out 4 x 4 cars that cost more than Lockhart earned in a year, pick-ups and drop-offs. And with drugs came violence. Guns, knives and acid.

Before Jess had gone missing, she and Lockhart had talked about starting a family. They'd even considered moving out of London. He wouldn't have wanted to bring up kids in the mansion block by a flyover across town where he and Jess lived, let alone here. But that was academic now. Still, he'd suggested enough times to his mum that she might like to move somewhere a bit safer. A quieter neighbourhood. But she wouldn't hear of it. *I'm not scared, love*, she'd say. *They can't get rid of me that easy.* And people said he was stubborn.

When he reached his mum's flat, Lockhart was pleased to see she'd shut the front door. He'd often reminded her about that, too, and had half-expected to find it ajar again this evening. He knocked and heard footsteps approaching from the hallway. They sounded unusually heavy. The door opened and Lockhart froze. It wasn't his mum standing there.

It was Jess's brother. Lockhart was struck anew by how much he looked like her and, for a moment, the unexpected memory of his wife rendered him speechless.

'All right, Dan?'

Lockhart stared briefly at the hand that'd been extended towards him and left it hanging. Then he raised his eyes to take in the man he hadn't seen for three or four years. Nick Taylor looked much as he had the last time they'd met. His blond hair, cropped close to his scalp, was a bit greyer than before. But his eyes were the same bright blue as Jess's, the dimples at the corner of his mouth identical to hers. He was clean-shaven and wore a parka jacket and dark jeans over work boots.

'What're you doing here?' said Lockhart.

The history between the two of them went back twenty years, to the early days when Lockhart and Jess were teenagers dating. Her brother, Nick, never approved of Lockhart and said he didn't think the lad from the estate had many prospects. As Jess and Lockhart had continued going out, the tension between him and Nick rose to the point where, one night in a local pub, words had been exchanged and the confrontation escalated. But Lockhart had only just turned eighteen; Nick was twenty-two, not to mention a lot stronger. The older man had kicked his arse outside the pub in front of a crowd of onlookers and Lockhart had never forgotten the humiliation. Neither one had apologised to the other and the grudge had stood ever since.

In some ways, though, that was just the beginning. The real animosity had started when, following Jess's disappearance, Nick had blamed Lockhart for it. *Off playing soldiers when you should've been there for her.* Since then, Lockhart had frequently felt the desire to start a second fight with him. Now, there would only be one outcome of that.

'Nice to see you too, mate.' Nick smiled.

'I'm gonna ask you again, what you doing in my mum's house?'

'Daniel!' Lockhart heard his mum's voice from down the hallway. 'Just come in, love, and let's talk about it.'

'About what?' said Lockhart, pushing past Nick and into the flat. 'Are you OK, Mum?'

She was in the kitchen, stirring a steaming pot of tea. Lockhart kissed her cheek and wrapped her in a big hug, careful not to squeeze too hard. She wasn't very strong these days, although her mind was as sharp as ever.

'I'm fine. My arthritis is playing up a bit more than usual, but I'll live.' She waved away his obvious concern. 'Your brother-in-law called and said he had something to tell us but hadn't been able to get hold of you.'

'That's cos he hasn't got my number,' Lockhart said.

Nick sauntered into the kitchen and took a chair at the small side table.

'Would you like some tea, love?' she asked him.

'Yes, please, Iris,' said Nick. 'Ta very much.'

Lockhart's mum tried to grip the teapot by its handle but could barely lift it off the surface, her hand trembling as she grimaced with the effort.

'Let me, Mum.'

'Thanks, love.'

He poured three mugs of tea and dumped in some milk and sugar. He handed one to his mum before smacking another down on the table in front of Nick and taking a seat opposite him with his own brew.

'Go on, then.'

Nick exhaled a long breath through his nose. 'Iris told me all about Whitstable,' he said. 'I don't know why you're bothering.'

Lockhart shot a glance at his mum but didn't reply.

'I just don't want you wasting your time. We're, um…' Nick drummed his fingers on the tabletop. 'Mum, Dad and I are seeing a solicitor to get her declared legally… dead.'

'What?' Lockhart immediately felt the rage bubbling inside him. He knew Jess's family had long held that belief. But making it formal was something else. A betrayal.

'Dan. Look, mate—'

'Don't call me that.'

'OK, whatever. She's been gone eleven years now. We have to face the facts. And we've got to move on with our lives.'

'You did that a long time ago,' said Lockhart. He jerked a thumb towards the front door. 'She's still out there, somewhere. I know she is. And I'll find her.' He held Nick's gaze, and it was his brother-in-law who looked away first.

Nick shook his head. 'I'm just trying to do the right thing for all of us.'

'Bullshit.'

'Anyway, I'm here to let you know we're going ahead with the claim.'

'No. You can't do that.' Lockhart's voice was low, menacing.

'Yeah, we can.'

Lockhart flexed his hands. 'I'll challenge it. *We'll* challenge it, won't we, Mum?'

Before Iris could respond, Nick spoke. 'Well, good luck with that. But if the judge finds in our favour, and she's declared dead, then we'll be entitled to a share of her estate. Which means you'll need to sell the Hammersmith flat, or buy us out.'

Lockhart snapped. He shot up from his chair, took two steps around the table and hauled Nick to his feet by the lapels of his jacket. His chair clattered to the floor. Lockhart walked him backwards to the kitchen doorway and shoved him through it. 'Get out! Go on, get the fuck out!'

'Daniel!' exclaimed Iris.

Nick didn't resist as Lockhart followed him down the hallway, opened the front door and pushed him onto the balcony. He stumbled and regained his balance, straightening his jacket.

'This is happening,' said Nick, his face flushed. 'The sooner you realise that, the better.'

'I don't want to see you here again,' Lockhart growled.

'You won't.' A smirk twitched at Nick's mouth. 'But you will hear from our solicitor. I'll tell Mum and Dad you said hello.' He walked away, casting one look back over his shoulder.

Lockhart watched him turn into the stairwell and disappear. Then he smacked his fist hard against the open front door. 'Fuck!'

He heard his mum from behind him and turned to see her in the hallway. Her eyes were wet. 'I'm sorry, love.'

'You should've let me know he was coming over.' Lockhart was still furious.

'If I did that, you wouldn't have come. He said there was something important. I knew it'd be about Jess, but I had no idea it was going to be that.'

'You told him about Whitstable, too.'

'I didn't think there was anything wrong with it. If you found something about Jess, he'd have every right to know. He's part of our family, like it or not. If we believe she's alive, we have to accept that.' She reached out a frail hand, touched his sleeve. 'But we'll get through this. You and me, together. Just like we've done ever since your dad died.'

Suddenly, the rage dissipated, and Lockhart drew her into an embrace. 'It's OK,' he said, hearing his own voice catch as his throat constricted. 'I love you, Mum.'

He held her closer this time. Partly because it felt good to be hugged by someone. And partly so she couldn't see the tears he was trying to fight back.

CHAPTER TWENTY

Martin Johnson was enjoying his round of golf. He was only five over par and, with just four holes left to play, it was shaping up to be an excellent round. Of course, solo rounds couldn't contribute to a handicap. The powers that be didn't trust golfers not to cheat when playing alone. They obviously hadn't realised that it was perfectly possible for two friends playing together to collude on a falsified scorecard. But he didn't care. It was Friday night, the air was pleasantly cool and dry, and this was his time. No one could bother him out here. No calls, no emails, no whining clients, no self-righteous judges. And no secretaries complaining about his touching. He hadn't exchanged more than a few words with Eva this week and briefly wondered if she was plotting something.

'Excuse me.'

The voice snapped Johnson out of his rumination, and he turned towards it.

'I've lost a ball. Would you mind helping me look for it, please?'

Johnson exhaled noisily. Normally, he wouldn't waste time assisting anyone. But he couldn't abide the thought of someone playing behind him.

'Fine,' he replied, leaving his trolley on the fairway and crossing to the rough. He carried an iron to prod the long grass under the trees.

'I think it's somewhere round here. Shanked the bloody thing.'

'Right, let's have a look,' he said, turning towards the thicket of mature evergreens. His strategy was to check for about half a minute, then tell this idiot to take a one-stroke penalty and play out from the edge of—

The impact spun him around and he dropped like a sack of potatoes, the club slipping from his hand. But he was still conscious, at least. What'd happened? Had he been hit by a ball? He felt his feet rising and, next, he was being dragged deeper into the trees where it was almost dark. He cried out and managed to grab something, but it was just a tuft of grass that came away in his hand. He scrabbled around desperately for anything that could help him.

Then an almighty blow connected with his ribs, and another, sending raw bolts of pain through his torso. Eyes shut, Johnson crossed his arms in front of him just as a fist connected with the side of his face. He tasted the warm tang of blood and turned away instinctively, confused and terrified. As the punches and kicks continued to rain down, Johnson curled up, shielding his head, desperate to protect himself.

But there was nowhere to hide.

DAY FIVE

CHAPTER TWENTY-ONE

It was mid-afternoon on Saturday by the time Lockhart arrived at the golf course. After the shock of the news he'd received from his brother-in-law, he'd risen early from a broken night's sleep and gone swimming in the Thames. Wetsuit, cap and goggles on, he'd battled upstream through the cold and foul-tasting water towards Putney Bridge. Now and then, the sheer physicality of struggling against the river would take his mind off Jess and the idea that she could be declared legally dead. But, each time, his thoughts quickly returned to her, and to the possibility of that terrible verdict. He'd fight it with every ounce of energy he possessed.

After drying off and changing out of his wetsuit, he'd driven back to their flat and spent the rest of the morning online, researching how to challenge a claim of death for a missing person. He'd not stopped, even to eat, until he'd received the call around 2 p.m. A flustered PC Leo Richards – one of the MIT's uniformed officers – had informed him that a body had been discovered at Wimbledon Park Golf Club. Lockhart had initially demanded to know why, at the weekend, the on-call team wasn't dealing with it. Richards had told him about the triangle drawn on the victim's neck. Then it had made sense. Since Porter was at City Hall, speaking at a conference on Crime and Policing, it fell to Lockhart to attend. Somewhat reluctantly, he'd shut down the laptop and grabbed his jacket.

Dropping his Defender in the golf club car park, Lockhart stepped out and glanced around. He saw a couple of white vans he knew belonged to the SOCOs, and a grey coroner's van, but there were also a dozen civilian vehicles he didn't recognise. At the sound of crunching gravel, he turned to see PC Richards walking across to him. He wore a blue Tyvek protective suit that'd been unzipped to the waist.

'All right, guv,' said the young man.

'Leo. What are all these cars doing here?'

'Oh, er, they've still got the bar and driving range open. Plus a few holes near the clubhouse. They said that—'

'I don't care what they said. Get inside and tell the manager to close the whole place down immediately. Any part of it could be a crime scene, if they haven't destroyed every bit of evidence by now. Jesus.'

'OK.'

'How did this happen?'

'The club was open when the body was found,' Richards explained. 'The manager told me they didn't want to scare the members, so they've kept it all quite low-key. Business as usual, you know?'

Lockhart rubbed his eyes. He suddenly felt exhausted. 'What about the HAT?' He knew the Homicide Assessment Team would've been first on the scene and might have crucial early evidence.

'They've gone, guv.'

'Gone?'

'Yup. Once I was here and they knew you were on the way, they buggered off. Called to a stabbing in Highbury, apparently.'

'They speak to anyone?'

Richards shrugged. 'The manager, I think. And the woman who found the body when she hit a shot into the trees on the fifteenth hole.'

'You got handover notes?'

'Nope.'

Lockhart tried to contain his frustration. He was on a very short leash. 'Please tell me some good news.'

'Er, the duty pathologist's here.'

'Which one?'

'Dr Volz.'

'OK.' That was a start, at least. 'What do we know about the victim?'

'Manager reckons it could be a Mr Martin Johnson. He signed in alone for a round at six p.m. last night and hasn't been seen since. They just assumed he'd left without signing out. But his car was still here this morning. That's it, there.' Richards indicated a black Porsche 911 across the car park. 'And they found an abandoned set of clubs, which probably belongs to him.'

'Right. I'll go and take a look. First thing I need you to do, Leo, is get in there and shut this place down. Completely. Find out the names of everyone who was here last night, staff or players, and ask any of them that are here now to stay put. Get the contact details for anyone else. Work out what CCTV we have access to.'

'Will do, guv.'

'The club should give us Mr Johnson's home address,' Lockhart continued. 'There might even be a next of kin listed. We need to confirm it's him and not some other poor sod. But don't make any death calls just yet, all right?' Lockhart took out his phone and began dialling Smith. 'I'll get some reinforcements.'

After changing into protective gear and registering with the Crime Scene Manager, Lockhart lifted the tent flap and entered. He found Volz inside, squatting beside a body. The scene was disturbingly familiar.

'Hi, Mary.'

'Dan.' Volz stood and slipped her mask down. 'PC Richards told me you'd be coming. This is very similar to the Charles

Stott murder. I haven't examined him a great deal, yet, but you can see that the facial injuries are worse than those inflicted on Mr Stott.'

Lockhart looked down at the corpse. It was a pitiful sight. The man was almost in a foetal position, as if still trying to defend himself, though Lockhart knew some of that was probably the result of rigor mortis. Where a face had once been, there was now a bloodied pulp. The front of the skull was caved in, some white teeth jutting grimly from red flesh.

'Christ.'

No sooner had he begun to imagine the brutal end to this man's life than the memory came to him. He was back inside the house in Helmand. The interior was smoky from the flash-bang grenade he'd dropped, but cooler than the baking, still air outside. He'd lowered his weapon onto the floor tiles so that he could climb in through the window. As he stood and the smoke dissipated, a man appeared in front of him. Lockhart recognised the sniper rifle slung over the guy's shoulder, the camouflage wrapping around its long barrel. He had to make a split-second decision. And, without further thought, he charged forward.

'What I would expect,' continued Volz, her voice snapping him back to the present, 'is that an attack this frenzied would've left some evidence. I'll make sure that the SOCOs gather plenty of samples here, and I can look for more back at the mortuary. Let's see if we can extract foreign DNA, fibres, that sort of thing.'

'Yeah.' Lockhart cleared his throat. Tried to gather his thoughts. His pulse was racing, his mouth dry. He swallowed. 'And the symbol?' He could see half of it already on the side of the neck that faced upwards.

'I presume that's why you were called,' Volz said. 'Quite apart from the other similarities.' She knelt and lightly drew away the collar on the victim's jacket. 'Appears identical to the one drawn on Stott's neck.'

'Except it looks like it's facing the other way. Pointing up.' He thought of Green's initial observation. 'Could the direction of it be significant?'

Volz angled her head. 'I don't know.' She paused. 'But what I can tell you is that this man has been dead for over twelve hours.' She took the victim's hand and applied some pressure to bend his arm and wrist back out, but it stayed in position. 'He's in the peak phase of rigor mortis. So, since we know that his golf round started at eight, you're looking at a similar time of death to the previous victim. Between seven and eleven p.m., I'd say. Might get a more accurate time from his stomach contents if you can find out when he last ate.'

'Thanks, Mary. Let me know if you find anything the killer might've left.' He glanced towards the tent flaps. 'We're in the dark right now.'

Lockhart stepped outside, somehow relived to be out in the open air again and away from the bloodied corpse, particularly after his flashback to Afghanistan. Why was this happening now? It was years ago that he'd been there. Must be the new case. Green would call this a 'trigger'. He ought to ask her about it. And he should probably also let her know that, now, they appeared to be dealing with a serial perpetrator.

CHAPTER TWENTY-TWO

The display on Lockhart's Suunto watch read 18:52. Having spent nearly four hours at the crime scene, this was the first chance he'd had to go to Jubilee House and brief DCI Porter. On the way back, he'd finally acknowledged that he was ravenous and made a pit stop at one of the local cafés. He'd grabbed a sausage-and-egg sandwich and inhaled most of it by the time he returned to his Defender. This was how the job ruled your existence: bodies, suspects and witnesses dictated your working hours and routinely trumped in importance anything else you were doing. Lockhart wondered if, should Jess return, he could continue to live such an unpredictable, all-consuming professional life. The thought vanished as he approached Porter's door and knocked. Inside, he could see the boss was still in his dress uniform from the conference. Porter finished a call on his mobile as Lockhart entered.

'Linked incidents then, eh, Dan?' The DCI looked quite pleased with himself. Lockhart didn't think it was cause for self-congratulation.

'Appears that way, sir. Significant similarities in the MO. And, more importantly, we never went public with the triangle symbol.'

'Of course, you know what that means.' Porter tilted his head. It reminded Lockhart of a schoolmaster. Or an officer from his military days. The exercise of authority. He understood what he was expected to say in reply, but he didn't want to play Porter's little game.

'That the killer was likely to have crossed paths with both Charles Stott and Martin Johnson at least once before the time of their murders, since it appears they were targeted.'

They'd tentatively confirmed the lawyer's identity less than an hour ago, after cross-referencing the clothing worn by the victim with CCTV from the golf club car park and reception. In those video images, his face was recognisable and matched the sign-in time on his membership. Volz would confirm it tomorrow with his dental records, probably, although such was the destruction of Johnson's face that even that wasn't a given.

'Perhaps.' Porter raised his eyebrows. 'And, crucially?'

'Well, unless Jemima Stott-Peters, Xander O'Neill or any of the women on our list who might've had a grudge against Stott also knew Johnson, we'll need to overhaul our suspect strategy.'

'Exactly. Which means leaving Ms Stott-Peters and her friend Mr O'Neill well alone. They're obviously nothing to do with this.'

Lockhart knew his boss could be right, but his gut told him he'd still need to clear them both for last night. 'Given their connection to the first murder,' he began, but Porter lifted a hand to silence him. 'I think we should—'

'Leave them alone, I said.'

Lockhart didn't respond. He wasn't going to argue about this now. But neither was he intending to follow orders. He concluded that, on this occasion, it was probably easier to seek forgiveness than permission.

'And, the wallet was gone?' asked Porter. 'Phone and car keys left?'

'That's right.'

'What about a watch?'

'Still on his wrist,' replied Lockhart.

'Hm. Well, cast the net wider on those violent muggers. Whole of the Greater London area.'

'Sir, my sense is that there's something more complex than a robbery going on here. There's the triangle symbol, and if Lucy can run the data, I reckon we can find the link between Stott and Johnson. There has to be one,' he added, hoping he was right.

Porter leant back in his chair and regarded Lockhart with something approaching sympathy. 'Go home and get some rest, Dan. You look like shit.'

'Thank you, sir.'

'You're welcome. I mean it, though.'

'About me looking like shit?'

'About getting some rest.'

'Right. I'll just write up some notes and rally a few more troops for tomorrow morning, then I'll be off.'

'Good man.' Porter pressed his lips into a half-smile and picked up his phone again. 'I'm going to convene a short press briefing.'

'Will you need me there?'

'No, that won't be necessary. Maybe you could do an appeal from the golf club, though, a bit like with the Stott murder on the Common. See if that jogs people's memories.'

Lockhart groaned inwardly. He'd do whatever was required to help progress the case, but he had no desire to be a media figure. And a cynical voice told him it was simply box-ticking by Porter, anyway. Investigating by numbers. He imagined the boss reeling off the checklist during his Superintendent's assessment: crime scene piece to camera, impact statement from victim's loved ones, simultaneous TV broadcast and upload to the Met's YouTube and Facebook channels…

'Sir.' He turned and walked towards the door. Gripping its handle to let himself out, he paused and swivelled back to Porter, who was already scrolling on his mobile screen.

'Maybe we should bring in a psychologist,' said Lockhart.

Porter scoffed. 'No way,' he replied, without looking up.

'If it's stranger violence, or something else signified by the triangle, then a victim or offender profile could really help us.'

'Not happening.' Porter finally stopped reading his texts and raised his eyes. 'I know where this is going. My budget doesn't stretch to your friend, Dr Green. We can't afford her, and I don't think we need her input to this case. I'll tell you what's going on here: an extremely violent mugger is attacking wealthy men who are out on their own at night in dark, isolated pockets of the city. There are your profiles. Now go.'

'With respect, sir—'

'Go! Get some rest, and we'll start again tomorrow morning. Bright and early.'

Lockhart bit back his frustration and nodded. He was already dialling Green's number before he'd returned to his desk.

CHAPTER TWENTY-THREE

Something needed to change, Lexi thought, as she allowed Netflix to skip the credits and automatically start the next episode. It wasn't the show that was the problem; *Unbelievable* was probably the best thing she'd watched on TV in a while. It wasn't even the fact that she was home, alone, lying on the sofa on a Saturday evening. She could cope without Sarah's company for one night while her buddy attended a family birthday dinner with her cousins; Lexi had been invited but politely declined. It wasn't that, either. It was the hangxiety.

It had started first thing, when Lexi woke up, groggy as hell and maybe still a little wasted from the night before. She'd felt horrible, throwing up twice in the toilet and unable even to look at the breakfast she normally devoured on a Saturday morning. Why did she drink so much last night? She'd found a receipt in her jeans pocket, from a quarter after two in the morning, for a round of drinks in a club that'd cost sixty pounds. One round. She couldn't even remember what it'd been or who it was for. She didn't have that kind of money to throw away on alcohol. Then there was the text from an unidentified guy asking her if she wanted a hook-up. Lexi had no recollection of giving out her number. Jeez, she needed to get a hold of herself.

But the hangxiety wasn't just about feeling awful and nauseous, and realising that you'd spent money you shouldn't have. It was a whole lot more than that. Wondering what the hell you'd done between 1 and 3 a.m. when there was just a big blank space in your memory. Hating yourself for spending an entire day on the couch, totally unproductive. She couldn't face a run or a CrossFit class and had barely been able to stomach so much as a coffee until this afternoon, but even that had only succeeded in making her more jittery.

Clinical psychologists were trained to solve human problems. To map symptoms to causes. To link thoughts, emotions and behaviour. To find strengths and tap into them to make things better. And she had to be honest. Deep down, she knew that her drinking was the result of what'd happened to her last fall. The case Dan had brought her into. It wasn't his fault; Lexi couldn't blame him. If anything, she owed him. She'd gone her own way and, though she'd been right, it was Dan who'd saved her. She could always have said no when he asked her to help. But she'd said yes, and that decision had ended up scarring her, physically and mentally.

Lexi had told herself a few times over the past couple months that she simply didn't have time to see anyone about those problems. That she could fix them herself. But it was a lie. She was in denial about how bad this was, about how her control over her life was slipping away. It was as much a reaction to losing Liam as it was the result of what'd happened to her. And her brother Shep's death by drug overdose years back was still a factor, too. She wasn't sure she'd fully dealt with that yet, either.

Maybe if she had a project, something to take her mind off it all?… She knew that wouldn't be enough, though. She'd been through some major traumas and needed to process them properly. That's what she spent all day telling her clients at the clinic. *We have to face up to these events and deal with them, rather than avoiding them. So that they don't scare us anymore.* What was that old phrase? Physician, heal thyself. That was it. Tomorrow, she would make a plan. And things would start to improve.

With that resolution, Lexi felt a little better. She returned her focus to the show and watched as Marie, the young woman at the centre of the story, found her life unravelling following a sexual assault. Nobody believed that Marie was telling the truth, because she'd dissociated during the attack and couldn't remember any details. It made Lexi think of her own experience, three years ago. It hadn't been anywhere near as bad, thank God, but she still remembered it clearly.

She'd been walking home from her work placement at a hospital in another part of town, and a man had followed her for a while before catching up with her and claiming that she'd dropped something. But when she'd stopped, he'd tried to pull her into an alleyway, grabbing her breasts before attempting to push her to the ground. She'd yelled and screamed and, though no one had come to help her, the guy had gotten spooked and run away. She was left sitting by a wall, crying, shaking and wishing she'd had some way of protecting herself. It had been six o'clock in the evening, and still light.

Lexi had reported it to the cops, given a description of her attacker as best she could. But she sensed that, because she hadn't actually been *raped*, they weren't taking it all that seriously. Like it was just a normal thing that happened to women. They never caught the guy. Lexi wondered how many more women he'd attacked since then.

A noise made her start and she looked up to see her housemate, Rhys, standing in the doorway. He wore his dressing gown and carried a whole pizza on a large plate. The smell of it made her stomach lurch; she'd still not eaten properly all day. Add hangry to hangxious. *Way to go, Lexi.*

'What's this?' he asked, his eyes on the TV screen.

'*Unbelievable.*'

'OK.' He came in and took one of the armchairs.

Great, thought Lexi. Just when she actually wanted to be on her own, for once, Rhys shows up and decides to be sociable. She told herself to be nice, make an effort. Let him feel welcome. It was a shared house, after all…

'You had a good day?' she said, hearing the fake cheer in her own voice.

'Not bad.' Instead of elaborating or reciprocating with a question about her day, he crammed in a whole slice of pizza and proceeded to chew it with his mouth open. The noise made her want to throw up again. Lexi tried to concentrate on the show and block him out. At some point, she glanced across and found that, rather than watching the TV, Rhys was staring at her. He immediately looked away. She felt icky, but tried to return her attention to the screen, nudging the volume a little higher to mask the sound of him eating. It didn't work.

'It's episode four,' she said, thinking that a little conversation might help. 'You want a quick recap of the first three?'

'No, thanks,' he said. 'I'll work it out.'

'Sure.'

As Rhys carried on munching his pizza open-mouthed, Lexi felt herself physically tensing. If it went on much longer, she was either gonna scream at Rhys, throw the remote at him, or go postal on his ass. Then her cell phone rang. It was Dan. On a Saturday night. OK, she thought, swiping to pick up.

'Lexi.' The way he said her name sounded serious.

'Hey, gimme a second,' she told him, hauling herself off the sofa. She felt some of the tension drop as she climbed the stairs and shut the door to her room. 'What's going on?'

'Sorry for disturbing your weekend.' He sounded stressed.

'It's all good. You OK?'

Dan paused a beat before responding. 'There's been another murder. Like Charles Stott. Middle-aged guy, beaten to death, triangle on his neck.'

'Oh my god.'

'So, listen, I wondered if you'd be able to do a profile for us. Two profiles, in fact. Suspect and victim. If he's murdered two people in a week, there could be more.' He was talking fast. 'We need to know who we should be looking for, and who he might attack next.'

'Dan, seriously, are you OK?'

She heard him exhale hard.

'There's some other stuff,' he replied. 'But it's not about work. I'll tell you another time.'

'Sure.'

'So, what do you reckon?'

'Uh, I thought you weren't really interested in my theory about the symbols—'

'That was then. We have two victims now. It's different. You can look at it with fresh eyes. No assumptions, like you said.'

'And what happens if you don't like my conclusion, again?'

'We'll cross that bridge when we come to it. For now, I just need anything you can give us.'

Lexi had that creeping sense of dread at getting into this further. But she needed something constructive in her life right now. To do something useful, make an impact. And she sure as hell owed it to Liam, and to Shep, to help wherever she could. If she could save a life, that would go some way to making up for her failures. She took a deep breath and closed her eyes.

'I'll do it.'

'Thank you.'

'All right, so, you want me to come in?' she asked. 'Like, tomorrow or something, read the files?'

'Yeah, that's where we might have a slight issue.'

'We?'

'Me and you.'

'Right…'

'Porter doesn't want you working on it.'

'Thanks a bunch. What'd I do to upset him?'

'Nothing. It's not personal. Well, maybe it is a bit. I suggested a psychologist, he said it wasn't necessary and we don't have the budget for you.'

'You know I'll do it for free, Dan.'

'Cheers. But the problem is, now he's said no, I can't bring you in officially. He's SIO, it's his decision.'

'So, what do we do?'

'I can copy some of the files,' he said. 'And take them home. So maybe you could come over and read them at my place tomorrow? I mean, if you're free.'

'Sure.' Had she agreed so quickly because there was an invite to Dan's apartment? 'What time?'

'Eight in the evening? Gives us a chance to do some analysis in the day, see what we can gather about the new victim.'

'Eight works.'

'Great.'

'Dan?'

'Yeah?'

'Could we get in trouble for this?'

'If anyone finds out, it'll all be on me. I'll protect you, I promise.'

Dan was the sort of guy who you believed when he said those words. But it didn't stop there being a risk. She was pretty sure that reading classified police material had to be illegal in some way.

'OK, then,' she replied. 'See you tomorrow night.'

'Cheers.'

Lexi rang off. Her dread of a few moments ago had started turning into a buzz. She hoped it wasn't just the hangxiety returning.

DAY SIX

CHAPTER TWENTY-FOUR

Smith brought the car to a stop and studied the large detached house set back from the road. Castelnau, the broad street running north to Hammersmith bridge, bisected the exclusive district of Barnes that was contained within a large meander of the Thames. The houses were all spotless white stucco and London brick, each with two or three upmarket vehicles in the driveway. She knew there wouldn't be a single property here under seven figures. It was the sort of area that Smith could only dream of living in, though it was well within the price range for a law firm partner like Martin Johnson.

'This the place, then?' She turned to Khan.

He nodded. 'Yup.'

Smith thought he seemed a bit down. He'd been quiet on the way over, and she suspected it was more than simply having to work both days of the weekend. 'You OK, Mo?'

'I'm fine.'

'It's just you look a bit… out of sorts, that's all.'

'Said I'm fine.'

'All right, I'm only asking. Come on, let's have a look inside.'

On a Sunday morning, the street was eerily quiet. Smith extracted the keys from her pocket, momentarily considering how, two nights ago, the very same bunch was in the pocket of a man who thought he'd be coming back here after his round of golf. Instead, he'd been beaten to death and, for some reason, had had a triangle drawn on his neck. The second middle-aged guy that'd happened to in a week. And Smith had a feeling this killer wasn't stopping at that. There was a message behind it. But she was buggered if she had a clue what that was. She reached out and inserted the key, twisting it and opening the door.

No sooner had she stepped inside than an alarm began blaring at her, angry and deafening.

'Christ's sake, Mo!' she shouted. 'Didn't you check if there was an alarm?'

'I-I must've forgot.'

Smith fished out her mobile and called the security company number listed on the box. She had to go back outside to be heard over the noise. After giving her rank, name and badge number, she was put on hold for a minute – the alarm screaming with increasing urgency – until finally the noise stopped. She thanked the guy and hung up. There was total silence, but she could still hear the alarm pulsing inside her head. A curtain twitched across the street and Smith turned to go back inside.

'That was not what I needed at this time in the morning,' she said.

'Sorry,' mumbled Khan.

'Big night last night, was it?'

'No.'

'So, what's your excuse, then?'

'What d'you mean?' His irritable tone reminded Smith of her son during his teenage years.

'How come you're not on your A-game today?' *Or this entire week.*

Khan shook his head but didn't say anything.

Smith closed the door gently and faced him. When he finally made eye contact, she spoke. 'You've not been yourself lately, Mo. What's up? Come on.'

She let the silence hang like she was running an interview; people couldn't help but fill it eventually.

'It's…' Khan sucked his teeth briefly. 'Just my family, innit.'

'Your parents?'

'Yeah. They're on at me the whole time about getting married. Some second cousin in Karachi they're trying to set me up with. Uncles and aunts and cousins and what-not all gettin' involved. Nice Muslim girl, wedding over there, she'll move here. All you have to do is say "yes", Mohammed.'

'Sounds stressful.'

'Damn right it is.'

'What do you think?'

'I think it's bollocks. I've been on a few dates with this girl I met online. Here, in London. She's great.'

Smith could see he was fighting his anger.

'But no way could I tell Mum and Dad about her,' he continued. 'She's not Muslim. She don't even believe in God.'

Smith thought for a moment. 'There any way you could talk to them? Let them know the arranged thing isn't what you want?'

'I tried. Only reply they gave me was that if I wasn't up for it, I can get out of their house.'

'Shit.'

'Yeah. It is shit. Where am I gonna go?'

Smith didn't have an answer for that. She knew Khan's finances were limited, on a new DC's salary and with student loan repayments. 'I'm sure you'll work it out with them.'

'You don't know them. Their rules are like… rigid. No debate. It's pissing me off.'

'All right, well. Let's do what we've got to do here. At least that'll take your mind off it for a bit, yeah?'

'Doubt it.'

They walked through into a large, open-plan living space which had obviously been re-fitted recently with a top-spec kitchen area and designer furniture. Together, they began checking the surfaces, drawers, bookshelves and cupboards for anything of interest. Any indication of something that might not be right in this seemingly perfect home. Any reason why someone might've wanted to kill Martin Johnson. But there wasn't much to go on here.

'Pretty sick how one guy had all this,' observed Khan, peering through a set of French doors into a landscaped garden.

'Doesn't seem like he had much love, though. No partner, no children. Parents dead. Just one younger sister who was living in Australia. PC MacLeod called her yesterday. Said she got the impression they weren't close. They hadn't even spoken for six months, and she was his nearest relative.'

'Not all families are close,' remarked Khan.

'And maybe some are closer than they'd like to be.'

'Yeah, right.'

'I don't think Martin Johnson was close to anyone.' Smith gestured to the walls and bookcases. 'Can you see a single photo of another human being?'

'Might be some upstairs.'

'OK. You take a look up there. I'll check out the study.'

Smith went through into Johnson's home office, hoping that she never became isolated in the way that their victim appeared to have been. She had her fella, and her son. Her folks were still around, too, though they'd moved out of London. She decided to give them a call after her shift. Something about the loneliness of Martin Johnson's life had pierced her professional armour. But it didn't take her long to snap back into work mode when she saw the document on his desk.

Neatly printed and laid out, as if he'd been examining it just before he left the house. Smith skim read the first few pages. It was a legal piece about sexual assault claims: how they were processed and investigated, and what evidence the Crown Prosecution Service required to reach a threshold of criminal charge. She took out her phone and began photographing the pages, turning them over carefully by the edges. She'd finish this and then see if there were any other similar—

The smash and tinkle of glass from upstairs made her freeze. Her first thought was that there might be an intruder, or someone in the house.

'Mo?' she yelled. 'Mo!'

Smith pocketed her phone and raced out of the study, heart thumping. 'Mo!'

An anguished cry came from the upper floor. Smith took the stairs two at a time. On the landing, she followed the sound into the bedroom.

'Jesus, Mo.'

Khan stood staring at the ground. In front of him was a large picture frame, face down, shards of broken glass spilling out from it onto the wooden floorboards.

'I think it was expensive,' he groaned. 'I wasn't concentrating, and I just turned around and then...'

'You know you'll have to fess up to the boss about this.'

'Come on, Max. Please.'

'What? Don't look at me like that. We can't just leave and pretend it didn't happen.'

Khan shook his head and stormed back downstairs, muttering to himself.

'Oi, Mo!' she called. But he didn't reply.

As they entered the MIT office, Smith took Khan by the elbow. 'You've got to tell him about the picture frame, Mo, or I will. There's insurance for this sort of thing. But you've got to be honest about it.'

Khan hadn't said a word the whole journey back, seething silently beside her. Smith remembered he'd been shouted at by both Lockhart and Porter for his work in the past week, and she didn't envy the task he now had.

'You want a brew?' she asked.

'Nah, I'm good.' Khan threw a piece of chewing gum into his mouth and walked across to where Lockhart was standing by Lucy Berry's desk, his shirt sleeves rolled up, studying something on the analyst's screen.

Smith went to the kitchen and flicked the kettle on. She needed to top up her two main fuel sources: caffeine and sugar. While she waited for the boil, she scoffed a banana and helped herself to a handful of chocolate digestive biscuits from a jumbo-sized team packet on the side. That wouldn't last long. She was just pouring the water into her mug when she heard raised voices – mainly Lockhart's – from the open-plan office. This was followed quickly by Khan stomping past her, shouting expletives as he threw the door open and left.

That went well, then.

She remembered mistakes she'd made in her early days as a detective. Everyone made them. But this would hurt for Khan. He looked up to Lockhart, regarded him as a role model, partly because of his military background. The guvnor hadn't shared many stories from his army days. In fact, Smith had the impression he didn't like to talk about it much. But they all knew he was hard as nails. There was a running joke about how many people he'd killed, only it wasn't really a joke.

Smith hadn't heard the exact words exchanged just now, but being chewed out in front of everyone by Lockhart would've seriously dented Khan's ego. He needed to learn and improve, but it was also a question of how those messages were delivered. A quiet word was usually much better than public humiliation. In the middle of a double murder investigation, though, that was easier said than done. She resolved to give Khan a pep talk later, when things had cooled down.

They all got stuff wrong. Even with the benefit of twenty years' experience, she did. Like last autumn on the Throat Ripper case. She had a sudden image of the suspect falling from the balcony, the sound of his scream followed by him hitting the concrete below. A pang of guilt stabbed her, and she wondered if she should perhaps go to visit the guy in the care home where he now lived, confined to a wheelchair and with a permanent brain injury. But what would she say to him? And would he even be able to understand her? She decided to leave that idea in the kitchen for now.

Carrying her mug through to the office, she walked over to Lockhart. He and Berry were looking at a webpage. Smith registered Martin Johnson's photograph and deduced it was his profile on the law firm's website.

'What's going on with Mo?' asked Lockhart, hands on hips. 'He's screwing everything up at the minute. Pretty soon he's gonna drop the ball big time. If we weren't short staffed, I'd tell him to take himself off and not come back until his head's screwed on properly. Porter's gonna love that accident with the artwork. I mean, what the hell? Was he searching the house blindfolded?'

'I'll talk to him, guv. I think there's some stuff going on.'

'We've all got stuff going on, Max.'

'Yeah.' He was right about that.

'So, apart from smashing the place up,' Lockhart said, 'you find anything useful?'

She took out her phone to show him the documents she'd photographed. 'Maybe.'

CHAPTER TWENTY-FIVE

Lexi stood outside the mansion block and checked the address that Dan had texted her. Yup, this was it. Traffic roared past beside her on the huge Hammersmith flyover – which carried one of London's biggest and busiest roads – while across the way a tube train broke the surface and rattled noisily along. How did Dan get any sleep here? Maybe he didn't.

She pressed the buzzer for his apartment and immediately realised that she hadn't brought anything over except her laptop, notebook and pen. Should she have gotten some takeout food for them, or at least brought a bottle of something? No, that probably wasn't appropriate. In any case, she knew Dan was trying to drink less; they'd talked about that a bunch of times in their therapy sessions. And she didn't need any more alcohol. Today was the first day of her new plan: getting her shit together. It starts with this, she thought, as Dan greeted her through the intercom and buzzed open the main entrance.

Three floors up, she found his apartment door ajar and cautiously nudged it.

'Dan?'

'Yeah, come in.'

She stepped through into the narrow hallway. The spot where she knew Dan had held his last conversation with his wife before he went to Afghanistan and she went missing. She guessed there would be a whole lot of painful memories for him in this place.

'Should I take my shoes off?'

'No, it's fine.'

Lexi walked through into the living room. The first thing she saw was Dan, tidying the small table that clearly doubled as desk and dining surface. He wore a white T-shirt and blue jeans. His dark hair was wet, and he looked as if he'd just taken a shower. He smiled at her, but she could see the effort behind it. He was under pressure, seemingly not just on the double murder case. Maybe he'd tell her what was going on, in his own time. Glancing to her right, the next thing she saw was the wall.

'Oh my god,' she whispered, unable to catch herself.

'Yeah, that's… well, you know what it is.'

She crossed to the montage of photographs, handwritten notes and other documents, all arranged around a large map of the UK with various pins stuck in it. It covered an area about six feet high by eight feet wide. The sum total of Dan's personal investigations into his wife's disappearance over more than a decade. At the top centre of the collection was an 8 x 12-inch photograph of a pretty young woman. She was mid-twenties, Lexi guessed, and blond, with blue eyes that shone out from the portrait. She had a broad smile and dimples in her cheeks. Jess. Lexi realised she'd never seen a picture of Dan's wife before, despite having talked about her with him for hours in her clinic.

Studying all this work, the embodiment of Dan's undiminished hope for Jess's return, Lexi felt an overwhelming sense of sadness. This was quickly followed by a powerful feeling of discomfort at intruding on the most intimate part of Dan's life. But she reminded herself that he'd invited her here and, more than that, they'd already spoken about his emotions, fears and traumas in a way that he probably hadn't shared with anyone else. Maybe not even his mom. Perhaps not even Jess. She was so absorbed in the wall of information that his voice made her jump a little.

'Do you want a drink or something?'

'Oh, sure. Thanks.'

'Beer? I might have some wine…'

'Water's good.'

'OK.' He held up a manila file in each hand. 'Here's the stuff. I'll get your water.'

Dan put the files down on the table and, as he left the room, she stole a final glance at the material on Jess, before sitting down. The apartment was neat and tidy; she wouldn't have imagined anything else, given Dan's military background. It was pretty much the same as how her dad has always kept their home. Everything was straight, lined up, clean. She was reminded of that old line that her mom used to tease her dad with: *You can take the boy out of the military…*

He came back in and placed a glass of water down in front of her. Then he pulled up a chair alongside hers, so close to her that she could smell the shower gel or whatever he'd just washed with. She flicked her eyes to him, but he was focused on the files.

'Here we go,' he began, opening them both. 'Let me take you through what we've got.'

Two hours later, they'd covered all the material. Lexi had asked Dan questions as he explained each piece, taking notes and stopping him occasionally to read a report.

He leant back in the chair. 'What do you think?'

She tilted her head. 'OK, so, this is just my initial profile sketch. I need a little more time to work on it, obviously. For the fuller picture.'

'Course.'

'Victims first.' She flipped a couple pages back in her notebook. 'Both were white men in their fifties. They were wealthy and wielded a degree of power from their jobs and financial positions. They both lived in south-west London, around three, four miles apart. Not super-close, but pretty nearby. Walking distance, anyway. And they were killed only like a half-mile apart.'

Lexi paused and Dan nodded that she should continue. 'Despite these similarities, it appears that the two men weren't known to one another. We don't think they were socially connected, and there's nothing so far that Lucy Berry could find to suggest an online association. Not even a mutual Facebook friend. And we don't believe that Martin Johnson ever acted as an attorney for Charles Stott, which would be the most logical professional relationship.'

'Correct. Not that we know of, at least. We're hoping Johnson's law firm can confirm that tomorrow, as well as giving some details of his clients, which might help us.'

'Right. So why were these two individuals targeted by the killer? The attacks weren't random. And I agree with you that they weren't robberies gone wrong. Whatever DCI Porter thinks.' She flashed a grim smile at him. 'The level of violence was too extreme, and the locations were unlikely.'

'Yeah.'

'So, the two victims were chosen, and the blitz attack MO – using the blunt object once and no more – suggests that the killer set out to murder them. But for what reason?'

'That's the question. If we can answer that,' he said, 'then we might have a chance of working out who he'll choose next. Because I think there's gonna be more.'

'Each victim was alone in an isolated place with no CCTV in the immediate vicinity,' she went on. 'Which indicates that the killer had planned it, maybe followed the victims or knew something about their schedules?'

'He gets pattern-of-life intel, then picks a vulnerable strike point. Makes sense.'

'And the obvious link between them in terms of a motive is that, as you've discovered, both of these guys had some kind of sexual assault association. Stott was notorious for it and had tens of victims, however low-level his actions. With Johnson, though, it's less clear. He only had a document on the legal aspects of sexual assault claims.'

'Which wasn't really his area of law. He mostly did injury compensation.'

'True,' she acknowledged. 'But there's potential overlap. Or maybe he was helping out a colleague or a buddy. We have no proof that he sexually assaulted anyone.'

Dan linked his fingers and planted both hands on the table. 'We might find that evidence tomorrow, though.'

'Be careful.'

'Of what?'

'Assumptions that could bias your investigation. You think this is about sexual assault. Like it's some vigilante who's doing this. And I agree with you up to a point. That is a possibility, but there's not enough data yet to be confident in that conclusion.'

'But a triangle *is* enough data for you to think it's about witchcraft?' He arched his eyebrows.

She sighed. 'That's not exactly what I was trying to say before.'

'Wasn't it?'

'No. This is what I was thinking: the triangle has meaning, but there are different ways of interpreting it. One way is as an occult symbol. The elements fire and water are triangles that point in opposite directions, as the drawings on the victims appear to do. But it could just as easily mean something else.'

'You said the triangle is a female symbol, too.'

'Amongst other stuff, yeah.'

'So, what if the killer's getting revenge for these guys sexually assaulting women?'

'You're into the offender profile, now.'

'But could I be right?'

'Well, that *is* the likely motive. But how would they know about the accusations?'

'I dunno.' He shrugged. 'Maybe it's someone who works in one of those sexual assault referral centres. They deal with victims every day, they know the stats about how few perpetrators are convicted, and one day, they snap. Start dispensing justice themselves.'

'Maybe. But we don't yet know that Martin Johnson attacked anyone. And it doesn't seem as if any of the women who accused Charles Stott of assault actually reported it to the police.'

'No. That's true.' He nodded slowly.

They sat in silence for a moment, looking over the documents spread across the table. What else connected these men? Was it something about the triangle, or was she totally off on that?

Eventually, Dan spoke. 'You know DS Smith is working on a case about serial sexual assault,' he said. 'Maybe we should ask her, see if there's anything she can tell us that might help. Characteristics of sex offenders or something.'

'Go for it. I'll stay out, though.'

'Why?'

Lexi pressed her lips together, her eyes widening. 'Well, she's not exactly the biggest fan of forensic psychology. Or of me, for that matter.'

'Don't mind her. She just wants to solve cases.'

'Same as I do.'

'There you go, you've got a common objective.' He started to gather the documents on the table. 'You want to talk to her, then?'

She held up her palms. 'Sure, whatever. If it'll help.'

'Cheers.' Dan grinned. 'I'll set it up.'

CHAPTER TWENTY-SIX

There he is. The smug bastard himself, staring back at me from the TV as the news headline runs beneath his self-satisfied grin:

London Murder Victim Identified as Lawyer Martin Johnson, 56.

The man who represents so much of what I hate. Some of that hate was purged as I kicked him to death. But there's still a hell of a lot left inside me. Thinking back to Friday night, though, I'm particularly pleased with my idea about getting him to help me look for a golf ball. Distraction, misdirection. Then whack! He didn't even have time to register that he'd been tricked. There was something comical about watching him go straight into survival mode. But that didn't work for him.

The portrait-headline combo on screen now was a re-run from the start of the story. The real highlight had been a moment ago, though, when Dan Lockhart had appeared, delivering one of those stupid pieces-to-camera that the police seem to think will bring witnesses forward. He was at the golf course, standing outside, wearing a North Face jacket. *We're hoping it'll jog people's memories*, that's what Lockhart had said. I find that pretty funny, because you can't remember what you haven't seen.

I could call their hotline and tell the cops right now that there was no one else there. Just me and Martin on that part of the golf course. Same as it was just me and Charles in the woods on

Wimbledon Common. Same as it's going to be me and the next guy when I crush him like one of those miserable little insects under that log in my dad's garden, the first time I ever ended a life. And the same as it'll only be me and Lockhart himself when the time comes. The thought of that brings a smile to my face and a jolt of excitement to my belly.

The rolling news has moved on now and is showing footage of a bus stop. At first, the fact it's not my stuff annoys me, and I consider flipping the channel – maybe seeing if there's a decent action or horror movie on John's Netflix, something with blood, anyway – but then the headline appears:

Police Seek Serial Sex Attacker in South London

That's interesting. I turn the volume up.

Eight documented attacks by this fella and counting. There's a woman with her face blurred talking in a disguised voice about what happened to her. She's describing a small, stocky man. A knife. It's kind of pathetic how she just let that happen to her. Women needed to be better at defending themselves, that was the simple answer. They can't expect anyone else to do it for them. The police clearly aren't capable of doing anything about it. But this guy can't hide for ever. Pretty soon, like the others, he'll get what he deserves.

I'm bored of sitting here, now. My limbs are stiff and aching, the pain worse than usual today, probably because of all the physical effort two nights ago. It's time to have some fun. I'm going out to a bar. I need to get laid.

DAY SEVEN

CHAPTER TWENTY-SEVEN

Lockhart added a few final updates to the whiteboards and turned to survey his team. They were gradually assembling for the early-afternoon briefing. Gradually being the operative word. For most of them, this was the seventh straight day that they'd be working a twelve-hour-plus shift, and they all looked knackered. He'd have to start rostering rest days for them this week. There was only so long people could keep that effort up; sooner or later, they started to make mistakes. Khan's accident in Johnson's house was a good example. But it wasn't just about making errors. In the absence of significant progress, your motivation started to fall away. Your fire started to go out.

He thought about how that applied to himself and his search for Jess. The Whitstable lead had been a breakthrough; had given him hope. Then his brother-in-law, Nick, had turned up on Friday night and made his announcement. Since then, Lockhart hadn't slept properly, anticipating the communication from a solicitor on behalf of her family to say they wanted her declared legally dead. Wondering whether a judge would rule in their favour. Whether that verdict would mean the Met closing her shelved missing persons investigation. And whether he could lose the home they had bought and made together.

As the final team members took their chairs, Lockhart tried to focus on what he needed to say. He glanced at his watch: 14:09. They were supposed to start at 14:00 sharp, but Porter still hadn't arrived.

'All right, let's get going,' he announced, clapping his hands. 'I'm guessing the boss will join us soon as he can, and we'll bring him up to speed. Luce, do you want to kick us off?'

'Um, OK.' Berry ran a hand through her bob-cut and held up her notebook, partially covering her instantly flushed cheeks. 'I couldn't find any online association between Charles Stott and Martin Johnson,' she began quietly. 'And I checked for links to Jemima Stott-Peters, too. There was nothing on open source, no social media. No telephone connections that we're aware of, either.' She paused, checked her notes. Lockhart knew that was unnecessary; she could probably recite the information blindfolded.

'And, er, I've been through the list of previous cases that Johnson's law firm finally sent to us,' she resumed. 'They didn't represent Charles Stott or, apparently, any third party related to his films. Johnson specialised in personal injury claims.'

Lockhart waited to be sure she'd finished. 'So, we don't think the reason why Stott and Johnson were targeted has to do with any business or legal issue that connected them.'

Berry shook her head in confirmation. The rest of MIT 8 sat impassively.

'Just on the subject of Ms Stott-Peters,' he added. 'I called her this morning. She gave her permission for us to make an appeal on social media about her husband's watch. See if anyone's seen it, maybe tried to buy or sell it. Priya, can I leave that with you?'

'No probs, guv.'

Lockhart didn't mention how he'd also asked Stott-Peters what she'd been doing on Friday night when Martin Johnson was murdered. Porter had already warned him off, but Lockhart wasn't about to let it drop. She and Xander O'Neill were still people of interest as far as he was concerned. Stott-Peters had told him that she and Mr O'Neill were having dinner together on Friday night, at her house. Lockhart didn't like the fact that there was no checkable detail, like a restaurant booking, or that they were each other's alibis.

'Anything else, Lucy?' he asked.

'No, um, that's it.'

'OK. Max, how did you and Mo get on at the law firm this morning?'

Smith turned sideways in her chair so she could see Lockhart as well as the others. 'Apart from getting them to send Lucy that list of cases, we talked to a few people that worked there.'

Lockhart glanced at Khan, who was sitting with his arms folded and a face like thunder. He looked as if he wanted to be anywhere but in this briefing. Probably still pissed off about the bollocking he'd got yesterday for breaking the picture frame and damaging the artwork inside. It'd turned out to be a Damien Hurst limited edition print worth upwards of ten grand. The property damage forms Lockhart had needed to fill out had been a nightmare; Porter had gone ballistic. But Lockhart didn't have much sympathy for Khan; he was lucky to still be allowed out after that, and his attitude now wasn't helping things.

'No one really had much to say about Johnson, to be honest, guv,' Smith continued. 'Except for one person. A secretary in the firm called Eva Kowalski, twenty-five years old. She suggested that there'd been a few occasions in the past where younger women working for Johnson had moved on from administrative positions quite quickly. Now, I thought, maybe that's not unusual. They're more junior, they might not want to stay long-term. But Eva said that she'd heard it was because of Johnson.'

'Because of him doing what, exactly?' asked Lockhart, though he already suspected.

'Sexual harassment,' Smith stated. 'There were even rumours of assault in one or two cases, according to Eva. Put that together with the document we found in his house and...' She didn't bother finishing her sentence.

A murmur ran through the assembled team and Lockhart caught the words 'shitbag' and 'bastard'. He held his hands up for calm as the volume of conversation increased. 'OK, OK. I know what some of you will be thinking.'

'That he had it coming to him?' The voice came clearly over the chatter. It was Andy Parsons. The large DC shifted in his chair, his expression defiant. 'Someone's getting revenge on rapists, aren't they?'

Lockhart remembered Green's caution about that conclusion when she'd reviewed the files last night. 'I acknowledge that is a significant overlap between the two victims. But we have to be careful about jumping to any conclusions.'

'Come on, guv,' Smith said. 'I'd say it's pretty obvious what's going on.'

'It's one theory,' replied Lockhart. He could feel the unease in his team and was aware that he probably sounded like Porter to them right now. Despite what you were told in your detective's training about neutrality, he knew it was the same for every copper, whether suit or lid. There were some victims you wanted to help more than others, and some you found it very hard to feel sorry for at all. He remembered how fired up their team had been last year, when the victims of a serial murderer had been innocent young women. That seemed a long way from this case.

'Whatever the reason for our perpetrator going after these men,' he went on, 'we have to stop him killing again.'

'Can't we all just take a week off, guv? You know, see what happens.' Parsons was smirking, while the rumble of laughter in the group showed general approval for his suggestion.

Lockhart was on a short fuse. He ignored the joke. 'Our job is to investigate murders, whoever the victims are. We can't pick and choose. I don't care if this guy is bumping off serial killers or terrorists or anyone else who we don't want on the streets. That isn't how justice works. We've all got to be professional about it. Does anybody have a problem with that?'

For a moment, the group was stunned into silence. He took a deep breath, squeezed his hand, and slowly let go. Someone slurped their tea.

'OK,' he resumed. 'Moving on. No DNA off the bodies, yet. Looks like our perpetrator covered up.' He indicated a pair of close-up photographs on the victim strategy board, showing the triangles drawn on Stott's and Johnson's necks. 'There's no forensic follow-up from the symbols. Our best guess is that they were done in ink, probably with a felt-tip marker pen. Which doesn't really tell us anything much.'

As some whispered discussions broke out, Lockhart saw that Berry had her hand raised, patiently waiting to speak, and gestured for quiet.

'Oi, shh. Go ahead, Luce.'

'Um, I was just thinking, well, do we know what the triangle means?'

Lockhart pressed his lips together. He couldn't let on that he'd briefed Green. In any case, her ideas about it were speculative at best.

'No, we haven't got a clue,' he replied.

'So, should we, I mean, could we maybe ask Dr Green if she has any, er, ideas? It must mean something.' Berry shrank into her chair.

'You're right, Luce, I'm sure it does mean something. But Porter says we don't need Green on this case, and that we haven't got the budget anyway.'

'We could 'ave a whip-round for her... a few quid each,' offered one of the older guys, a lascivious grin on his face. 'I'd put me hand in me pocket.'

'We don't want to know where you'd put your hand,' said Smith. Her line was greeted with raucous laughter.

Lockhart was about to tell them to show some respect when the heavy footfall from across the office got his attention. Porter stomped over and stood in front of them, brandishing an iPad. The laughter died immediately. The DCI scanned their faces then held the tablet up so they could see its screen. Lockhart glimpsed a news website.

'"Wimbledon murders",' Porter boomed, reading the headline. '"Victims linked to sex offences".' He prowled in front of the whiteboards, letting the words sink in. 'Quoting unnamed sources,' he added, his voice straining with rage. 'Close to the investigation.'

No one dared speak. Lockhart had no idea who was responsible for the leak. But he knew it wasn't going to help them one bit. His next thought was that it wasn't going to do much for his boss's promotion chances, either.

'Is somebody going to explain this to me?' Porter's eyes were wide and unblinking, his jaw set hard. 'Or should I just assume that I can't trust any of you?'

The only noise in the room was the DCI's angry breathing. Lockhart looked out across the team. They were all watching Porter. All except Khan. He was staring at the carpet.

CHAPTER TWENTY-EIGHT

Smith placed the tray of steaming cardboard cups on the corner table.

'Let me give you a hand.' DS Eddie Stagg leant forward and reached out but stopped himself mid-air. 'Sorry, Max. When I said "hand", I didn't mean—'

'It's OK. Honestly.' She cocked her head. 'What, you think you're the first person who's said that to me, accidentally or otherwise? I've had this hand for forty-four years. And I've been doing the job for twenty-two. Everyone called me "claw" when I first joined. There's not much you can say about it that bothers me.'

'Right.' Stagg nodded and sat back again. 'For the record, though, it wasn't deliberate.'

'No harm done.' Pinning the tray with her 'different' hand, Smith extracted a tea for herself, then another for Stagg and slid it towards him. 'Milk, two sugars, right?'

'Spot on, cheers.'

She removed the other two drinks – a black coffee and a green tea – and placed them on the opposite side of the small table. 'Guess whose is whose?' she said with a smile. Stagg chuckled.

'Speak of the devil.' Smith raised a hand as Lockhart and Green crossed towards them, though she needn't have. At six p.m., there was hardly anyone else in Lavender Hill police station cafeteria. A young detective grabbing an armful of sandwiches to go; four uniformed officers eating dinner before a night shift, clearly engrossed in some gossip. Then a load of empty tables, and the four of them. Plotting like Guy Fawkes and his mates.

'All right, Max?' Lockhart nodded to her. 'Dan Lockhart,' he said, shaking Stagg's hand.

'I know who you are, sir.'

'Don't worry about the "sir". Dan's fine.' He sat down. 'Max, you know Lexi.'

'Yeah, I remember you from last year. The Throat Ripper.' Smith extended her hand and Green shook it. The psychologist looked as if she'd seen a ghost but snapped out of the trance when Stagg introduced himself to her.

'Nice to meet you,' replied Green, taking her seat too. 'Thanks for the tea.'

'Do I detect an accent there?' Stagg arched an eyebrow. 'From the other side of the pond, perhaps?'

'Yeah.' Green flashed a smile.

'You American?'

'Guilty. My mom's British, though. I was born here, grew up over there, then moved back here when… I moved back a few years ago.'

'I love American stuff, me.' Stagg nodded enthusiastically. 'Was over there at the start of the year. Florida. Beautiful, it was. Lovely and warm.'

'Awesome.'

'Dr Green works in the NHS,' said Lockhart. 'She's a clinical psychologist. With forensic experience.'

'Thanks for coming in, doctor.'

'Lexi, please.'

'You got it. I'm Eddie. First names all round, eh?'

Smith glanced to her left. Stagg was clearly charmed by Green. But – she had to admit – who wouldn't be? The woman was young, smart, beautiful, and nice. No wonder Lockhart liked hanging out with her. There had to be a catch, though, Smith thought. Nobody's perfect.

Stagg turned to Lockhart. 'Heard about your work on that Throat Ripper case last year. Bloody good job that was.' He raised his tea in salute.

'Cheers.' Lockhart acknowledged the compliment with a slight dip of his head. 'But it was basically Max and Lexi who found him.'

Smith felt herself reddening at the praise.

'And we're hoping you can help us find our Operation Braddock man.' Stagg winked. 'Both of you.'

'You might be able to help us out, too,' said Lockhart.

'Great. Sorry we can't meet in the CID office.' Stagg glanced around. 'It's just, my boss wouldn't be best pleased if she knew what we were discussing.'

Lockhart sipped his coffee. 'Same here. Our gaffer's paranoid about press leaks, so he wouldn't want us talking to anyone about our double murder case.'

Smith unfolded a map of south-west London. 'That's why we're doing this the old-fashioned way.'

'Christ,' exclaimed Lockhart. 'A paper map. Haven't seen one of them for years.'

She chuckled. 'So, I've marked the two murders on here with red dots, OK? The eight blue dots are Op Braddock incidents, the last four of which have been actual attacks.'

'They're all in the same area,' observed Green.

'Not just that.' Smith tapped a finger on the map. 'It's the type of location that overlaps in both cases, too. Remote, isolated spots where the victims are alone. They all have trees nearby which offer the attacker shelter while they wait for the victim, and when they escape afterwards. Virtually no camera coverage. Add in savvy perpetrators who aren't leaving their DNA behind, and it's a nightmare to investigate.'

Stagg placed his hands palms-down on the table. 'We don't have a clue who we're looking for, despite the victims' description.'

'A shorter than average, larger-built guy, who wears a black ski mask and black jacket, and carries a knife,' said Green. 'I saw it on the news.'

Lockhart wiped a hand over his face. He looked tired. 'So, we've got a serial sex attacker and a serial murderer operating in the same part of London at the same time.'

'And the murderer seems to be targeting middle-aged men who've sexually assaulted women,' added Smith.

'We don't know that for sure,' said Green.

Smith felt a stab of irritation.

'You guys work on sexual assault cases, right?' Lockhart asked Stagg.

'Yeah, since they closed down Sapphire.'

Smith knew exactly what he was talking about. The Met had formed the network of specialist sexual assault teams a decade ago but disbanded them in 2018 after repeated instances of incompetence and malpractice. These included detectives encouraging rape victims to withdraw allegations to reduce the number of 'unsolved' cases and improve stats. Officers had been sacked and even jailed over it. It was the Met's borough CID teams who picked up the slack since then.

'Lexi's trying to profile our killer,' said Lockhart.

Smith caught his eye. 'I thought Porter didn't want that.'

'You guys aren't the only ones hiding stuff,' he grinned. 'So, *a* theory is that our murderer is going after guys who've been accused of sexual assault but never prosecuted.'

'A vigilante,' Stagg said. He looked as though he approved.

'How could someone access that information?' asked Green. 'I mean, to target sex offenders.'

Stagg blew out his cheeks. 'I dunno. Websites? A victim support network, maybe?'

'What about someone who works on rape cases?' suggested Lockhart. 'Someone who's in the system.' Smith noticed he was watching Stagg closely.

The big man held Lockhart's gaze silently. Then he burst out laughing. 'What, you think it's one of us? You've gotta be joking.'

'I didn't say that.' Lockhart spun his coffee cup. 'Just wondered if you had any ideas. We don't have much to go on, either. And the fact that both of our victims were accused of sexual assault is one line of inquiry.'

'There's a lot of people that hear about sexual assault every day. Lawyers, nurses, counsellors, charities.' Stagg shook his head. 'I wouldn't know where to begin. Sorry.'

Green shrugged. 'It's only one hypothesis about motive, right now, anyway.'

'Wouldn't be surprising if it's correct, though,' Smith said. 'Do you know how many rape allegations result in a successful conviction?'

Lockhart shook his head.

'Not many?' offered Green.

'Four per cent. Or, put another way, there's a ninety-six per cent chance that if a woman accuses a man of raping her – and it's almost always that way round – nothing will come of it. Assuming that the allegations aren't made up, we're talking about twenty-four out of every twenty-five rapists in this country getting away with it.' She slapped the tabletop. 'Can you believe that?'

'Shit,' said Lockhart.

'Makes your blood boil, doesn't it?' Stagg nodded at him.

'Yeah, it does.' The reply came from Green.

'So,' Smith cleared her throat, 'anything you might be able to tell us about the perpetrator, you know, psychologically speaking, could help.'

Green looked at her. There was a trace of surprise in her expression, but it disappeared quickly. 'Sure. You, uh, you want me to come in and look at the files?'

'Be great if you could,' Stagg said. 'Whenever's convenient.'

'OK.'

The big man shifted awkwardly in his seat. 'And, unfortunately, our budget isn't very—'

'I'll do it for nothing.' Green's eyes flicked to Lockhart. 'I'm getting used to that.'

'Thank you.' Stagg took a card from his shirt pocket and handed it to Green. 'Email me and we'll fix a time.'

'There's something we'd like your help with too, Dan,' said Smith. She pointed at the map. 'See these yellow dots? They're all bus stops that Eddie reckons are most likely to be the locations of future sexual assaults.'

'We don't have enough manpower – sorry, er, *people*power – to put surveillance on all of them. So, we're thinking cameras.' Stagg lowered his voice. 'Max said you used to do this sort of thing in the army. Surveillance and all that stuff.'

Lockhart didn't reply.

'So, you know, we were hoping you might be able to give us some advice,' Stagg continued. 'Even set it up, maybe?'

'I'm guessing you've already tried to do this officially?' said Lockhart.

Stagg hesitated. 'The thing is—'

'Brass rejected it,' Smith stated. 'Because they're idiots.'

Lockhart drank some coffee, then said: 'You realise that if a camera does pick him up, it'll be inadmissible in court?'

'We'll find another way to get him,' replied Stagg.

There was a moment's silence as they watched Lockhart study the map. He rubbed his fingertips along the stubble on his jaw.

'What do you reckon, guv?' asked Smith hopefully.

'Well—'

'Sir!' The high-pitched sound came from across the canteen. It was DC Roland Wilkins from the CID team. He was clutching some papers and hurrying towards them. 'There you are, sir.'

Smith snatched the map away and folded it closed as Wilkins approached the table. He was slightly breathless.

'I was looking everywhere for you,' said the young DC. Then his gaze alighted on Green and he proceeded to stare at her without speaking.

Green smiled awkwardly back, and Smith noticed her eyes drop briefly to the hole in the end of his nose.

'We're just having a meeting here, Roland.' Stagg sat up straight. 'Is it something urgent?'

'Oh, just…' He held up the papers. 'There's an overtime form here, and a leave sign-off sheet. Needs your signature, sir.'

'Does it have to be done right now?'

'Well, I'm going home soon, and I wanted to submit it, you know—'

'OK, fine.' Stagg held out a meaty paw. Wilkins passed him the papers, and after a cursory examination, he took a biro from his pocket and scrawled something illegible on both documents. 'There you go. All right, see you tomorrow, then.'

'Thank you, sir.' Wilkins checked the forms, then cast a final glance at Green, before scuttling back across the cafeteria and out.

'Sorry about that.' Stagg drained his tea. 'So, what do you guys think? Can you help us catch this scumbag?'

'For sure,' Green replied instantly. 'I mean, I'll do whatever I can.'

Lockhart pressed his lips together for a few seconds. Then he gave a single nod. 'All right.'

CHAPTER TWENTY-NINE

Lexi was deep in the psychology zone. Following the meeting with Dan and his colleagues, she'd taken a bus home to Tooting, headed straight up to her room and gotten to work. She was sitting on her bed, laptop on her legs, with some chilled lo-fi hip hop beats on to help her concentrate and a mug of strong tea to keep her alert. She wasn't just thinking about Dan's murder cases, but also the serial sex attacker whom she'd agreed to profile.

She briefly wondered if she'd taken on too much by offering to help with both investigations. Well, it was too late now. And besides, she was engaged in something useful, something that could make a real difference. Lexi felt a sense of motivation that she hadn't experienced in a long while; a feeling that any amount of drinking couldn't produce, especially not when you'd sobered up afterwards.

Obviously, she didn't have details of the Operation Braddock crimes, yet. But that didn't stop her wondering if there was any more than geography and sexual assault that linked those cases with the murders. She'd already pulled up a research paper that described a theory relevant to both, called the Pathway to Violence. It described the progress from feeling a grievance to planning an attack, researching a target and finally acting. This wasn't bar brawls, road rage or crimes of passion; it was about the mindset of causing deliberate physical harm to others. The thought made her shiver.

Focusing on the killer, Lexi tried to map the theory to her clinical model of the five Ps. The first P was Predisposing: what made the individual likely to kill? In this case, Lexi was interpreting the sheer brutality of the act as evidence of psychopathy; a total lack of regular human empathy. Psychopaths don't just start behaving like that one day; they usually show signs of callousness and cruelty for years, even back to childhood. Early exposure to violence was common, as was the desire to dominate and exploit others.

Of course, it was possible that the killer had acted aggressively in the past but avoided detection and punishment. Or perhaps they'd served time but just been released. That could answer the 'why now?' question, or Precipitating, as another P in the model was also known. Someone who'd recently come out of prison, with scores to settle… but many such people would be electronically tagged and not easily able to move around, especially at night. And their targets were more likely to be criminal associates. She wasn't convinced it was an ex-con. Which suggested a psychopath who'd gotten their kicks some other way up till now. A smart one.

Thinking about the Pathway to Violence, Lexi guessed there was a significant recent trigger. A trauma of some kind that'd created a grievance, a hatred projected onto specific individuals or a group. This had – via some degree of planning and decision-making – led the perpetrator to target a film director and a compensation lawyer in the same part of London.

Were the victims' professions relevant? Or was it simply their demographic: middle-aged men? She couldn't ignore the sexual assault link, though if these were revenge attacks with that motive, she might've expected something more sexually symbolic in the homicide MO or signature. Mutilated genitals or penetration, maybe. Jeez, that was dark. She briefly imagined how many other twenty-nine-year-old women were sitting alone thinking about that right now. Probably not a whole lot.

From what the MIT knew so far, the two victims appeared totally unconnected. That indicated to Lexi that they were probably symbolic rather than directly responsible for the killer's trauma. According to the psychology research, symbolism was common in premeditated violence. But what did Charles Stott and Martin Johnson symbolise?

Lexi was tapping out some notes on her laptop when there was a knock at her bedroom door. Without waiting for a response, Sarah entered, leaving the door open.

'Hiya, what's up?' she said, beaming her gigantic smile.

'Hey, Sarah.'

She pointed an accusatory finger at Lexi. 'You finally getting busy on that dating website?'

'Hell, no!'

'You're not working, are you?'

'Trying…'

'Soz.' Sarah came over and hopped onto the bed. 'Didn't mean to distract you. Much.'

'It's cool.' Lexi closed the laptop. 'I needed a break anyway. There's only so much violence you can read about in one evening.'

'Tell me about it. That sounds like my job. Most days, anyway.'

'Yeah, right.' Lexi grabbed her mug and took a sip. The tea had gone cold. 'How's it going in that team?'

'Same shit as when you were there.' She sighed. 'The number of kids I see who get such a rough deal… If the parents are even around, one or both of them is regularly hitting the kids, or the kids see parents hitting each other. And you know how that usually goes.'

'Dad hitting mom. Or another man hitting mom.'

Sarah pulled a tress of her long, frizzy hair and wound it around her finger. 'It's gotta affect the kid, hasn't it? I mean, witnessing that all the time.'

'It does. Permanently, in some cases.'

'You believe people can change, don't you, Lex? You've got to, otherwise you wouldn't do what you do.'

Lexi knew that, at some level, Sarah was right. But when you saw evidence to the contrary, it made you question that fundamental view of the world. Whether it was a serial perpetrator of violence whose behaviour stemmed from childhood roots too deep to excavate, or a traumatised individual like Dan struggling to deal with personal loss and grief, people often didn't seem able to change. Did that apply to her, too? Shep, Liam, the memories of her attack last year, even the sexual assault three years back. How had those experiences altered her?

'Sure, I do,' she replied. 'But the change isn't always in the right direction.'

'People surprise you though, don't they?' Sarah's eyes widened. 'The things they can overcome.'

'Absolutely.'

'Anyway, talking of change.' She prodded Lexi's shoulder. 'It's about time we got you out on a date.'

'I don't wanna go on a date,' Lexi countered immediately.

Sarah ignored her. 'There's this trainee doctor in our team, Raj. He's tall, really lovely. Oh, and he's hot.'

'Sounds great, but—'

'And I just happened to find out today that he and his girlfriend split up last month and, apparently, he's interested in meeting someone.'

'I don't know…'

'Come on, Lex. You can't sit around being single for ever. We'll just do some drinks or whatever, no pressure. I'll come too, maybe Raj can bring another guy friend. It'll be fun.'

'I'm trying not to drink so much.'

Sarah snorted. 'Since when? What happened to the gin monster?'

'She needs to rest her liver. And help the cops.' Lexi tapped her laptop.

'Help Dan, you mean?' Sarah puckered her lips.

'No! Well, yes, but not because of… never mind.'

'So what? You've got a side gig. Doesn't mean you can't still have a good time, does it?'

'Um…'

Sarah turned that infectious grin on her once more. Lexi was powerless. 'I'll find out when Raj and his medic mates are free. Later this week, maybe?'

Lexi was caving.

'Come on…' Sarah began prodding her gently in the ribs. It was too much to resist. 'You. Know. You. Want. To.'

'Oh, all right, OK,' she conceded. 'Sure.'

'Yay!'

'Well, if we're going out,' said Lexi, opening the laptop, 'then I'd better get back to this.'

Sarah got up off the bed and moved across to the full-length mirror, throwing a few celebratory dance moves in front of it.

'By the way,' added Lexi, 'watch yourself if you're taking buses, OK?'

She stopped dancing and spun round. 'Oh God, you're talking about that bus stop rapist guy?'

'You saw the news?'

'Er, yeah.' Sarah shook her head briefly. 'I'm gonna get a personal alarm I reckon.'

'I was thinking of buying some pepper spray.'

'Good plan. There's a lot of weird guys out there.' Sarah took a step away from the mirror towards the door.

Lexi screamed.

'Jesus Christ!'

Their housemate was just outside the doorway, suddenly visible in the mirror from Lexi's position on her bed. Just standing there, staring at her in the reflection.

'What're you doing, Rhys?' asked Sarah.

Before he could answer, Lexi cut in. 'How long have you been there? Were you listening to our conversation?'

'N-no,' he stammered. 'I wasn't really listening. Just something about going on a date this week with a doctor. The door was open, it was... Anyway, I found this downstairs.' He held up a piece of paper. Lexi recognised it right away. A credit card statement.

She sprang off the bed and walked to the doorway. 'Lemme see that.' She snatched the document from his hand and scanned it.

'I only opened it cos I thought it was for me,' he explained. 'Sorry.' He reached inside his dressing gown and scratched his belly.

'This is mine!' she yelled at him. 'What the fuck, Rhys?'

'Don't worry. I didn't really read it, anyway.'

'You didn't *really* read it? So, what, you read like half of it? Jeez, this is not cool. It's private. Check the goddam envelope properly next time.'

'It was an accident.'

The bill was over six hundred pounds. Bars, clubs, some new ankle boots she probably didn't need. Definitely didn't need. Her spirits suddenly dropped with the reminder of how she had literally no money. She thought of all the work she'd be putting in for the police, for free. But that was worth it. And at least she was seeing her private client tomorrow; that'd bring in an extra hundred pounds, after her costs. The moment of relief that gave her was immediately countered by heart sink at the realisation it meant spending an hour with Oliver Soames venting at her. Reminding Lexi of her aborted pregnancy...

'And in future,' she snapped at him, 'don't just stand in my doorway, got it?'

Rhys mumbled a reply she didn't catch as he retreated towards his room. He went inside and shut the door.

'You don't have to bite his head off, Lex.'

'I mean, seriously. He just...' Lexi felt her body tensing. 'Whose side are you on?'

'All right, chill.' Sarah laid a hand on her shoulder. 'Be in a better mood than this when we go for drinks with Raj and his mates, yeah?'

Lexi didn't reply. She already regretted having agreed to Sarah's matchmaking plan.

CHAPTER THIRTY

Graveyards are strange places. I've always thought that. A bunch of dead people shoved into the ground, with little stones on top of them to let you know who the desiccated pile of bones underneath belonged to. Kidding ourselves that they matter, that we keep some connection to them, that there's anything left beyond worm food once the lights have gone out.

For each bouquet of flowers laid, I can picture a sentimental loved one pulling the blooms out of a plastic bucket at a petrol station or supermarket and thinking *Gladys* – or whoever had croaked – *would like those*. Tearfully wishing that person was still alive as they place the overpriced stems on the stone where, within a day, they'd be dead too. I can't imagine being that attached to someone.

I felt nothing when a doctor called to say my old man was dying; I didn't even stop filming to go and visit him in hospital. As for that useless woman who once called herself mum, before deciding she preferred heroin to her family, I don't know or care if she's even breathing. The idea of actually *crying* when you're told a person has snuffed it is ridiculous. So, maybe it's just people that are weird, not graveyards.

But they do make good places for murder, especially at night. Quiet, dark, plenty of trees. No cameras spying on you. And no people. Not living ones, anyway. Except the occasional idiot who cuts through to shave two minutes off a journey. So, this is where I'll do it, tomorrow. My newest victim. Another one who has to pay. I wonder if he'd want to be buried here, given how he always walks home this way from his stupid dance class? I could ask him as I'm kicking the shit out of him. On the other hand, when his relatives see the state of his corpse, they might opt for cremation.

I watched the news earlier. It's obvious the police don't get what's going on, not even Dan Lockhart with all his skills and tricks. And, if he thinks the first two were hard to understand, this next one is going to confuse the hell out of him.

I can't wait.

DAY EIGHT

CHAPTER THIRTY-ONE

It had been a rough night, though Lockhart had no one to blame but himself. After he'd got home from Lavender Hill station, he'd crammed in a plate of scrambled eggs and baked beans on toast and continued researching how to dispute that a missing person was dead. *A missing person.* Jess. He could never lose sight of her, no matter what legal proceedings ensued with her family.

But, thinking about it all, he'd just got more and more stressed, until his autopilot had taken him to the fridge, where he found himself reaching for a can of Stella. Just to take the edge off. He hadn't intended to drink. But one beer had led to another, and a third – he'd counted nine cans on the floor this morning – and things were hazy after that. Next thing he knew, he'd woken up at 5 a.m., his neck aching from the weird position he'd fallen asleep in, fully clothed on the sofa.

Despite that, Lockhart had been up early this morning. He had a little job to do and reckoned he had half an hour before he needed to be at the MIT office in Putney. Porter had called a morning briefing and Lockhart could guess what the priority would be. His boss was still furious after yesterday's press leak about the murders. The DCI had obviously incurred the wrath of his superior, Detective Superintendent Burrows, who was head of the whole MIT. She didn't pull her punches. But Lockhart reckoned that Porter was even more concerned than her about the impact of negative publicity, given his upcoming promotion assessment.

Now, Porter was determined to identify the source who had gone to the media and, Lockhart guessed, line them up for the firing squad. He briefly remembered Khan's body language when the news of the leak had dropped. The young DC had been underperforming lately, but selling his team out to a journalist? That was something else. Betrayal. Would Khan do that?

Lockhart wished he had Green's psychology brain at times like these. He wondered how she was getting on with her profile, and whether anything she could see in the details might unlock the case for them. He needed to give her a bit more time; not only was she working for free, but she was also helping Smith and Stagg out with their hunt for the serial sex attacker.

Pushing open the door to the small electronics store in Shepherd's Bush, Lockhart went straight over to the guy behind the counter.

'Can I help you, sir?'

'Yeah.' He extracted a piece of paper from his jacket pocket and handed it to the sales assistant. 'I need eight of these.'

The man read the note. 'Eight?'

'Yup.'

'I'll see what we've got.' He rummaged behind the counter, opening and closing cupboard doors but evidently failing to locate the product. 'Just give me a moment, please.' He walked towards what Lockhart guessed was the storeroom and keyed in a code to open it.

Lockhart willed them to have the stuff. There was always a trade-off with things like this; the big shops were better stocked, but sometimes asked more questions, and kept more careful records of purchases. And he needed this to be deniable, or as close to that as possible. The less he had to explain, the better. He didn't want this coming back to bite him.

The guy seemed to be gone for ages, and Lockhart was aware of a camera in the corner, watching him. That was why he'd worn the baseball cap. Finally, the storeroom door flew open and the guy emerged with an armful of small cardboard boxes.

'You're in luck,' he said.

'Nice one. You take cash?' Lockhart felt in his other pocket for the thick bundle of notes Eddie Stagg had given him.

'Certainly, sir.' The guy cracked a wide smile. 'With pleasure.'

CHAPTER THIRTY-TWO

Lexi had stayed up late working on her profile. She'd read about instrumental violence and other psychopathic behaviours until she could barely keep her eyes open. By the time she'd finally shut down the laptop, it'd felt like progress. But she was paying for it now with her inability to concentrate today in the clinic. Or maybe it was just her client, Oliver Soames. Lexi forced herself to tune into his monologue again.

'…and so it's like, I can't stop picturing all the things that my son and I – because I know it would've been a *he* – could have done together.'

'Mm-hm.' Lexi made an affirmative noise. 'Tell me more about that,' she said. The classic question if you happened to have stopped listening.

'Well, what else do I say?' He stared at her aggressively, and she briefly worried he was going to call her out on not paying attention. But then he sat back in the low armchair and his eyes darted around the room.

'Trips to the park to kick a football around,' he went on. 'I mean, I don't play, but I know *we* would have. And he would've been great at it. We could've gone to matches.'

She nodded, jotting another note on her pad about something which had just occurred to her that might be relevant to Dan's murder cases.

Re: target prep, check reports of low-level stalking in area – escalation?

Chris Merritt

'We would've built stuff together, in a shed. Or the garage. Woodworking.' He flapped a hand. 'It's all on YouTube, these days.'

'Uh-huh.' She continued to write.

More background on triangle symbolism

'And hikes. We would've done long, tough hikes up mountains. A father-and-son team.'

Lexi glanced up from her notes to see Olly shaking his head ruefully. He was short, pale, and kind of overweight. She figured he didn't spend too much time outdoors, let alone hiking. He had once told her he'd taken up running, but she wasn't sure if that was as much fantasy as the stuff he was talking about right now.

The whole piece sounded to her like make-believe. He'd imagined an idyllic future with his unborn child, sharing what he believed were masculine activities, with no recognition that they weren't things he ever did, or even confirmation that his child was male. Parents living out their own personal fantasies through their children was definitely a thing, but projecting all that onto a foetus was a new one for her. She had to say something; letting him ruminate about this for an hour was unprofessional.

'It sounds like you'd really thought a lot about your future together, Olly. But I'm just wondering how much of that planning you did *after* you found out about the abortion?'

'What are you trying to say?' he retorted.

'Only that sometimes we can let ourselves get stuck on what might've been. Rather than focusing on the present. And the future we're thinking about is like this perfect world where—'

'Are you telling me I'm making all this up?' he cut in.

'No, that's not what I meant. Sorry.' She paused a beat. 'How does it make you feel when you imagine that future?'

He inhaled deeply through his nostrils and gave a quick, hard breath out. 'Depressed. No, worse than depressed, whatever that is. Hopeless. And angry. So bloody angry. Like I've been robbed.'

'OK, I hear that. So, I guess what I want to ask is: how helpful do you think it is, right now, for you to be going over all this stuff every day? These what-ifs?'

He wagged a finger at her. 'I see what you're trying to do. You're trying to get me to tell myself I'm wrong. But I know how I feel.' He jabbed the finger into his own chest.

'Of course, you do, Olly. You're the expert in you.' That was a cliché, but it never hurt to mention it now and again. 'I guess I'm just wondering—'

'Anyway, what would you know about it?' His voice oozed bitterness.

Now wasn't the time to tell him that, in fact, she knew a whole lot about it. That she'd been in the exact same position as his partner. That she'd made the same choice. That her boyfriend at the time, back at college in the States, had been as selfish about it as Olly was being now. And that, through all of it, she hadn't told her parents anything. She'd figured that they were still grieving after Shep's death, and they didn't need a load more stress. At the time, it'd seemed like the best call but, looking back, it'd left her almost completely isolated.

'We're not here to talk about me,' she replied gently. 'These sessions are a space for you.'

He nodded firmly, as if her answer proved him right. 'I suppose I should tell you that we've separated, as well.' He gestured to her pad. 'You can note that down.'

'I'm sorry to hear that, Olly. Is it something you want to talk about today, or should we devote time to it next week?' She discreetly checked the clock: ten minutes left.

'It happened a few weeks ago,' he continued, not exactly answering her question. 'Became official this weekend, though. We are no longer a couple.' Olly met her gaze and Lexi immediately felt a little uncomfortable. She looked down at her paper.

'And how are you doing?' she asked.

'How do you think I'm doing?'

Jeez, this was exhausting. Not to mention infuriating. She kept the pleasant veneer but inside she was losing any shred of sympathy she had left for him. This douchebag was everything Lexi hated about male privilege; the entitled sense of owning a woman's body just because he'd put his dick inside her and gotten lucky with one of his sperm. Exactly like her old boyfriend. She wanted to reach out and slap him. The fantasy of her doing so was broken a moment later when she realised that he was speaking again.

'…I didn't deserve to be treated that way. It was fifty-fifty, I mean, if anything sixty-forty in my favour because I earn more…'

The subject of body autonomy made her think of Operation Braddock. She had Eddie Stagg's business card in her bag. Once Olly had left, she'd email him and fix a time to read the case material. Maybe she could even head to the police station this evening after work? She'd planned a run in the park tonight as part of her new regime, but this was way more important.

'…the idea that she can just do whatever she wants, it makes me so angry. Like… like I want to break something, to let it out somehow, make someone pay…'

Lexi badly wanted to help with the serial rape case. She was so enraged by the idea of this man assaulting lone, vulnerable women in *her* city that a part of her even wanted to go looking for him herself. Was helping from her armchair enough? Max, Eddie and the others were out there on the streets, interviewing victims, checking the crime scenes. She hoped her profiling would do some good. It had to. Then she realised Olly had stopped talking. They sat in silence for a few seconds. She pretended to make a couple more notes, flicked back through her pages, then looked up.

'Thank you for being so open with me, Olly. That takes real courage.' She smiled, picturing the money hitting her bank account. 'So, same time next week?'

CHAPTER THIRTY-THREE

According to scientific research, Tuesday was supposed to be the worst day of the week. But Ernesto Gomez didn't believe that. The study he'd read about said that most people rated Tuesday as their lowest point in the week. It was distant enough from Sunday for the weekend's feel-good factor to have worn off, but it still seemed a hell of a long way until Saturday. Ernesto supposed that Tuesday could be a bad day, if you hated your job and didn't have much outside of it to look forward to. That didn't apply to him, though.

Ernesto loved his work as a set designer. He'd started out as an interior designer, drawn to the combination of artistic expression and practicality. Creating spaces for people to work, play, and live in together. It was a beautiful thing. But, one day about six years ago, a friend had asked for his help building a film set. Ernesto jumped at the chance – he was a huge movie fan and the opportunity sounded like too much fun to miss out on. He'd expected it to be a one-off project. As soon as he'd got on set, however, it was as if something lit up inside him.

He'd never gone back to his old work after that, although someone in the business had once described set design as being like interior design, only on speed. That summed it up perfectly: all the sensory aspects and creativity of interiors, but with action, deadlines and adrenalin. There was nothing more satisfying than seeing an actor step into your set, into the world you'd created, and watching it shape their performance. Or attending a premiere and, while the stars were the ones who got papped on the red carpet, you could sit back quietly in your seat and think: *I made that set.*

But it wasn't only his love of set design that was making Ernesto happy on this particular Tuesday. Far from it! Tuesday was also one of the best days in his week because it was Zumba night. After a long day of technical drawing, sourcing props or making 3D models, there was nothing Ernesto loved to do more than jump into the dance studio and get sweaty. The drums, the energy, the movement. Reggaeton style was his favourite.

And then there was Paul. Kind, lovely, gorgeous Paul. They'd met online two months ago, and from that first coffee there'd been a connection. Ernesto felt it somewhere in his soul. Things had been going great so far and, he hoped, there was a serious possibility that he and Paul could be together long-term. If he was allowed one complaint, though, it was that Paul didn't want to come to Zumba. Ernesto had told him that you didn't need to be a great dancer, that it was more about music and fitness, but Paul was still a little shy. Maybe he'd try it another night. There was plenty of time for that in the future Ernesto was imagining for them.

He took out his phone and texted Paul:

Thinking of you x

Not *Love you*. Not quite yet. But almost. Ernesto smiled to himself and went back to his work. It wasn't long before the reply pinged on the table next to him. He couldn't resist taking a peek.

Same here x

He felt as though his heart might burst with happiness.

CHAPTER THIRTY-FOUR

From the passenger seat of Stagg's car, Smith watched the bus stop across the road. An older man in a flat cap with a walking stick was perched on the bench, while a younger woman leant against the shelter, scrolling on her phone without so much as a glance up. Did the woman realise how vulnerable she was? Had she even seen the news about the 'bus stop rapist', as the tabloid press was calling him? Was the mere presence of a man – albeit an elderly and clearly infirm one – enough to dissuade the attacker, should he be lurking nearby?

Beside her, Stagg was doing a crossword, rustling the folded newspaper and scribbling occasionally with his biro. It was gone ten p.m. and they'd been waiting like this for almost half an hour. She glanced behind her. In the back seat, Lockhart had his eyes closed. Smith remembered him telling her that the ability to sleep anywhere, at any time, was one of the most prized skills in the military. She couldn't tell if he was asleep or not, but she hoped – despite the illegal act they were about to commit – that he was relaxing a bit, at least.

The guvnor definitely hadn't been himself the past few days. Smith didn't know what was up; Lockhart kept himself to himself as much now as he had seven months ago when he'd joined their MIT. Ultimately, she didn't mind that. Everyone had their right to privacy. And experience taught her that a colleague who was a closed book but a good operator was much better than the reverse.

A long single-decker bus chugged into view, pulled up with a hiss of brakes and the man and woman waiting got on board. Once the few passengers who'd disembarked had walked far enough away, Lockhart spoke.

'Let's go.'

They strolled across to the shelter and Lockhart extracted a small toolkit and two boxes. Smith and Stagg observed as he drilled a hole in the corner of the shelter's metal frame, plugged it with a screw, then carefully mounted the little camera he'd purchased that morning. As he covered it with a discreet, dark grey box in which he'd cut a tiny aperture, Smith surveyed the immediate area. There were dark trees behind them, no one around, and the nearest houses were set far back with their blinds or curtains shut. She couldn't see a single camera, apart from the one they'd just installed, obviously. It was the exact type of location their attacker would target. He was a guy who understood the local geography, who knew the buses and discreet routes on foot, to and from the stops. Well, she thought, hopefully his disgusting campaign of terror ended here.

Lockhart pocketed the multi-tool he'd been using as a screwdriver. 'It works on a motion sensor,' he said, taking out his phone. 'We sync it to the app on this. I'll set it up for you guys, too.'

'High-tech,' observed Stagg.

'Pretty standard, actually. Come on.' Lockhart gestured for them to move aside with him, a few yards away. 'Go on, Eddie. Walk over to the stop.'

Smith watched as Lockhart's phone screen came to life with footage of Stagg ambling past the shelter. It was pretty clear, a decent quality feed despite the limited street lighting.

'Cool,' she said.

'It's a good bit of kit,' remarked Lockhart. 'Camera works well in low light. We used to use the old version of these in… never mind. Cheers, Eddie.'

'You wouldn't even know it was there,' said Stagg as he returned to them. 'Does it work, then?'

Lockhart showed him the footage and explained how to call it up. 'OK. Basically, we're going to capture every person who walks past this bus stop and trips the motion sensor. Multiply that by eight once we've installed every camera, and that means a ton of false positives.'

'I don't care if there's nine hundred and ninety-nine ordinary people on here,' replied Stagg. 'If the thousandth is our bloke and the footage gives us any chance of identifying him, that's a result in my book.'

Smith nodded. 'I'll second that.'

'To be honest, though,' added Lockhart, 'there's not a lot of chance of catching him in the act. Unless you monitor all eight feeds simultaneously from dusk till dawn.'

'We'll check it as often as we can,' said Smith. 'We might get lucky.'

'All right, then.' Lockhart pocketed his phone and picked up his mini toolbox. 'We'd better move on. There's seven more of these to do.'

Smith knew it was going to be a long shift. But she'd go without sleep or food all night if it meant one less woman was sexually assaulted in her city. Something about meeting the victims of this bastard had ignited a fire in her that was burning fiercely. She just hoped she wouldn't lose her job because of it.

CHAPTER THIRTY-FIVE

I hate waiting. Patience isn't one of my strengths. I despise the whole idea of *delayed* gratification. Shrinks always talk about that being a predictor of kids' success in later life. As a child, can you stop yourself eating a marshmallow for ten minutes if you know you'll get two at the end of that time? Me, I couldn't. I'd eat the marshmallow immediately, then find the person with the bag and bite, scratch or kick them until they gave me the rest. That's how life works, survival of the fittest. If that was one thing Mum's and Dad's failures taught me, it was never to let anyone or anything be stronger than you.

I imagine that Dad had been strong, once. But his life collapsed after he came back from the Gulf War in '91. I was a baby, but from what he told me years later, he couldn't deal with returning home. First, he started drinking every day. Then, he began punching Mum, which made her go back to sticking needles in her arm, like she used to do before they met. He hit me, too, but never enough that people asked serious questions.

Eventually, Mum left, and it was just me and him, but when he was chucked out of the army, the pub became his new full-time job. Sometimes he'd take me along and sit me down in a corner with a colouring-in book while he sank pint after pint. But, most of the time, he'd just leave me in our shitty little flat, where I watched whatever movies I wanted and fantasised about being the one doing the violence.

When I was twelve, I came home from school one day to find him preparing a noose to hang himself. He didn't go through with it, but from that moment I knew that the only person I could rely on was myself.

It was war that changed Dad. Dan Lockhart would get that, same as he understands what it's like to kill someone with your bare hands, for which I respect him. Not many people have the balls to do that. But, after tonight, he's only got a few more days to find me before I come for him. His skills had better be up to scratch. Better than Dad's, at least.

My watch says it's almost ten thirty. The guy I've been waiting for should be coming any time now. The mallet in my pocket has a reassuring weight. I like the *thump* sound it makes when it connects with bone. One surprise strike is all I need, then the fun can begin. The payback, the justice.

It's almost completely silent in the graveyard. There's just the rustle of tree branches in the slight wind, the occasional chirrup of a robin, and my own breathing. Then a new sound. Footsteps on the path. Getting louder.

Showtime.

*

Ernesto was buzzing. The Zumba class had been amazing. It was as if the music had taken over his body and, once he'd felt that start to happen, he'd just let go. They'd moved and danced for almost a full hour straight, but it'd seemed like only a few moments. Now, walking home, he could feel his thighs trembling from the exertion. The night air was helping him cool down, but he was looking forward to a shower when he got to his flat. That wasn't the only thing he was anticipating.

Earlier, Paul had texted to ask what he was doing after Zumba. Since Paul knew the class ended at 10 p.m. and they both had work tomorrow, his question wasn't about going out afterwards.

Back in Colombia, where Ernesto had grown up, it wouldn't be unusual to start your night out at ten thirty. But here in London people didn't do that. *He* didn't do that, not on a weekday, anyway. Ernesto wasn't one of those party-animal guys who was on the scene every night. And Paul knew that. Which meant his message was about one thing, and one thing only. And that was absolutely fine with Ernesto.

As he strolled through the graveyard, thinking again what a cool set it would make for a movie – so gothic and creepy – he let himself begin fantasising about Paul. He was picturing the bathroom of his apartment, clouded with steam, warm and inviting. He imagined hot water against his skin, flowing over his body. Then Paul, opening the shower door and stepping inside with him. The texture of his beard, the touch of his strong hands…

His excitement growing, Ernesto took out his phone. They'd agreed he would text Paul when he got home to say that he was in, and Paul would come over. He lived in Brixton, which was only ten minutes in an Uber. From the graveyard, it was still another fifteen minutes' walk to Ernesto's house, but he couldn't wait. If he texted now, Paul would get there even faster.

He went into his messages, tapped on Paul's last one, and began a reply. Then he heard something behind him and stopped, turned. No one was there. He blinked, squinting into the darkness. Ernesto had never seen another soul walking through here at night before. Probably because the place shut in the afternoon. At this time, he always hopped over the low wall to get in. That was a little naughty, but the dead didn't mind. And it was so worth it for the most atmospheric shortcut in town. Satisfied he was alone, he continued walking.

Seconds later, he heard the quick footsteps and spun just in time to see a dark shape coming up on him, a swinging arm. Ernesto raised his hands, but he was too slow. The impact on the side of his face sent him backwards, sprawling, flailing, and he smacked into the path, his phone flying from his grip. The wind was knocked from him and he clutched his stomach. He tried to shout but somehow couldn't form words, only panicked, mangled noises. Then a body was over him. Another almighty blow connected with his ribs, and this time he screamed louder, screwing his eyes shut and desperately clawing air until his nails raked flesh. A face.

The attacker growled in what sounded more like annoyance than pain, as if Ernesto's best efforts to defend himself were merely an inconvenience. He opened his eyes again and tried to keep fighting, thrashing his limbs. But then he saw the object raised again, high above him, and when it came back down and connected, everything went black.

DAY NINE

CHAPTER THIRTY-SIX

As Lockhart reached the crime scene perimeter, he surveyed the vast expanse of gravestones and grass, interspersed by old trees. Streatham Cemetery was one of the few large burial sites in London he hadn't been to before, not that he was crossing them off some morbid mental list. It was a typical Victorian cemetery; a massive plot of land set aside to meet demand for places to bury the dead. A hundred and fifty years ago, London's population was swelling through migration by those searching for work, but life expectancy in the city was just forty. The maths was simple, and the answer was big graveyards.

Londoners might live longer these days, but their ultimate fate hadn't changed. The capital drew people in from all over the world but remained indifferent to their existence. Whatever they succumbed to, they all ended up six feet underneath her surface. Decaying, disintegrating and eventually merging with her soil. London literally absorbed its citizens; they became part of her fabric in death as much as in life.

Lockhart briefly wondered if this gloomy train of thought was the effect cemeteries had on him. Then the voices got his attention. He followed the sound and saw a couple of reporters and a photographer making their way towards him, shouting questions. *Did he know what was going on? Was it another victim of the serial killer? What could he tell them?* He deflected everything with a single palm, firmly raised, and the words: 'no comment for the minute'. Before they could intercept him, Lockhart flashed his warrant to the PC at the outer cordon who swiftly raised the tape for him to duck beneath. He spotted DCI Porter on his phone over by one of the two chapels. After signing in with the CSM, Lockhart walked over to his boss and caught the end of his call.

'Of course, ma'am,' said Porter. 'I'll have a full update for you within the hour.'

Lockhart knew it would be DSI Burrows on the line, channelling pressure from the Chief Super above her down to Porter. Pressure that would surely make its way to the rest of the MIT before long.

His boss rang off and tucked the phone inside his jacket, peering over Lockhart's shoulder towards the journalists.

'Jesus Christ, Dan.' Porter spoke in hushed, angry tones. 'How did that lot get here so bloody fast?'

'No idea, sir.' Lockhart shoved his hands in his coat pockets. 'Probably have to give them something soon, though. They're already asking if this is linked to the other two. And it doesn't look as though they're going anywhere.'

'All right. I'll deal with my own media strategy, thanks very much.' He ran a hand over his smooth, shaved head. 'Three bodies in nine days. Fuck knows I didn't need this right now.'

Lockhart said nothing. He felt the urgency of catching this killer as much as Porter. But for him, homicide cases were always about the victims, not about the investigators. Now wasn't the time to call the boss on his lack of empathy, though. Lockhart wasn't the one going for promotion, despite what Porter had said a few days ago. And he guessed that if the big man found out about him briefing Green, let alone the bus stop covert cameras, it'd be more than the acting DCI role he could lose. A scuffing of shoes came from behind them and they turned to see Khan approaching.

'And I don't need this, either,' muttered Porter.

'Sir.' Khan acknowledged Lockhart with a small nod. 'Boss.'

'Anything?' asked the DCI wearily.

'Just spoke to the groundsman who found our victim this morning. He was in the gatehouse last night – he lives there – but he didn't hear nothing. Then again, he had the telly on, and the attack was—' Khan pointed but Porter cut him off.

'I know where it was. Right over the other side. There's a tent there. With a body in it.'

Khan didn't reply but his jaw worked aggressively at some gum.

Porter sighed. 'Have we started house to house?'

'No.' Khan frowned. 'I thought the uniforms were gonna do that.'

'Well, there's only two of them here at the moment, and as you can see, they're busy keeping uninvited press out of our crime scene. So, get over the road and start knocking on doors.'

For a second, Khan looked as if he was going to protest. But he bit his lip, mumbled an affirmative reply, and went off. Lockhart watched him leave, remembering his reaction to the press leak. Khan was one of the first on the scene here today, and the journalists hadn't been far behind. Lockhart didn't want to throw accusations around, but something was definitely going on with Khan. Maybe he'd have a word with Smith, later; she spent more time with him than anyone else in the MIT.

Porter had indicated that he thought one of them was responsible for unauthorised contact with the media and said that an email audit would be conducted in due course. This had damaged morale and trust in the team at a time when they needed everyone to put in extra hours and effort. Lockhart wondered what they'd find in his emails. He was pretty sure his contact with Stagg and Green had been by phone only… But he couldn't worry about that now. The most useful thing he could do was focus on this crime scene.

'We got a duty pathologist?' he asked.

'Nope.' Porter shook his head. 'There's nobody available. Even though that's what "duty" meant, the last time I checked.'

'Right.'

'I haven't even seen the body yet,' said Porter. 'Let's suit up.'

CHAPTER THIRTY-SEVEN

Lockhart had run towards the Taliban sniper inside the house in Afghanistan, taking him to the ground and throwing wild punches with a kind of uncontained rage that seemed to belong to someone else. The guy had defended himself, at first, blocking Lockhart's early strikes while trying to squirm out from under him, and managed to land a couple of knees to his stomach and ribs. But that wasn't enough. When Lockhart's fist slammed into his face, the sniper's resistance seemed to evaporate. Perhaps Lockhart should've stopped there. But it was as if that alien force was still in control of his body. All he could see was the corpse of Private Billy Ross, the young lad from his unit this guy had just shot. And he kept punching.

'Dan!' Porter's voice brought him sharply out of the scene. 'I said, do you agree?'

Lockhart felt nauseous. His heart was palpitating. Now he understood why these flashbacks were coming to him. 'Er… sorry, sir, I wasn't quite—'

'Do you agree, it's the same killer?'

Green used to tell him that those physical reactions were just part of the memory. It might feel as though the event was happening again, but he was safe. Trying to get his fight-or-flight response under control, Lockhart stooped to examine the victim.

The dead man lay on his back, his face bruised and swollen. Trails of blood had dried around the nose and mouth. Again, there was a triangle drawn on his neck, but this time it had a horizontal line through it.

'Looks that way,' observed Lockhart. 'Apparent ambush MO, isolated location. Symbol's a bit different, though.'

'Hm.'

'And so's the victim. For a start, he's much younger than Stott and Johnson.'

Porter was about to reply when the tent flap opened and one of the SOCOs came in holding a brown paper evidence bag. 'iPhone,' she announced. 'We found it in the long grass just behind the tent. Could be the victim's.'

'Good.' Porter jerked his head towards the body. 'I assume he's not been rolled yet?'

'No.'

'Right, let's do it and see what's in that rucksack.'

Two minutes later, they had removed the backpack, confirmed no obvious external wounds lay underneath it, and carefully returned the body to its original position. The SOCO placed the bag down and gently unzipped it, probing inside.

'Damp clothing,' she said. 'Smells sweaty. Gym kit, most likely.'

'Let's find out where he was training,' Porter commented.

'Hang on.' The SOCO paused, then extracted a small, dark object. A wallet. She opened it and pulled out a driving licence, scanning the front before offering it to Porter.

'Ernesto Gomez.' The DCI scrutinised the photo and handed the card to Lockhart. 'Born 1985. Address in Streatham. I'd say it's him.'

Lockhart agreed. 'Is there money in the wallet?'

The SOCO flipped the divider and tugged out the corners of some notes. 'Forty quid.'

'I don't think this was a random robbery,' offered Lockhart. 'I reckon Mr Gomez was targeted. Like Johnson and Stott. Someone knew he was coming through this cemetery.'

Porter shook his head. 'Killer could've followed him in here, taken the opportunity of darkness and tree cover to attack. Maybe he just didn't find the wallet. He panicked and fled without taking anything.'

'Can I see that phone?' Lockhart asked the SOCO. She passed him the evidence bag. He took the mobile out, taking care to hold it by the edges, and moved it towards the victim's hands. This had worked for him once before, last year. He lifted Gomez's fingers, noticing that the nails were long and darkened with dirt.

'Dan, what are you doing?' asked Porter.

'Make sure we get samples from under these nails,' he told the SOCO. 'OK?'

'Sure, I'll get a swab kit.' The SOCO stood. 'By the way, if you're thinking of trying to open that phone, it won't work. iPhone X doesn't have fingerprint ID.'

'Right.' Lockhart glanced up to her and back to the phone.

'Try his face instead. His eyes are open.'

Lockhart held the phone over the victim's face, tilting it, but nothing happened.

'Let me have a go.' The SOCO crouched next to him. He gave her the phone. 'It works on infra-red sensors,' she explained, angling Gomez's head to the other side. 'It checks for a match on shape, so the contusions and swelling on his left side might confuse it.'

She swept the phone over the right-hand side where Gomez's eye was open, staring ahead, unblinking. Nothing happened. The SOCO repeated the motion, but the device stayed locked. She tried again, and suddenly the screen came to life.

'There you go,' she said. 'I'll get that swab kit, now.'

'Genius.' Lockhart stood and, together with Porter, examined the home screen. There was a notification on the call log. Lockhart tapped into it.

'Five missed calls from someone called Paul,' he said.

'Check the texts,' suggested Porter.

Lockhart tapped into them and found the thread he was looking for at the top. Paul had sent Gomez several messages between 11 p.m. and midnight, asking if he was home, then if he was OK. A further three texts today expressed Paul's hope that Gomez was all right, ending with a request to call him. Scrolling up, Lockhart read the texts from earlier that day. They were affectionate and flirtatious, signed off with kisses, and culminated in a plan to meet up last night.

'We need to speak to this guy,' said Porter.

Paul wasn't the only person they needed to speak to. Green had warned Lockhart about jumping to conclusions, and it seemed as though she'd been right. He was already dismissing the theory that their killer was a vigilante attacking middle-aged straight white men accused of sexually assaulting younger female colleagues. Apart from being male, Ernesto Gomez didn't appear to fit a single part of that profile.

Lockhart needed to find out more about Gomez and give Green the new information. Just as soon as he could get some distance from Porter.

CHAPTER THIRTY-EIGHT

Smith emerged from Brixton tube station into a wall of sensory overload. Above heavy traffic, she could hear shouted conversations, fire-and-brimstone preaching, pleas for spare change, and drumming. The meaty aromas of street food grills mingled with exhaust fumes and cigarette smoke. And there were people, everywhere. Bustling, shoving, loitering; a great mass of humanity collected at one huge crossroads.

Faced with all that, she wouldn't blame an unsuspecting visitor for heading straight back underground. But this was London, and Smith loved it. She never wanted to lose touch with the streets of her home. That said, she might've preferred to drive to Paul Newton's residence, but the simple fact was that no cars were available. It was either a sign of how many extra staff had been loaned to MIT 8 today, or of how strapped their resources were. Most likely a combination of both.

After the body of Ernesto Gomez had been discovered early this morning, and initial examination had suggested he was their killer's third victim, things had stepped up a gear. Make that two gears; three if you were talking about Porter's stress levels. DSI Burrows had even visited their office, which happened about as often as a solar eclipse, mainly to announce that the series of three linked killings had been given the name Thorncross.

Met ops often took their titles from English villages and, in this case, a quick Google search showed that Thorncross was just a stone's throw from the beautiful Isle of Wight coastline.

Smith briefly imagined the sandy beach, the waves, a walk with her fella and no violent crime to deal with. She could just about remember what that was called: a holiday. Maybe she'd get one when Thorncross and Braddock had been cleared up. But no way would she even consider leaving London until then.

Reinforcements from MIT 11 in Lewisham had been bussed like tourists into Jubilee House this afternoon. They were already hot desking, though Smith's aggressively labelled personal biscuit collection and photographs of her loved ones made it clear that *her* desk was not available. Smith had been one of those temporary transfers herself a few times, so she appreciated how important it was to be welcoming. Which, of course, she would be. Just as long as no one sat in her chair or pilfered her snacks.

It wasn't just the activity levels that were changing. Smith had been forced to confront her earlier certainty that these serial murders were about revenge for unpunished sexual assaults on younger women by older men. Gomez was thirty-five, Latin American, and gay. In terms of motive, it felt as though they were back to square one. But she reminded herself that she still knew very little about Gomez, and that the allegations against both Stott and Johnson hadn't emerged until the MIT had spoken to their colleagues. That aspect of their victim strategy wouldn't be so easy for Gomez, because he was a self-employed freelance designer. Still, the Lewisham lot were making themselves useful by tracking down his professional contacts, as well as liaising with the Colombian embassy in Knightsbridge to locate his family in Medellín.

Meanwhile, it was up to Smith to follow up a key lead: Gomez's boyfriend, Paul Newton. He was a cardiologist at the nearby King's College Hospital but had been given the day as compassionate leave when he was informed of Gomez's death.

As Smith walked to Newton's flat, she took advantage of the few spare minutes to review some footage on her phone from their

Braddock bus stop cameras. There was a lot of material and Smith already knew they'd struggle to keep up with watching it all. It was 3 a.m. by the time they'd finally finished putting everything in place, which meant she'd only managed four hours' kip before she was up again and into Jubilee House. She was feeling the effects of that late night – or maybe early morning was more accurate – but at least the cameras were in place.

Nothing of interest had cropped up so far, and a text to Stagg this morning confirmed he hadn't seen anything, either. But a result on their first night would've been almost too good to be true. At least the feed was working, and no one seemed to have discovered, vandalised or nicked the cameras, which was a major plus. This was London, after all.

At the new-build apartment complex, Smith pocketed her phone and rang the buzzer for Newton's flat. Once inside, she found his door on the third floor open, a slim black man standing on the threshold. He had a short, neat beard, and wore chinos and a thin woollen sweater over a collared shirt. Smith would've described him as handsome, ordinarily, but his face seemed to have lost all vigour. She imaged he was still in shock.

'Doctor Paul Newton?' she asked.

'Yeah.' He blinked. 'Just… Paul's OK.'

Smith introduced herself, adding: 'Please call me Max.'

The open-plan living room and kitchen had a circular dining table in the middle, where Smith found her team's FLO, PC MacLeod, sitting amidst several mugs and crisp packets. There was an iPad to one side.

'I'm very sorry for your loss, Paul,' said Smith. 'And I apologise for intruding here, too.'

Newton nodded quickly. 'It's all right. I understand.' He slumped into his chair and peered into an empty mug. Smith felt as though the energy had been sucked out of the room.

'Shall I put the kettle on for us?' asked MacLeod gently, reading the situation. Once again, Smith was grateful for her emotional intelligence.

'Thanks,' whispered the doctor.

MacLeod glanced at her.

'Oh, well…' Smith was gasping for a brew, and sometimes sharing a hot drink did help break the ice a bit. 'If you don't mind. Cheers, Rhona.' She took a seat beside Newton.

'So sudden,' he said, unprompted. 'We were supposed to meet up last night. I was meant to go over to Nesto's place. Then he just didn't answer me. I wasn't sure if he'd run out of battery or lost his mobile, or if something had happened…' Newton tailed off, his face still blank. He shrugged. 'I don't know what I thought. But I didn't want to just turn up at his place, you know?'

'Yeah, of course. Sounds like you were worried, Paul. And it's hard to know what to do in situations like that,' Smith said. But she needed to go back a step. 'How long had you known Mr Gomez?'

'Only a couple of months. But it was getting serious,' he added. 'We saw each other three, four times a week. More, recently.'

'So, you were spending a lot of time together?'

'Mm.'

'And do you know of anyone who might've wanted to hurt Mr Gomez? Was he in any kind of trouble?'

'No… nothing. I mean, not that he ever mentioned to me. And we were very open with each other. We had to be, since we couldn't be open with our families about… us.' Newton continued to stare at the table. 'Nesto was the sweetest guy in the world. He never had a bad word to say about anyone.' At this, his voice cracked, and he began to cry silent tears that shook his body. 'I'm sorry,' he mumbled.

'It's fine,' said Smith quietly. 'Take your time.'

They sat in silence for a moment while MacLeod brought the mugs of tea over. Newton gradually stopped crying and took some deep breaths, warming his hands on the mug.

'You see death every day at work,' he said, almost absent-mindedly. 'And you care about the patients on the ward. But you never get too attached. You can't. So, I guess I thought I could handle it. Death, I mean. Then when it's someone you love…' He stopped and looked up at Smith. 'God, I *loved* him. That's the first time I ever said it. I hadn't told Nesto yet. And now I…' Newton's head dropped and his shoulders began to shudder once more.

'I'm sure he knew how you felt about him.' MacLeod leant towards Newton and laid a hand on his shoulder. 'You're coping so well with this, Paul.'

'I don't think I am,' he said, his voice rising in pitch.

'You'll find your own way through it,' said MacLeod, her soft Scottish accent soothing, reassuring. Newton turned to MacLeod and, suddenly, wrapped his arms around her. The FLO held him and rubbed his back. Smith found herself moved by the simple, human gesture. The flame began to kindle inside her, as it had done so readily for Op Braddock.

When the time was right, Smith resumed her questions. 'Can you tell us about Mr Gomez's work, please?'

'Oh.' Newton sniffed and massaged his eye sockets with the heels of his hands. 'Nesto loved what he did. Set design, for films and TV.'

'He worked in film?' Smith recalled Lockhart's mantra: he didn't like coincidences. And neither did she. How likely was it that two of the victims' professions were linked by the same industry? But if that was the connection, how did Johnson, the lawyer, fit into it?

'Yeah. You can see some of his stuff on Instagram.' Newton reached for his iPad and tapped the screen a few times. 'Here you go,' he said, proffering the tablet to Smith. 'He put half of his life on there, to be honest. They wouldn't let him post photos of sets where the production hadn't been released yet, he told me. It was pretty cut-throat, apparently. You could get fired just like—' he clicked his fingers, 'that. But he could put some stuff on there, older work. And,' Newton hiccupped a small laugh, 'he always posted his Zumba. He was mad about it. Tried to get me to go.'

Smith was scrolling through the pictures. Gomez had added details of the places, times, and events of his life. It wouldn't be hard to find out where he was going to be, she thought.

'Oh God,' moaned Newton. 'If I'd said yes to going with him last night, we'd have been walking home together and, maybe… this wouldn't have happened. I should've—'

'This is not your fault, Paul,' said MacLeod. 'Not at all.'

'It was the fault of the person who attacked Ernesto,' said Smith, realising she'd used the victim's first name. That was a sure sign this was becoming personal for her. 'No one else.'

Newton raised his wet eyes and met her gaze.

'And I'm going to find him,' she added.

CHAPTER THIRTY-NINE

According to the clinical psychology textbooks, a patient not turning up for a session should be a cause for concern rather than relief. But relief was exactly what Lexi felt when her 3 p.m. client, a young Syrian asylum seeker, had failed to show. It wasn't the first time, and since Lexi knew he was unreliable rather than risky, she could use the DNA – Did Not Attend – time to work on her profiling rather than chasing him up.

Like most clinicians, she had a mountain of paperwork to get through. But that could wait. Because none of it was as important as helping to catch a serial rapist operating in her part of south-west London. A guy who was preying on young women waiting alone at bus stops after dark. She'd been in that position herself many times, taking public transport home on her own. It could be her. The thought scared her, and had made her more vigilant of late, but it also made her angry as hell. Or maybe she was already angry, and this asshole sex offender was just someone against whom she could channel that rage more productively than she had been doing with her binge drinking.

Despite feeling strong emotions about the case, though, Lexi had to be objective about profiling the Operation Braddock attacker. She needed to apply the theories she'd studied to make an educated guess about who this was, and what was driving him. That was how she could be most useful. Of course, she was still writing a profile for Dan's double murder case, too, but she was kind of stuck on that, and planned to come back to it this evening.

Last night, Lexi had dropped by Lavender Hill police station, where Detective Sergeant Eddie Stagg had supplied her with the details of all eight Braddock incidents so far. She'd been given a desk in the CID room and, after Stagg had talked her through the basics, she'd been left with printed copies of the victims' accounts. It made for tough reading, because Lexi realised that she fell into the same demographic as those being watched, harassed or attacked: female, white, age twenty to thirty-five.

And her personal discomfort hadn't improved when she'd caught Detective Constable Roland Wilkins staring at her several times, his jaw slack, a wad of gum visible inside his mouth. Gross. Each time she'd busted him, he'd looked away sharply, acting as if nothing had happened. It was creepy, but the experience would be familiar to a lot of women. Whether on a train, in the street, the gym or a café, shopping, in a bar or wherever, men stared. And those stares, eyes roaming over your body as if it were their property, left you in no doubt as to what they were thinking.

In the case of the Braddock rapist, though, his thoughts had escalated to actions. He'd begun simply by watching women. Then, twice, he'd demanded the women expose their breasts to him. His next two reported attacks had involved assault by touching. Every time, he'd run away. The reluctance, almost shyness with which he acted, coupled with the fact that he made no threats and used no weapons in those first six attacks, made Lexi believe he fell into the sexual motivation category of stranger rape.

These rapists typically had poor social skills, limited sexual experience with women, and did not intend to hurt their victims. Research showed most rapists tended to attack women of similar age and ethnic background to themselves. So, Lexi was developing a picture of their suspect as a young white man, maybe twenty to thirty-five years old, awkward and introverted, a little quiet or passive, definitely single, and most probably a loner. She also figured that, given the geographical knowledge demonstrated in the attacks, he lived locally – probably within the area formed by the locations of the offences.

They knew from the victims' statements that he was shorter and stockier than average. Lexi wondered if he believed his physical appearance made him unattractive to women, particularly if the 'stocky' part of his build was fat rather than muscle. Maybe he'd been rejected by women when expressing his interest towards them and had developed low self-esteem as a result.

This type of rapist also tended to start out stalking or spying – a 'Peeping Tom' – which fitted with the Braddock reports. He would often feel that he had an emotional connection with his victims. Crucially, this meant he was unlikely to seriously harm the women he attacked. So far, so good on the profile, she thought, until she tried to factor in the two most recent attacks.

These had both involved the use of a knife to make threats of violence. The intended victim in incident seven had managed to get away from him, but victim eight had not been so lucky. The violence, the weapon, the aggressive act of dragging the woman into the vegetation behind the bus stop all pointed to a different category, more about anger. These offenders were typically more 'alpha', assertive, confident and physically stronger.

But the threats he'd made towards the victim even indicated a little sadism, which was another type altogether. The type that most often graduated to murder. Since there had only been one violent attack, Lexi couldn't say for sure where this guy fitted.

She was lost in thought, tapping her pen on the desk and re-reading her notes for anything she might've missed, when her phone vibrated. It was Dan.

'Hey, what's up?' she greeted him. 'Listen, I'm gonna do some more on the profile tonight, although I don't really know—'

'Have you seen the news?' he interrupted.

'Uh, no.' Lexi could feel her pulse going a little faster. 'I've been in with clients all day. Why? What's happened?'

'There's a new victim. Same killer, as far as we can tell.'

'Holy shit. Really?' Lexi was already calculating: three victims in nine days.

'Yeah.'

'Um, OK.' She grabbed her pad and flipped back to the notes she'd taken in Dan's apartment. Her memory of the visit made her picture his wall about Jess. And she remembered him, vulnerable, grieving. She felt that fierce desire to help him, once more. Then his voice brought her back to the present.

'I think you might've been right,' he said.

'About what?'

'About it not being related to sexual assault.'

'Huh.' Lexi clamped the phone between her ear and shoulder and pulled up the BBC News website on her work computer. One of the minor headlines under UK news ran:

Murder Victim Discovered in Cemetery

Posted three hours ago with the tag 'London'.

'Jeez, the press are all over this,' she exclaimed. She clicked into the article and scrolled down. It was just a few paragraphs and lacked detail.

'Tell me about it. We haven't even held a media briefing yet. Porter's going nuts. The journos are linking it to the first two murders, and they know about the symbols.'

'That sucks.'

He hesitated. 'Er, I'm assuming you haven't said anything to—'

'Hell, no! Come on, Dan. I mean, I literally just found out there was a third victim.'

'Sorry. Course. Just checking…'

'Is that why you called?' She could hear the irritation in her own voice. 'To accuse me of leaking information to the press?'

'Nope, not at all. Forget I said that.' He paused. 'In fact, I want to tell you more about it.'

She took a breath and leant back in her chair, still a little offended. 'OK.'

'Have you got a few minutes?' he asked. 'I really need your help.'

Lexi suppressed the small, ridiculous burst of pride she felt at the idea of Dan *needing* her and glanced at the clock. Her next client wasn't due till four and it was a quarter of, now. 'Sure,' she replied. 'Go ahead.'

CHAPTER FORTY

I'm aching. Badly. It's always like this, now, the day after physical exertion: sex, violence or any other fun stuff. The combined pain of broken bones, torn tendons, and busted ligaments that have supposedly healed but don't appear to have got the memo about being fixed. After it happened, they put me in a coma, at first, because my body was so shattered. Operated on me a dozen times. Shoved metal plates and screws and all kinds of stuff under my skin to hold me together. Kind of like Hugh Jackman's Wolverine character in the first X-Men film. Minus the claws, unfortunately. And except for the fact that he recovered in, like, a day. I needed months to get used to my injuries. Months more after that to rehab and get my strength back. But I'll never be the same as I was before the accident. It's like my whole body holds a memory of it and can't let go. Can't let me work like I used to. Can't even let me live a normal life. Not that my life was particularly normal up until a year ago, but that was how I had wanted it to be. It was *my* life.

And that's why they have to pay for taking it from me. I couldn't let that go unpunished. Who did they think they were, doing that to me?

That pathetic creature last night put up a bit of a struggle. Maybe because he was younger, fitter. But it didn't make any difference in the end. Just like being younger, fitter and tougher won't make any difference to Dan Lockhart when I come for him in a few days' time. But first, there's someone else on my list. Another one who colluded to screw me over, and who needs to suffer for it.

Usually, I haven't got the patience or interest to research stuff in detail. I like making decisions impulsively; things are more exciting that way. When it comes to murder, though, some degree of planning and preparation is needed to avoid getting caught.

That's why I'm in John's apartment, lying on his sofa, eating his food, drinking his beer, and using his laptop and his Wi-Fi to research my next kill. It's nice to know that I could count on John for an alibi if the police ever came knocking. But I don't think I'll even need him to lie for me. By the time they find me, it'll already be too late for them to stop me.

And too late to save Lockhart.

DAY TEN

CHAPTER FORTY-ONE

Lockhart had woken long before his alarm. He'd checked the clock on his phone, seen it wasn't even 5 a.m. yet, and tried to go back to sleep. But his brain had been a vortex of thoughts from which he couldn't escape: the bodies of Ernesto Gomez, Martin Johnson and Charles Stott. The Taliban sniper in that Afghan house. The Op Braddock rapist and cameras set up to catch him. The possibility of losing his job if their illegal surveillance was discovered. And, running through all of it, Jess. The image of her smiling face, then the unthinkable idea of her being declared 'officially' dead.

He'd tried to relax, but it was no use. After half an hour watching the bus stop feeds had failed to distract him, he'd decided to get up. Green had always told him in their therapy sessions that whenever he got mentally 'stuck' in his own stress, the best thing was to do something different. So, just as the sun was creeping over the horizon he'd grabbed his wetsuit, cap, towel and a flask of tea and set out in his Defender for the river.

A scrap with the Thames had done the trick and, by the time Lockhart had got back to Hammersmith, he would almost have said he was feeling good. Invigorated, at least. He dropped the Defender around the corner from his block and walked to his front door with three tasks in mind: grab a quick, hot shower, get some porridge down him, then head to work. Just ahead, the postwoman was wheeling her red delivery trolley away from the building, and the sight of her prompted Lockhart to add a fourth item to his list. Check the mail inside their communal entrance.

Among the usual takeaway menus and estate agents' circulars was a white envelope, his name and address typed behind its small clear window. It'd been posted yesterday, first class. Instinctively, he knew what it was. His heart was already sinking as he took the stairs two at a time to get back to his flat. He needed the privacy and safety of his home to confront this. Dropping his swimming kit inside the front door, he tore the envelope open. The heading stood out in bold type:

Claim for Declaration of Presumed Death

Lockhart had understood that this would be coming. Even so, something about seeing those words in print, black on white, made his gut lurch and his throat constrict. He wanted to tear the letter up immediately, throw it away, set fire to it. Pretend it didn't exist. But he had to face this. He forced himself to keep reading.

> *We are writing in regard to your wife, Mrs Jessica Lockhart (née Taylor), who was officially registered as missing…*

He was no stranger to legalese from the hundred court cases he'd seen during a decade in the Met. When the subject of this measured, neutral and technical language was his wife, though, it jarred, and he began to feel anger stirring in his belly. Still, he read on:

> *…and, given that the time elapsed since her disappearance has substantially exceeded seven years, our clients, the Taylor family, are seeking an official declaration of presumed death, which…*

Did Jess's parents no longer care about their own daughter? Did that wanker Nick not believe, deep down, that his sister was alive? The rage grew for Lockhart, snaking through his limbs and making his fingers and toes tingle. He could feel his face flushed with blood as his eyes ran over the next paragraph. And he could scarcely believe what he was seeing.

> *…whilst we must also recognise that an adult has the legal right to disappear, should he or she not wish to be found…*

Impossible. No way had Jess left him of her own free will. She couldn't have. He wouldn't believe it. That was the final straw. The fury had taken over, now, and he was dimly aware of the edges of his vision clouding. Without thinking, he ripped the letter in two and reached out, grabbing the first thing his hands found. He hurled the object against the nearest wall, bellowing as he released it. The smash and tinkle of glass made his vision clear instantly, as if he'd broken the surface of water he hadn't known he'd been under. He was suddenly conscious of the near silence in his flat, his heavy breathing the only noise.

Then he realised what he'd done.

Lying on the ground, its large frame cracked and glass shattered, was the photograph of him and Jess on their wedding day. Holding one another and grinning as if they had the rest of their lives together. It was more than Lockhart could take.

With shaky legs, he stumbled backward, made contact with the wall. Then he slid down it until he was sitting on the floor. He reached out for the two halves of the letter, taking one in each hand, and screwed them up as his head sank to his chest.

Then he began to cry.

CHAPTER FORTY-TWO

'You OK, Dan?' Lucy Berry stopped typing and swivelled her chair to face him.

Lockhart guessed she could see the dark bags under his red-rimmed eyes. Even if Berry hadn't been one of the more skilled analysts in the Met, she could've worked out that something was amiss.

He cleared his throat. 'Yeah, I'm all right. Just didn't sleep well, that's all.'

'I've got two little ones,' she replied with a wry smile. 'Welcome to my world.'

Lockhart forced himself to acknowledge the joke with a chuckle. He tried to push the letter and its implications out of his mind and focus on work.

'Thorncross,' he said. 'Any word from the lab on DNA?'

'Nothing yet,' she replied. 'I'll chase them up in a bit.'

'We need a break on this.'

'With DNA, you never know.'

A sample of skin cells harvested from beneath the fingernails of Ernesto Gomez had been sent to the specialist DNA unit at King's College London for expedited analysis. Its profile could be automatically compared to the six million records in the national database. Lockhart had known cases where that process had given investigators a suspect name, almost always from someone who'd previously offended. Occasionally, the hit was from someone who was in the system for professional reasons: emergency services workers, detectives, crime scene staff. Usually, those latter cases were accidental, the result of transfer from contact with a victim. Sometimes, labs mixed things up and contaminated samples. And, very rarely, the presence of a professional's DNA was there for another reason. One Lockhart didn't like to think about.

'We have got a potential lead on Charles Stott's watch, though,' Berry added. She pulled up an electronic note on her screen. 'From the social media appeal.'

'Oh yeah?' He leant in to read it.

'Yup.' She pointed to the key details. 'Second-hand jewellery shop owner called Wayne McGarrahan emailed to say someone had tried to sell him a Breitling watch with the inscription we knew was on the back: "To our Charlie, happy fortieth". Says he refused to buy it because they didn't offer ID.'

'Did he describe the seller?'

'Just says a "young" guy.'

Lockhart was already thinking. 'Cheers for letting me know about this, Luce. Where's the shop?'

'Bethnal Green.'

He groaned inwardly at the thought of the journey. The East London district was ten miles away, right on the other side of the city. But if his hunch was right, he needed to go there in person. 'OK. Leave that one with me, I'll follow it up. Can you mark it as actioned?'

'Will do. Sure you don't want to send Mo or another one of the DCs?'

'No, it's fine.' He lowered his voice. 'By the way, do you think Mo's been a bit... off, lately?'

Berry considered this, then shrugged. 'I guess he's had a couple of unlucky things happen on this case. Maybe he's taken that personally.'

'Or maybe it's a personal thing that's affecting his work.'

'Don't know. He's not mentioned anything to me.'

'Thanks, Luce.'

Lockhart glanced around the MIT office. There was no sign of Porter.

'Do you know where the boss is?' he asked.

'Haven't seen him yet today,' replied Berry.

'Probably talking to a lawyer about how he can hack our emails and phones to work out who tipped off the press.'

Berry laughed. 'Yeah, he seemed pretty worked up about that. Who do you reckon it was?'

'Not a clue,' answered Lockhart, though he had his suspicions.

'I mean, could it maybe have been the killer?'

Lockhart considered this. 'It's possible. But the article talked about the sexual assaults, and if we don't think that's the reason why these victims are being chosen, then it's a bit of a coincidence if the killer also knew those allegations against Stott and Johnson.'

'And you don't like coincidences.'

'Right. So, more likely the leak came from an investigator.'

'Makes sense.'

'All right, I'm heading out. I'll catch up with Porter later on.'

The DCI's absence was a good thing, Lockhart reflected. Because there was no way Porter would agree to what he was about to do.

CHAPTER FORTY-THREE

'I don't want nothing to do with that sort of activity.' Wayne McGarrahan crossed his thick arms and shook his head theatrically. 'This is a reputable establishment.'

The sign that read *Cash for Gold* immediately above his head didn't exactly reinforce the assertion, but Lockhart wasn't here to debate that with him. He'd come across enough wheeler-dealers like McGarrahan in London to know that the ethics of buying and selling second-hand goods of uncertain origin were flexible, dictated more by the likelihood of being caught than by some absolute moral standard. And a personal inscription raised the chance of an item being traced a hundredfold.

'Glad to hear it,' replied Lockhart, his eyes running over rows of watches, rings and necklaces in glass cabinets behind the proprietor.

'I mean, I took one look at that Breitling and I knew it was vintage, fifteen years at least. If it was legit, I could sell it for five grand, minimum. Six, maybe. Would've given him two or three for it.' His eyes widened. He was clearly enjoying telling the story. 'But I says to meself, hang on, Wayne. That's gotta have a history, a piece like that. But could the lad tell me what it was?' McGarrahan raised his eyebrows expectantly.

Lockhart waited.

'Course he couldn't. See, I've got a nose for these things. Comes with the job.' He gestured expansively to the collection of valuable items around him. Lockhart spotted another sign offering a pawn service with what appeared to be exorbitant fees.

'What *did* he tell you, sir?'

'Some rubbish about a relative giving it to him, but I could tell it was a load of bollocks. So, I says to him, sorry mate, no can do without ID. He claimed he didn't have none. And off he toddled.' McGarrahan jerked a thumb towards the shop door.

'Can you describe this man?'

The pawnbroker narrowed his eyes. 'Sort of posh. Shorter than me. Well-built though, like a rugby player.'

'Did he give you his name?'

'Nope.'

Lockhart produced the six-pack of mugshots he'd put together earlier. He'd copied the photos from the internet, because using actual police mugshots would've made the one image he really wanted to test stand out.

'Take your time,' said Lockhart, spreading them out on the counter.

McGarrahan glanced at the portraits and snorted a laugh. 'Him,' he said, instantly jabbing his finger on the face of Xander O'Neill.

'You're sure about that?'

'No doubt. The two moles on his cheek, there. And I've got a good memory for faces, me. Part of the job, cos I've gotta be careful about—'

'We might need you to come in to make a statement to confirm that.' Lockhart handed over one of his cards.

A broad smile grew on McGarrahan's face, revealing a set of crooked teeth. 'Course, Inspector. Anything to help.'

Lockhart imagined that McGarrahan was calculating what help he'd be due in return. He'd cross that bridge when he came to it. For now, he had to work out how to make the arrest of a man his boss had categorically ordered him to leave alone.

He was almost at Bethnal Green tube station and about to head underground again when his phone rang. It was Berry.

'Luce, what's up?'

'The DNA results are back,' she said quickly.

'Yeah?'

'No trace.'

'Fuck.'

'But there is one thing,' she added. 'I thought you'd want to know.'

'Go on.'

'The sample had XX chromosomes.'

'You're saying?…'

'Yup. It belongs to a woman.'

CHAPTER FORTY-FOUR

Lexi sprinkled some chilli flakes over her avocado toast. It was a quick dinner, designed to give her more time to work tonight, but it didn't hurt to make an effort. That was a part of her new plan: less booze, better food, greater purpose. She'd wondered if she should cook something a little more advanced, since Dan was coming over, but in the end, she hadn't had time to go to the grocery store after finishing up late at the clinic. So, she'd just doubled up the avocado toast, reminding herself that dinner wasn't the reason for his visit; it was work. Lexi wasn't sure exactly *what* work, since he'd been a little cagey on the phone and wouldn't say what he wanted to discuss.

She was filling a glass of water from the tap when she heard footsteps behind her and turned. Rhys was in the doorway, wearing an anorak and baseball cap, a rucksack slung over his shoulder. He didn't acknowledge her, instead dropping the pizza box he was clutching on the floor next to the fridge.

'Uh, hey, Rhys,' she said, already aware of her harsh tone.

'What?'

She pointed at the box. 'That goes in the recycling. Remember our conversation last week?'

'Oh… yeah. Where is it again?'

'Jeez,' she muttered, crossing the room and opening a cupboard. 'In here.'

'OK.' He picked up the box, lumbered over and tossed it inside.

'Goddam it!' she barked, rearranging the box. 'Can't you just put it in there properly? Do I have to tidy up all your shit?'

Rhys cowered slightly. Lexi didn't know where her outburst had come from; she guessed the anger was still there, right below the surface.

'Sorry,' she said.

He stood silently in front of her, still looking terrified. Then the doorbell went.

'I'll, um…' He waved a thumb towards the front door and sloped out.

Lexi wiped a hand over her face. She knew she needed to be way more zen about this, but the fact was that Rhys just wound her up. Every time she saw him, she thought of the man he'd replaced in their home: Liam. And that made her feel sick to her stomach, guilty and heartbroken all at once.

The door slammed and, next she knew, Dan was in the kitchen right where Rhys had been standing a few seconds earlier.

'Friendly chap,' he said, jerking his head towards the front door.

'He's a douchebag.'

Dan frowned slightly. 'You all right, Lexi?'

'Uh, yeah, I'm good.' She nodded, trying to get her shit back together. 'Thanks.'

'Cheers for making time for me.'

'No problem.' She paused a beat. 'Oh, you want some food? I literally just made this…'

'Great.' His eyes widened. 'I mean, if you've got enough.'

'Sure. I made extra. Just in case. Grab a seat.'

She brought the plates over to the kitchen table. Dan took his jacket off, hung it on the back of his chair and sat down opposite her. Only then did she notice that his eyes were raw, the whites bloodshot, deep purplish bags underneath. Immediately, she found herself forgetting her own stuff and going into empathic mode. That was easy with Dan; he brought that response out of her. She knew he'd almost never opened up about his mental health, and she wanted to respect that trust he'd placed in her to talk about his deepest fears. To show her his vulnerabilities.

'Are you OK?' she asked gently.

'Yeah.' He sighed and looked up from the food. 'Actually, no. Not really.'

'What's up?'

Dan was gripping his knife and fork so tightly that his knuckles were white. 'Jess's family want to have her declared officially dead. Like, legally.'

'Oh my god.'

'Yeah.'

'I'm so sorry,' she said, instinctively reaching out a hand and laying it on his forearm. She wouldn't have done that in a therapy session, but he wasn't her patient anymore. He didn't flinch, but she withdrew her hand anyway after a moment. 'You wanna talk about it?'

He looked as if he was about to say yes, but then it was like he caught himself and something closed up again. 'Not now.'

'OK.'

'Cheers, though. I'd prefer to talk about the case. Thorncross, I mean.' He sawed off a large piece of the avocado toast and somehow fitted it in his mouth. He murmured with satisfaction and, despite everything they were discussing, Lexi felt pleased. Then she felt ridiculous for feeling that. Jeez, a psychologist's awareness was a pain in the ass, sometimes.

'Sure,' she replied.

'I didn't want to go into detail over the phone,' he said through a mouthful of food. 'Porter's paranoid about us all leaking to the press, so I wouldn't put it past him to tap our calls.'

'Seriously?'

'Probably not, but you never know. I wouldn't want to get you in trouble.'

'Appreciate it.'

Dan swallowed. 'This is good, by the way.'

'Thanks. Not exactly Michelin-star, but hey.'

'I'm not complaining. We OK speaking here?' He waved his fork around the kitchen.

'Yeah, Sarah's out at a spin class. And Rhys, well. I didn't even know he *went* out, but apparently, he does. And I confirm we are not being bugged.'

Dan smiled briefly, but she could see the effort behind it.

'OK, so, I've been thinking,' she went on, 'about those symbols that the killer's been leaving on the body. The third one proves they're occult. Or, more accurately, pagan. Basically, you can think of them as like pre-Christian religious signs. They represent the elements, and so far, we've had water, fire, and air.'

'There are four elements, right?' He shovelled in some more toast. 'Those three, plus earth.'

'Uh, actually there's five.'

Dan stopped chewing. 'Five?'

'Yeah. The fifth is spirit. They're represented on a pentagram.' She reached for her laptop, opened it and clicked a few times to bring up a file. 'Look.'

He stared at it for a few seconds before turning to her. 'So, we can expect two more murder attempts?'

'I guess so.'

'That's useful. Any idea what it means?'

She drew in a long breath. 'It's possible that the symbols have some idiosyncratic meaning…'

'Idio-what?'

'Idiosyncratic. Like, personal.'

'Right.' Dan looked a little embarrassed. 'Carry on.'

'But we may never know what that is unless we find the killer and they tell us, or they've documented it somewhere.'

Dan nodded slowly. She could see his frustration.

'Anyway,' he said, 'there's an update from my side.'

'Yeah?'

'We found skin cells under Ernesto Gomez's fingernails. Probably from trying to defend himself, though we can't be certain. Result came back earlier. They were from a woman.'

'No shit?'

'Yup.'

She sat back in her chair.

'And there was another development today, too. You remember Xander O'Neill?'

'The actor you don't like, who may or may not have been having an affair with Jemima Stott-Peters?'

'That's the one.'

'Yeah, I remember him.'

'We have a witness who says he tried to sell Charles Stott's watch in a second-hand jewellery shop.'

'Really?'

'Yeah.'

Lexi considered this. 'Doesn't mean he killed Stott, though, does it? I mean, if he was seeing Jemima, he might've had access to the watch at their house. Maybe he stole it before Stott was murdered.'

'Maybe,' he conceded. 'Or perhaps she and O'Neill were in on it together.'

'You think the female DNA on Ernesto Gomez's body was hers?'

'Could be.'

'Do the two of them have any connection to the other two victims?'

'No.' He drew the word out into two syllables. 'Not that we know of. Yet.'

'So…'

'I'm telling you, Lexi, I don't like him.'

She snorted. 'Is that evidence?'

'Remind me again: how many murder investigations have you run?'

Lexi bristled. 'I don't need to be a cop to see that, for some reason, you think this O'Neill guy is a killer, and you're fitting the data into that conclusion. Not drawing your conclusions from data.'

Dan jabbed his finger on the tabletop. 'At the very least, he's got to explain why he was trying to sell the watch of a murdered man, and how it came into his possession. I'm heading round to his place later for a chat. We'll see what he says then.'

'You're not gonna arrest him and do it under caution?'

'Yes, thank you, that had occurred to me.'

'OK, because—'

'Porter won't have it. He's already told me twice to stay away from Stott-Peters and O'Neill. I need to find another way. He trips himself up, he's still got the watch, whatever.'

Lexi ate some avocado toast while she thought. 'So, say you do that. O'Neill comes up with a credible reason why he had the watch, and there's no other evidence against him. What then?'

'Well,' Dan blew out his cheeks briefly, 'in that case, we'd most likely have to move on.'

'And find another suspect.'

'Yeah.'

'One with a link to all three victims,' she added.

'Ideally.'

'Except, you probably need to do that within, like, two days, because based on this killer's pattern of behaviour, that's when we can expect their next attack.' Lexi folded her arms and a few seconds' silence hung between them.

'Have you got a drink?' he asked, eventually.

'Tea? It's a little late for coffee, but—'

'I was thinking of something alcoholic, actually.'

She hesitated. It would be easy to open a bottle of wine. Even easier to do it with Dan, in her house, and nobody else here. Potentially a dangerous combination. 'Uh, I'm not sure that's such a great idea.'

'You're probably right. Tea's good. Thanks.'

Lexi got up and went across to the counter. She filled the kettle and flicked it on.

'Let's assume you're correct and it's not him and Stott-Peters behind this,' Dan said. 'How else could we profile the killer?'

'OK.' She reached for a couple of mugs. 'Well, you have three unconnected victims, right?'

'Far as we know.'

'But two of them worked in film. And the third was a compensation lawyer. So, how about this: someone who worked in film, with one hell of a grudge against some people in the industry.' Lexi threw a tea bag in each mug. 'Maybe they want compensation for something that happened to them, but haven't gotten it, and this is their revenge. And they have some kind of spiritual belief that makes them draw the symbols.'

'Could still be Xander O'Neill…'

'Enough with that theory, Dan!'

When he was her patient in the clinic, she'd never have expressed this kind of irritation with him. But things were different, now.

'What do we know about the attacks?' she asked, exasperated. 'They were brutal, savage. We also think they were premeditated due to their isolated locations and timings. It's got psychopath written all over it in great big letters.'

'Thanks for pointing that out,' he said drily.

'The important thing is that this kind of behaviour is a psychopath's default state. Something was keeping a lid on it until this, this film incident, or whatever, and now it's been activated. The question is, what was this person doing before that stopped them killing? That'll be the most useful piece of a profile. I think they had a job that was satisfying those urges for violence.'

Dan didn't reply. The kettle clicked off and she poured the boiling water.

'OK, put it another way,' she continued, getting some milk from the fridge. 'In what professions would psychopathic characteristics be helpful? Lack of fear, no empathy. We can narrow it down with a connection to film, assuming that's no coincidence. What do you think?'

'I don't know,' he shrugged. 'Some kind of fighting, martial arts thing.'

'Now you're catching on.' She flashed him a grin as she poured the milk. 'Security, bodyguard, stunt person, military advisor…'

'Military?'

'Sure. The so-called warrior gene.'

'What?'

'It's a thing in human biology about predisposition to violence, which can be triggered off by stuff like abuse or hardship in life. And it links to a theory from anthropology about why violent and antisocial people evolved. You need someone to defend your group from threats, right? A person with a low threshold for violence can do that way more easily, especially when they feel they've been wronged and want revenge. They could kill someone and not even blink.'

'Really?'

'Yeah. And, so long as you reward that person, keep them happy, and their identity aligns with yours, you're safe. It's when they turn that violence against their own people, or start using it alone, for themselves, that you're in trouble.'

She put the tea down in front of him.

Dan stood. 'I've got to go,' he announced.

'You OK?'

He grabbed his jacket off the back of the chair and marched out.

'Dan?' she called after him.

She heard the door slam and his footsteps fading.

CHAPTER FORTY-FIVE

Lockhart had needed to get out. It was the talk of warrior genes and killing without blinking that'd done it. He was picturing the recent victims and then, suddenly, he'd been right back in that house in Afghanistan. His heart was pounding, his palms sweaty, mouth dry, and all he knew was that he couldn't be there, in Green's kitchen, talking about murder. Now he'd put some distance between himself and her house, and his panic had subsided, he could think a bit more clearly.

Green's theories had given him a lot to mull over. Her ideas made sense, and her arguments were persuasive. But there still wasn't much hard evidence behind them. She'd linked the pieces of the puzzle with some fancy words that he didn't completely understand, like *anthropology* and *idiosyn*-something or other. Remembering what she'd said, he briefly wondered whether defending others was programmed into *his* DNA. Did he have this 'warrior gene' or whatever it was? It would certainly explain some things.

There hadn't been much time, however, to contemplate that further before he'd arrived at Xander O'Neill's house. The two-storey building was a squashed mid-terrace on one of the streets that ran off Balham High Road, about a mile north of Green's home. Scanning the exterior, Lockhart could see it was clearly in need of maintenance. It barely looked big enough to fit the five people O'Neill had told him lived here. A small roof window suggested that there'd been a loft conversion, which was about the only way Lockhart could imagine them all squeezing in. He guessed it was a rent-saving set-up; O'Neill had said he was struggling to find work.

Lockhart could hear voices inside as he pressed the buzzer; then laughing, the baseline of some music. Nothing happened. He pushed it again and, eventually, the door was opened by a fit-looking young woman with large, inquisitive eyes and masses of dark curly hair. A huge glass of red wine dwarfed one of her hands. The other rested on the lintel, forming a barrier across the threshold.

'Sorry to disturb you,' he said pleasantly, holding up his warrant card. 'I'm with the Met. Is Xander O'Neill in?'

'Oh my God!' she exclaimed, her face lighting up with intrigue. 'What's he done? Naughty boy!'

'Is he at home, please, Ms?…'

'Rosamund.' She cast a glance over her shoulder down the hallway to where a dinner party was obviously gathering pace. Or maybe this was just a normal Thursday night at Xander O'Neill's home.

'No, he's out. I think. Xandy!' she yelled up the stairs.

Lockhart peered past her. He was tempted to see if he could talk his way in, perhaps even check out O'Neill's room for the stolen watch or anything else he might be hiding, but he had no authority for that. He'd need to wait. Better to keep his powder dry, for now.

'Yeah, sorry, he's not here,' she said, shrugging and eyeing Lockhart.

'OK, thanks anyway. I'll call back another time. It was just a few follow-up questions from a chat we had last week. Nothing urgent,' he added.

As Rosamund closed the door, he could've sworn her expression was one of relief. She hadn't even asked his name.

*

By the time Lockhart had driven back to Hammersmith and climbed the stairs to his flat, he was exhausted. It'd been a long, stressful day, although he felt as though he had little to show for his efforts. He couldn't remember the last time he'd had a good night's sleep and, despite being knackered, there was no reason for him to think that would change tonight.

Green would probably have had some advice to help him relax, but he didn't want to burden her with all his shit. He'd told her about Jess earlier, but the conversation had ended there. And he hadn't even mentioned the flashbacks to Afghanistan, the image that tormented him of that Taliban sniper. How similar the guy's corpse had looked to the Thorncross killer's victims. The logical conclusion that, in some ways, he probably understood the murderer they were trying to catch better than anyone. And, yet, he felt as though he knew almost nothing about them.

Without quite knowing how he'd got there, Lockhart found himself in front of his fridge, reaching for a cold can of Stella. He cracked it open and swallowed a mouthful. Immediately, something in him eased, just a bit. He took another swig, exhaling with satisfaction. It'd help him sleep, he told himself.

Pulling out his phone, he tapped into the camera app and began checking the footage from the Op Braddock bus stops. He didn't find anything of interest. Before he knew it, he'd finished the can. Automatically, as if guided by some alien force, he extracted another beer from the fridge and wandered into the living room.

Then he saw the crumpled paper on the table. Two halves of the letter he'd torn and screwed up because it claimed Jess was dead. Lockhart drank some more, a deep draught. He chucked his phone on the table and, after smoothing out the letter again, he carried it over to Jess's wall.

He pinned the two pieces side by side and stood back, gulping down Stella, his gaze shifting between map, documents, notes and photographs.

She wasn't dead.

He *knew* that.

Now he just needed to prove it.

He crushed the empty can in his hand and went back to the kitchen to get another.

CHAPTER FORTY-SIX

I was bored, again, so I'd decided to go out. Since I was heading to a club, I showered and dressed up. You need to look good if you want to get laid, right? But, again, I found myself waiting. This time, my impatience was directed at a bus I wanted to hurry up and come. I was being lazy, I knew that. But it was just a bit too far to walk to the nearest tube station from John's place. The new shoes I'd bought with the two hundred pounds he 'lent' me were still that bit too stiff. And my body was still aching that bit too much. Another couple of days and I'll be back to normal. Ready for some more action. In the meantime, something to take away the pain would be nice. Ketamine, maybe? Should be easy enough to get hold of some in the club.

John has also kindly supplied me with a top-up for my pay-as-you-go phone, courtesy of his borrowed bank card. I'll drop the card back into his wallet tomorrow morning, before he even realises it's gone. When he gets the statement, he'll either be too timid to ask, or it'll be too late for him to get the money back, anyway. Thanks to the top-up, I was passing the time by streaming a YouTube video of the Ultimate Fighting Championship's 'most brutal' knockouts. That was when I heard the voice.

'Make a sound and you're dead.'

I looked up. A short, chunky man was standing beside me, his face covered in a black ski mask that left only his eyes visible. The bottom half of the mask shifted with the movement of his jaws as he chewed. Funny what details you notice. So, this was the guy, the bus stop rapist. I glanced back at my phone. Heavyweight MMA fighter Alistair Overeem was pounding the head of an opponent he'd taken to the ground. The crowd went crazy and the referee stepped in, signalling the end of the fight.

'I'm serious,' said the guy. 'You scream or even think about calling 999 and I'll hurt you.'

I put the phone away, wishing I had my mallet. I'd just have to get by without it. There was no question of this little prick raping me, but I had to do something. I really couldn't be bothered, though. I knew it'd hurt and probably mess up my clothes. But there was no sign of the bus, so he wasn't going anywhere. And, in these shoes, I couldn't run.

'Get up and walk behind the bus stop,' he commanded. 'Do it now.'

I felt like laughing. Then I went for him.

In one movement I stood and threw a haymaker with my right hand. It connected with the side of his head, but not cleanly, and he stumbled, trying to reach for something. I aimed a kick at his chest and sent him flailing backwards into the road. He hit the tarmac with a dull sound. I grabbed his feet and dragged him up onto the pavement. I didn't give a fuck, now, that this was in full view of anyone who cared to drive past. He was going to die.

I kicked and stamped on him a few times with my heels, then got on top of him, pinning him to the ground between my legs. I began striking down at his head, then decided I wanted to see the face of the man whose life I was about to end. I grabbed the mask and he tried to hold my wrists to keep it on. He was stronger than he looked. For some reason, he took his hands away and I ripped off the mask. Our eyes met for a second.

Then it was as if someone had set fire to my ribs.

I gasped, fell sideways off him. He got to his feet. In his hand was a hunting knife, the tip of its blade dark red under the dim streetlight. I rolled away, clutching at my wound with one hand.

It stung like a bastard. I looked up at him. He was shaking, terrified. I pushed myself up on one hand, tried to get to my feet. He threw the knife away and ran. I managed a few steps before I fell, again. The pain was too much, and I roared as he ran into the park behind the bus stop, disappearing into the darkness.

DAY ELEVEN

CHAPTER FORTY-SEVEN

It was Stagg who had been the first to see the camera footage from the bus stop in Colliers Wood, just south of Wimbledon. He'd sounded as though he was choking on his breakfast during the call he'd immediately made to Smith. Coat and car keys in hand before Stagg had finished speaking, she was already on her way when she'd rung Lockhart who, fortunately, had excused her from working on Op Thorncross this morning to follow-up. After a hasty drive south west, she'd arrived at the scene of the stabbing and attempted rape. Stagg, who lived closer, was already there. The place was eerily quiet.

Smith felt sick to her stomach. It was the same uncomfortable feeling she'd had more often than she cared to remember in recent months, any time she thought of that suspect falling from the balcony. The sounds of his scream and contact with the ground three storeys below. The gnawing, niggling sense of something you could've done differently, and the knowledge that it was too late, now.

'We should've seen it,' she said.

'I'm as angry as you are, Max.' Stagg thrust his hands into his pockets. 'But the fact is, it's happened. And there's nothing we can do to change that.'

She shook her head. 'I should've been keeping an eye on it.'

'At eleven thirty at night?'

'Yeah.' Smith knew exactly what she was doing last night at the moment that bastard rapist accosted a woman at this bus stop. She'd been in bed with her fella, having a great time, her phone still in her bag in the hallway. The guilt was eating her up, the regret intolerable. 'We could've got straight out after him.'

'Come on. You've seen the clip. The whole thing was over in, what, less than a minute. By the time you'd have started your car engine or called a patrol unit, they'd both have long gone. Even if you were monitoring the app, you'd have needed to be looking at the right feed to see it happening. That's a one-in-eight chance.'

She clenched her jaw, staring at the bus stop. He was right.

'I feel shit about it, too,' Stagg went on. 'My phone battery died while I was watching telly, and I didn't even realise till gone midnight. Dan didn't see it, either. We all failed. But what we need to ask is: what can we do about it now?'

Smith was grateful for his pragmatism.

'OK,' she replied at length. 'Anyone reported the assault?'

'Nope.' Stagg pushed out his lower lip. 'I don't get it. I mean, it looked like a stab wound, right? But no one in the local hospitals matches the injury description and timing, and no one's called us or contacted The Havens about it yet, either. They're all primed to bell me, though, if anybody even vaguely resembling the victim shows up. Shame we didn't get a clear image of her face.'

'Whoever it was that fought him off, she's hard. That little pervert picked on the wrong woman this time,' Smith said, with a mixture of anger and admiration. She couldn't believe what she'd seen in the footage: a rape victim who'd actually beaten up her attacker, punching him in the face until he pulled out a knife and stuck it in her side. 'I just hope to God she's all right, if she's not had any medical treatment.'

'Why do you think she didn't call an ambulance?' he asked.

'Dunno.' Smith thought about it briefly. She recalled a case years back of a stabbing victim who hadn't sought medical treatment because he was an illegal migrant and was scared of being deported. 'Could be lots of reasons. Immigration status. Wound wasn't as bad as we think. Or she's a criminal who doesn't want the police getting involved,' she added with a snort.

'Well, when we find her, we can get her into A & E, make sure she gets whatever she needs.'

'*If* we find her.'

'We will,' Stagg said. 'We have to. And, I hate to say this, but it's not just about checking on her health. She saw his face.'

'I know.'

'She could give us a photofit. We put that out in the press, online, etcetera, and guaranteed someone'll know who he is. This isn't like a gang incident with a code of silence, it's a sex offender. The public are gonna be desperate to help.'

Smith concurred. It was a cast-iron lead, if they could find the woman. 'Can you look at CCTV from the area, see if we can spot her walking away? She must've gone somewhere. And we've got a clear timeframe.'

'I'll try. Maybe I could tell Wilkins to get off his arse and requisition local footage.' Stagg smirked. 'Give him something useful to do.'

'Good plan.' She hesitated. 'Only problem is explaining to the brass how we got here. No crime's been reported.'

A sly grin spread across Stagg's face. 'Leave that to me. Quick phone call to our tip line from an eyewitness too scared to come forward, and that's all the justification we need to be here.'

Smith knew the technique was dodgy, but sometimes that was necessary. If you were at A and you knew B was your destination, you just had to find a way to get there. There was a bag of tricks coppers used to achieve that. Smith drew the line at manufacturing or tampering with evidence, but for something like a fake tip-off, she was happy that the ends justified the means. She'd made Op Braddock a personal crusade against this vile sex offender, and she wondered how far she'd go to catch him. The way things stood, pretty damn far.

'I'll pretend I didn't hear that,' she said. 'Let's have a look around.'

They began a detailed search of the area around the bus stop. The ground in the park behind it was dry and compacted after a couple of days with no rain, and the chance of finding footprints was minimal. Ten yards away, she could see Stagg combing a patch of long grass. She scanned the park, wondering which direction the rapist had fled and whether that might offer a clue as to where he lived. She remembered the Wimbledon Prowler, a serial burglar who broke into large, empty homes in the affluent suburb. He'd travelled to London from Manchester for the crimes. Was she barking up the wrong tree believing this was a local man? She made a mental note to call Green later. Perhaps the psychologist's profile would give them—

'Max!'

She whipped round to see Stagg gesturing to the ground. 'What've you got?'

'Come see.'

Smith half-jogged over to where he stood and looked down. At his feet was a hunting knife, its distinctive six-inch steel blade bloodied at the curved tip. She took in the serrated spine and winced inwardly at the thought of it penetrating her own skin, imagining the pain and hoping once more that the victim was all right. The weapon was grim proof of the attack they'd witnessed on camera. But it was exactly what they'd hoped to find.

CHAPTER FORTY-EIGHT

As he drove to Croydon Magistrate's Court, Lockhart was pretty sure that his pounding headache and sloth-like reactions indicated he was still over the limit. When he'd woken up and wandered bleary-eyed into the kitchen, he'd found a dozen cans of Stella in the sink. He cursed himself once more for being such a bell-end. Again.

Not only had his drinking binge made everything slow and painful this morning, but it hadn't even succeeded in giving him a decent sleep. To make matters worse, he'd been lying on his sofa, wasted, when the bus stop attack had occurred last night. Smith's call was the first he'd known about it. And, as if that wasn't enough, he knew that the real punishment was still to come, when DCI Porter discovered what he was up to now.

Lockhart reached for the cardboard cup in the holder by the gearstick and swallowed down a mouthful of the black coffee he'd bought in the office half an hour ago. It was stone cold. He fought back the nausea of it hitting his empty stomach, accepting the small act of penance. There would be more of that before the end of the day.

Croydon, in central-south London, was not the closest court to Putney, but Lockhart hoped that by going further away from home turf, he'd buy himself some extra time before Porter could find out what was happening. He knew his boss had friends at their local magistrate's court in Clapham's Lavender Hill and reasoned that, if he'd gone there, his plan could be kyboshed before it'd had a chance to work.

He'd arrived early at Jubilee House, before most of the MIT was in, and typed up an arrest warrant for Xander O'Neill. Lockhart's intention was to bring the young actor in on suspicion of theft and handling stolen goods, the rationale for the arrest being that they needed to execute a search of his home to find the watch in question, without giving him time to dispose of it.

If they were lucky, the search might turn up something else connecting O'Neill to the murders, like the size eight Nike Flex shoes or other clothing. Then the MIT could lean on him to name the woman involved, if there was one. If they didn't find anything else, then they could use the lesser charge of theft to get O'Neill's DNA and fingerprints for comparison. And, if that failed to pin anything more serious on him, then at least they could get the cocky little shit for theft, and he'd be on the national DNA database for the future.

Yet, as Lockhart parked and entered the court building, he recalled Green's words last night: *you think this O'Neill guy is a killer, and you're fitting the data into that conclusion.* Was she right? Was he simply clutching at straws in the absence of a better lead on the killer? His brain was too tired to consider the arguments for and against. Right now, he just needed to apply the military tactic of sticking with the decision he'd made and seeing it through. Even if there was a possibility that he was wrong.

Lockhart paced up and down the public waiting area, clutching the warrant and checking his watch more often than was necessary to know that all the judges were still busy. A constant stream of witnesses, defendants and lawyers – sometimes distinguished only by their briefcases – milled around him, whispering urgent conversations and being ushered in and out of the courtrooms. He was considering asking the clerk for another update when his phone rang. It was Smith.

'Max.'

'All right, guv.'

'What's happening?'

'I'm back at Jubilee House.'

'OK. How'd it go at the scene?'

She described Stagg's discovery of the hunting knife. 'Eddie's getting it sent to the lab on the hurry-up. We're expecting the blood on it to be our victim's. That means when we catch the bastard, we could get him on attempted murder as well as attempted rape. Even if it's downgraded to GBH, it'll add years to his sentence.' She sounded aggressively zealous.

'Good.'

'And, if we get a break, they'll find the guy's DNA on the weapon, too. Gives us a point of reference for anything else connected with Braddock. Eddie's trying to run down purchases of that specific type of knife, too.'

'Now we just need to find the victim to give us his face and tie it all together.'

'Exactly. Eddie told me he's going to set DC Wilkins to work on it today, getting hold of any local CCTV.' She paused. 'Normally they'd have someone a bit more experienced, but they're strapped.'

'Guess beggars can't be choosers,' said Lockhart. 'Anything else?'

'Only that Eddie's done a little media appeal for the victim to come forward. He reckons she's an illegal migrant who's worried about her status.'

'Wouldn't be the first time.'

'So,' she went on, 'he's given an assurance of help with anything like that and tried appealing to her sense of protecting other women who could be attacked.'

Lockhart heard his name being called from across the hallway. 'Gotta go, Max. See you back in the office.'

He rang off and crossed towards the clerk, a small, stern-looking man with a clipboard whose gaze roamed around the waiting area. 'Detective Inspector Daniel Lockhart?'

'That's me,' he said, producing his warrant card.

'Judge Gibson-Parry will see you in her chambers now. Follow me.'

Lockhart tried not to show his relief. Elizabeth Gibson-Parry was known to be one of the judges who leant in favour of investigators. Last year, she had granted him a search warrant based on limited intelligence, but it'd proven accurate and led to the discovery of a murder weapon. Lockhart just hoped she was in a good mood this morning. Or a better mood than him, at least.

It was late afternoon by the time that Lockhart, DC Andy Parsons and PC Leo Richards arrived at Xander O'Neill's house in Balham. Lockhart knew he couldn't execute the arrest warrant and conduct a search alone, and reasoned that he could trust those two not to blab to anyone about the plan for a couple of hours, at least. Parsons and Richards had made a 'routine' call on Jemima Stott-Peters, under the guise of a welfare check, which had established that O'Neill wasn't at her place. A visit to the climbing wall confirmed he wasn't there, either. So, unless he was out auditioning, he was likely to be at home. The ideal time to hit a residence for an arrest was early – what the military called 'stupid o'clock' – but if they waited till tomorrow morning, Porter would probably find out and put a stop to it.

Lockhart pressed the buzzer and waited. Pressed again, then once more. The sound of footsteps running on stairs grew louder and the door was opened by the man they were seeking. Xander O'Neill wore a tight vest and jogging pants, the muscles of his upper body bulging. His face was red, and Lockhart noticed a graze on one cheek. He was slightly short of breath and looked as though he'd been working out. The actor's eyes flicked from Lockhart to the others and back.

'What do you want?' he demanded.

'Alexander O'Neill,' Lockhart stated, 'we have a warrant for your arrest on suspicion of theft and retention of stolen goods. The warrant also allows us to search the property for said stolen goods.'

'Is this a joke?'

'No, Mr O'Neill. It's not.'

The young man nodded slowly a few times. Then he turned and bolted up the stairs. Lockhart was after him instantly, lunging forward and grabbing his ankle. O'Neill kicked back but Lockhart held firm and, in seconds, Richards and Parsons were up the stairs and pinning O'Neill down. Richards cuffed him and began reciting the police caution. Lockhart waited for him to finish before he spoke.

'Something to hide?' he asked.

An hour later, they were booking O'Neill in at Lavender Hill police station. As Lockhart informed the custody sergeant of the charges, Parsons brought the brown paper evidence bags through to be logged.

At the back of O'Neill's sock drawer, they'd found a silver Breitling watch, inscribed with the words: "To our Charlie, happy fortieth". There was also a quantity of what appeared to be cocaine in his bedside cabinet, though it wasn't enough to charge him on possession with intent to supply. A personal stash wouldn't get him much more than a rap on the knuckles, but it was extra ammunition. The real test would be the clothing they'd bagged up. There were no Nike Flex trainers, but they'd found a hoody and some other tracksuit bottoms with what appeared to be mud on them. Lockhart was satisfied they had enough to make O'Neill lose his swagger over the next twenty-four hours. His arrogance had already shifted into a look of murderous rage every time he met Lockhart's eyes.

After confirming his personal details, the custody sergeant behind the desk asked O'Neill if there was anyone he wished to be informed of his detention.

'Oh, yes,' he replied, turning to Lockhart, 'there is.'

CHAPTER FORTY-NINE

I could kill someone right now. Anyone will do. It doesn't even need to be that little fucker who stuck his knife in me last night, although he'd be top of my list today. John's lucky he's out at work, to be honest. I've put the bloodied bedsheets in his washing machine, but if he asks, I'll just tell him it was my time of the month.

I don't want to explain to him or anyone else what happened. It's not that I'm embarrassed about the guy getting the better of me in a fight. He had a concealed knife. I should've anticipated that and taken it off him. Then buried it deep in his gut and let him bleed to death. I don't want to tell anyone because I know the police are looking for me. And knife wounds in hospitals attract a lot of attention. Especially when they've put out an appeal for me to come forward and help identify my attacker. I've no idea how they know about it. I didn't think there were any witnesses, but I might've been wrong. To be fair, I had other things on my mind at the time.

I could play the victim for the cops, of course. Describe the face of the man who attacked me. But they'd want my details, they'd ask after my background. Probably take my DNA to help build their case against the guy, too. And I don't want to have to deal with the consequences of that. It'd be the end of everything. So, I've decided to keep my head down. Which means sorting out the wound myself.

How did it come to this? I was one film away from the big time. Now I'm sitting naked in John's bathtub, trying to clean the bleeding two-inch wound I've just opened again by removing the tape I'd closed it with last night. I've bought a needle and some fishing line to pull my skin back together. I've taken John's vodka to sterilise my little home-made surgery kit. And to drink.

I thought I was good at dealing with pain, but now I'm thinking twice about piercing my own skin. I'm not scared, just preparing myself. I need to man up and do it. The sooner I stitch myself up, the sooner I can get back to my real objective. The arsehole from the bus stop can wait; he'll get what he deserves. I'm talking about the other two who need to pay for my accident. There's one more professional, who shouldn't be too hard to find. And then there's Dan Lockhart. The thought almost cheers me.

Time to get to work.

I take a big slug of vodka and pick up the needle.

Deep breath.

DAY TWELVE

CHAPTER FIFTY

It wasn't yet midday, but Smith had already been pounding the streets for several hours. This wasn't necessarily how she would've wanted to spend her Saturday morning, but her fella understood that her work didn't neatly fit into sociable hours. He'd gone off to the football with his mates while Smith set out to locate their victim from the latest bus stop attack. In a perfect world, DC Wilkins would've already obtained any useful CCTV footage yesterday and all she'd need to do was follow it up. But Wilkins hadn't even come in to work yesterday – calling in sick, according to Stagg – which meant Smith had to do almost everything herself. She didn't mind, though.

This was Smith's style of investigating; old-fashioned graft, legwork. Like detectives did back in the day, before everything became about sitting in front of a screen, trawling mobile phone records and running computer searches. There was something satisfying about getting out there, knocking on doors, talking to real people. It didn't even bother her that she'd drawn a blank so far. She was systematically working through each street that led away from the area of the bus stop and knew that, sooner or later, she'd find what she was looking for. If there was one thing she'd learned in life, particularly living with a disability, it was that determination paid off. If you had the grit to keep going, you'd succeed where others gave up.

Despite going 'old school', however, there was one piece of new technology that Smith intended to exploit. There had been a recent trend for doorbell cameras, which people could operate through their smartphones, much like the devices they'd placed on the bus stops. Because they were generally activated by movement, Smith hoped that someone nearby would've captured the victim's journey away from the crime scene. If she was very lucky, it'd lead all the way to the woman's front door. But Smith would settle for narrowing it down to just one street.

On her fourth residential road, she clocked something even better on one of the houses: a home CCTV system. Its front camera pointed out towards the pavement. Anticipation stirring, she walked up the path and pressed the buzzer.

*

Lockhart stopped pacing the waiting area of Lavender Hill police station long enough to check his watch. Less than sixty seconds had elapsed since he last looked at it, but he knew that every minute counted. Time was running out before they'd either need to charge or release Xander O'Neill. The actor's lawyer – who seemed too well-presented for O'Neill to afford on his own – had stretched out every conceivable meal break, rest, consultation and medical check-up, squeezing the period available for interview to the bare minimum. They hadn't even had time to take his DNA yet.

Lockhart needed to go in and get to work, but he'd asked Green to be there too. Smith was about the only other person he'd trust to join him, but she was out trying to find the Braddock victim. He was hoping that, with Green observing the interview on a video feed, she might pick up on things he'd miss and get a sense of O'Neill's pressure points. Two pairs of eyes were better than one, he reckoned. Especially when the second pair belonged to Green. She'd agreed to help, and he'd dashed off the paperwork for her to attend.

The only problem was that she wasn't here yet. Another five minutes, he told himself, then he'd have to make a start without her. He'd just resumed his pacing when the automatic doors whirred open and Green shot in, breathless.

'Sorry I'm late,' she said, her cheeks flushed. 'There were, like, no trains. Saturday closures, I guess. So, I had to take the bus, and then the road was shut off for repairs, so I walked—'

'Never mind,' he interrupted. 'You're here now. But we don't have long.'

'OK.' She wiped her brow on the sleeve of her jumper.

Lockhart lowered his voice. 'We can probably manage two interviews before I'll need to call the CPS for authorisation to charge, depending on what O'Neill says, obviously. Happy with that?'

'Uh, sure. So, I just watch and listen, and we talk between the two interviews?'

'Exactly.'

His attention was drawn by some movement behind him and he turned to see one of the uniforms from the custody suite opening the door behind the reception. Then, unbelievably, O'Neill stepped through, wearing his own clothes.

'Have a pleasant day, sir,' the officer told O'Neill.

Lockhart stepped forward. 'What's going on?'

O'Neill froze for a second as he registered Lockhart's presence, then his face lit up. 'Inspector! Didn't they tell you? I've been released.'

'What?'

The actor shrugged. 'No charges to answer to.'

'But...' Lockhart blocked O'Neill's exit and raised his voice to the uniform. 'You're letting him go?'

'That's correct.'

Lockhart watched as O'Neill's gaze shifted from challenging him to obvious interest in Green. The younger man's eyes dipped and rose again, widening in appreciation. Lockhart felt a protective impulse accompanied by a powerful urge to punch O'Neill in the face. He could aim right for those moles on his cheek. But, beyond a few moments of satisfaction, that wouldn't achieve anything.

'Are all of your team this good-looking?' he asked Lockhart, gesturing to Green.

Lockhart ignored the question. 'The stolen watch,' he stated.

'Oh, that. Given to me by my dear friend Mimi,' replied O'Neill breezily. 'Not stolen at all. Must've been a misunderstanding.'

Lockhart felt his limbs tensing.

'What's your name?' O'Neill asked Green.

'None of your damn business,' she replied.

The actor made a small dismissive noise and moved towards the main doors.

Stepping sideways, Lockhart blocked his path.

'What are you going to do, Inspector?' O'Neill looked up at him defiantly, puffing out his chest. 'Assault me again? I can add that to the complaint which my lawyer's already preparing. Excessive force used by you and your officers at my home, yesterday.'

'You little prick,' blurted Lockhart.

'Dan.' Green's tone was cautionary.

Lockhart could feel the rage swelling like a tide within him. His hands were tingling and his fists were already balled. He was one more smug comment away from violence. Then his phone rang.

'Better get that,' said O'Neill, nodding to Lockhart's jacket.

Lockhart stood still, breathing heavily through his nostrils, then broke eye contact and reached into his pocket. He looked at the screen. It said *DCI Porter*.

'Good luck.' O'Neill grinned and walked past Lockhart towards the street. The automatic doors buzzed open to let him out as Lockhart answered.

'Sir.'

'Whatever the fuck you think you're doing,' said Porter, his voice cold and precise, 'I want you back at Jubilee House and in my office, immediately. That's an order.'

CHAPTER FIFTY-ONE

It was slow, but Smith was making progress. The house with the home CCTV system had captured a figure moving past at 11.47 p.m. on the night of the attack. With the distance and wide-angle lens, the detail wasn't great, but it was good enough for Smith to identify the woman who was attacked at the bus stop some ten minutes earlier. The key was her walk.

She moved with difficulty, favouring her right leg while clutching one hand to her left side, just above the hip. The obvious effort made Smith think again of the pain this poor woman must have endured, hauling herself home with a stab wound on top of the trauma of an attempted rape. Whoever she was, she was mentally and physically as tough a person as Smith had encountered in twenty-two years of policework. She found her respect for this victim renewed, her motivation to track her down redoubled.

But even the boost of seeing the woman on film couldn't temper Smith's frustration. After finding the footage, she'd since knocked on two dozen doors with no result. She was starving, having already scoffed her supply of bananas and Jaffa Cakes, and desperately in need of caffeine. Shut up and keep going, she told herself. That's what the heroic woman had done two nights ago. Smith owed her that much.

Reaching the next house on the street, she rang the bell for the lower of two properties in the maisonette. Moments later, the door was opened by a small man with short, thick curly hair.

His compact features, at once inquisitive and timid looking, reminded Smith of a rodent. She held out her warrant card for him and introduced herself.

'Oh, how can I help, officer?' he replied. His fingers knotted together.

'Sorry to trouble you, sir. Is this your home?'

'Mm, yes.' He glanced over his shoulder, inside. Smith could hear the crowd noise and commentary of a football match coming from another room. 'Yes, it is.'

'And is it just yourself in the property, then? Or does anyone else live here?'

His hesitation was barely a second, but Smith caught it. 'Just me.'

Smith gave him a moment to change his mind, but he didn't say anything else.

'You may have seen on the news that we're looking for a woman who we believe walked down this street late on Thursday night. She may have been seriously injured in an assault and we'd like to find her, to make sure she's OK.'

'Right.' He nodded quickly.

'Did you see or hear anything late on Thursday night? It would've been around 11.45 p.m.'

'No, nothing.' He gave a nervous laugh. 'I'm a very deep sleeper.'

Smith doubted that. 'All right. Well, thanks anyway. Let me give you my number, in case you think of anything else from late Thursday night or early Friday morning.'

'Of course.'

She patted her pockets. 'Sorry, I don't have a pen. Would you mind?—'

'Sure.' He turned around, searching for something to write with. Smith took the opportunity to look past him, her eyes sweeping the interior. Unremarkable. Then she spotted it. At the bottom of the stairs, so small she could easily have missed it. A hairband. Like the kind in almost every woman's pocket or handbag. And this guy's hair wasn't long enough to need tying back.

'Actually, you could just put it in your phone,' she said.

He laughed awkwardly and pulled a device from his pocket. Smith gave him the number for her work mobile.

'Sorry, I didn't catch your name, mister…' She let the words hang.

'John.'

'Thanks for your time, John.' She gestured towards the television noise. 'Who's playing?'

'Oh, er, Chelsea.' He didn't sound certain.

She grinned. 'That's my team. Big cup game today, isn't it?'

'Yeah. Massive.'

'Well, I'll let you get back to it.' She gave a mini-fist pump. 'Come on the Blues.'

The smile he gave her as he shut the door looked almost painful. John hadn't wanted to talk about football. And there was no cup game today. Someone else had been watching the match in his home.

Smith stepped back and searched the windows, but they were shuttered. It might be nothing. But her copper's nose was usually on the money, and it told her something about John wasn't quite right. She jotted his house number down and made a note to check him out when she got back. Which, judging by the length of the road, wouldn't be for a while. That was OK. She'd long since cancelled any plans she had for her Saturday night.

CHAPTER FIFTY-TWO

'It's been a pain in the arse, to be honest.' Eddie Stagg gave a backward glance as he led Lexi across the CID room. 'Just crap, mostly. No, in fact, all crap.'

'No leads on the latest victim, then?' she asked, as they reached his desk.

'Not from here,' he replied, flapping a hand at his computer, which was surrounded by crisp packets, chocolate bar wrappers and mugs. 'Max has been on the streets all day, though, trying to work out where the woman went after she was attacked. I get to deal with the time wasters. But you never know, we've had good intel off of social media appeals before, so...' He shrugged and dropped heavily into his chair. It creaked under the weight of his large frame. 'Grab a seat.'

Lexi pulled one up and sat. 'Hey, you might catch a break.'

Eddie cast another forlorn look at his monitor. Lexi saw that he had the Wandsworth Police Facebook page and Twitter feed open side by side.

'Wilkins should be doing this kind of work.' He jabbed a finger towards the screen. 'Apparently, he's laid up at home. Fell down the bloody stairs. Can you believe it?'

'Jeez, I hope he's OK.'

'Well, he's not in hospital, so it can't be that bad.' Eddie shrugged. 'Anyway, cheers for dropping by. You've not got anything better to do with your Saturday afternoon, then?'

'Actually, I was already meeting Dan here. He wanted me to observe an interview with a suspect. Related to a murder case.'

'Is that allowed?' Eddie frowned. 'I mean, you being there.'

'I guess so.' Lexi shrugged. 'It was just watching the video feed. Dan said he'd done the paperwork.' She hoped none of this would come back and bite her in the ass.

'What happened?'

'They let the guy go before he could be interviewed.'

'Shit. Bad luck.'

'Yeah, Dan was really pissed about it. He had to head back over to Putney to go see his boss.'

'Who I expect isn't best pleased about that outcome.'

'Yeah, right.' Lexi took a notebook from her handbag. 'So, I wanted to give you a little update on my profile for Op Braddock.'

Eddie's face lit up and he rubbed his hands together. 'Cracking. Do you want a cuppa tea?'

'No, thanks, I'm good.' She paused. 'And, uh, don't get too excited. There are no firm conclusions.'

'Until we find our victim, wobbly conclusions are better than nothing.'

'Sure.'

'All right, then,' he said, 'let's hear it.'

Lexi took him through her work so far. Mapping the initial six incidents to the 'Peeping Tom' type, graduating from stalking to assault, with a sexual motive. A shy, younger man, awkward around women. Low self-esteem, repeatedly rejected, but desperate for sexual contact.

'OK.' Eddie steepled his fingers over his belly, his brow furrowed in concentration.

'He doesn't want to hurt his victims,' Lexi continued. 'In many cases, he actually believes he has a connection to them. Almost like he's looking after them, in a weird way.'

'Serious? How do you even begin to understand these psychos?'

Lexi stopped herself challenging his incorrect use of the term *psycho*. 'I mean, that's one theory, but it's well-evidenced by interviews of these guys after they've been caught. Sometimes, it's fantasy for them. Other times, they've totally misread a woman's verbal or non-verbal cues as meaning she's interested in them.'

'Christ. OK, that's helpful.' Eddie nodded, pressing his lips together. 'But, er… what about the knife?'

'That's where it gets complicated. The last three attacks have involved violence or threats. Serious threats. With a little sadism, even, the way the witnesses described it. That's a different profile: aggressive. We're usually talking about bigger, stronger, so-called Alpha-type guys here. The sort of man who likes to believe he can just take what he wants. And who likes hurting women. For some guys, their sexual arousal is triggered by the woman not consenting, even actively resisting.'

'Really?'

'Uh-huh. It's even got a name: raptophilia.'

'Rapto…?'

'Philia.'

'I see.' Eddie nodded a few times, then frowned. 'So, what, he's two different blokes?'

'Right. That's what I don't get, either. Is he a quiet guy with a hidden streak of violence that's starting to emerge, or a confident guy who didn't need to use violence before?'

'Didn't *need* to use it?'

'Yeah, so, if he was, like, successful or whatever. Then something changed.'

'Hm.'

Lexi could tell Eddie was confused. 'Oh, and, uh, he's probably white, because most of the women he's attacked have been white, and rapists generally target their own ethnic groups. And most likely he lives in the area, given his knowledge of the locations.'

'We thought as much.'

'Right.' A wave of disappointment crested in her. She wasn't helping at all.

'Anything else?'

'Nope.' She scanned her notes. 'That's about it. I mean, it's just one psychological interpretation of the perpetrator's behaviour. Sorry,' she added.

Eddie cleared his throat. 'Well, look, thanks, Lexi. I really appreciate the work you've put into this. And when we catch this bastard, we'll see which of your two types he is.'

She put the notebook back in her bag, suddenly wanting to leave. To take her useless theories home and let the real investigators do their work.

'Would you mind giving Max a call and telling her what you told me?' asked Eddie. 'I think, you know, you'll explain it better than me.' He gave her a lopsided smile. 'What with all the long words and stuff.'

'Sure. I've got her number.' Lexi guessed Max wouldn't be as sympathetic to her profiling efforts as Eddie. Her stomach was already tightening at the prospect of that conversation.

CHAPTER FIFTY-THREE

Lockhart hadn't always had a problem following orders. In his early army days, he'd just done what he was told. As a teenage private, he hadn't really known any different. Once he'd got a bit older and joined the Special Reconnaissance Regiment, though, he'd had to learn to think for himself. The officers could set out whatever plan they liked from the comfort of their headquarters. But when he was out, alone, undercover in Belfast or Baghdad, he was the one making the decisions.

The ability to operate independently had served Lockhart well in the SRR. His problem was going back to taking orders once he'd joined the Met. Particularly when he didn't agree with those orders; doubly so when he thought they were designed to serve the career interests of an ambitious senior officer.

'What did I tell you a week ago? And don't bullshit me by pretending you can't remember.'

That was Porter's opening line as Lockhart entered the DCI's office. He'd known this was coming since he'd decided to continue investigating Xander O'Neill. Now, he had to take his punishment. Before he could reply, Porter spoke again.

'I told you specifically to leave Mr O'Neill, and Ms Stott-Peters, alone.'

'I know, sir, but—'

Porter raised a hand to silence him. 'I'm sitting here, SIO on the Thorncross murders, thinking I know what's going on and what my team's up to. Next thing, I'm being called by the grieving widow of a deceased man whose killer we're trying to find, asking me why her friend, who was supposed to be helping arrange her dead husband's personal effects, has been arrested.' His boss spoke calmly and carefully, an undertone of menace in his deep voice.

'Now, I know you're not stupid, Dan,' Porter went on. 'So, I'm going to give you a chance to explain to me why you disobeyed a direct instruction from your DCI.'

Lockhart linked his hands behind his back and stood up straight. 'We obtained information from a member of the public that the watch belonging to Charles Stott had been brought to a second-hand jewellery store, by a man who matched the description of Mr O'Neill. The shop owner, who provided the intelligence, identified Mr O'Neill from a six-pack of photographs, so we effected an arrest before he had time to dispose of the stolen item. We found the watch in his house.'

'Using a warrant I knew nothing about.' Porter's volume was rising.

'We needed to act quickly, sir.'

Porter pulled a theatrical face of confusion. 'Who's this "we"? Are you trying to claim this was someone else's fault?'

'I mean, me.'

'The watch is irrelevant, anyway. Ms Stott-Peters says she gave it to Mr O'Neill as a gift. So, you haven't even managed to solve a theft.'

'There was cocaine in his room, too.' Lockhart knew the argument was weak even as he said the words.

'One gram?' Porter scoffed. 'It's nothing we wouldn't find in half the bedrooms of London if we searched them. And you know the CPS aren't going to prosecute anything less than intent to supply. So, forget about the drugs.'

'Sir.'

'And you went to Croydon to get the warrant signed off?'

There was no point making excuses. Porter knew exactly what he'd done. Lockhart nodded.

'I didn't catch that.'

'Yes, sir.'

Suddenly, Porter slammed his palm on the desk and rose up from behind it. 'Not. Fucking. Good enough!' he yelled.

Lockhart said nothing. He didn't know what would douse the flames now. He became aware that activity in the open-plan area outside Porter's office had reduced as the rest of the team listened while pretending to keep working.

'You want to screw up your own career, that's fine by me,' he shouted, thrusting a finger at Lockhart. 'But I am not carrying the can for this bullshit.'

'I made a mistake,' said Lockhart quietly. Though he didn't really believe he had.

'Why do you have to make life so difficult for yourself?' continued Porter, still visibly enraged. 'All you had to do was follow my instructions, do a half-decent job on this, and you could've become acting DCI when I leave.'

'You're leaving, sir?'

Porter ignored his question. 'If we weren't so thin on the bloody ground, I'd take you off this investigation altogether.' The DCI sat down and tugged at the sides of his jacket, took a breath.

Lockhart wondered if he'd weathered the storm.

'I have an official complaint against you by Ms Stott-Peters for causing her emotional distress.'

'But—'

'And Mr O'Neill's lawyer has indicated that a further complaint will be made for the brutality of you and two other members of MIT 8 when you arrested his client yesterday.'

'That's not—'

'Shut up and listen!'

Lockhart bit his lip.

'From now on, Dan, you run everything by me on Operation Thorncross, and you do exactly what I say. If you can manage that, then when this is over, I will consider – and I'm only saying *consider* – not passing those complaints on to the DPS for full inquiry. Understand?'

The DPS, or Directorate of Professional Standards, were the police who investigated the police. If they upheld a charge of misconduct, you could lose your job. You might even get a criminal record. Possibly go to jail. DPS were three letters no copper ever wanted to hear.

'Sir.'

'Get out.'

Lockhart felt the urge to be home before he'd even set foot outside Porter's office. He'd stocked his fridge with a dozen more cans of Stella. And they were calling to him.

CHAPTER FIFTY-FOUR

Lexi swallowed the last of her wine and stood, a little rocky on her feet. The bar they'd chosen on Old Street was so crowded and noisy that she felt momentarily disorientated and needed to steady herself on the stool.

'Who wants a drink?' she said, looking at the glasses on the table.

'I'm good.' Sarah tilted her bright red cocktail. Whatever the hell it was, there was plenty of it left.

Raj and Harvey – the two doctors Sarah had invited out – both raised their half-full pint glasses and shook their heads. 'Thanks, though,' said Raj, his gaze lingering on her.

'I'm going to get another,' Lexi announced, pointing to the bar, then realising the gesture was unnecessary.

As she turned away and pushed into the crowd of drinkers, she felt a hand grab her arm and steer her away from the table.

'You OK, Lex?' Sarah hissed.

'Never better.'

'Come on, you're two drinks ahead of everyone else and you've barely said a word. What's up?'

For a second, Lexi thought about telling her the whole story. The two cases, her useless theories, the fact she hadn't done jack shit to help the police catch two serious offenders despite working on profiles for days. Not to mention that she'd done all that for free when she still had bills to pay. Damn. It was the call to Maxine Smith that'd pushed her over the edge. Max was tough, and not a psychology fan, but she'd reached out to Lexi on Braddock only to slap her down when the profile came. Her words still stung: *Good job we're not relying on you to stop anybody else getting raped.*

Sarah squeezed her arm a little harder. 'Lex, what's up? Tell me.'

'It's nothing.'

'All right, well, just… take it easy, yeah?' She dropped her voice to a whisper, barely audible over the pumping dance music, and flicked her eyes back towards their table. 'These two are hot. We're single.' She grinned. 'Do the maths.'

'I'm really not interested,' Lexi replied loudly.

'Are you mad?' Sarah's eyes widened in horror. 'Can't you forget about your detective for one night?'

'It's not about him.' Maybe it was about him, she thought. Just a little.

Sarah's expression relaxed into one of resignation. 'Whatever. At least don't screw it up for me, then.'

'Sure.' Lexi pulled her arm free and went to the bar. There had to be something more she could do to help. She felt the desire to be out there, hunting for the bad guys, like Max and Dan. When it came to Dan, that wasn't the only desire she felt. Sarah was right. Lexi chastised herself for the thought when Dan was dealing with the whole thing about his wife being declared dead.

She tried to bring her mind back to the two cases. She was missing something on the profiles, she knew it… but with the people and the chatter and the music and the alcohol, she couldn't think straight. She ordered more wine, not bothering to look at the menu, and carried it back to the table.

'It's just biology,' she heard Harvey saying as she took her stool.

'What is?' she said, taking a quick gulp of her drink.

'Having babies,' replied Raj.

'I'm telling you, it's weird. And scary.' Sarah held up both palms. 'That's all I'm saying.'

'You guys are built for it,' said Harvey, looking from Sarah to Lexi and back.

'Trust us.' Raj grinned. 'We're doctors.'

Sarah shook her head and laughed.

'Look,' Harvey said, 'I did a rotation on the maternity ward. You just take all the drugs they offer, pop it out, start breastfeeding. Seriously, it's not that bad.'

'How would you know?' Sarah glared at him playfully, her lips twitching into a smile. 'Have you been pregnant? Given birth?' She paused. 'Didn't think so.'

'And have *you*?'

'No, but…' Sarah shrugged.

Lexi considered explaining what morning sickness was like. Or simply the knowledge that another life was growing inside you. And how deciding to end that life was the about the single hardest choice anyone could make. One that stayed with you for ever. She drank some more wine, her irritation growing.

'OK, so, as an expert in the human body,' Harvey continued, 'especially female anatomy, I can tell you that you're perfectly designed to do this.'

'Maybe,' replied Sarah. 'But that's easy for—'

'And what the fuck are you designed to do?' blurted Lexi. 'Stick your dicks in us for like two minutes, if that, shoot your load and then congratulate yourselves on getting us pregnant? *Hey, good job, man*,' she mimicked a male voice. 'Jesus Christ.'

'Whoa, Lexi!' Sarah put a hand on her shoulder. 'Where did that come from?'

Harvey took a mouthful of beer. 'Time of the month?'

'Excuse me?' Lexi thought she might smash her wine glass into his stupid, smug face. 'What the hell did you say?'

'Just kidding,' he added hastily, looking to Raj for help.

'Don't listen to him,' said Raj, shaking his head. 'He's not all there. Too many night shifts, right?'

'Yeah.' Harvey swiftly finished his pint.

'Anyway…' Sarah shifted awkwardly in her seat.

'There's always surrogacy,' Raj offered.

Something clicked in Lexi's brain.

'We were chatting about that the other night,' said Sarah.

'Oh yeah?' Harvey raised his eyebrows.

'I mean, it's not like I'm thinking about babies right now.' Sarah rattled the ice cubes in her glass.

'Not at all.' Harvey inclined his head.

'It depends what you want,' Raj went on. 'We see surrogate pregnancies more and more in the hospital now. Women with careers, usually, who don't want—'

'Surrogates,' stated Lexi.

'Yeah, you know, when another woman—'

'I have to go.' Lexi stood, grabbed her jacket off the bar stool.

'What? Where are you going, Lex?' Sarah got up too.

'I've gotta… I'm sorry.' She manoeuvred around the table and pushed her way out of the heaving bar.

CHAPTER FIFTY-FIVE

I stink. Just took a sniff of my armpit and realised that I hadn't showered in two days. Can't risk getting the knife wound wet now that it's beginning to heal up. Amazing how you can start craving something as basic as hot water and soap when it's taken away from you. I've never been big on appearance. Haven't ever worn much make-up, unless I'm going out to get laid. I dress however I like. And if people don't like my muscles, that's up to them. But I draw the line at being offended by my own smell.

Still, there are more serious things to think about. I know the police are looking for me – as a victim, for now, at least – and John said they even came around here, asking if he'd seen a woman they believed had been stabbed. I've hidden the injury from John, but if he thinks something's up, he's clearly too awkward or scared to talk about it straight out. I've noticed him paying more attention to me since that visit, though. Asking a few times if I was feeling OK. He needs to be careful.

My relationship with John is based on three things. One, he idolises me. Two, he's a pussy who lets me do whatever I want in his home. Three, he never asks any questions. If that's going to change, our relationship might have to come to an end.

It wouldn't take much to make that happen. And it wouldn't turn out well for him.

I'd probably drown him in his own bathtub. Then message his current employer from John's email account to say he's going to be off sick for a while. And carry on living in his house while

I finish what I set out to do. Let's hope it doesn't come to that. It'd be a shame to kill John. He's a good sound editor, and there aren't many of them.

It does remind me though.

I've got some research to do.

CHAPTER FIFTY-SIX

Once outside, Lexi hadn't even taken three steps in the direction of Old Street tube station before she called Dan.

'Lexi.' He sounded dejected.

'I've got it,' she yelled, her voice still at bar volume.

'OK, what?'

'Surrogates!'

'Eh?'

'Surrogates,' she repeated. 'I think the reason our Thorncross victims are unconnected is because they're surrogates. They're not the people who actually did something bad to the killer. They just represent those people.'

'Where are you?' he said. 'Are you on a night out?…'

'Never mind that,' she countered. 'We need to look someplace else for the whole film injury thing. Maybe even abroad.'

She heard him sigh, then what sounded like a can opening. 'I don't know, Lexi. Doesn't seem all that likely.' Even in her state, she could detect the little slur in his words.

'It's the best explanation that fits the data,' she said quickly. 'I knew there was something missing from the profile. This is it!'

'All right,' he replied calmly. 'Cheers for calling.'

'Wait!' she barked. 'You're not taking this seriously, are you?'

'I'll look into it.' There was a gross slurping noise on the line.

'Jeez, Dan. Fine. Drink your… whatever that is, and ignore me if you like.'

'I'm not ignoring you, it's just…' He tailed off.

'Well, I'm going home right now,' she interjected. 'And I'm going to find your killer.'

She ended the call before he could respond.

DAY THIRTEEN

CHAPTER FIFTY-SEVEN

Lexi woke with a start. For a few seconds, reality blurred with a nightmare she'd been having, where she was shut in a room with no door. Her heart was still racing as she recalled the panic of the dream, scrabbling in vain to find a way out. But she quickly realised she was in her bedroom, pale morning light seeping through the blinds. She was safe, although she noticed the door was open, which was a little weird. And she was lying on her bed, fully clothed and on top of the duvet. She felt her laptop resting against one leg and, in a second, she remembered exactly what she'd been doing.

Then came the dull throb of a headache, somewhere behind her eyes, from all the wine she'd drunk too fast in the bar last night, plus the strong coffee she'd made to help her work through when she got in late. Now, her stomach felt hollow and achy. But Lexi didn't care. She'd been on to something that was too important to ignore.

When Raj had mentioned surrogates in the bar, a thought that'd been bubbling away for a week had finally crystallised. She remembered an FBI report she'd read which said that victims of planned violence may not be connected to the attacker. Instead, the perpetrator might target innocent people who symbolise the source of their anger. In other words, surrogates.

This had led Lexi to spend half the night trawling the internet for the person who fitted her profile. Some kind of film performer, she reasoned, with a grudge against a director, a set designer and a compensation lawyer, possibly related to an event outside the UK. She'd googled film-set injuries and lawsuits and medical cases until her eyes glazed over.

After three hours, she'd only found one article of interest: a small piece by 'staff writers' buried deep in the *L.A. Times* about an accident last summer on the set of a superhero movie, which had left a stunt performer with serious injuries. The person wasn't named, and there appeared to be no follow-up articles. Evidently, the film studio had made some kind of injunction, or perhaps reached an out-of-court settlement to avoid the negative press and reputational damage of the incident. But there was one clue to the stunt performer's identity: it was a woman.

She recalled Dan's description of the female DNA under Ernesto Gomez's fingernails. And she remembered her own, brief thought – when Dan first told her about Charles Stott's murder – that a woman could've carried out the attack herself. That there were some women capable of such violence.

Lexi had felt the buzz of excitement at her discovery, only to experience the frustration of the lead going nowhere without either the stunt performer or the journalist's name. So, she'd had to think around the problem. Surfing into the chatrooms of movie fandom, she happened upon a site called NerdCave. Here, movie geeks exchanged all kinds of trivia, from the minutiae of actor biographies to the finest details on film sets, costumes, gaffs and plot holes.

She'd posted a message, citing the *L.A. Times* article, asking about the accident and whether anyone knew either the film or the stuntwoman's name. Then she'd started researching psychological theories of female killers. She figured she must've dozed off some time around three or four in the morning.

Opening her laptop now, she refreshed the browser window. A flurry of comments had been added beneath her post, forming a thread where a handful of self-proclaimed 'super-nerds' had given their opinions. The consensus seemed to be that the film in question was *Leopardess*, a futuristic fantasy movie from a major studio, due for release in the summer. There was some debate about who the stuntwoman was, but in the end, an expert calling himself CaptainCali had weighed in with what he said was the definitive answer. Lexi's pulse quickened as she read to the bottom.

The stuntwoman hadn't worked again in Hollywood, to anyone's knowledge, since the accident. Because she was a foreign national, the nerds speculated that she'd returned to her home country, perhaps even being deported from the US following the expiry of her work visa.

She was rumoured to be British.

And CaptainCali had posted her name.

CHAPTER FIFTY-EIGHT

Smith had risen early, given her sleeping fella a peck on the forehead, and taken the bus into Jubilee House. The canteen wasn't open on Sundays, so she'd treated herself to a ham and cheese croissant and a fancy coffee from one of the posh bakeries in Putney. Comfort food was instant morale for long hours on an investigation. Fuelled up, for a while at least, she set about her work.

First, she reviewed the footage from their bus stop cameras during the previous night. It took her almost two hours to check all eight feeds, but finally she was satisfied that nothing of interest had occurred. Then, she messaged Stagg, who confirmed that no one had come forward yet as the victim of Thursday night's stabbing and attempted rape.

Stagg also told her that he'd be at his desk in Lavender Hill station all day, down the road in Clapham, and invited her to head over at some point if she wanted to chat anything through, check the responses to their public appeal, or just grab a brew. Smith appreciated the offer; weekend working could be pretty isolated.

By this point, though, others from MIT 8 were starting to come in, following leads on the Thorncross murders. Lockhart had arrived, looking terrible. He gave her a nod as he sat down a few desks away, coffee in hand. She wondered what he'd got up to last night. She texted Stagg back to tell him she might come over later, but that chances were she'd be given some work on their serial murder case. That was fine by her; since meeting

Ernesto Gomez's boyfriend, Paul Newton, she was fired up for a result on Thorncross, too.

Smith then set about checking out the 'John' she'd met yesterday. A search for his address against the electoral roll revealed one sole occupant of the property: Jonathan Foster. He was about the right age to be the guy she'd spoken to. She looked up his name and address on the Police National Computer, finding nothing more than a small car of which Foster was the registered owner. He had no criminal record, not even an unpaid parking ticket. A model citizen. So why had he been so evasive when she'd visited?

There were all sorts of reasons people might behave that way. Usually, in her experience, it was a personal cannabis stash or some illegal TV box they didn't want discovered. Maybe she was being paranoid. The hairband on John's carpet could've belonged to a girlfriend or female friend or relative. Or a bloke with a man-bun, for all she knew.

Nevertheless, Smith trusted her instincts, so she tried to search online to see what John did for a living or if there was anything else that she could find about him. But his name was too common, and she quickly drew a blank. She fired off an email to Lucy Berry, on the off-chance the analyst could put in a few hours at home, asking her to trace him in more detail. If anyone could drill down into this Jonathan Foster's life, it was Berry.

Smith was considering how early she could reasonably get her lunch, and whether she should see if Lockhart wanted to head out, too, when her mobile rang. It was Stagg.

'Max. The lab's come through.'

She couldn't immediately place which request he was talking about. 'Yup.'

'There's a match.'

'OK, great. Of what, exactly?'

'The knife.'

She gave a rapid intake of breath. 'It's a registered offender? Have we got a name for the rapist?' This was a serious breakthrough in tracking the scumbag down. It was what they'd been hoping for.

'No. Not the offender. The victim.'

'What?'

'Yeah. The blood on the knife that stabbed the woman we can't find. Her DNA was in the system.'

'Seriously? She's been attacked before?'

'You tell me. It's your operation.'

'Eh?'

'Thorncross.'

CHAPTER FIFTY-NINE

Lockhart felt like shit. It wasn't just the physical punishment from having drunk another skinful of Stella last night. It was the mixture of fury and disgust at himself for letting his discipline drop so low. OK, so he'd screwed things up with the Xander O'Neill arrest, and now Porter was gunning for him even more than usual, dangling a DPS case over his head that could spell the end of his career in the Met. Most people would crack open a beer or two to ease the stress of that. But he hadn't stopped at a couple. And it was the second night in a row. There had been others in the week. It was unacceptable.

People were depending on him. Potential victims of a serial murderer on whom they had bugger all in terms of decent leads. Women who wanted to travel by bus at night without fear of being raped. A team of detectives, uniforms and civilian staff who were looking to him for leadership, while Porter was busy schmoozing in his press conferences and senior briefings. And, most importantly of all – as far as Lockhart was concerned – Jess. Not only was she out there, somewhere, but now her family wanted her declared dead. It was up to him to keep her alive by challenging that in court. Her own relatives had abandoned hope. He was all she had. He couldn't let her down.

And what was his response? Make a plan, face up to it all and get stuff done? No. It was to drink can after can of Stella until he passed out on his sofa and woke up at 5 a.m., with a mouth like sandpaper, still wearing his jacket and shoes, desperate for a piss.

Brilliant job, mate. Well done.

He reflected that, perhaps, things had been better when he'd been having his therapy sessions with Green. Her support had kept him going through tough times, given him some tools for managing his stress and not letting his emotions get the better of him. He missed having someone to talk to about how he was feeling. He looked around the MIT room. No way was he telling this lot about all the shit going on in his life; apart from the issue of trusting them, it'd undermine his leadership. Then the thought occurred to him that he didn't just miss the sessions. He missed Green.

He immediately felt another surge of guilt to add to his self-loathing and tried not to think about her. But, as Green had told him, trying *not* to think about something usually meant you just thought about it more. And now he was recalling their conversation from late last night – both of them drunk – where she'd told him something about surrogates and finding the killer. What had he said in response? He couldn't remember, exactly, but he didn't think it was positive.

Lockhart rubbed his hands over his face and whispered to himself that he needed to step up his game. This wasn't good enough. Then another voice cut into his self-criticism.

'Guv.'

He looked up to see Smith standing by his desk.

'I've just got off the phone to Stagg,' she said. 'The blood from the knife we found at the bus stop was a match to the skin sample taken from under Ernesto Gomez's fingernails.'

Lockhart wished he wasn't hungover. He tried to process it through the fog in his brain.

'It wasn't the attacker who was stabbed at the bus stop,' he stated. 'Which means the Braddock victim who fought back against the rapist is...' He frowned. 'Our Thorncross killer?'

'Looks that way,' replied Smith. 'Especially given how tough we know she is. You saw her defending herself in the video. I reckon she could beat someone to death.'

He considered this a moment. 'Green was right.'

'What about?'

Lockhart picked up his phone. 'She told me right at the start of this, just after Charles Stott's murder, that the killer could be a woman. Based on the occult symbol being female or something. I didn't give her theory enough credit.'

'Come on, Dan. She was crystal ball gazing. We had no evidence back then. We weren't going to discount half of the population from our suspect pool based on her opinion about a triangle.'

'We *did* discount half the population, though. The wrong half.'

Smith shrugged. 'You can't worry about that,' she said firmly. 'It was anyone's guess at that point. Can't argue with the DNA, now, though.'

'Right.' Unlocking his phone, he saw a missed call from Green and a text to call her back. He held the screen up to Smith and tapped to ring Green. 'OK, then. Let's see what she has to say.'

CHAPTER SIXTY

Lexi reached to her armband and selected the song 'Reapers' by Muse from her cellphone. Then she cranked up the volume and began her sprint home. The heavy guitars and angry lyrics seemed to capture her mood right now. Irritated, pissed, mad. Her legs pumped hard as her feet pounded the sidewalk, her teeth gritted against the fatigue that was now setting in. Running on a hangover was always tough, but she had to do something physical or she was going to go crazy.

She could recall word for word Max Smith's response yesterday to what the detective had described as Lexi's 'psychobabble', and the confusion on Eddie Stagg's face as she tried to explain the mixed profile of their rape suspect to him. Then, several large glasses of wine and a few gins later, there was the conversation with Dan about the serial murders. His vague, non-committal response to her idea of surrogate victims. And the fact he hadn't even picked up when she'd called him mid-morning today.

Lexi wanted so badly to help with both of those cases, and it frustrated the hell out of her that she couldn't do something more. That she couldn't apply her theories in any kind of useful way. And that the cops weren't listening to her, or that she couldn't *make* them listen. Her sprint built up pace to the point where she was almost losing control of her body. She let out an anguished cry just as the song cut out and was replaced with the tone of an incoming call.

'Dammit!' she yelled, before slowing and glancing at the screen, strapped to her arm. Dan. She dropped her jog to a walk, took a couple breaths, and answered.

'Hey.'

'Lexi, you all right?'

'Yeah. I'm—' she gasped, spat, 'I've been running.'

'Good effort. Listen, I've got Max here with me. You're on speakerphone in the office.'

'OK,' she said warily. Lexi never felt as sure of herself with Max there, her scepticism at Lexi's work almost palpable. 'I tried to call earlier. I think I know who your murder suspect is.'

'So do we,' he replied. 'Kind of.'

'What? How?'

He explained the DNA match from the murder scene to the attempted rape.

'Holy shit,' was all she could say when he'd finished. As she turned into her road, there was a brief silence on the line and Lexi wondered if they were expecting her to offer some instant interpretation.

'We're following a lead on her location,' said Max.

'We wanted to know if you had anything else for us,' added Dan. He cleared his throat. 'I know you tried to tell me something yesterday, but—'

'You weren't listening.'

'Sorry.' Dan sounded as though he meant it.

Lexi felt her rage subside a little. 'Just give me a second,' she said, walking up to her front door. 'Better I talk someplace more private. Hang on.'

She let herself in. The house was silent. 'Rhys? Sarah?' she yelled, but there was no answer. She went through into the kitchen and sat at the dining table.

Dan's voice came through her headphones. 'Lexi?'

'Yeah, I'm here. OK, so, the most important thing is that I think your killer's name is Blaze Logan. She's a British stuntwoman who was injured on a film set in the States. After the accident, there was some kind of—'

'Whoa, whoa,' Dan interjected. 'Blaze Logan?' he repeated.

'Yeah.'

'How did you get her name?'

She told him about her online trawl, the *L.A. Times* article, and the NerdCave chat thread.

'How can you be certain it's her?' Max made no effort to hide her doubt.

'It makes total sense,' Lexi replied. 'First of all, we have to ask why the murder victims aren't connected.' She didn't wait for a response. 'It's not as if the killer is targeting a particular location, or even one particular type of victim, right?'

'Go on,' said Dan cautiously.

'Something links the three victims. It has to, because the attacks aren't random. They're planned. The killer knows the target's pattern of life. She knows where to find them alone, at night, in a spot with no cameras or witnesses.'

'Agreed.'

'And I don't buy the idea that Charles Stott's and Ernesto Gomez's jobs aren't significant. A film director and a set designer? It has to be connected.'

Silence.

'So,' Lexi continued, 'it's probably something about film. But where does Martin Johnson, the compensation lawyer, fit into it? Gotta be a lawsuit relating to something in film, right? Some event that left the victim – our killer, or maybe someone real close to them – with a grudge that'd make them kill.'

'That could be one explanation,' replied Dan.

'That's not all. The attacks are blitzes, right? We know the victims were punched, kicked and stamped to death. And in at least one case, the assault continued long past the point of death.'

'Yup.'

'So, we're almost certainly talking about a psychopath. I don't mean just your average investment banker. I mean stone cold psychopath. No feelings, no empathy, no remorse. It fits with the Explosive Avenger type of female killer.'

There was a laugh on the line. 'The what?'

'Explosive Avenger. I looked it up. Female killers are rare, and usually fall into one of two stereotypes. There's the Black Widow, poisoning a husband or rich relative for financial gain, and the Angel of Death, murdering weaker individuals in her care, on a kind of delusional power trip. But there's a third documented category too. Explosive Avenger.'

'Sounds like a piss-take of a superhero.'

'Well, it's for real. Extreme violence as retribution for some past wrong, like abuse. You heard of Aileen Wuornos?'

'Sure,' replied Dan. 'The sex worker in Florida who murdered her clients.'

'There you go. One example. We don't credit women with the capacity for violence, right? We think it's something that men do. Like it's in their DNA.'

'Maybe.'

'It's true. If a woman kills,' she continued, 'our interpretation is totally different. A female killer is either labelled hysterical and insane, or just selfishly scheming after men's wealth. A violent murder by a woman isn't considered to have been her choice. It was an accident, self-defence against a guy's aggression. Or a man coerced her into it. It's because we're taught to see men as warriors, women as nurturers.'

'Fair enough, but—'

'What I'm saying is that there's a very small number of females who, under certain circumstances, could beat someone to death. Psychopaths.'

'How does that support your theory about this Logan woman?' asked Smith.

'OK. Think about being a stunt performer. What psychological qualities do you need? You've gotta be able to manage your own fear. Psychopaths don't feel fear. Perfect.'

'Mm.'

'They crave excitement, too. They get bored easily. What better way to get your kicks than doing one of the coolest jobs going? You move from gig to gig, you don't need to commit to anything for more than a month or two. There's no regularity or routine. Just a shit ton of excitement and action. And status. It's the ideal job for someone with a psychopathic personality.'

'So, you're saying this stunt person had an accident?'

'Right, that's my theory. Now she can't work because of the injuries, or she was blacklisted, or the studio sponsoring her visa kicked her out of the US. It's the end of her life, basically. She's smart enough to know that if she goes back to the States and attacks the actual people she holds responsible for what happened to her, the cops will be all over it. She doesn't want to be caught. So, she's selecting unconnected victims who are surrogates for the real targets of her hatred.'

There was a pause. Lexi heard a noise and turned to see Rhys shuffling into the kitchen. He seemed to be limping slightly, and there were a pair of dark circles around his eyes, like he'd walked into a door. She caught his eye and glared at him, pointing to her phone. He nodded, dropped some trash into the recycling bin, then left quickly.

'Er, you lost me a bit at the end there,' said Dan. 'Surrogates?'

Lexi sighed. 'Yeah. It's a theory. René Girard.'

'Who the hell is that?' Smith's tone was openly hostile now.

'He was a philosopher who wrote about mythology. Basically, he said that humans need to make sense of chaos in our lives. We try to blame bad stuff on specific people – even when they're not involved – so we can vent our rage. It's happened throughout human history, worldwide. It's in a bunch of religions, across cultures. Scapegoating. When we've made someone else responsible for our actions, they can take the blame, even for our violence towards them.'

'All right, I get the idea, I think. It's a bit academic, but…'

'Dammit, Dan! Forget about the academic part. This isn't a college lecture. Scapegoating and surrogacy are just things humans do. And serial killers have done it before. You know I'm right.'

'You sure about that, Lexi?' His voice was irritatingly measured.

'Yeah. I mean, it's all there. Blaze Logan is the woman you're looking for. She's your killer. And you know what? I'm willing to bet she'll kill again if you don't get your shit together and find her.'

Dan gave a long outbreath. 'We'll look her up.'

Lexi couldn't believe this was all the thanks she was getting. 'Do you want me to come in?' she asked, exasperated. 'I can help. Write all this down, explain it to the team. Try to work out who she might target next.'

She could hear Max and Dan whispering but couldn't make out the words.

'Cheers, Lexi,' he replied, eventually. 'We'll manage OK without you.'

CHAPTER SIXTY-ONE

'Yes! Go on, Freya!'

Liz Jennings watched her daughter kick the football vaguely in the direction of the opposition's goal, then chase after it along with a bunch of other ten-year-old girls. Despite the coaches' best efforts, the under-elevens matches were mayhem. Screaming, shouting, running, and laughing, too. Liz smiled and wrapped her arms around herself on the touchline. These moments were precious, she knew, and all the more so since Peter had left last year. Peter was her husband – soon to be ex-husband – and Freya's dad.

He'd just announced one day that he'd had enough, and that he was relocating to the Channel Islands where he'd got a new job managing offshore accounts for high net worth individuals. Liz hadn't even known he was applying for anything. That turned out to be just one of several secrets he'd been keeping from her, which included a girlfriend he'd been seeing on the side of their marriage for the past eight months. Or was it more accurate to describe *her* as the one who'd been on the side in Peter's life? Either way, he'd made it clear that he didn't expect Liz, or indeed Freya, to follow him to Jersey. *It'll be best if she stays in her school. She'll need you here.* And other excuses.

Just like that, their sixteen-year relationship was over.

In the following months, there'd been some dark days, but she was coming through those, now. She was lucky that her parents didn't live too far away. They were ten miles down the road, in

Surbiton, and both retired, which meant that one of them was able to collect Freya from school every day, take her home to Earlsfield, cook her dinner, and look after her until Liz got home from the office.

When Peter was here, she had done the school run most days, but without him – and before any kind of financial settlement was reached – Liz needed to work twice as hard. She didn't want them to lose their home, to have to move or even put Freya in a new school.

But those extra hours came at a price. She hated being apart from her daughter in the evenings, counting the minutes on her train ride back from the City and subsequent walk from the station to home.

She'd always text Freya to let her know she'd got off the train at Earlsfield and would be home in fifteen minutes. Freya would text back to say what bedtime story she'd chosen. Most nights, it was *The Tiger Who Came to Tea*. Liz wondered whether the father coming back at the end was Freya's favourite bit. Whatever the reason, that time together at the end of the day was sacred, and it always helped Liz unwind, too.

Her job as a loss adjustor was stressful, particularly when she saw first-hand the impact of a disaster on someone's life, and still had to value down their insurance pay-out. Just this week, she'd reduced a middle-aged man to tears when her assessment of the fire damage at his home failed to match up to the exorbitant claim he'd made. She didn't enjoy those types of encounters, of course, but loss adjusting was what she knew, and she did it well. She'd always been thorough, had an eye for detail. And having the work was vital now it was just her and Freya.

Liz had spent her professional life valuing other people's losses. But what was the cost of losing Peter, she wondered? Not even so much for her, but for Freya. How often would she see her father, now? She didn't yet understand why he was gone. And, when eventually she did, how would that affect her, as she grew into her teens?

The thought brought a lump to Liz's throat. She blinked away the prickling sensation in her eyes and hugged herself a bit tighter. Then, as loudly as she could, cheered again for her daughter.

CHAPTER SIXTY-TWO

Lockhart took a deep swig of hot, strong coffee; just what he needed to blow away the final cobwebs of his hangover. It was nearly 4 p.m. and, finally, his brain was starting to work a bit more effectively, thanks to the caffeine hit and a few more hours elapsing.

He and Smith had gone out for takeaway coffees and brought them back to the canteen. The place was empty, the serving shutters down for the weekend, but at least there was a bit more privacy here than at the Starbucks down the road. They needed to take stock and plan their next move.

'What you make of it all, Max?' he asked.

Smith pushed out her lower lip, shook her head. 'I don't know, to be honest, guv.'

After Green's call, he'd passed the name Blaze Logan to their MIT analyst, Lucy Berry. She was giving up part of her Sunday at home to research the stuntwoman. Smith had just explained how, earlier today, she'd also given Berry a name to check out – Jonathan Foster – based on his occupancy of a property close to where the victim was last caught on camera.

Lockhart rotated the cardboard cup slowly in his hand.

'Let's think about what we *do* know,' he said. 'There's a woman who was attacked at a bus stop three nights ago, by the man we believe to be our Op Braddock rapist. We get her DNA from a bloodstain on the knife he used to stab her. That DNA matches the profile of a skin sample taken from our third Thorncross victim,

Ernesto Gomez. Foreign DNA in a fingernail is usually an indicator of defensive action. And we saw the woman fighting the rapist. We know she's capable of violence. Those are the facts. So, our initial conclusion is that the bus stop victim attacked and killed Ernesto, which means she probably also murdered Charles Stott and Martin Johnson. But we can't definitively prove the murders, yet.'

'Yup,' was all Smith said.

'And beyond that,' he continued, 'we don't actually know anything about this woman or her motive. Lexi's got her theory about it being a stuntwoman called Blaze Logan, based on the victims' professions, the personality of a psychopath, an article in the *L.A. Times* about an accident during production of a movie, and the opinion of an online film nerd.' He tapped a fingertip on the table for each point.

Smith snorted. 'It is pretty vague, when you put it like that.'

'You think there's anything in it?'

'Impossible to say. It's like talking to one of those psychics, isn't it?' Smith closed her eyes and held up her palms as if summoning the spirits. 'I'm getting a *John*,' she said, grinning.

'John Foster?'

'It was the first name that came into my head.'

'Lexi would say that was your unconscious, or something.'

'Whatever.' Smith rolled her eyes.

'Until we know more about Logan and Foster, maybe the bigger question is how we present any of this to Porter.' Lockhart grimaced. 'He's already told me he wants everything I do on Thorncross run by him. And he's holding a DPS case over me if I don't toe the line.'

'You can tell him about the DNA link, right?'

'Yeah. But the name Blaze Logan came from Lexi. And she isn't supposed to know anything about this case. Porter told me not to brief her. Then the fact we know our victim's a fighter came from unauthorised camera surveillance.'

She took a sip of coffee. 'So, don't tell him *that* stuff.'

'Serious?'

Smith nodded. 'The DNA link is enough. Stagg will cover us on how we identified the bus stop victim.' She made quotation marks. 'His little "tip-off", remember?'

'So, we just say that the woman who we think was stabbed is now a person of interest in our murder inquiry?'

'Exactly.'

Lockhart considered this. It could work. 'All right,' he replied. 'You want to come with me and tell the big man about it, then?'

Before Smith could reply, his phone rang on the table. It was Berry.

'Luce,' he said, switching to speakerphone. 'Max is here, she's listening too.'

'Um, OK, great,' replied Berry. 'Hello, Max. I've got something for both of you, actually.'

'Really?' Smith glanced at Lockhart, her eyebrows raised.

'Go ahead, Luce.'

'Well, er, so it seems as though Blaze Logan isn't a real person. I mean, there's no one in Britain called Blaze Logan. So, it could be an alias she uses when working, like a stage name or something.'

'Hm.' Lockhart knew that would immediately make any tracing ten times harder, especially if the name change wasn't official. 'Any luck on her previous identity?'

'Not yet…'

'Bollocks.' Lockhart felt the weight growing in his neck and shoulders, his head suddenly heavy. What if Green was right, and they failed to find Logan at all?

'…but…'

He should've let Berry finish. 'Yup?'

'I did discover that Jonathan Foster is a freelance sound engineer. He works mostly on film and TV productions, and has a one-man company registered to his home address.'

There was a pause, then Lockhart said: 'You know how I feel about coincidences, Luce.'

Berry gave a small laugh. 'Well, um, you're going to like this one, then. Jonathan Foster worked on two films in the past four years which featured stunts by Blaze Logan, before she went off to the States about eighteen months ago.'

Lockhart and Smith stared at one another in silence.

After a few long seconds, Smith spoke. 'I knew he was hiding something.'

'Thanks, Luce. That's bloody good work.'

Berry listed the movies and Lockhart noted them down. He checked there was nothing else and ended the call.

'Well,' he said, 'Porter can wait. I think we need to pay another visit to your mate John.'

Smith nodded. 'My copper's nose never fails.'

CHAPTER SIXTY-THREE

'Pull in here,' said Smith. Lockhart braked and reversed his Defender into a kerbside space on the quiet residential road. He cut the engine and cracked a window.

Smith watched him check each of his mirrors before scanning the street ahead. Gone was the hungover wreck of earlier today. In its place was her usual guvnor, sharp and alert as a hunting dog. Smith could see that he'd switched into operational mode, now that he'd got the scent of a lead, and was reminded of what he used to do before he joined the Met. Given who they might find in this house, she was glad he was here with her.

'Which number?' he asked.

'Forty-three A,' she replied, making a subtle hand gesture towards the property. 'About thirty yards down on the right.'

He shifted in his seat, craned his neck. 'Green door, just before the one with the estate agent sign outside?'

'That's it.'

'Flat?'

'Yeah. Top half of a maisonette.'

'Fire escape at the back?'

'Don't know.'

Lockhart nodded. 'What do we reckon? Five p.m. on a Sunday. Is he going to be in?'

'More likely than if we came at this time on a weekday, I guess.'

He glanced at her. 'What does your copper's nose tell you?'

'Piss off.'

'Well, we've got eyes on now, at least.' Lockhart settled back in his seat.

'Can't see from here if anyone's in or not,' she observed. 'Can you?'

'Nope. I could always do a walk past in a bit, though. John doesn't know me, so if he is curtain-twitching, it won't spook him.'

'OK. You want to wait till Stagg arrives? He shouldn't be much longer.'

'Yup, let's hang on.'

When Smith and Lockhart had decided to drive to John Foster's house, they'd called Eddie Stagg over at Lavender Hill. Stagg had jumped at the chance to get away from his desk and see some potential action, especially connected to Op Braddock. His role was to park up at the other end of the street, sealing off at least one escape route in case this Blaze Logan character was inside, and chose to run. Which would be a crazy thing to do given she had a stab wound that, as far as they knew, was still untreated in a hospital. Crazy, but not impossible. People had taken much bigger risks to get away from the police.

Right now, the link between Logan, Foster, and Operations Braddock and Thorncross was largely circumstantial. There was no slam dunk, as the Americans liked to say, to confirm that Logan was the woman involved in either crime, or that Foster was hiding her. That meant there was little chance of getting the duty magistrate to sign off on an arrest or search warrant, especially on a Sunday. They were relying on Foster's co-operation, if he was home. And Smith knew they had to handle it sensitively.

So far, this Blaze Logan – whoever she was – had no crime to answer to. Their plan was to see if she was in Foster's apartment, or if he knew her whereabouts. Then, they'd ask to speak to her as a probable victim of the bus stop attack. If they managed to bring her in, that was a start. They might obtain a DNA sample from her as the victim of a violent crime, and they might get access to the property, where she could be storing items related to the murders.

That was the idea, at least. But if Logan was there and decided she didn't want to come, then they could have a serious problem. There was no Territorial Support Group – the boys and girls in riot gear who went in mob-handed for arrests of dangerous suspects. It was just Smith, Lockhart, and – when he finally got here – Stagg. She had her handcuffs, but she'd also seen this woman fighting in the camera footage. And her heart had been beating at about twice its normal rate since they'd left Jubilee House.

They'd been in position a few minutes when Smith's phone vibrated in her lap: Stagg. He told her he was at the north end of the road, meaning Foster's property was now sandwiched between them.

They were good to go.

'Let's see who's home,' said Lockhart.

Smith took a deep breath and let herself out of the car.

There were no signs of life at the windows as they approached the door. They knocked and waited. Smith leant in, listening carefully. Nothing.

Then her phone went again, sending a pulse of adrenalin through her body. She picked up.

'Lone male heading your way,' said Stagg. 'IC1,' he added, giving the description for white ethnicity. 'Short, curly hair. Matches the description of the occupant. You should be able to see him now. He's got shopping bags.'

Smith stepped back and squinted down the road. John Foster was walking towards them, head down. After a few more steps, he looked up and froze. He appeared to be considering his options. Apparently realising there was no way he could reasonably turn around now that she'd seen him, he proceeded cautiously towards them.

'Hello, John.' Smith kept her tone friendly.

'Hi.' His eyes flicked from her to Lockhart and back.

'Sorry to bother you.' She flashed a smile. 'This is my colleague, DI Lockhart. Do you mind if we come in for a minute?'

'Er, what do you want?' There was a tremor in his voice.

'We'd like to ask a few more questions about the other night, when we believe a woman who'd been seriously injured was in this area.'

'I… there isn't anything else I can tell you.' The supermarket carrier bags he was carrying rose and fell as he shrugged. He walked past Lockhart and put the bags in his right hand down while he fumbled in his pocket, eventually producing a set of keys.

'We'll only take a couple of minutes of your time,' Smith said pleasantly.

'It's not convenient now.' He moved past Smith and, with a shaking hand, threaded the key into the front door lock.

'Are you sure?' Smith asked.

'I can't help you,' he said, heaving the bags over the threshold of the open door.

'Max! Did you hear something inside?' Lockhart called from the path.

'I think I did, guv. Sounded like someone shouting for help.'

'What?' Foster turned in his hallway, dropping the bags.

But Smith was already inside, Lockhart right behind her.

'Wait!' yelled John.

CHAPTER SIXTY-FOUR

I was lucky I came back when I did. Any earlier and I'd have been in John's house when Lockhart and his mates arrived. Any later and they'd have been inside when I got there. As it was, they were helpfully standing right outside John's front door as I turned into the road, clearly trying to talk their way in. Dan Lockhart himself. I could hardly believe it.

John's a little mouse, so I didn't expect him to offer up any resistance to the police. But to his credit he did try to protest, and held them up before they pushed their way inside. I should thank him for that; it shows he had some loyalty. It still made me think, though, that I should've killed him earlier. That I shouldn't have been so lazy. Because I'm sure he's giving me up to the cops, right now. Everything he knows, at least. Which isn't much, but it's enough.

Standing down the road, watching this unfold, I started making a plan to follow them inside. To take advantage of Lockhart being there; to surprise him. Beat him to death there and then, along with that claw-handed sidekick of his. But, just as my excitement at the possibility grew, I noticed another guy heading for the house. A big bloke, barking into a mobile phone. And I began to wonder how many of them there were. If reinforcements were on the way, there was no chance of me getting out. It was an easy choice: escape first, fight later.

So, I pulled up my collar, turned around, and walked off back the way I came.

John told me yesterday that the police had visited, looking for the woman who was attacked at the bus stop. But, for them to return in a group, they must've found something more to link me to the address. Whatever that was, John is probably spilling his guts already. Which means I don't have much time to find somewhere to go.

It's not going to be easy. At least I've got one of John's bank cards. Sooner or later, he'll realise it's gone. I have my unregistered pay-as-you-go phone. My passport, which I always carry with me. And the clothes I'm standing up in. Nothing else.

The safest, most sensible option would be to travel to Victoria station, get on the next coach to France and disappear off somewhere in Europe. Never be seen here again.

It's tempting. Get away, start somewhere new.

But I haven't finished what I started here. And I'm not letting Lockhart get away with it that easily.

I think I'll stay for now.

DAY FOURTEEN

CHAPTER SIXTY-FIVE

There was a buzz of excitement as the MIT office filled up on Monday morning. It wasn't yet 9 a.m., but every desk was taken, and people had already resorted to standing. That, or thieving chairs from the neighbouring financial crime team at the other end of the open-plan office.

From his vantage position at the front, Lockhart looked out around the room. He counted every member of their twenty-four-strong MIT 8, plus a half-dozen extra detectives he knew had been seconded to them from MIT 4, in south-east London.

He caught the eye of two of those Lewisham detectives he recognised, DI Zac Boateng and DS Pat Connelly. Lockhart nodded and they both returned the acknowledgment. The pair had played a blinder last year on a murder in Deptford, spotting the similarities to other deaths Lockhart had been working on and passing the case to him immediately. Lockhart was pleased they were here.

There was a smartly dressed, competent-looking young woman sitting with them, who had 'fast track' written all over her. Lockhart didn't know who she was; he couldn't keep tabs on all the temporary staff Porter was drafting in to help on Op Thorncross. The more people working on this, though, the better. And if she was part of Boateng's team, that was good enough for him.

In addition to the Lewisham group, Lockhart noticed DS Eddie Stagg and DC Roland Wilkins sitting off to one side. Stagg was chomping on a bacon roll and simultaneously swigging from a large mug, while Wilkins stared at his phone screen, the young

DC's concentration and jerky hand movements suggesting he was playing a game. They'd be here for the Op Braddock links.

In fact, he thought, the only person who'd been involved in Thorncross who wasn't here was Lexi Green. Despite his – and Smith's – scepticism, Green was the one who had provided them with the name Blaze Logan. But inviting her here would mean admitting to Porter that he'd been keeping her in the loop all along. And he wasn't about to shoot himself in the foot like that. He'd just have to find a way to keep her included.

He'd already dismissed her ideas on this case at least twice. When was he going to learn? Whether casework or therapy or simply talking, Green made things better in his life.

Before he could interrogate that observation any further, the activity and volume began to rise, and Lockhart realised that DCI Porter had entered the office. The two of them would be delivering the briefing this morning for what now constituted a manhunt. Or, more accurately, a *woman*hunt. He'd never heard that term before. Then again, he didn't think he'd ever come across someone like Blaze Logan before.

Anyone who wasn't already in position for the meeting wheeled a chair across and crammed themselves into the space. The size of the crowd and the few unfamiliar people made the team update feel more like a press conference. They hadn't held an actual press conference, yet, but Lockhart had no doubt that Porter would be planning how best to cover the sizeable media angles on the operation, as soon as this briefing was over.

'All right,' boomed the DCI, 'gather round everyone and listen up. I can see some new faces here. But there are so many of us that if we did introductions we'd be here till lunchtime. So, I'll get straight into it and the faster we finish, the faster you lot can get cracking.'

Lockhart saw Khan fiddling with his phone. He looked as though he was texting. Then he happened to glance up and met Lockhart's gaze. Furtively, he pocketed the device.

'Now,' Porter announced, 'I have one word of warning before I ask DI Lockhart to bring us all up to speed. Many of you will have seen details of our ongoing murder investigation in the papers over the past week or so. Some of that information was privileged and known only to us. I want to make it absolutely clear that any unauthorised contact with the media will be dealt with swiftly, and decisively. And anyone who does decide to talk to a journalist without my say-so will be looking for a new job before the end of the week. Does everyone understand that?'

There was a good deal of murmuring, but Lockhart saw plenty of nodding heads and heard several *yes, sir* replies.

'Good. And that applies to discussing the details of this case with anyone outside this room, too. Right, Dan, over to you.'

'Thank you, sir.' Lockhart stood and moved to one side of the whiteboard they were using as a projector screen. He surveyed the assembled group; more than thirty faces focused on him.

'We have a new person of interest on Operation Thorncross,' he began. 'She goes by the name Blaze Logan, though we believe this is an alias. We're working to find out her real name, which should give us a passport photograph and further background intelligence.' He pressed the clicker in his hand and bullet points appeared on screen under the heading of the op name. Helpfully, someone had inserted an image of a blank face with a '?' in the middle of it.

He clicked again and a second picture came up. It showed a woman in motorbike leathers astride a dirt bike, crash helmet under one arm. With the lighting and grainy quality, her face wasn't clear. 'Luce has found a few photos online that we think are of her. This one's probably the best. As you can see, it's not great.'

'We discovered Logan almost by chance,' continued Lockhart. 'Because we believe she was the victim of a stabbing and attempted rape four nights ago. That attack was one of a series of sex crimes in south-west London which DS Eddie Stagg, over there—' he indicated Stagg, who half-stood up, hastily wiping his mouth with a napkin, 'has been working on in Wandsworth CID, along with DS Max Smith from our MIT, under the banner Operation Braddock.'

He paused to let the information sink in a moment. People seemed to be following so far.

'The perpetrator of those assaults is unknown, so keep in mind that we may uncover evidence of his identity during this investigation. In fact, we believe Logan is the only one of his victims to have seen his face, because she fought back and removed his mask.'

'How do we know that?' Porter snapped.

Lockhart froze momentarily. He wasn't sure if he'd said too much. He took a sip of coffee to give himself a moment to think before he answered.

'The morning after Logan was attacked,' he said, 'an eyewitness came forward to say that they'd seen a woman possibly being assaulted at a bus stop in Colliers Wood, between Wimbledon and Tooting, the previous night. Officers attended the scene and discovered a bloodstained knife. Analysis of—'

'Why didn't the eyewitness call 999 at the time of the attack?' interjected Porter.

Lockhart didn't respond immediately. *Because the 'eyewitness' was drunk on Stella and passed out on his sofa…*

'We don't know, sir.' Stagg spoke loudly and confidently from the side of the room. 'He or she may not have been sure of what they saw, at first. They described a fight, so it may not have been clear who was the victim until they thought about it later. It's also possible they didn't have access to a telephone immediately. They might've been scared of reprisal. And, of course, there are members of our community who are very wary of contact with the police. We suspect it's the latter reason, hence the fact it was an anonymous tip.'

Porter frowned, but he didn't say anything more. Lockhart had to hand it to Stagg, he was a good bullshitter.

'Analysis of the blood on the knife,' Lockhart resumed, 'provided a match with a sample taken from the body of Ernesto Gomez.' He clicked again, bringing up a photo they'd been given by Gomez's boyfriend, Paul Newton. It showed the Colombian set designer holding a beer and smiling in what looked like a pub garden. 'The material was under Gomez's fingernails, which indicates a probable defensive wound. Our hypothesis is that Logan attacked Gomez and may therefore be a suspect in Op Thorncross. Given the identical MO and signature of the three Thorncross murders, she could also therefore be responsible for killing Charles Stott and Martin Johnson. At the very least, she's a significant person of interest.'

Lockhart could already see one or two expressions of puzzlement among the group.

'Now, some of you might be wondering how we were able to identify the victim from the bus stop as Blaze Logan,' he continued. 'This was the result of painstaking work by DS Stagg, DS Smith and our analyst, Lucy Berry.' Lockhart spotted Berry in the group and gestured to her. She immediately blushed a deep red and shrank slightly in her chair. 'Based on the eyewitness report of the attack, we traced the journey of the victim away from the bus stop into neighbouring streets, where home CCTV supplied by a member of the public gave us a range of properties into which the victim could've gone.'

Another pause. He noticed a couple of nods.

'House-to-house inquiries found that one of these addresses was occupied by a man named Jonathan Foster. He initially behaved evasively but eventually disclosed to us that he had a female friend named Blaze Logan staying with him who was out on the night of the bus stop attack and came back shortly after what we believe to be the time of the assault. In his bathroom bin, we found a quantity of bloodied tissues consistent with a serious injury, as well as a used needle and some fishing line, suggesting that she'd sutured her own stab wound.'

This was met with a smattering of audible winces, gasps and expletives from the room.

'We also found clothing in the room she'd been staying in at Mr Foster's home, which matched the outfit the eyewitness described the woman at the bus stop as wearing. Further discussion with Mr Foster gave us the backstory of Blaze Logan.'

Lockhart went on to describe Logan's work as a stuntwoman, her move to the US, the accident that left her seriously injured and the lack of compensation she received before being deported to the UK.

'There is a strong possibility,' he added, 'that her motive for the murders is something connected to her profession as a stunt performer, since two of the victims also worked in the film industry. Though what her exact connection to those individuals is, we have yet to discover.' Now wasn't the time to share Green's theory of surrogate victims. He was only just getting his head around it himself.

'Great work, Dan.' Porter leant back in his chair. 'What are the priority follow-up actions?'

Lockhart clicked on to the next slide and brought up more bullet points.

'We need to find out Blaze Logan's real name. Our best bet for that is the US embassy, because they'll have a record of a visa application for her some time around eighteen months ago. Luce assures me there are very few professional stunt performers in the UK, so tracing her application should be possible. If we go through our FBI liaison in the embassy, we'll have an answer within a couple of hours. We're also checking with the British Stunt Register in case she's on their books.'

'Good.' Porter made a note.

'We have Foster's laptop, too, which he said Logan used regularly during the time she was staying in his home. We can request data exploitation on that, see if her search history gives us any clues on her intentions.'

'Excellent.'

'Max also got Mr Foster to check his personal possessions, and he discovered that his emergency bank card was missing from his wallet. It's not a card he uses often, and it only has a few hundred pounds in the account. He wanted to cancel it, but Max persuaded him to leave it in case Logan has it. Might enable us to trace her movements.'

'Fine.' Porter tapped the notebook with his pen, then said: 'Is she using a phone?'

'We don't know, sir.'

'Double check with Foster if he knows anything about it.'

'Sir.'

'The second you have a confirmed photograph, get it out to the UK Borders, airports, ferry terminals, anywhere else she might go. And all boroughs for patrol units, obviously, plus every other police force in the country. She's had, what, a seventeen-hour head start on us? She could be anywhere by now.'

Lockhart nodded, but he didn't agree with Porter's final point. Green had told him about humans' natural response when faced with a threat: fight or flight. And he didn't think Logan was someone to flee from danger. She was like him. She was a fighter.

CHAPTER SIXTY-SIX

I wake up, blink a few times, then remember where I am. There's a warm, slumbering body next to me. Still fast asleep. I think I wore him out last night. What was his name, again? Joseph? Or was it Gareth? Doesn't matter. The only thing that mattered was that he was there, last night, in the club. A brief conversation confirmed that he was single, and that he lived alone. Those were the only two things I cared about. The fact that he wasn't hideously unattractive was a bonus. His job was something to do with web design… user experience, maybe. He said his clients were mostly in the US, and he didn't need to start work until midday, so he was having a big Sunday night. I hope his clients won't miss his services too much. Actually, I don't give a shit about his clients, just as long as no one comes searching for him anytime soon.

I take another look at him, lying there, one arm thrown above his head, fingers splayed as if he's waving to someone. Maybe he is, in a dream. It's the sort of thing he'd do; he seems like a nice guy. His only mistake was – like most men – thinking with his cock. It didn't occur to him to ask why a woman who was out of his league was picking *him* up in a club, why I was so interested in the *privacy* of his apartment. Why I gave him almost no information about myself. Why I made him leave without telling his mates.

I feel a burst of excitement as I push myself up into a kneeling position, pick up the pillow I've been sleeping on, and straddle him. He stirs as my weight settles on top of him. I lift the pillow, just as his eyes open a fraction. He registers that it's me, and there's half a smile on his face as he closes his eyes again. Perhaps he thinks I want some more of him. That this is my special way of waking him up. But he couldn't be more wrong.

It's my way of making sure he stays asleep.

A muffled sound escapes his lips as I press the pillow onto his face and hold it firmly down. I know he isn't strong enough to resist me. Still, he starts to struggle, presumably as he realises this isn't a kinky game. It takes a surprisingly long time, perhaps almost two minutes, before the flailing and thrashing is over and he stops moving.

When I'm certain he isn't breathing any longer, I roll back onto my side of the bed. Remove the pillow I just suffocated him with, sit up and use it to support my lower back, which is hurting almost as much as my stupid stab wound. I reach across to the bedside table for his MacBook laptop. I open it and take his limp right hand from beside him. Touch his index finger to the corner button on the keyboard. And it opens. Thank you, Joseph. Or Gareth.

I fire up the web browser.

There's work to be done.

CHAPTER SIXTY-SEVEN

Lexi threw the teaspoon into her kitchen sink, took a slurp of tea too soon, scalded her mouth, and growled. She was still mad about getting cut out of the Thorncross case, after discovering the name of Blaze Logan. She deserved better than that. She'd given Dan's team their serial murder suspect on a plate, working for free, and all he'd promised was to 'look her up'. And she hadn't heard anything more about it since.

She tried to reason with herself. This case wasn't about her. She didn't need recognition; she wasn't a narcissist, right? It should be enough to know that she'd done something useful. And yet, it gnawed at her. Did she want Dan's approval, was that it? Or did it go deeper than that? Was it about trying to compensate for those other losses she could've prevented? She thought of her brother, Shep, and of her old flatmate, Liam. The sense of guilt made her feel a little sick.

There had to be more she could do. What about Operation Braddock, the bus stop attacks? She'd only succeeded in confusing and alienating the detectives with her profile on that, because it wasn't clear – but how many cases were? Models and theories were always neat, reality was a whole lot more complicated. She was doing her best, all things considered. But it wasn't enough. Lexi resolved to take her tea upstairs and do some more research.

At the top of the stairs, she noticed that Rhys's bedroom door was open. That was odd. Normally, he kept it shut. She paused, throwing a glance back down the stairs. Should she?… No, it was his space. He was entitled to his privacy. But she *was* the main leaseholder, and he wasn't home. She hesitated a little more. Then her curiosity got the better of her and she went inside.

Rhys's room smelled how she remembered Shep's room smelling as an unwashed teenage boy; sweat, dirty clothes, stinky shoes and other odours Lexi didn't want to interrogate too closely. She moved across to Rhys's desk and put her tea down next to his computer. It occurred to her that she really knew very little about him at all. Surely, she had a right to know about the guy she was sharing a house with. Didn't she?

She scanned the items on his desk: several half-empty bottles of those mega-caffeinated energy drinks, a games controller whose cable went to the PC, some letters with the hospital logo at the top, a copy of *WIRED* magazine, and a plain book.

Lexi reached for the book, and flipped it open at random. It was a journal, handwritten. She read a line, having to work hard to decipher the messy scrawl:

…not that I don't want a girlfriend, it's just better that I'm not involved in anything now because of what happened…

She snapped the diary shut and put it back. She should leave right away.

But she didn't follow the thought. Instead, she held still a second, listened. There was no sound.

Unable to stop herself, she moved to the set of drawers beside the desk and eased open the top one. It contained Rhys's socks and underwear. She assumed they were clean, but it was still gross. She was about to close it again when something smooth at the back caught her eye.

She eased the balled socks and boxers to one side. And couldn't believe what she was looking at. A knife.

Not just any knife, a long-bladed, curving, serrated, evil-looking thing.

Her mouth was dry, pulse thumping in her neck.

'What are you doing?'

The voice almost made her heart stop and she whipped round to see Rhys in the doorway. How had she not heard him come in?

'Rhys, I was, uh—'

'Why are you looking in my drawer?'

She needed to get a hold of herself. This was serious. She couldn't back down, now.

'There's a goddam knife in here,' she said.

He stepped over and peered in. Lexi could smell his body odour. She moved slightly away, conscious of how close they were. Sarah wasn't home yet and she felt suddenly vulnerable.

'Oh, yeah,' he replied. 'That.'

Her gaze involuntarily rose to the birthmark on his forehead, but she brought it back down again and made full eye contact. 'What the hell is a knife like that doing in this house, huh?'

'It's... um, it's a collecting thing. Like a, sort of a hobby.'

'A hobby?' She raised her eyebrows. 'Are you kidding me?'

'No. It's a zombie knife.'

'What the *actual* fuck?'

'I swear.' He shrugged. 'You collect them. You know, it's like, from films and video games and stuff.'

'Is it real?'

'Well, er, it's made out of metal, if that's what you mean. But I don't think it's sharp—'

'I'm calling the cops.' She took out her cellphone.

'Hang on.' Rhys held up both hands. 'Sorry. I'll get rid of it.'

Lexi snorted a breath through her nostrils, her lips pressed tight together.

'Today,' Rhys added. 'I promise.'

Lexi jabbed a finger at the drawer. 'Go put it in a knife amnesty bin right now.'

'Yes,' he said meekly. 'Where is it, again?'

'Jeez.' She sighed. 'There's one in Brixton. Just Google it or whatever.'

Her phone vibrated in her hand. The screen flashed up to show it was a text from Dan. When she looked back up, Rhys was squinting at the screen.

'I mean it.' She held up the palm of her free hand. 'Get that thing out of this house, like, immediately. And if you don't, or if I see anything else like that here ever again, you'll be finding a new place to live. Got it?'

Rhys mumbled another apology.

Lexi grabbed her tea, its presence on the desk a reminder that she shouldn't have been in here at all, and walked out. It was only when she got inside her own room and shut the door that she realised she was shaking.

She took a sip of tea and opened the text from Dan.

It read:

Sorry. You were right again. Need your help. Please call.

CHAPTER SIXTY-EIGHT

I've found her. It took all day, but she's in my sights, now. There are plenty of loss adjustors in London, all greedily trying to get their little commissions by screwing over insurance claimants. But I wanted one who lived within walking distance of my new home in Clapham. The home that belonged to Joseph (not Gareth, his driving licence confirmed it) until this morning. Technically, it's still his. He just doesn't need it anymore.

It wasn't enough, however, simply to find a loss adjustor who lived in south-west London. He or she had to have a predictable life, so I could locate them easily. Most people who work in insurance have a routine existence. That goes hand in hand with their choice of profession. It doesn't necessarily mean you can find out where they live. Thank God for mummy blogging is all I can say.

Liz Jennings. She's posted all about juggling work and motherhood. About her beautiful little daughter, Freya, who loves to play football. And about her journey to and from work. Why do people feel the need to overshare like that? Would they just tell strangers this stuff in the street or on a train? Probably not. But, somehow, if it's online, that's OK. *Here's my entire life…* If they knew how much it made them a target, though, they'd think twice.

I've borrowed a jacket and baseball cap from Joseph.

It's gone 7 p.m., and Liz will be leaving work soon.

Time to go and take a look at her.

DAY FIFTEEN

CHAPTER SIXTY-NINE

'Millicent Dimmock.' Lockhart studied the enlarged passport photograph on one of Lucy Berry's monitors. It was hard to reconcile the friendly sounding name with the actions of the woman who had been calling herself Blaze Logan for the past five years.

'Millicent Susanne Dimmock, born July twenty-first, nineteen eighty-nine,' stated Berry.

Smith leant in. 'No wonder she used a stage name. Doesn't sound like a stunt performer.'

'Or a serial killer,' added Khan. He was standing slightly behind them.

Lockhart suspected that few – if any – serial killers sounded like serial killers just from the names they'd been given at birth. He imagined Green would have some clever theory to explain how we associated the names of the most infamous ones with murder, even though there was nothing special about their names. Probably because killers weren't as different to the rest of us as we'd like to think. Even if some were psychopaths – as Green had explained again to him last night on the phone – they were still members of our society, and at least a part of their actions was explained by the way society had treated them. If anyone understood how fine the line was between a killer and everyone else, it was Lockhart.

Khan cleared his throat. 'Is it wrong to say she's pretty hot?'

'Yes, Mo, it is.' Smith turned to him; her expression severe. 'It's not relevant. If our suspect was a bloke, you wouldn't be saying that at all.'

'Would you, though?'

'No.'

There was a moment's silence.

'It could be relevant,' said Lockhart. 'If she uses her looks to charm people, to help her get what she wants. People always talk about how Ted Bundy did that. It's a psychopathic characteristic, superficial charm.'

'Maybe,' conceded Smith.

'It is,' Lockhart said. 'Dr Green told me.'

'Hm.'

'Doesn't look like her name change was official,' said Berry, clicking into another window on her second screen. 'Then again, it is legal to just start using a different name.'

Lockhart briefly wondered whether his wife, Jess, had changed her name after she disappeared. Whether she was living somewhere under a completely different identity. He forced his focus back to the screen.

'I guess it suited her to have at least two identities,' he observed. 'Have we run down everything we can get on Millicent Dimmock?'

Lockhart wasn't fully up to speed on yesterday's progress; after calling Green, he'd spent a large part of the evening meeting Ernesto Gomez's parents, who'd flown in from Colombia that morning. He and Porter had explained what they knew and what they were doing to catch their son's killer, all through a Spanish interpreter. Smith had texted him the key updates around 10 p.m., but this was the first chance he'd had to see the results for himself.

'Not yet, Dan.' Berry gestured to the screen. 'Info only came through from the US embassy late yesterday afternoon. We're expecting confirmation of her biodata from the British Stunt Register this morning, which might give us more to work with. It's a start.'

'As I mentioned last night, guv,' said Smith, 'we shared the photo with Foster. He says it's Logan. Told us her hair's a bit shorter now, but otherwise she's recognisable from that image.'

'Good.' Lockhart rubbed his chin. 'And the image has gone out to UK Borders and all police forces nationally? As well as every London borough team?'

'Yes,' replied Berry. 'DI Boateng was in charge of that. He stayed late with his Lewisham people to get it done.'

Lockhart nodded. He made a mental note to thank Boateng for his work. 'Has it been circulated more widely?'

'Not yet, guv,' said Smith. 'We haven't gone full press and public.'

'Press?' came a deep voice behind them. It was Porter.

They each greeted him with a *sir*, except Berry, who called him Marcus. Civilian staff mostly avoided ranks and titles.

'I think we should call a press conference for eleven a.m. today,' Porter said, as he walked over to their group. 'We bring the media up to speed on the new Thorncross developments and get the image out there in every newspaper and on the web. Flood social media. See what comes back.'

Lockhart wasn't sure that was the best tactic. 'With respect, sir—'

'We control the narrative,' Porter held up a hand. 'That way, we get our story in ahead of potential leaks.' He paused, scanning their faces. 'Not that I'm anticipating any more, obviously.'

'On the other hand,' Lockhart countered, 'if we keep the search low profile, we avoid spooking Logan. Then there's more chance of her making a mistake, and of us catching her. We'd have the advantage.'

That was how they operated in Lockhart's old military unit, and they usually found the people they were looking for.

Porter shook his head, as if Lockhart's suggestion was hopelessly naive. 'Our best *advantage*,' said the DCI, 'is to use the public. Get them on our side. Community policing.'

'It may not help, sir,' protested Lockhart. 'Logan is someone who's used to changing her appearance. She's done it professionally for years in her stunt work. She may already look different to how Foster described her.'

'But someone must've seen her since she left his house.' The DCI folded his arms. 'She might be physically capable, but she's not invisible.'

Lockhart was aware that the atmosphere had become strained, and others nearby were listening to the disagreement now. He tried to keep his tone level. 'We could generate leads on her whereabouts by other means.'

Porter arched his eyebrows. 'Such as?'

'Foster's bank card, for one.'

'And have we had any hits on that?'

Lockhart didn't know. He looked to his team.

'Nothing so far,' Berry said.

'We can check again this morning,' added Khan.

'I hear what you're saying, Dan,' Porter nodded thoughtfully. 'But the fact is that going public is also a deterrent to Logan attempting any further murders. Which is what we believe she was planning, right?'

'Yes, sir. Two more.'

'Two?' Porter folded his arms. 'How do you know that?'

Lockhart cursed himself for saying too much. He had to explain, now. 'It's the symbols we think she's drawn on the victims. There are five elements in ancient alchemy or wicca, whatever. She's drawn one on each of the three bodies so far.'

'Since when did you become an expert in reading occult symbols?' Porter looked incredulous.

'I'm not.' Lockhart decided it best not to elaborate. But there was one more thing Green had told him last night, which he wanted to share. 'I'm not sure going public will be a deterrent, sir. From the violence she's carried out already, we believe Logan's a psychopath. That means she's likely to be a thrill-seeker, a risk taker. A media circus could give her even more reason to attack. She'll take it as a challenge. A chance for publicity, even.'

Porter emitted a noise somewhere between a snort and a laugh. 'Where are you getting this stuff from, Dan? It sounds like you've been speaking to that psychologist. Which, obviously, would be against my direct instructions to keep the details of this case strictly within the investigative team.'

'I understand that, sir.' He paused. 'I might've mentioned a few aspects of the case to her, informally, as part of a general discussion. But no more than what has appeared in the papers.'

Porter stared at Lockhart for a few seconds, his mouth slightly open. 'I hope not, for both of your sakes. We can prosecute civilians for disclosing details of police operations, too.'

No one spoke.

'Right,' said Porter, 'that's decided, then. We're going public.'

'Sir—'

'Get back to your actions. I'll expect another update at four p.m. And I want a predictive analysis of who our suspect is likely to target next. That can go in the media briefing. Enhanced public safety.'

Lockhart swore under his breath as Porter marched away towards his office. No one spoke until he'd gone inside and closed the door.

'Predictive analysis?' Smith sounded baffled.

'I think that's what you call crystal ball gazing, Max.'

'Do we have any idea who she's going after next?' asked Berry.

'We don't,' replied Lockhart. 'But I know someone who might.'

CHAPTER SEVENTY

Lexi jotted the word *NerdCave* on her notepad. She needed to go back to the movie forum and ask CaptainCali for any more details he had on the accident that injured Blaze Logan. She also planned to re-read the *L.A. Times* piece. Right after this session with her private patient, Oliver Soames. She forced herself to tune in to him.

'…she was the first woman I'd really loved, you see. Or felt anything for at all, in fact. I mean, apart from my mother, of course.' He shifted in his seat. 'I think that was partly why it hurt so much. Why it made me so upset, so… so angry.'

'Uh-huh.' Lexi nodded slowly, aware she'd missed the beginning of what he'd said. 'Can you tell me a little more about that please, Olly?'

'More?' His face creased in confusion, and then he winced, and his hand went to a large Band-Aid on his cheek.

'You OK?' she asked.

'Bloody well cut myself shaving this morning. Like an idiot.'

'Right.' She wondered whether to gently challenge his self-criticism. But she decided to leave it, for now. 'So, yeah, uh, can you say some more on that?'

'Which bit?' he asked.

Lexi was momentarily wrong-footed. She'd been a terrible therapist today, barely listening to Olly's usual ranting about his ex-partner and the abortion. She knew she should be more sympathetic, particularly considering she'd been through the same thing with her ex. But Olly wasn't using the sessions how she'd intended, and every attempt she made to bring them back on track met with resistance from him.

Private patients were sometimes like this; they thought their money bought them the right to dictate the agenda, the course of treatment, even. A good therapy session should be collaborative. But she hadn't felt a sense of co-operation once with him, despite trying hard. Besides, since Dan's call earlier to ask for her help in profiling Logan's potential victims, she'd thought of little else. Now, she had a chance to make a difference on something that really mattered.

'The part about, uh, loving her,' suggested Lexi, latching on to a word she did remember him saying. 'Feeling something for her.'

Olly crossed one leg over the other. 'Well, I hadn't had much luck with women before I met her. Not even really luck. Just… experience. Inevitable consequence of an education in boys-only schools, I suppose. None of us had any clue how to talk to them. You. Women, I mean.' He shrugged and gave a brief, self-deprecating smile.

Just for a second, Lexi caught a glimpse of what Olly might've been like before the abortion. Charming, in a kind of awkward, British way. Hugh Grant in *Notting Hill*. Only less hot. Like, a lot less hot. Lexi felt her mouth making an involuntary smile and covered it with her hand. Jeez, she was being so unprofessional. Olly might be an entitled douchebag who oozed male privilege, but he deserved better than the service she was providing right now. *Get your shit together, Lexi.*

'But it sounds as though that changed when you met her,' she commented.

He closed his eyes briefly, nodded. 'It did. I remember our first date.'

'Why don't you tell me about it? What you guys did, what attracted you to her.'

'Really?' Olly fished in his pocket, produced a piece of gum, and popped it in his mouth.

'Sure.' Lexi quickly rationalised the request by telling herself this was a good way to help Olly access a positive memory. To bring him out of his irritable low mood for a while. To model a different connection between thoughts and emotions.

But the reality was that him talking for another five minutes would give her more time to think about Blaze Logan's potential victims, and take them up to the end of the session, when she could get back online. Lexi hoped she'd find something useful to tell Dan. She needed the good deed to balance out how she was treating Olly. Otherwise, she was definitely going to hell. Or wherever it was that bad therapists were sent.

CHAPTER SEVENTY-ONE

Smith had timed it to perfection. She'd brewed her final coffee of the day and positioned herself beside the 'snack table'; that spot in any office where biscuits, cakes, chocolate and general leftover food were all placed for the locusts to graze. Importantly, her advantageous eating position hadn't compromised her view of the big-screen TV.

Most of the team had paused their work and had gathered round to watch. Andy Parsons nudged the volume higher as a BBC London News anchor threw to the room at New Scotland Yard where Porter and Lockhart were taking their places behind a desk equipped with microphones. Behind them, a large screen displayed tiled Met Police logos interspersed with the strapline: *Working together for a safer London.*

The next shot from the back of the room showed the assembled media: journalists crowded in, photographers and cameramen standing around the hacks. The occasional flash popped off, casting a ghostly glow over the boss and the guvnor for a split second each time. Porter was decked out in his full dress uniform, hat under his arm, evidently comfortable in the limelight. He looked every inch the Detective Superintendent-in-waiting.

By contrast, Lockhart looked as though he didn't want to be there at all. Despite the smartness of his suit and tie, he clearly hadn't shaved, and his face and eyes bore the stress of two weeks in which Smith knew he hadn't slept much. His body language was unusually sluggish as he walked in and took his seat, and it seemed as though he'd rather be anywhere but in that room. Smith had a pretty good idea why.

Lockhart had made no secret of his opposition to Porter's idea to go public on the identity of Blaze Logan, aka Millicent Susanne Dimmock. She knew that the DCI was a political, media-savvy, career-minded operator. Lockhart didn't give a shit about any of that. He just wanted to catch killers using whatever techniques were best to get the job done. If Smith had to choose between the two approaches, she'd take Lockhart's one every time.

But the guvnor wasn't without his faults; most notably his insistence on bringing Dr Lexi Green and her psychobabble into the tent. Smith still wasn't sure what was going on between them. She knew Lockhart was a married man – albeit that his wife was missing, as she'd discovered through a Google search one evening a few months back – but was he interested in Green? That was the most likely explanation, but Smith understood their relationship about as well as she understood the mind-reading stuff.

She got that criminals made decisions about their acts; that was half of the basis of our legal system for prosecuting them. But she had no time for delving into childhood experiences, for fancy phrases like *raptophilia* and endless speculation about how someone might've been feeling when they attacked another person with a mallet. She dealt in facts, hard evidence. That was what secured convictions, not Dr Green's Mystic Meg-style lottery predictions. Smith had given that a go on Op Braddock, largely out of desperation, but it'd got them nowhere, proving her right.

Porter had started speaking and Smith was nibbling on a Jaffa Cake, admiring his stage presence, when there was a whisper behind her. An educated, female voice.

'DS Smith?'

She turned. 'Ah, DS… Jones, isn't it?' Smith obviously knew the smart young woman's name. She just didn't want her getting ideas above her station. Especially not in *her* team.

'Can I have a word, please?' She was holding a laptop.

'Er…' Smith glanced back to the screen. 'Can it wait?'

'Not really.'

Smith sighed gently and finished her Jaffa Cake, taking another one for the road. 'Come on, then.'

In a quieter section of the office, Jones displayed the laptop screen to her. There was a spreadsheet of neatly arranged columns and rows, each containing tiny text.

'We've been cataloguing the technical exploit from Jonathan Foster's laptop,' said Jones. 'Which he told us Logan was using while she stayed at his house.'

'OK.' Smith planted her hands on her hips. The thought occurred to her that this woman was just a kid, twenties at most, but had already achieved the same rank as her. Smith had probably been in the Met almost as long as Jones had been alive. Something about that annoyed her.

'There's a clear pattern of research into the three victims so far,' continued Jones confidently. 'Charles Stott, Martin Johnson, Ernesto Gomez.'

'I know who the victims are.'

'Of course. Well, it's just that, between victims one and two, Logan appears to have spent a lot of time reading about DI Lockhart.'

Smith pushed her lips out. She was tempted to make a joke about how many members of the MIT had probably done the same, out of curiosity at the guvnor's mysterious military past, or his missing wife.

'If you look at this list of searches and links followed,' added Jones, tapping her fingernail on the screen, 'you can see she was trying to go quite deep into his past.'

'Hm.'

'Including archived news articles about his wife.'

'I see.'

Jones waited. She was clearly expecting more of a response.

'And what's your concern about this?' asked Smith.

'Only that, well, could there be a risk to DI Lockhart?'

Smith exhaled slowly. 'Look, it's not uncommon in major investigations for perpetrators to try and find out about the coppers involved,' she explained. 'Sometimes they're thinking about coercion, pressure on family members. Other times, it's just plain curiosity. I wouldn't worry about it too much. I think the guvnor can look after himself.'

The young woman clearly wasn't satisfied by this. 'Well, I'll log it in my write-up. Just thought I'd mention it to you, since, you know, you're in his team.'

'Thanks. He'll appreciate that.'

'Right, then.' Jones closed the laptop. But she didn't move away from the desk.

'Anything else?' asked Smith.

'Um, yes, there is one thing, actually.' Jones leant in, lowered her voice. 'I just thought I'd let you know about the guy who's joined us from Wandsworth CID.'

'DS Stagg?'

'No, DC Wilkins.'

'Oh, I see. What about him?'

'Well, it's probably nothing, but he and I used to be in the same team. Cyber Crime.'

Typical, thought Smith. Stick the graduate on the computers while the real coppers were out on the streets.

'It's just that, in the Cyber team, he was a bit, well… creepy.'

'Creepy?'

Jones nodded. 'Watching, staring. Then the occasional bump into you, a brush against you, that kind of thing. All deniable, of course. But I still felt pretty uncomfortable with it, to be honest.'

Smith wondered if this was naivety on Jones's part. She was a pretty young woman and, wherever she went, men of all ages were going to check her out. Especially in a job where eighty per cent of her colleagues were male. As far as Smith was concerned, that was her cross to bear; the beauty 'tax'. Smith was no oil painting, but even she got the odd lewd comment. It wasn't right, but it happened. You dealt with it, told the guy to piss off, and usually it was fine. End of.

'I'm just letting you know, as a woman,' Jones added, with a kind of awkward, flat smile.

'Appreciate it.' Smith nodded towards the TV. 'Shall we get back and see what the boss is saying?'

'Sure.'

As they crossed back towards the main group, Khan approached and intercepted her. Could she not just watch her colleagues on the news for quarter of an hour in peace?

'Max,' he said urgently, 'we've got something.'

'What is it, Mo?' She had one eye on the screen. Porter was speaking while Lockhart sipped water, his head bowed. Behind them, a giant photograph of Logan filled the screen.

'It's Foster's bank card,' said Khan.

The words got her attention. 'It's been used?'

'Yup. In a club in Clapham. Two nights ago. The payment's only just come through.'

Smith accepted that listening to the press conference was a lost cause. She finished her coffee. 'All right. Let's get over there, then.'

CHAPTER SEVENTY-TWO

When I dreamt of seeing my face on the big screen, I didn't imagine it'd be a wanted poster.

Stunt performers are usually in the background. We get smashed into walls and thrown off buildings, we're blown up and set on fire. And we don't really get much acknowledgment for any of it. Our names appear three-quarters of the way down the end credits of any movie or TV programme, long after everyone's left the cinema or switched off Netflix. Which is fine by me.

I never wanted to be an actor. They have to emote, and I don't really do emotions. Except perhaps blind rage. I do that pretty well. But actors have to cry on demand, and I don't… I mean, I can't remember ever doing that.

Stunt work, on the other hand, was made for me. I loved it. I'd found my thing in life. And it was enough, among those who knew, to be considered good. That gets you more work, which means more money, so you can buy the stuff you want. Stuff you never had growing up. And there's plenty of free time to do whatever the hell you like.

I nearly got there. *Leopardess* was supposed to be my break. But the only thing that ended up broken was my body, when I slammed into a concrete wall that shouldn't have been there. The director had insisted I do the stunt without a co-ordinator on set, because everything else was ready to go. Before the take, the designer moved the wall, and the wire I was on pulled me into it at full speed. Then everything went black.

When I came to in hospital, much later, and discovered they'd blamed it all on me, that was the moment I switched. The moment I decided to give in to the fantasy I'd held since I first stamped on all those insects under the log. To make them pay.

Speaking of which, I'm across the road from Earlsfield train station, hat and scarf on, waiting impatiently for her to appear. The mummy-blogging loss adjustor. I'll follow her home, and work out where I'm going to strike. That point where she's alone, with no witnesses, no cameras, no help. Not that it matters too much, now that they know who I am.

Maybe Lockhart and his mates thought that by putting my face all over TV and social media – even the free London newspapers, I've just discovered – they'd scare me off attempting the next murder. But they're wrong about that. Their publicity hasn't put me off. It's just given me even more reason to get on with it quickly.

And, right on cue, here she is.

*

Liz Jennings emerged from the station amid the usual throng of people. Jostling and shoving, desperate to get through the ticket barriers and make their way home. This evening hadn't been too bad, although she'd needed to stand up for the entire journey, because it was so crowded. But on the days when it was cold and wet, leaving home in pre-dawn darkness, returning after dusk, and commuting in and out of the centre of town on delayed trains like so many sardines rammed into a can, she did wonder. Was there another life, with more sunlight and fresh air, more movement and happiness? Perhaps there was. There had to be.

But Liz couldn't just think about herself. Her priority now was Freya, and whatever she needed to do to keep life going. That was all that mattered. And if long, miserable commuting days were what was required, she'd do it for a hundred years if it meant she and Freya could have a few hours of happiness together in their home.

Once she was free of the melee at the station entrance, Liz pulled out her phone and texted her daughter.

Walking back now. Hope you've been good for Grandpa! What story would you like sweetie? xx

Spurred on by the thought of seeing Freya in just a few minutes, Liz dropped the phone into her bag and picked up her pace.

*

I follow her away from the station, around corners and along streets. Keeping my distance, on the other side of the road, shielded by parked cars on both sides. She's got her head down, not even slowing as she plucks a phone from her handbag and taps out some kind of message before shoving it back in there.

Gradually, the other commuters drop away, turning off onto side streets and into their homes, until it's just me and her. I'm trying to find the best place to strike. There are no parks, unfortunately, nowhere that's easy to slip into and out of, unnoticed. It's residential housing, terraces as far as you can see in every direction. It'll have to be here.

When I left Joseph's house earlier, I didn't think I'd do it tonight. This was just going to be another recce, building on last night's research. There's no particular rush, I told myself. The cops might know who I am, but they don't know *where* I am. Lockhart and his gang have finally stepped up their game and risen to my challenge. But they're still some way off. It's just a recce…

On the other hand, she and I seem to be alone. Sooner rather than later gives the police even less chance to stop me. And, once I've taken her out, I can move onto my grand finale: Lockhart. I feel a surge of excitement at that prospect.

So, fuck it. Why not do it now? Nothing's stopping me.

The more I'm looking at her, the more I'm thinking about the loss adjustor who did me over. The bitch who screwed me out of the compensation I was due after the accident. Who almost certainly took some kind of bung from the studio to find in their favour. Loss adjustors are supposed to be independent, impartial. In my case, it was bullshit.

And the more I dwell on that, the more this woman striding ahead of me becomes her, the one responsible. The more that anger grows inside me, rippling through my body and taking it over. I see *her*, the one who did it to me. She needs to take the blame. I'm going to make her pay.

I cross the street towards her.

*

Liz wasn't far away now. A couple of minutes at most. She knew every corner and how far it was in minutes between there and home. She was longing to see Freya, to wrap her in a big warm hug and hear all about her day at school, before perching on the side of her bed and reading the story. If it was a cold night, or if Freya wanted to, they'd even snuggle together under the covers.

When they'd finished the book, Liz would put her light out and head downstairs. Have a bit of dinner and a chat with her dad, who had been looking after Freya this evening. Then Dad would head home and Liz could slip into the bath for half an hour, once she knew Freya was asleep. Sometimes, she thought those simple things alone were enough for her to be content.

Her phone buzzed in her bag. She removed it and glanced at the screen, though she already knew what it would say. She smiled as her prediction was confirmed. Freya had written:

Tiger who came to tea please x

Liz didn't need to text back, now that she was so close. She locked the phone screen and slung it back in her handbag.

Then she heard a noise behind her.

CHAPTER SEVENTY-THREE

Lexi pushed open the door of Fishers, the restaurant in Fulham where Dan had told her he was eating. The smell of frying chips hit her immediately, and she could almost taste the tang of salt, lemon and vinegar on the air. It made her realise that she'd barely eaten since leaving the clinic. It was nearly 10 p.m., now, and she'd been working solidly at home, preparing something to share with Dan after his request earlier.

At this time, the place was almost empty, and she quickly spotted him in the corner, a solitary figure hunched over the huge plate of fish and chips he was devouring. He'd already seen her and waved. She pointed to the counter and he gave her a thumbs-up. Lexi ordered sweet potato fries and a soda and went over to join him.

'Sorry to drag you all the way up here,' he said, through a mouthful of food.

'It's cool,' she replied. 'It's not that far. And I guess you're a little busier than me.'

Dan smiled, but just for a second. He looked exhausted, she thought.

'I've been coming to this place for years,' he said, glancing around the small, simple interior. 'Jess and I used to get takeaway here and walk along the river. If it was pissing with rain or freezing cold, we'd sit in the window, just over there…' His eyes lost focus.

Lexi turned to look at the window table. She knew he'd be picturing the last time he and his wife had been here together.

Was it a little weird that she was here with him, now? Or was it a good sign that Dan felt able to invite her here, somewhere he used to share with Jess? She didn't know.

'It's nice,' she commented, turning back to him. 'Cosy.'

He seemed to snap out of the memory. 'And there's no chance of Porter seeing us here. He'd never cross the river to get his dinner.'

She chuckled. 'That's a bonus.'

'You get the bus up?' he asked.

'Uh-huh.'

Dan frowned and pointed his fork at her. 'Be careful at those bus stops, yeah?'

'I can look after myself.' She reached into her bag and pulled out the pepper spray and personal alarm she'd bought online. 'See?'

He nodded approval. 'OK. Just… until we catch this guy, taking the bus at night probably isn't the safest option.'

'How else am I supposed to get around?' She shrugged. 'I can't afford to take cabs everywhere.'

'Fair enough.' Dan speared a few chips and put them in his mouth. 'Maybe try not to travel alone, then.'

Lexi raised her chin defiantly. 'I'm not scared of that guy, you know.'

She didn't add that she'd been thinking about the bus stop rapist pretty much non-stop since they'd asked her to help on Op Braddock. That making some contribution to catching him would be a way for her to banish the ghost of the assault she'd experienced. To make sure at least one man who thought he could get away with rape would be punished. She'd find him herself, if she had to.

Dan looked as though he was about to reply with some more man-advice, but they were interrupted by the server bringing Lexi's fries and soda to the table.

'Thank you.' She waited for the guy to leave before speaking again. 'What's the latest on Logan?'

He lowered his voice. 'We've traced her to a club via a bank card she stole and used there. A couple of the team are on night shift, going through the CCTV footage. They were still working on it when I left half an hour ago. We think we've got her inside the club, talking to a guy. Next step is to try and ping her leaving, see where she went. If we're lucky, we'll have somewhere to visit first thing tomorrow.'

'That's positive.' She grabbed a handful of fries, dipped them in some ketchup and stuffed them in her mouth. They were crispy and salty and delicious. She thought for a second. 'You think she was trying to pick up a guy? You know, to have somewhere to stay.'

'Could be.' Dan stopped chewing. 'Do you reckon she'd attack him? Or even kill him?'

Lexi cocked her head. 'Hard to say. I mean, her victim choice seems to be relatively defined. At least, if my theory's right. She stayed with John Foster for, like, two months and didn't hurt him. If someone's useful to her, she won't attack.'

'Reassuring.' He resumed eating.

'That said,' she continued, 'the second anyone becomes a threat to her, they're at risk. Don't forget, we're talking about a psychopath here. A person who uses violence as a tool to get what they want, and has no conscience about doing so. If she went home from that club with a man, he's in danger.'

Dan nodded and sawed off a piece of battered fish. She could tell he didn't want to hear that, even if it was true. It was one more thing to worry about.

'So,' he said, 'who's she going for next?'

Lexi cracked open her soda and took a sip. 'OK, so this is, like, very preliminary.'

'Hit me.'

'I believe she's targeted individuals who symbolise the people who screwed her over after her accident on the movie set.'

'Surrogates, like you said.'

'Right. Director, set designer, compensation lawyer. The question is, who else was involved in it? There's a kind of conspiracy theory on the movie website about the studio paying people off to sweep the incident under the carpet.'

'Someone in… what? The finance department of a film company?'

'Maybe, but that's a little vague. The news article mentions an insurance claim that was independent of the legal settlement. That's my best guess.'

'A person who works in insurance?'

'Yeah.'

Dan gave a long, slow breath out. 'Is that it?'

'Not quite. One of the movie geeks thinks the conspiracy extends to the LAPD. That the studio paid off a cop to ignore evidence or whatever.'

'Does he have any proof of that?'

'Not that he shared with me, but—'

'Hang on,' he cut in. 'You're telling me this is just what some bloke on a website reckons?'

'There must've been a police investigation,' she countered firmly. 'It's possible that she's blaming a detective for not investigating it properly, at least. Corrupt or legit.'

There was a silence and Dan appeared lost in thought. Lexi glanced across to the server, who was, understandably, observing their exchange. She made eye contact with him and he looked away quickly, resuming his wipe down of the counter.

'What is it?' she asked Dan.

'Logan was looking me up on Foster's laptop,' he replied. 'Researching stuff about me. Military stories, Jess.'

'Maybe I'm not the only one who should be careful, then,' she said.

He picked up a chip and waved it casually. 'It's probably nothing.'

'Still.'

'It's fine.' He threw the chip in his mouth.

Lexi arched her eyebrows. 'You can look after yourself, right?'

Dan grunted. 'Anything else?'

'Well, I kinda had the idea she might pick on a reporter, too. You know, because they didn't give her the coverage she wanted.'

Dan chewed, swallowed. 'So, we're looking for someone who works in insurance, a police officer, or maybe a journalist?'

'Yeah.'

'Do you know how many of those there are in London?'

'Hey, I said it was preliminary.'

'*Very* preliminary.'

'Jeez, I'm trying to help.'

He nodded slowly. 'I know. Sorry. I just wish we had more.'

'We do have a little more.' She sipped her soda. 'Firstly, we believe she travels to and from the location of the attacks on foot. Maybe to avoid leaving a transport trace. Maybe because she's lazy and it's more convenient, I don't know. Her victims were all murdered within a twenty-minute walk of John Foster's flat, where she was staying. My guess is she's going for someone in that area, or within a similar distance of wherever she's staying now.'

'OK.'

'And we think she does her research online, right?'

'Yeah. She used Foster's laptop to find out about her previous victims.'

'So, we're looking for people with relatively high profiles, who've got stuff on the web about where they work or what they do in their spare time.'

'Probably.'

'If you filter the jobs of insurer, cop and reporter by geographical area, then check for those with detailed social media, blogs or whatever, the numbers will be a whole lot smaller.'

Dan was staring at his plate.

'And,' she added, 'if we predict that she's targeting a total of five victims – the five elements in her symbols – then my best guess is she's only looking at two out of those three professions.'

He raised his head, pulled a face. 'We can notify police in the area, sure. But as for the others… it'd do more harm than good to just issue a public warning to anyone local in insurance or news. The press is already going nuts over a female serial killer. Can you imagine what they'd make of it if they thought they were targets, too? Even Porter won't want to brief that to them.'

Lexi began to feel pissed off, again. She'd done her best, with minimal data, and Dan didn't seem grateful at all. 'Well, you asked for my victim profile, and this is what I've got. Sorry it isn't good enough. But I'm not psychic.'

'Unfortunately. I wish you were.' He shovelled in the last piece of fish. 'Actually, no I don't. You already know more about what's going on in here than anyone else,' he added, indicating his forehead with the tip of his knife. 'You don't want to know the rest of it.'

Dan gave her a little smile and, despite everything, Lexi felt herself blush.

DAY SIXTEEN

CHAPTER SEVENTY-FOUR

Lockhart had been woken by the call just after 6 a.m., by which time more than ten hours had passed since the incident yesterday evening. Details were still thin, but Lockhart was furious that it'd taken so long for anyone to connect the violent assault on a forty-three-year-old woman named Liz Jennings with Operation Thorncross and Blaze Logan.

He suspected there were several reasons for the delay. The main one was the fact that, miraculously, Liz was still alive. The out-of-hours Homicide Assessment Team would not, therefore, have been called and the priority would've been her immediate medical care. The victim being female, and a vague description of the attacker wouldn't have helped attending officers make the link to Logan, either. And any overnight investigative work had probably been hampered by the lack of night shift resources in the strapped Merton borough team, who were covering the area where the assault took place.

Liz had been attacked in a quiet residential road in Earlsfield, south-west London, just one street away from her house. A man had witnessed the incident from his window and called the police before having the courage to run into the road and confront the attacker, who had fled, leaving the man to stay with Liz until the ambulance arrived ten minutes later. The intervention had probably saved her life; if the witness had looked out of his bathroom window any later, it might've been too late for Liz.

But that was where the good news ended.

Liz had received serious head wounds and had been taken straight to Accident & Emergency at St George's Hospital in Tooting. Following triage, she'd been moved to the Neuro Intensive Care Unit in the neighbouring Atkinson Morley Wing, where Lockhart was now climbing the stairs to visit her.

He was sickened to think that he'd been stuffing his face with fish and chips and chatting with Green about who Logan might target while, a few miles south, that person was already in hospital, fighting to stay alive. They hadn't been fast enough, or good enough, and Liz's life hung in the balance because of that failure. The guilt gnawed at him with each step he took up towards her.

Lockhart was buzzed into the NICU. He'd never been on this ward before, but he knew the drill. He took a squirt of alcohol gel from the wall dispenser and rubbed it into his hands, then produced his warrant card and introduced himself to the nurse at the desk before signing in.

'She's in a medically induced coma for the time being,' said the nurse, a young black woman with close-cropped hair, whose ID card read: *Grace Adebayo*.

'Does she have family here?'

'Yes, her father has been with her.'

'Is there a partner?' asked Lockhart.

'I believe so. But the father said he's not around at the moment.'

'OK. Does Liz have children?'

'One girl. Her mother is looking after her.'

Lockhart nodded. 'Can I see her, please?'

Nurse Adebayo hesitated. 'Yes, but she's not conscious. She can't talk to you.'

'I know. I just want to... see her.'

'All right. Come with me.'

Adebayo led him through the ward. There were cubicles to left and right, separated by blue curtains drawn far enough around to offer some privacy and dignity for the patients while still allowing medical observation. Every bay was taken, the occupants lying in beds with rails on the sides. There were several free-standing machines behind each patient's head. Lockhart saw respirators, intubation, drips and wires. Beyond the equipment, he also saw people whose lives would never be the same again. Near the end of the ward, they came to a stop a few feet outside one bay.

'This is Liz,' said the nurse quietly. 'I can see Arthur has stepped away.' She indicated an empty chair pulled up close to the bed. 'He was sitting there all night.'

Lockhart didn't reply. His mouth was already dry as he looked through the curtains at the woman who was, in all probability, Blaze Logan's latest victim. One arm was in a cast from elbow to hand. Her facial features were barely recognisable between the swelling, bruising, and gauze dressings. Lockhart felt the rage towards Logan begin to grow inside him. It was rapidly followed by the image that invaded his mind: the Taliban sniper in that house in Afghanistan. And then Lockhart was right back in that moment.

On top of the man, batting his hands away and throwing punch after punch. Until the decisive one landed in his face, followed by another, and another. The sniper's head slapped the floor tile beneath him, just as Lockhart connected again, caving the guy's cheek in this time, his own knuckles bloodied and raw. As the film played in his mind, Lockhart could see the sniper lying beneath him, completely still. He could feel his weight pressing down on the body. He could even smell the residue from the stun grenade he'd thrown moments earlier.

Now, his heart was hammering in his chest and he felt sweat prickle his temples and lower back as he struggled to remember what had happened next…

'She has a subdural hematoma,' said Adebayo, her words pulling him back to the present. 'Are – are you all right, officer?'

Lockhart blinked. 'Fine. Subdural hema—?'

'Hematoma. It's a bleed on the brain. The consultant is monitoring it and we're hoping there's no need to operate, because that carries an additional risk.'

'Yeah, of course.' He felt nauseous, shaky. Angry at Logan. And, because they hadn't located her, he found himself looking for someone to blame. Him, for not catching Logan earlier. Green, for not being more specific in her profiling. Porter, for going public and perhaps forcing Logan's hand on this attack. Maybe they all shared a measure of responsibility.

Lockhart wondered what would happen when he did find Logan. Right now, he felt as though he could kill her himself. He had no doubt she wouldn't think twice about beating him to death if she got the chance. And if what Smith had told him about the research on Foster's laptop was more than just idle curiosity…

He heard footsteps approaching and turned to see a man in his seventies with a full head of grey hair, liver-spotted skin and deep bags under his eyes walking towards them. He wore a cardigan over corduroy trousers and was holding a cardboard drinks cup in one slightly trembling hand. His tired eyes flitted from Lockhart to the nurse before he craned his neck into the bay.

'Has something happened?' he asked.

'There's no change, Mr Simpson,' the nurse answered gently. 'This is Detective Inspector…'

'Dan Lockhart.' He extended a hand and the older man shook it. 'Metropolitan Police. I'm investigating the attack on Liz.'

'Arthur Simpson. I'm her father. Lizzy still uses her married name, you see.'

Lockhart nodded. He didn't quite know what to say to this man whose daughter was in a coma because of a psychopath his team had not been able to stop. Pleasantries seemed pointless.

'My wife's been with her daughter all night,' continued Simpson. 'We haven't even told little Freya what's happened yet. I mean, how do you begin to explain something like…' He gestured towards his daughter with his free hand before letting it drop to his side where it hung limply.

'I'm so sorry for what you're going through,' said Lockhart. 'And for what happened to Liz.'

'Why would anyone do this to her? My Lizzy wouldn't hurt a fly. And whoever it was didn't take anything from her. Apparently, they just kept kicking her before they ran away. That's what I was told. It's senseless.' Simpson's mouth remained open in obvious disbelief.

'I know.' Lockhart paused. 'But I promise you, I will do my best to make sense of it. My whole team will.'

'Thank you,' replied Simpson, his eyes moist.

'Can I get anything for you?' asked Adebayo. Simpson indicated that he was fine. The nurse moved into the bay, checked the machines quickly, then said: 'I'll leave you to it.' She walked off back towards the desk. Lockhart made a mental note to speak to her on his way out about security. They'd need an officer here on the ward in case Logan guessed where Liz was and decided to finish what she'd started. Changing Liz's name on the patient list, too, would offer some extra protection against Logan, as well as reducing attention from the press.

'Mr Simpson, I realise this must be a very difficult time, but do you mind if I ask you a couple of questions about your daughter?' Lockhart planned to send their Family Liaison Officer, PC MacLeod, over to see Simpson later this morning, and to visit his wife and Freya, too. He knew MacLeod would do a great job on the welfare side. But for now, he needed facts.

'Of course,' said Simpson. 'What do you want to know?'

Lockhart thought back to Green's words last night. Her predicted professions. 'What did Liz do for a living?'

Simpson looked slightly taken aback at the question. 'She was a loss adjustor.'

'Insurance.'

'Yes, well, she worked on behalf of insurers. Why – do you think it was something to do with her work?'

'It could be.' Lockhart hesitated. 'We have to keep all our lines of inquiry open at the moment.' He hated parroting those meaningless Porter-style lines, but he couldn't disclose their suspect strategy to Simpson. Especially when it wasn't even official.

Green had called it correctly. That was four out of a probable five victims. Would Logan make a second attempt on Liz's life, now? Would she target another person who worked in insurance? Or would she move on to her final victim?

Following Green's logic, that would either be a journalist, or…

Lockhart felt a shiver go through him.

Twenty minutes later, Lockhart was driving to Jubilee House when his phone went. He answered it on the hands-free in his Defender and Smith's voice filled the interior.

'Good news and bad news, guv.'

'Gimme the good news, Max. I need some.'

'Right you are. Well, we think we've found Logan leaving the club with a man on Sunday night, early hours of Monday.'

'Result. Any idea where they go after that?'

'Looks like they get into a Toyota Prius around half midnight.'

'Uber?'

'Most likely. We got the car reg and traced it to a guy who, according to the PNC, lives in Kingston. We're heading round there now to find him. Or find out where he is.'

'He'll have a record of the drop-off address on his app.'

'Exactly.'

Lockhart drummed the steering wheel. 'Can't imagine Logan risking a hotel. Do we reckon they went to the guy's flat?'

'It's a decent shout.'

'Two-and-a-bit days ago. Whether she's still there or not is anyone's guess. It's gonna depend on how safe she feels.'

Smith cleared her throat. 'Er, that might be the bad news, guv.'

'What?'

'Yeah. Once we had a half-decent image from the club, Porter put it straight out online.'

'What?' Lockhart couldn't believe it. It was as if the boss actually wanted Logan to stay ahead of them. Without thinking he made a fist and slammed it sideways into the door beside him. Then he did it again. Swore a few times. 'Find the cab driver and get that drop-off address ASAP,' he said.

'On it right now.'

Lockhart ended the call. Then he bellowed as loud as he could. And stepped on the accelerator.

CHAPTER SEVENTY-FIVE

Smith finished her banana and, for want of anywhere to put the skin, dropped it in the footwell. That was one major downside of surveillance; the longer you sat in a car, the more skanky it got. And that was multiplied by the number of people. In this case, three: her, Lockhart beside her in the passenger seat, and Khan behind them, tapping away on his phone.

'Stay outside or go in?' she asked, keeping her eyes on the house. This was where they'd traced the cab drop-off in the early hours of Monday morning: a basement flat in a converted Victorian terraced house in Gipsy Hill, south London. It belonged to a thirty-five-year-old man named Joseph Dobbin, who had taken the taxi here with Blaze Logan.

'If we'd found this place before eight a.m.,' replied Lockhart, his voice tight with frustration, 'I would've said wait. Get eyes on, stake it out, observe any activity.'

'But now?'

'Now Porter has put the CCTV image from the club online, chances are Logan's seen it. That raises the threat assessment for Joseph Dobbin. My call would be go in.'

'So… why don't we?' Khan's voice came from the back seat, accompanied by the noise of gum chewing, which got louder as he leant forward.

'Because Porter told us to keep still until the TSG arrives,' Lockhart said.

The TSG – or Territorial Support Group – were the Met's muscle, called in for tasks like crowd control, or arrests of potentially dangerous suspects. Logan certainly qualified, but Smith wondered how the testosterone-pumped men of the TSG were reacting to the order to deploy in numbers for a woman.

'Ah, right.' Khan sat back again.

'In the absence of any activity, we've got no way of knowing if Logan's still there. Or even if Joseph's safe.' Lockhart breathed out heavily through his nostrils.

Smith glanced at him. 'How long will TSG be?'

'They couldn't say. They're on another job, apparently. For Trident.'

The Trident units around London dealt with gang crime; frequently their operations involved multiple consecutive arrests and forced entry of premises. That could take hours.

'I won't hold my breath, then.' Smith reached for her flask of tea. She hadn't even unscrewed the top when her phone rang. It was DS Stagg.

'Eddie,' she said, clamping the phone between ear and shoulder as she poured the tea.

'All right, Max? What you up to?'

'Surveillance,' she replied.

'Oh yeah?'

'Thorncross.'

'Decent lead?' he asked.

'Maybe. Hard to say. We'll take anything we can get.'

'I know that feeling.'

Smith gave a small laugh. 'What's going on? You working on Braddock?'

'I'm checking all the feeds from last night, but there's nothing much happening. Looks like our bloke's taking a bit of a break. And as soon as it calms down, the boss starts piling on other cases.'

'Tell me about it.'

'But this is exactly when we need to be making progress on it. Proactivity.' The exasperation in his voice was clear.

'Well, watching the cameras is a start.'

'True. Anyway, I called because I've got a fella called Xander O'Neill downstairs. Says he wants his clothes back. Apparently, Lockhart took 'em in a few days ago and they haven't been returned yet.'

'Oh, right. Hang on.'

Smith turned to Lockhart and relayed what Stagg had said.

'Make him wait,' said Lockhart.

'You sure, guv?'

'Yeah.'

The gesture seemed somewhat petty to Smith, but she didn't care enough about O'Neill to fight his corner. The guy was no serial killer, but he was still a bit of a prick, so if Lockhart didn't want to give him his stuff back immediately, it was no skin off her nose.

'Tell him I'll come over and do the paperwork tomorrow,' said Lockhart. 'If I've got time.'

Smith informed Stagg, who seemed to find it quite funny. 'He's not gunna have time, is he?'

'Doubt it,' she said.

'I'll go down and tell Mr O'Neill myself,' he said with a chuckle, and rang off.

A few moments passed in silence while Smith drank her tea. She was wondering about putting the radio on low, or maybe even listening to some music through one headphone, when Lockhart sat up straight.

'I'm going for a walk,' he said, reaching for the door handle. 'Take a look from the back.'

'Isn't Parsons on the back?'

'Yeah.' He opened the door. 'Wait here.'

'Guv?'

Lockhart didn't respond. He was already outside and closing the car door softly.

*

The annoying thing about using someone else's bathroom is that you don't know where all the stuff is. I rifle through the cabinet, looking for something antibacterial. Something to clean up my stab wound, which has started oozing. But it seems as though he hasn't got anything, the dickhead. And I can't find a first aid kit anywhere else. Water and soap will have to do.

I close the cabinet and take a good look at myself in the mirror. To most observers, it'd appear to be a pretty decent body. Fit, strong, muscular, athletic. But it's a shadow of what it was. A pale, weak apparition. A phantom. I've lost size and tone. I'm covered in surgical scars from God knows how many operations; I was still in a coma when they did most of them. And there are the wounds you can't see, beneath the scarred skin. Torn ligaments and tendons that will never heal properly, meaning I can't go back to stunt work. The only thing left of the old me is the tattoos.

I've got a ton of them: the angel and devil on opposite shoulders, the rolling dice, the butterfly. Then there's the Ghost Rider astride a motorbike, skull engulfed in flames – the comic book character Johnny Blaze. In the stories, he was a stuntman who did a deal with a demon to become the spirit of revenge, or something like that. I got it at the same time I took his name, because I thought it was badass. It was nothing to do with vengeance. But I couldn't have planned that one any better if I'd tried.

And there's the pentacle. The five-pointed star in a circle with an elemental symbol at each point: fire, water, earth, air and spirit. Someone in Hollywood who saw it asked me straight up if I was a witch, or a wiccan. Did I do pagan sacrifices and that type of thing? I know a lot of people believe a ton of weird shit in Hollywood. But I told him I didn't believe in anything except myself.

And those elements that make all of us. It seemed appropriate to mark them on the people who took my body and my spirit from me in that accident. One for each of them.

Looking at the little circle for spirit reminds me of who's going to get that one.

Not long now.

*

Lockhart turned his Airwave radio to silent as he entered the street that backed on to the property of interest. He could see the unmarked Ford Mondeo with his teammates Andy Parsons, Priya Guptill, and Leo Richards inside. They clocked him and he gave an almost imperceptible nod as he crossed to the small, modern church halfway down the road, marking the point where the Victorian houses ended and a new, low-rise estate began.

They'd probably be wondering what the hell he was doing. While the occasional 'walk-past' was common in surveillance, depending on the target, Lockhart was planning something even more direct. He entered the churchyard and strolled to the back where a short brick wall and wooden fence marked the border with the row of houses they were looking at. Shielded by the church building, he climbed onto the wall to get eyes on the basement flat.

Peering over the fence into the garden three doors along, Lockhart noticed a light on in Dobbin's flat. He didn't need to think about it any further. Pocketing his radio, he was quickly up and over the fence, using a tree to stabilise himself, and dropped into the garden. He crossed two low walls and slowly approached Dobbin's back door. Listened carefully, but couldn't hear anything. Tried the door handle.

It was unlocked.

He eased it open and stepped carefully inside, keeping his footfall as silent as possible. He was in a living room with a desk and computer against one wall, two sofas on the other side, and a door in the middle. The lights were off here, meaning the one he'd seen was in another room. The vaguest memory of that house in Afghanistan came to him; entering the darkened interior alone… but it stopped short of a full flashback. He swallowed, breathed, kept going.

Lockhart moved, slow and steady, across the floorboards towards the closed door. There was a half-drunk mug of tea on a table between the sofas. He stooped and touched a knuckle to it: cold. As he took the final step before reaching for the handle, the board under his right foot gave an almighty groan. He froze, cursed himself for not testing it better first. Held his breath, waited.

Twenty seconds later, Lockhart was satisfied that nothing had responded to the sound. He gently turned the knob and pushed the door in. Advancing into a gloomy hallway, he could make out three doors: two open, one closed. A cursory glance told him the open rooms were a small kitchen and a bedroom at the front of the house. So, the closed door was probably the bathroom, and the source of the light from the back. There was a hum from inside, probably an extractor fan. And the faint smell of something organic, too.

Lockhart took a breath and grasped the handle. Then in one rapid movement he twisted and threw the door open. Light spilled into the hallway and his arm flew up instinctively to shield his mouth and nose from the stench.

Lying in the bath, eyes open, was a naked, dead man. His skin was marbled with the early signs of decomposition. He smelled like a butcher's bin on a hot day. Lockhart could taste bile in the back of his throat as he extracted his radio and turned it up again.

'Get a scene of crime team in here.'

'Guv?'

'On the hurry-up. Body found. Looks like our man.'

There was a brief delay before Smith responded. 'Received.'

Lockhart shut the bathroom door to preserve the environment. Then, alone in the dim hallway, he sank to his haunches, covered his head with his hands, and cursed himself once more.

But there was no time for self-pity.

A clue to Logan's whereabouts could be somewhere in this flat. If he could find it – and stay ahead of Porter, too – then he might just have a chance of catching her.

CHAPTER SEVENTY-SIX

I finally finish cleaning myself up. It takes ages, because I can't just have a regular shower or a bath. Not with a massive, weeping gash in my side. Still, given that the cops have managed to track me twice – first to John's house and then, I guess, from the club to Joseph's place – things could be a lot worse.

On the run, the easy option would've been to look for a squat. Talk my way in, dish out some booze to keep people happy, then bed down in a dark corner with a cheap sleeping bag I could've bought using John's bank card. Another possibility was to make my way up to St James's Church in Piccadilly and sleep among the homeless who are allowed in there overnight. Or I could've gone properly hardcore, off the grid in a park or underpass.

But those options have their dangers. The unpredictability of other homeless people on the street, looking for anything they get. Addicts, alkies, and crazies who think they can hear the voice of God. Even in my weakened state, I'm pretty sure I could take them. But I don't need the stress or the hassle. I need to rest. This place is perfect for that.

And I've got it all to myself.

I remembered reading in the paper once that the London borough of Kensington and Chelsea has nearly a thousand empty houses – ghost homes, they're called – bought by millionaires as investments or ways to launder money. They're known as 'buy-to-leave' properties; left empty because their owners live elsewhere, usually in warm, sunny tax havens, and they don't need anyone in there paying rent. But they often like to keep the place going, ready for them to drop in on a business trip, or for the summer months when their families stay in town.

It took a while to find one that wasn't alarmed. But once I'd jimmied a basement-level window and climbed inside, the place was mine. Hot running water, electricity, and a huge, comfy bed. They even have Wi-Fi, with a password kindly written on the back of the router. I've still got my PAYG smartphone, which I topped up the other day, so it's time to get online and do some work.

The first thing I find on the news websites is that the bitch I tried to kill in Earlsfield isn't dead. I suspected as much, because the neighbour came out of his house before I was done. I had to make a call, and I decided to run. I'd choose escape over finishing the job every time. Living to fight another day. Protecting myself. That's the smart thing to do.

And I'll *always* do it.

I could try to track Liz Jennings down, tiptoe into whichever hospital is treating her, and cover her face with a pillow, like I did to Joseph. Or maybe pull out some of the wires keeping her alive. But I have to imagine Lockhart is anticipating that.

He'll have security in place.

Which means there's only one thing left to do: go for him.

Time for some more research.

CHAPTER SEVENTY-SEVEN

Following the arrival of the SOCO team, Lockhart had donned his paper Tyvek suit, overshoes, mask and nitrile gloves, and was back inside the flat with Smith and four SOCOs. One was dusting surfaces for fingerprints, another was in the kitchen swabbing crockery and cutlery for saliva and bagging samples for touch DNA, while the other two were in the bathroom. With the corpse of Joseph Dobbin.

Lockhart could still picture the body in the bathtub, could still smell its early decay. Despite that, seeing Joseph hadn't set off his PTSD. He tried to work out why not, thinking back to his therapy sessions with Green last year. She used to talk about 'triggers': sensory stimuli that were similar in some way to the original event. It must be the facial beating, the blood, swelling and bruising of Logan's victims that was doing it...

'Found anything, guv?' Smith asked him.

They were in Joseph's bedroom. He was going through a chest of drawers while Smith was examining the inside of a large wardrobe.

'Nope. Sod all.' He shut a drawer and opened the one next to it.

'How do you think he died?'

Lockhart lifted a stack of T-shirts one by one. There was nothing of interest between or behind them. 'Dunno. Definitely not her usual MO.'

'Strangulation?'

'Suffocation, most likely.' He shut the drawer and switched his attention to the bed. 'Maybe in his sleep. Perhaps even the first night she came back here.'

'So, she might've stayed here for two days with a dead body? That's sick. I've heard some stories in my time, but...'

'It's like Green said. Logan's a psychopath. That sort of thing wouldn't bother her. You read about Dennis Nilsen back in the day?'

'Of course.'

'He kept his victims' corpses under the floorboards. Used to get them out, sit them in chairs and chat to them.'

Smith made a mock vomiting noise. 'When you put it like that, she seems *almost* normal...'

Lockhart noticed the two bedside tables. One had a well-thumbed paperback, eye mask, radio alarm clock, and small box of earplugs on it. He guessed that was Joseph's stuff. The other table had nothing on it except a half-drunk glass of water; that was probably Logan's.

'I reckon I could work a hundred years in a murder team,' continued Smith, 'and never get my head around that kind of... I don't even know what you call it.'

'Ask Green,' he said, squatting down beside Logan's side of the bed and inspecting the mess on the floor. There was torn food packaging, a free London newspaper, and the wrapper of a used condom.

'I'd rather not,' said Smith.

He prodded around in the detritus. 'Prefer to trust your copper's nose, would you?'

'It's never failed me so far.' She cleared her throat. 'Almost never.'

'So, what's the difference between a copper's nose and a psychologist's... mind, then? They both rely on intuition, don't they? Both backed up by evidence of a few facts and plenty of personal experience.'

Whatever Smith's response was, Lockhart didn't hear it properly. He'd just seen a small piece of paper. Extracting it from the pile of crap that Logan had managed to produce in just two days, he unfolded it. And he knew he'd struck gold.

'Guv? You listening?'

'Eh?'

'Is that supposed to be funny?'

'Sorry, Max.'

She clearly registered from his tone that the banter was over. 'What've you got?'

He hesitated. 'A receipt. Top-up voucher for a pay-as-you-go phone.'

Smith crossed the bedroom and he held it up.

'We wondered if she was using a phone,' she said, a smile on her face.

'Until now, though, we had no idea what it was.'

'We still don't,' she said, scrutinising the paper. 'Except that it's on the O2 network. And she bought it yesterday. With a bank card that I'm guessing is John Foster's.'

'Right. But if we know which number that top-up credit was applied to, we have a decent chance of finding the phone.' He looked up at Smith. 'And Logan.'

Inside his jacket, his phone vibrated. He unzipped the paper suit enough to take it out. It was DCI Porter. 'I'd better get this,' he said. 'I've ignored him twice already. Time I got my bollocking.'

'Bollocking? You found a body, guv.'

Lockhart cocked his head. 'Yeah, but I also entered a premises without a warrant.'

'Threat to life?'

'Porter didn't think so, did he?'

'He wasn't on the ground.'

'True.' He handed her the receipt.

'What do you want me to do with this?' she asked. 'Get it back to the office so we can draw up a warrant on it for the telcom?'

Lockhart glanced at the phone screen. Porter wasn't giving up. 'That's what we should do,' he acknowledged.

'But?...'

'I've got a better idea,' he replied. 'Bag it up.'

'Guv.'

'And don't log it.'

CHAPTER SEVENTY-EIGHT

Porter hadn't been as angry as Lockhart had expected. Maybe it was because Joseph's body had been found, and even Porter had to admit that wouldn't have happened for another day or more without Lockhart's intervention. Perhaps Porter had pulled his punches out of sensitivity for the two most recent victims, one of whom was still in hospital with potentially life-changing injuries. But Lockhart suspected the real reason was that Porter was storing up one almighty smackdown for the end of the case, with every chance that Lockhart's days in the MIT were numbered. No SIO, not even one as blinkered and stubborn as Porter, would chuck a DI off a live manhunt for a killer. Womanhunt.

However, Lockhart had already crossed a few lines, and he was about to do it once more. He knew what the official, recommended investigative procedure after finding the receipt should be. Bag, log, then back to Jubilee House to write a warrant compelling the telcom, O2, to tell him what phone number that top-up voucher had been applied to. They could even get other data in case Logan switched handsets or SIMs. Then they would receive frequent updates on Logan's whereabouts as her phone logged on to different cell towers.

That was the textbook answer.

But he'd had enough of Porter screwing up the investigation, of tipping Logan off by sharing every piece of intel they got on her through social media and news websites, in the vain hope that a member of the public would come forward. The boss had disregarded Lockhart's advice, twice, and they'd lost Logan, twice. Lockhart had reached his tipping point. He didn't care anymore what happened to him; he was going to do whatever it took to find Logan. Especially if there was a chance that she'd target a cop next.

Lockhart made his way out of Jubilee House and walked the hundred yards or so to the river. He didn't want anyone overhearing this call. From the contact list in his phone, he selected 'Jock' and tapped the call icon. It was answered after a few rings.

'Sarge! Y'alright, big man?' The Glaswegian accent was even thicker than Lockhart remembered. Must be the result of Barry Dalgleish, aka Jock, moving back home since leaving the army. Jock had joined the Special Reconnaissance Regiment from the Scots' Black Watch regiment, who were proudly known as The Jocks because they hailed from north of the border. He was a signaller – a communications and tech expert – and wasn't just one of the most skilled Lockhart had ever worked with; he was one of the most trustworthy, too. Which was ironic, since he now made a living as a 'white hat' hacker, paid by banks and businesses to penetrate their electronic systems and find the holes to plug.

'Ah, you know,' replied Lockhart. 'You?'

'Cannae complain. What's up?'

'I need your help.' Lockhart glanced around him. No one was even close. 'Which telcoms' systems can you access?'

Jock chuckled. 'Pretty much most a 'em.'

'O2?'

'Aye.'

'OK. I've got a top-up voucher for an O2 PAYG phone.'

'And you wantae know what number it's been used on?'

'Exactly.'

'Handset IMEI, all that, too?'

'Yeah,' replied Lockhart. 'Whatever locates it.'

'Real time?'

'Yup.'

Jock hesitated. 'And do I need tae know why you're asking me for this?'

'No.'

'Lucky I trust ye, eh? All right, you got the voucher number?'

'Yeah.'

'Give it me, then.'

Lockhart switched his phone screen to the photo he'd taken of the receipt earlier, and read out the code.

'Stand by, then, Sarge. Might take a wee while. Depends how wide O2's left their back door open. And what your target's doing with his phone.'

'Her phone.'

'Oh aye?' There was a pause, and when Jock spoke again his tone had softened. 'It's not…'

'No,' said Lockhart. 'It's not her.'

'Right. Gimme a few hours.'

'Cheers, Jock. I owe you, mate.'

'Dinnae worry about it. I'll take it out your bank account.'

'Don't joke about that.'

'I'm not.'

'There's no money in there anyway.'

'Didnae think so.'

Lockhart rang off. There was every chance that Jock would find something, if it was there to be found. But he had to keep going on the regular Thorncross investigation, too. If Green was right, Logan was planning to attack one more surrogate. And Lockhart would be damned if he'd let it be one of his own.

CHAPTER SEVENTY-NINE

Since learning of the attack last night on Liz Jennings, Lexi had been beating herself up big time. She'd read about it while checking the news online during a break at work. Had sat there blankly staring at the screen, barely able to believe it. Once the initial shock had passed, she'd tried calling Dan a couple times, but he hadn't picked up. Eventually, the briefest text arrived from him:

Can't talk now

Whatever. In some ways, Dan didn't even need to say anything. Lexi knew that she'd failed, again. It was so messed up.

A cursory Google search had revealed via LinkedIn that a woman named Elizabeth Jennings, whose CV put her somewhere in her mid-forties, worked as a loss adjustor in the City. A loss adjustor! Lexi should've seen this – it would've been the person responsible for assessing Logan's post-accident injuries, and calibrating the payment, whom she wanted to kill. If only Lexi had been able to work that out, maybe they could've given a warning to loss adjustors in London rather than doing nothing because – as Dan had argued – there were simply too many people working in insurance.

She found herself getting mad at Dan for ignoring her… but mostly at herself for not seeing the detail that could've made the difference. And she felt the desperate pull of regret, that mixture of not wanting to accept what's happened, but knowing that it has, and not being able to do jack shit about it. The poor woman was still alive – just – but the news article said that she'd sustained injuries that would probably be life-changing.

Lexi tipped some more gin into her glass and downed it, grimacing at the neat liquor's harsh taste, as if it were a punishment she deserved for screwing up so badly once more. Sarah was out at a spin class, and Rhys wasn't home either – she neither knew nor cared where he was – so it was just her, alone, at the kitchen table with a bottle of gin. That was not a good look. To anyone observing, it would've been a sad sight, but nowhere near as tragic as the fate of those victims she'd been unable to help – both on Thorncross and Braddock.

'Goddammit,' she said aloud. Poured herself another gin and chugged it down.

She needed to do something about all this… There had to be *something* she could do. And almost anything was better than sitting here on her own, drinking.

There was no way she was going to find Blaze Logan alone… she wouldn't even know where to start. But as for the bus stop rapist, well, what did he do? He attacked women, at night, at isolated bus stops in south-west London. Lexi checked the time on her phone: 9.40 p.m. Then the idea came to her: she'd go out looking for him.

Yeah. That's what she'd do.

Lexi reached for her bag and fished around inside. Checked the pepper spray cannister and the little rape alarm were there. Then she grabbed her jacket from the hallway, went back to the kitchen, poured herself one more gin, downed it, and marched out of the front door.

She was going to find this son of a bitch.

DAY SEVENTEEN

CHAPTER EIGHTY

Despite a liberal supply of her twin fuel sources – caffeine and sugar – Smith was struggling this morning. It was the cumulative effect of working more than two weeks straight of long, intense days. Any downtime she'd had before or after shifts, or on the single rest day she'd been rostered during Op Thorncross, had been spent helping Stagg track the serial rapist on Op Braddock. There was no two ways about it, she was knackered.

The effort was taking its toll at home, too. Smith and her fella hadn't properly spent time together in over a fortnight, and they'd had a completely unnecessary argument last night over stacking the dishwasher. It was a sure sign of stress, of work invading her private life. She knew things couldn't go on like this.

But she sensed they were close to something on both ops; Blaze Logan couldn't hide for ever, and nor could that scumbag keep attacking women at bus stops without giving his identity away, somehow. She just had to push on, grind it out. That was the way you got results. Then maybe life would get back to normal for a while.

Whatever normal was.

Smith realised she'd zoned out for a moment and brought her attention back to DCI Porter. He was standing in front of their assembled team – which appeared to have grown even larger today – and summarising the current state of their investigation and search for Logan. Following the discovery of poor Joseph Dobbin's body yesterday, they'd identified his next of kin, confirmed through fingerprints that Logan had been in his house, and gone door to door in his street canvassing for potential witnesses to her departure. Unsurprisingly, no one had seen anything useful.

Joseph's post-mortem was scheduled for later this morning. Dr Mary Volz was due to examine his body to establish a cause of death, likely to be suffocation. Smith felt queasy just thinking about what that must've been like for the young man, and wondering whether – had she been the one fighting for her life – she'd have been strong enough to resist Logan. In some lucky cases, the post-mortem also sparked new investigative angles through evidence found on – or in – the body. Today, though, they already had a lead; Berry had mentioned it to Smith just before the briefing.

'With John Foster's permission, we've been monitoring transactions on the bank card Logan stole from him,' stated Porter. 'We learned early this morning that the card was used last night in a grocery store near the King's Road in Chelsea. I need two volunteers to get over there right after this meeting and requisition any CCTV they have which might show us what she's wearing, whether she's altered her appearance, where she may have gone afterwards, etcetera. Who's taking that action?'

Smith raised her hand; it was exactly the kind of concrete, practical task she thrived on. Several others had also indicated their interest, and, looking around the room, she noticed Khan volunteering. Good for him, she thought. Getting stuck in was the best way to break out of his recent slump. Porter scanned the arms, stared at Khan for a moment, then pointed at DC Parsons beside him.

'Andy, you can go, with…' he cast around. 'Max.'

She saw Khan's head drop and made a mental note to give him a pep talk later. See how he was doing. If she got a minute to ask, that was.

Porter distributed more actions, and as he marked off names against tasks on the large whiteboard, she caught Lockhart's eye.

He was standing to the side of the group, leaning against a pillar, shirt sleeves rolled up and arms folded. He looked as though he hadn't slept in a week, which was probably about right. He gave her a tiny nod, which she returned, but she couldn't read anything more into his expression.

Smith didn't know what he'd done with the phone top-up voucher and she intended to get an explanation off him later for his decision. She'd gone out on a limb by not logging that piece of evidence from Joseph's flat. She trusted Lockhart, but there were limits, and her arse was on the line, too, if it came out that she'd been party to whatever parallel investigation he was running. Combined with the bus stop cameras, Smith was racking up enough serious misconduct charges to lose her pension. Christ! What was she doing?

Porter's voice cut in again.

'Now, I don't need to remind you all – but I'm going to do it anyway – about the public attention to this matter. You've all seen the news, and you know the media is focused on everything we do. Every development we brief officially is on the web and social media in near-real time, and in the papers within hours. That's the inevitable consequence of modern, accountable policing, but we need it to work in our favour. If we keep the public – and the media – on our side, sooner or later, they'll give us the tip that unlocks this case.'

Smith glanced at Lockhart. He was rubbing vigorously at the stubble on his jaw, eyes fixed on the floor.

Porter distributed further actions before asking, 'Anyone got anything else to add?'

Without unfolding his arms, Lockhart raised a hand.

'What is it, Dan?'

'Victim choice, sir. I just wanted to say that I've consulted Dr Lexi Green, who some of you will remember from Op Norton last year.' He paused. 'The Throat Ripper case.'

There were some murmurs around the group. Unbidden, the image of that suspect falling, screaming, came into Smith's head and she held her breath as the film of it, pin-sharp and with full audio, played in her mind's eye.

The noise he made as he hit the ground.

'We're all well aware of that,' replied Porter, his tone severe. 'And I'm sure I don't need to remind you that any unauthorised contact with anyone outside of this team will be dealt with fully and punished appropriately once this investigation is concluded.'

'Dr Green only knows what we've briefed publicly, sir.'

'I certainly hope so, given the press leaks we've had to manage.'

'Well, I think it's worth sharing what she had to say. She believes that Logan is taking revenge for an accident she suffered on a film set, which ruined her career as a stuntwoman. The victims she's choosing represent those she holds responsible for what happened to her, both in the accident itself and its aftermath.'

'OK.' Porter looked deeply sceptical, and Smith had to admit she shared his doubt.

Lockhart went on to explain Green's surrogacy theory and what each victim represented. How the symbols drawn on their bodies – with the exception of Liz Jennings, where Logan had fled the scene – indicated that there was likely to be one more victim. This sparked a good deal of chatter, but Lockhart raised his voice over it to finish his point.

'She believes there's a strong chance that Logan's final victim will be someone in the police.'

At this, a hush descended over the assembled group. Smith, like most others, found herself staring at the photographs which Porter had printed large-scale and stuck to a whiteboard. Before and after. Each victim, in life, smiling and posing for a portrait. Then, in death or coma, battered, bloodied, unrecognisable. And she knew they were all thinking the same thing: will it be me on that board next? Even Porter had turned to study the images.

Then the boss appeared to regain his focus and cleared his throat.

'I'm not saying she's right, Dan. But we should all be that extra bit careful. This is a very dangerous individual we're dealing with. Priya,' he added, searching for DC Guptill, 'can you draft a threat warning for the Intranet? Run it by me first, then clear it with Comms and have them issue an email to all addressees in The Directory.'

'Sir.'

The Directory was the Met's internal contact list: all forty-plus thousand staff. Smith was a bit surprised that Porter was taking the psychobabble quite so seriously. But maybe he just wanted to cover his arse in case Green was right.

'Right, then.' Porter clapped his hands a few times. 'Let's get to it, people. Find Blaze Logan.'

CHAPTER EIGHTY-ONE

So far, I've relied on surprise. Ambushing unsuspecting victims who are going about their daily business with no idea that they're being stalked like game. And, apart from the loss adjustor, it's worked. But Lockhart is way too savvy for that. He's a detective, and an ex-soldier who worked on reconnaissance and surveillance, covert ops. I'm not going to catch him off-guard outside his flat, in Hammersmith, or his office, in Putney.

I need to find another way to get to him.

Everyone has their weak point, though. Their Achilles Heel, their blind spot. Something that makes them lose their cool, forget their training, act on impulse, and make mistakes. It's just a question of identifying it, then exploiting it.

For most people, family is the obvious place to start. Of course, Lockhart's lovely wife, Jess, is no longer around, so it can't be her. I've gone back over the articles I found about Lockhart's military career and the disappearance of his wife. And there are two people very close to him who feature in coverage of both events. Celebrating the first with him during a medal ceremony, and commiserating with him in the second.

His parents.

According to one article, they're from Bermondsey. That was a few years ago, though. So, I need to find out if they're still around and, if they are, where they live now.

I know exactly where to start looking.

CHAPTER EIGHTY-TWO

Lockhart had just got off the phone to Dr Mary Volz, who had given him her initial readout on Joseph Dobbin's cause of death. As expected, it was suffocation. There was no doubt that Logan had murdered him, but they still needed to evidence that by testing whatever she'd done it with – most likely a pillow – for his saliva and her prints or DNA.

Given the limited forensic evidence at the other crime scenes, such a clear link would have Logan banged to rights when they caught her. Even if they couldn't *prove* anything else beyond doubt, one murder conviction would get her life in prison.

Lockhart took a swig of his coffee, which had gone cold long ago, and decided to head to the canteen for a fresh brew. He checked his phone on the way and saw a message from Jock saying he had an update. It'd arrived ten minutes ago, while he was speaking to Volz. He stopped dead in the corridor, jabbing the screen to make the call. There were no greetings.

'Got a hit, Sarge.'

Jock had already identified the phone number Logan was suspected to be using, as well as the handset and other data, placing the phone in the vicinity of John Foster's flat in Collier's Wood, Joseph Dobbin's home in Gipsy Hill, and in Earlsfield when Liz Jennings was attacked. That was great, but what they really needed was its location right now.

'Go ahead.'

'Target pinged on a base station in Chelsea,' Jock said.

'How recent?'

'Late this morning. About an hour ago. It's off now.'

Lockhart clenched his teeth, tried to stay calm. He was pissed off about the delay, but he knew there was nothing he could do about it. Jock couldn't check every action on the phone as it happened; sometimes there was even a time lag while the telcom's systems updated. Then he needed to communicate it to Lockhart, who had to be free when the call came through and not on the phone to a forensic pathologist. It wasn't Jock's fault.

'Text me the co-ords,' said Lockhart.

'Nae worries, big man.'

Lockhart rang off and tapped into his Telegram app. The secure messaging service, beloved of criminals and terrorists worldwide, was the best way to exchange the kind of data you didn't want anyone else to be able to see. Moments later, a set of numbers which Lockhart recognised as GPS co-ordinates – longitude and latitude – popped up on the screen. He copied the numbers and pasted them into Google Maps, then brought up the Street View image of the road.

The spot where Logan's phone had been logged was an upmarket area of housing around Onslow Gardens, just north of the King's Road in Chelsea. One of the most exclusive parts of the capital, populated by millionaire baby boomers and wealthy foreigners who bought flats there as an investment, often leaving them empty or allowing a child to live there while he or she studied in London. Logan didn't fit the demographic at all.

So, what was she doing there?

During his military days in the SRR, Lockhart had learned the old adage: think like your enemy. What was your enemy's intention? What action would best serve their interests? Being able to interpret signs or predict with any accuracy what an adversary might do could give you a crucial tactical advantage. He supposed that, in a way, it wasn't too different to what Green did with her profiling. He needed to apply that now, to think like Logan.

Had Logan somehow talked or threatened her way into one of these homes? Were there other members of the public in danger, as Joseph Dobbin had been? For one terrible moment, he pictured the young man's lifeless body in the bathtub, the coloured patches on his pale skin… and wondered if Logan had perhaps already killed someone else simply to give herself a place to sleep. Or was it possible that she had an ally, a confederate who lived there? If so, why had she not gone there earlier?

Think like your enemy.

Given that Logan had left Gipsy Hill the previous morning at the latest, she'd have needed somewhere to sleep last night. It fitted with the use of the bank card nearby, around the same time. The area of phone activity was residential, so chances were she was staying there, rather than reccying a target in the area – though he couldn't rule that out. If Lockhart was on the run, what would he look for? A flat, preferably empty so you didn't need to worry about the occupants… As cold-blooded as Logan was, all predators knew there was a potential cost to attacking every prey.

So, an unoccupied residence in that area, perhaps. That was the best he could come up with for now. The next question was: what to do with this new intelligence? He could make an excuse to the others, drive out there himself, alone, and try to find her… although the chance of actually seeing her on the street was low, particularly with the phone currently off. He needed the team's involvement. But none of them knew about the phone, yet, except Smith, and he hadn't even told her much about it.

Then an idea came to him. What had Porter been preaching for the past two weeks?

Community policing. Tip-offs from the public.

Lockhart switched windows on his phone, selected the number, and dialled.

'Daniel! What a lovely surprise.' The enthusiasm of her greeting made him smile. 'You working?'

'Yeah, Mum. Actually, I need your help.' He checked around him. No one was in earshot.

'What is it, love?'

'Can you make a call for me?'

CHAPTER EIGHTY-THREE

I was grateful for that fact that no one seems to use libraries anymore. John Harvard Library on Borough High Street is a massive, ugly building that few people would even notice, much less want to visit. The interior is a bit better; they've made an effort with tables, chairs, even a little café. It's got a ton of books, obviously, banks of computers, and every kind of reference material you could want. There just aren't many customers, or whatever you call them, inside. Which suits me fine.

At first, I wondered whether the fact that staff outnumbered visitors meant someone was going to be eyeing me suspiciously the whole time, with the chance that they'd recognise me off the news. I took precautions, obviously. Borrowed a nice headscarf, large sunglasses, and a big jacket from my new home. But no one seemed to pay attention.

I gave them a story about tracing estranged relatives and, without requiring any further explanation, I was shown the full electoral register. It's a weird thing, a big old-school printed document which is basically a massive list of addresses and everyone living in the area who's registered to vote. Any person has the legal right to look at it, under supervision and usually not for more than ten or twenty minutes. Long enough to check something. There are rules about not photographing or copying it, but that doesn't matter when there's only one thing you're after. One piece of information you need to remember.

It's a hassle finding what I want, because the register is organised by address rather than name, and because it's printed, you can't just type in a search. But the librarian is extremely helpful, and thankfully Lockhart isn't that common a name. It doesn't take us that long to find her.

Iris Margaret Lockhart.

Living alone, in flat eighty-two of a 'square' – which sounds like a block in an estate – on Clements Road in Bermondsey. I guess the husband's croaked, and the old dear lives alone now. Even better.

Now I know exactly how to get to Lockhart.

And I've got nothing else on tonight.

CHAPTER EIGHTY-FOUR

'I mean, it's lovely and everything. But I'm not sure I'd like to live round here,' observed Smith.

She and Lockhart were walking down Old Brompton Road in Kensington, close to Onslow Gardens where the eyewitness 'tip-off' had put Logan earlier today. Checking each shop, café and pub they passed. They had an A4-size print of Logan's passport photo, and were asking in anywhere local she might've visited.

'Got something against West London?' asked Lockhart.

'Course not, guv.' She flashed him a grin. 'Just doesn't feel like there's much of a community.'

'That your only objection?'

'That, and the house prices.'

'I knew it. You'd secretly love to have a place here, wouldn't you?'

'I could never move north of the river.'

'Course you could.'

'No, I couldn't. Feels a bit weird just visiting.'

Lockhart shook his head, managed a laugh. The banter was flowing easily enough – the only alternative being working in silence, which no sane copper wanted on a job like this – but she knew they were both on edge. Turning over stones, waiting for the trigger that could lead them to Logan. Imagining what they'd do if she strolled around the next street corner.

Picturing those bloodied, battered bodies.

They'd just drawn another blank in a burger restaurant. The clothing boutique beyond it was shut, so the pizzeria two doors down was their next port of call. CCTV had indicated that Logan went north after her last card transaction, yesterday, which would place her somewhere around here. It was needle-in-haystack stuff, but this was the kind of tried-and-tested, hard-graft detective work that Smith loved. Once the bit was between her teeth, she didn't give up. And she knew Lockhart was the same.

Stubborn idiots, the pair of them.

Smith was grateful for the guvnor arranging the anonymous tip-off about Logan being seen here. However he'd done it, Porter was now fired up, believing his strategy of regular media appeals and public intelligence sharing was working as planned, just in time for his Super's promotion assessment. And she was relieved that it just about put her in the clear over the receipt they'd found in Joseph Dobbin's apartment.

One less dodgy thing she'd done to worry about.

Porter was taking the tip seriously, partly because it tallied with the use of the bank card nearby, and partly because they had little else to go on. He'd deployed about half of the core team on surveillance around Chelsea, going door to door with the image of Logan or clapping eyes on transport hubs. Berry and another analyst were putting in an overtime shift in the MIT office with a facial recognition software package. And there was the possibility that Lockhart might get another 'anonymous tip' of his own any moment, wherever they were coming from. Smith knew better than to ask.

She pushed open the door of the pizzeria and the smell of the wood-fired oven, of dough and cooked tomatoes and melting cheese, hit her square in the nostrils. She began to salivate and wondered if they could get a cheeky takeaway… but quickly told herself there'd be time for that later, when they weren't searching for a serial killer.

Smith took out the photo and moved towards the manager, whose beaming welcome rapidly became a frown when he saw the warrant card she was holding up in her other hand. As a detective, you got used to having that effect on people.

She glanced over her shoulder. Lockhart was standing by the entrance, phone in hand.

He was texting.

CHAPTER EIGHTY-FIVE

Lexi told herself she was doing the right thing. What she'd done last night was pretty dumb – wandering around a half-dozen dead little bus stops alone, drunk – and she'd been lucky to get away with nothing more than a sore head this morning. Needless to say, she hadn't found the man she'd been looking for. Or, rather, he hadn't found her. But it wasn't the act itself of searching for this serial rapist that was stupid; it was the way she'd gone about it.

Tonight, she'd do it better. Prepared. Sober.

It was a little after 8.30 p.m. The sun – such as it was today – had retreated and darkness had closed in, not that it ever truly won that battle with the city that never slept. London had its own version of night, a yellowy-orange glow to the sky from a million lights that made clouds look like cotton candy and rendered all but the brightest stars invisible. And yet, in pockets of the city where trees and greenery won out over concrete, it was still possible to find yourself alone in the dark.

Lexi was surprised by how scary that was.

She thought of Logan's victims, who had all been out, on their own, at night. She imagined the poor women waiting at bus stops, with nothing more on their minds than going out or getting home. The moment each of them realised that someone meant to harm them. And that there was no one to help them.

These thoughts brought her quickly back to the time she had been assaulted. The powerlessness and terror she'd felt. Now, she was doing something about it. Something to stop it happening to another woman. She'd rather her efforts had been part of the police's operation, but if Max Smith and even Dan didn't want her help, then she had to do what she could alone.

You're doing the right thing, for sure. Aren't you?

Lexi briefly wondered if this search could be less about other women, and more about her… About finding her own surrogate for the man who'd attacked her in that alleyway and gotten away with it. Was this just a selfish way of dealing with her own trauma? And did that mean she had more in common with Logan than she cared to admit?

She came to her next bus stop. A quiet road, a few closed stores behind, a bunch of trees opposite that led onto a small park with a children's play area.

She sat down, scanning her surroundings and staying alert, but trying to look as if she was just chilling, waiting for a bus.

Lexi was ready for this dude. If there were assholes who carried around a rape kit, then she had an anti-rape kit in her bag. Pepper spray, personal alarm, mobile phone charged and ready to call the cops or take photos, whatever was needed.

Her heart was beating a little faster.

Bring it on, she thought.

CHAPTER EIGHTY-SIX

This is the boring part, before the fun starts. After I'd found the address for Lockhart's mum at the library, I realised there was no point travelling all the way back to Chelsea only to have to return to the same part of town after dark. That would've been pointless. So, much as I hate doing it, I've been waiting.

Thanks to Lockhart and his team, though, I had to keep my head down. Not spend too much time in any one place. Keep my sunglasses and headscarf on. It's such as pain in the arse. It briefly made me think about what life will be like after I've killed him. Once it's done, and the slate is wiped clean, but my name and face are still out there. I'll need to move away somewhere else – overseas, probably – and start again.

Take a new name.

That's pretty inconvenient, but it's not like there's much keeping me here, anyway. It might even be exciting, depending on where I go. And, I remind myself, it's what I wanted. I set Lockhart the challenge of catching me, and he's got close. I'll give him credit for that. But, ultimately, he's been too slow. And I'm a step ahead of him, again, tonight.

From the bench where I'm sitting, I stare out across the river. I stuff in the last of a roast beef sandwich I bought for dinner. Time to pay dear old Iris Lockhart a visit.

I take out my phone. Even though I was bored, I've kept it off the past few hours to save the battery. I switch it on. Type the address into Google Maps and press 'Directions'.

It's a fifteen-minute walk.

Off I go.

*

Lockhart was pissed off. There'd been no sign of Logan in the area where her mobile had pinged earlier today. And the last time he'd checked in with Jock, an hour ago, the phone had still been switched off. Jock was doing his best, but it was at times like this that Lockhart missed the resources of his old unit.

If he was still in Special Forces, or if he was working for MI5, for instance, and Logan was a wanted terrorist planning a mass-casualty attack, they'd have every piece of tech available at their disposal. Phone-finding kit you could use on the ground that was so powerful it'd put you right next to the bloody thing.

But, in the cash-strapped Met, with *only* a common-or-garden serial murderer as their target, he'd be lucky if someone lent him so much as a compass. There'd been such a dearth of unmarked pool cars free for their surveillance this evening, Lockhart was having to use his own vehicle. This was the level of resourcing he was operating with. He'd had no choice but to ask for Jock's help. That's what he told himself. It was justified. It was about finding Logan.

He'd already suggested that Smith – who had worked thirteen hours straight today – should go home and get some kip. Recharge her batteries, ready to go again tomorrow. Being the sort of copper she was, she'd refused. Instead, she'd gone to get them both a cup of coffee while Lockhart kept watch in his Defender. A couple of the others had already gone: Khan, Guptill. He'd send the rest home soon, too.

He opened up the Telegram app on his phone. No update from Jock. He refreshed the app, just to be sure. Nothing.

Normally, he didn't mind waiting. He could spend hours on surveillance, sitting patiently in the same position, staying alert.

Tonight, though, whenever things were too quiet, his thoughts returned to Jess. To the prospect of appearing in court and trying to convince a judge she was still alive, based on little more than some vague, old intel, and a gut feeling that told him she was out there. That she *had* to be.

Lockhart shut Telegram and put the phone back in its holder on the dashboard. Checked the time: 10.23 p.m. He planned to give it until midnight, then call it a night and send everyone home. Maybe he'd stay longer. One, perhaps 2 a.m... It wasn't as if he was going to get much sleep at home, anyway.

He tried to maintain his focus on the street, checking each face that passed, screening and dismissing them one by one. But his eyes kept flicking to the phone screen.

Waiting for the call from Jock.

*

Lexi was waiting. This was the fifth bus stop she'd visited tonight, building on the half-dozen she hit last night. She'd chosen them based on Stagg's map of the attacker's likely hunting ground, to maximise her chance of finding the guy.

She had been sitting in the shelter at this stop for a half hour and her butt had quickly gone dead on the hard plastic. After ten minutes, a bus had come and gone, the driver perplexed as to why she didn't want to climb aboard. He'd held the doors open for a few seconds longer before shrugging and closing them. Then he and his handful of passengers were on their way and Lexi was alone again with nothing more than the distant sounds of city life for company. The occasional rise and fall of a car engine in nearby streets, aircraft passing overhead, the rumble of a train she couldn't see. Then the screech of a fox, a shrill noise that seemed full of pain. Lexi had seen a nature documentary once that said it was a mating call. Or was it a danger signal?—

'Don't fucking move.'

Lexi froze. She could hear chewing.

'Not a sound, yeah?' said the man.

The vague sense that she recognised his voice came to her… but was rapidly overtaken by another, more urgent thought: her survival instinct telling her simply to do whatever he told her.

Then her rational brain kicked in, and she reminded herself why she was there. What the whole point of putting herself in this situation was. This was what she'd come looking for. The chance to do something about this son of a bitch.

She tried to breathe, keep as calm as she could, although her whole body was tingling, the fight-or-flight response kicking in.

'OK, sure,' she replied, looking up at him. 'You're the boss.'

He stood a few feet away in a black jacket and ski mask. A shorter, stockier man who looked as though he was carrying some weight. She could see a few inches of knife blade glinting in his hand.

Lexi noticed that he'd stopped chewing, and it now appeared as though he was the one who had frozen, staring at her. She briefly wondered what was happening. But she wasn't going to ask any more questions.

She took her chance.

CHAPTER EIGHTY-SEVEN

I'm only two minutes away. I can see the building where Iris Lockhart lives. An eight-storey monolith of flats, built in a giant U-shape around three sides of a square that's completed by a separate, lower block of four-storeys. There are stairwells and walkways attached at the ends for getting up and down. It looks like the kind of place you'd shoot an urban action movie, where someone like me would run and jump and climb between the structures like David Belle in *District 13*, doubling for heroine or villainess. Leaping gaps in a harness and wires, a crash pad of cardboard boxes below, not that I'd need them.

That gives me an idea of what to do next. How to make sure I draw Lockhart out. And how to get away afterwards.

Now I just need to find flat eighty-two. I hope Iris is in; I don't want to be wasting my time here. Having to come back again tomorrow. Then I think about the chances of her being at home and smile to myself.

It's ten thirty at night. She's a seventy-year-old widow.

Where else is she going to be?

*

Lexi made her move. Jabbing a hand into her bag, she grasped the cannister of pepper spray. Pulled it out with her thumb already over the trigger button and, before her attacker had time to react, she'd raised it and fired a burst. But the direction was off, and she watched as the initial stream arced to the ground beside his body.

She immediately adjusted her aim.

The man took a step back and threw up an arm to shield himself. But he was too slow.

The jet hit him, its impact spread somewhere between the arm he'd raised and one side of the ski mask covering his face. Its open eyeholes were small targets. But that's what she was going for.

'What the f—?' he cried, trying to wipe it off.

Lexi stood. Sprayed him again. Longer, this time. More precise.

He screamed, and she knew she'd got him full in one eye.

'You bitch!' he yelled.

She went for a third burst, but the spray died before it reached him. Lexi realised the cannister was empty about the same time he did.

The man turned and started to run, making for the park across the road, bathed in blackness behind the trees.

Lexi was just a few feet behind him as he barrelled through the trees and into the dark beyond. He moved with surprising speed. Some part of her mind recognised that it was dumb to be chasing a guy carrying a knife into a deserted place like this. Especially when her pepper spray had run out. That she could wind up getting stabbed, like Logan. But another voice told her she had him on the ropes. And no way was she letting him get away with this.

'Hey!' she yelled, pitching forward across the grass. 'Stop!'

She could see him right in front of her, hear the gasps of his ragged breathing.

He glanced backwards, and Lexi caught his eye. She could've sworn, right then, that he was scared. Of her. Well, fuck him.

Her legs were a little wobbly with the adrenalin, but she knew she had a kick to her sprinting, and she was gaining on him. Almost close enough to reach out and—

Her foot hit a dip and crumpled beneath her, the twist in her ankle producing an awful *pop* as her leg gave way. Next, she was on the ground, pain surging through her foot and lower leg.

'Stop!' she screamed, again. 'Stop, goddammit!'

But she knew it was useless. All she could hear was the slight echo of her own voice and that asshole's heavy steps getting farther away from her. His footfall quickly dissolved into silence that was broken only by a single noise. It took Lexi a moment longer to realise that it was the sound of her own crying.

*

Lockhart took a sip of coffee, glanced at the phone. *Come on, Jock.*

'How late we gonna stay?' asked Smith.

He grunted. 'Thinking I might do an all-nighter.'

There was a pause. Smith shifted in her seat, looked at him. 'You're serious, aren't you?'

'Dunno. Maybe.'

They drank their coffees. A radio crackled and Parsons checked in. He had nothing to report.

'Do you think she'll show, then?' Smith nodded in the general direction of the street.

Lockhart shook his head slowly. Not a *no*, more a *no idea*. He was considering how best to express that without sounding too pessimistic when his phone rang.

The initial surge of excitement was tempered when he saw who was calling. It wasn't Jock, but Green. His first thought was to reject the call to keep the line open in case Jock tried to get through. But then another possibility occurred to him.

Green was the smartest person he'd ever met. She got stuff wrong, of course. Made mistakes, just like him and everyone else. But whatever she did, she believed in it. And she wasn't a time waster. So, if she was calling so late, there was probably a good reason. It was going to be something important.

Smith leant across and looked at the screen. 'What does she want with you at this time of night, eh?'

Lockhart ignored the question and swiped to answer.

'Lexi,' he said.

At first, the only sound was a sob. Then she spoke.

'Help me, please.'

'Lexi, what's happened?' he demanded. 'Where are you?'

'It was him,' she moaned. 'I was at the bus stop and then he was there, and…'

'Are you hurt?'

'Not really.' She hiccupped. 'Not like *that*. He ran off.'

'Where are you?'

She told him the park and nearest road.

'Stay there,' said Lockhart. 'Keep talking to me. I'm on my way. We'll get a patrol car over to you as well.'

Smith was already grabbing the radio and making contact with the Met's communications centre.

'OK.' Green sniffed deeply, exhaled.

Lockhart started the Defender's engine. 'Do you need an ambulance?'

'No.'

'Sure?'

'Yeah.'

He turned to Smith. But he didn't even need to ask.

She nodded. 'I'm coming too.'

CHAPTER EIGHTY-EIGHT

'I'm good.' Lexi pulled the jacket a little tighter around herself. 'Seriously. I'm fine.'

'You don't look fine,' Dan said.

He probably had a point. She could feel herself trembling, despite being inside Dan's Land Rover, with the heating on, and his jacket draped around her. A cop car had arrived a few minutes after her call, while Dan and Max had reached her not long after that. She couldn't gauge the times accurately. It'd all happened so fast.

'I mean that in a nice way,' he added, with a little smile.

Despite the situation, she gave a laugh and looked down at her foot. 'It's just my ankle that's busted.' It was already swelling.

'Could've been much worse than that.' Dan's smile faded and his expression was suddenly stern. 'He had a knife, you said?'

'Yeah.'

'Christ, Lexi. What were you thinking?'

'I just…' she faltered. 'I wanted to catch him. That's all.'

Dan didn't say anything. He just breathed out slowly through his nostrils.

'Sorry,' she added.

'Anything could've happened.'

'I know.'

They sat in silence for a few seconds.

'That was the closest we've got to him,' she said. 'Like, real time. We nearly had him.'

'And he nearly stabbed you. Or worse, he could've…' Dan didn't finish the sentence.

Lexi swallowed. She'd not even thought about that.

'I'll drive you to St George's,' he said. 'Get that ankle X-rayed.'

'Don't they need you here?' Max and the uniformed cops who'd turned up were searching the park in case the guy was hiding out.

'They'll be OK without me for a bit. We've still got half a dozen people over in Chelsea looking for Logan, too. I can always head back there later.'

Lexi hesitated. She felt that pull of safety that she'd always got around Dan. 'Well, if you're sure. I mean, I can take a cab, if—'

'Come on. Let's go.' He grabbed the radio and told Max what he was doing. Then he put the Defender in gear and pulled out.

As the streetlamps flashed past, something occurred to her. As if her brain had taken this long to process the attacker's behaviour.

'It was weird,' she said.

Dan glanced sideways at her. 'What was weird?'

'The way he stopped and stared at me, like he wasn't sure of himself anymore.'

'Maybe he just saw the pepper spray.'

'No, it was still in my bag at that point.'

'Hm.'

A tingle crept over Lexi's skin, and she shivered. 'I think he knew me.'

*

It's started spitting with rain and, despite the protection of the walkway overhead, the wind drives a few big drops into my face. I wipe them away, knowing I'll soon be indoors, because I'm here. Four floors up, outside apartment eighty-two.

I tap my knuckle on the door three times. Loud enough to be heard, but not too hard; I don't want to scare the old dear. At first, there's no response, and I begin to wonder if I've picked the one night of the year when Iris Lockhart stays at bingo till midnight or takes her annual holiday at the coast or somewhere. I raise my fist to knock harder in case she's deaf. But then I catch a shuffling noise from within. Growing louder, coming towards me.

I can make out a slight wheeze from behind the door. It's taken it out of her just getting here from the living room or wherever she was. Or maybe her lungs are just shot to pieces from smoking or a lifetime in the city, or both. She clears her throat and then a hoarse London accent asks, 'Who is it?'

'Oh, hello, Mrs Lockhart,' I say, putting on my friendliest voice. 'Very sorry to disturb you. I'm a colleague of Dan's. We work together in Putney.'

'Daniel? Is he all right?' Her tone is concerned, now. I've got her interested.

'He's fine,' I reply. Then I speak more quietly, for dramatic effect. 'But he's doing a sensitive operation at the moment and he asked me to give you some news about him.'

'What news? What's goin' on?' She sounds a bit panicked.

'It'd be easier if we can talk inside. I know it's late, but it won't take a moment. I can't really explain from out here, though, due to the nature of the job. I'm sure you'll understand…'

I hope she doesn't call my bluff by ringing Lockhart to check.

'What did you say your name was?'

'Detective Constable Amy Lucas.'

She doesn't respond. I make a *brrr* noise, followed by another sound of obvious discomfort.

'Are you all right?' she says.

'Yes, it's just – ah – it's started raining out here.'

There's a silence, and I wonder if I've blown it. If I'm going to need to use force or threats rather than charm to get to her.

Then she says, 'Hang on, love.'

A lock clicks over and I hear a chain sliding back.

The door opens.

*

The rain began to fall as they drove to St George's Hospital, and Lockhart flicked on the wipers to clear the windscreen. He was trying to process what Green had just told him.

'You think the Op Braddock rapist knew you,' he said. 'As in, you also know who he is?'

'Yeah, well, I don't *know* who he was. But I think I may know him. Or have met him. It was how he looked at me, you know? Like he recognised me. And his voice...'

'Could it be someone you came across professionally?'

'I dunno.'

Lockhart turned his head and saw that she had her eyes closed, her mouth drawn into a kind of grimace. She'd wrapped her arms around herself. He willed her to think, to remember something, anything about this guy. But he knew he had to go slowly; she'd still be in shock, and there would be plenty of time for her to give a full statement tomorrow. Maybe it'd come back to her after she'd slept on it. If she was able to sleep. He was wondering whether to leave it or ask her something else when the trill cut through his thoughts.

His phone was ringing.

It was the call he'd been waiting for all night.

He swiped at the screen.

'Jock.'

'It's active, Sarge.'

The adrenalin stabbed in his belly and coursed through his limbs. He felt a tingle in his hands and feet. 'OK, where?'

'Bermondsey.'

Lockhart's mouth was suddenly dry, the sensation in his stomach turning to a creeping coldness.

'Sarge?'

He blinked a few times. 'Is the target moving?'

'Aye. Well, it was a minute ago.'

'Send me the co-ords right now,' Lockhart said, though he already had a good idea where they would put the phone, and Logan with it. He should've seen this coming. But now wasn't the time to think about that.

'Nae problem.' Jock rang off.

'What's going on?' asked Green.

'Sorry, Lexi.' He stamped on the brake and swung the Defender round in the road. 'That X-ray's gonna have to wait.'

CHAPTER EIGHTY-NINE

Lexi instinctively braced herself with one hand on the dash and the other on her door as Dan hit the gas. She saw the needle pass fifty miles per hour and heard the blaring of horns as he wove in and out of traffic on the crowded roads. The rain was coming down harder now, the Land Rover's headlights cutting through it as the windshield wipers fought against the barrage.

'I can drop you somewhere on the way,' he said.

'Hell, no,' she replied. 'I'm coming with you.'

Dan glanced at her, but didn't say anything. His face was illuminated every couple seconds by oncoming cars and Lexi could see his features were set hard.

'What can I do?' she asked.

'Grab my phone,' said Dan. 'Open an app called Telegram.'

She did as instructed and described what she could see: a message from Jock containing a bunch of digits.

'OK. Copy those numbers and paste them into Google Maps.'

'Got it.'

Lexi held her finger on the screen and noticed her fingers were shaking. Maybe it was the after-effects of what'd just happened to her in the park. Perhaps it was her body's response to being driven through London at twice the speed limit. Or maybe it was because Dan had just told her who they expected to find at these GPS co-ordinates.

Blaze Logan.

He'd offered her the chance to bail out. Despite being terrified of this woman, and knowing the danger she posed to anyone who got in her way, Lexi had refused. She wasn't sure why she'd done that, only that it felt like the right thing to do.

Google Maps brought up a crossroads in Bermondsey. 'Corner of Clements Road and Drummond Road,' she stated.

'That'll be the nearest cell tower,' he said. 'I'm betting it's no coincidence that it's the same place that I grew up.'

'Serious?'

'And where my mum still lives.'

'Jesus, Dan.'

Lexi was suddenly thrown right and then left as he spun the wheel one way then the other to overtake a van.

'I need you to call Max Smith,' Dan said, nodding at his mobile. 'She's in my contacts. Tell her where we're going and to get herself and the units in Chelsea over there on the hurry-up. Get Khan and Guptill back in. Tell her who's involved.'

'Sure.'

'And make sure she keeps the backup low-key. I don't want Logan getting spooked and… You know, if she's got my mum.'

Lexi nodded, then instinctively pushed herself back in the seat as they ran a red light. Pain shot through her ankle and she screamed. Dan slammed his hand on the steering wheel and the horn blasted as they ploughed across a junction, causing squeals of brakes to both sides.

'Sorry,' he said.

A stupid thought came to Lexi about Brits apologising all the time and she almost laughed.

She opened the contacts list to find Max Smith. She'd typed *M-A* when the screen switched to an incoming call. She held it up for him to see who it was.

Mum.

*

I've told him what I want. Where he needs to meet me. What's at stake if he doesn't do exactly what I say. What will happen if he asks for backup or tries to seal off the area. Those instructions were so much more effective coming from his dear mother. Particularly as it took her a few goes to get the words out through her whimpering and stammering.

I told her that no one needs to get hurt. That I just wanted to speak to her son. Clearly, that's not true, and I don't think she believed it. She asked me if I was that woman off the telly, the one in the news about the recent murders. Iris Lockhart may be old, but she's not daft, I'll give her that. There was no point denying it. She thought about this for a minute before asking me if I wanted to kill her son.

Since she knew who I was, I didn't think there was much point denying that, either.

She went very quiet. Then she told me that her son wouldn't be scared of me. That he'd killed people, too. More than me, in fact, as if it was a competition. That he didn't like it, but he did it when he had to. When he had no choice. And that he'd kill me if need be. I said he'd be welcome to try.

The fact is, I'll always have the edge over him, because he has something I don't. He's got a conscience. I wouldn't think twice about throwing an old lady off the roof of an eight-storey apartment block. And while that would haunt Dan Lockhart every day for the rest of his life, I wouldn't lose a wink of sleep over it. He knows that.

And that's why he'll do what I say.

Now I just need him to arrive. I can hear the rain hammering on the balcony. No sense going outside yet.

Probably got time for a cup of tea while we wait.

*

Lockhart was driving so fast that he half-expected to be pulled over by a police car. Or cause an accident. But he didn't care. After hearing the terror in his mum's voice there was only one thing on his mind. And he'd already decided he wasn't responsible for whatever happened to Blaze Logan.

He'd disregarded her instructions and ordered backup anyway, stressing to Smith that there should be no blues and twos, just unmarked vehicles and as little sound as possible. Lockhart was confident that Logan wouldn't be escaping this time. But the priority had to be Mum's safety.

They arrived outside the building that held so many child-hood memories for him, now dark and eerily silent in the lashing rain. He brought the Defender to a hard stop and unbuckled his seatbelt.

'Stay here,' he told Green and, without waiting for a response, he was out of the Defender and running across to Mum's block.

Logan had told him to head up to the roof. But she thought he was twenty minutes away, oblivious to the fact that he'd traced her phone and was almost there when she'd got his mum to call. That gave him an advantage.

Think like your enemy.

If Logan was in his mum's flat, she'd take the nearest walkway to the roof. Which meant that if he took the fire escape at the side, he might get there first.

Lockhart picked up his pace to a sprint.

CHAPTER NINETY

I grab Iris Lockhart by the arm and half-pull her up the stairs. She's shuffling and groaning with the effort, making a massive deal out of it. As if I'm trying to make her climb Everest without oxygen. I could live without this. But there's no other way up, given that the piece of shit elevator is out of action. It takes for ever, but eventually we reach the top.

'Get out there,' I tell her, shoving her through the door and onto the roof.

She stumbles, falls forward and crashes to the concrete, crying out at the impact. Probably broken her wrist or hip or something, like old people do when they fall over. The rain is hammering down and already soaking into her nightdress. I feel no pity for her. She looks up at me defiantly, clutching her arm.

'Daniel won't let you get away with this,' she says, a hard edge to her voice. Then she grimaces in pain and rolls onto her back on the wet ground.

'Shut the fuck up,' I tell her.

Now I just need *Daniel* to arrive. He won't do anything risky when he gets here, not with his mum one good kick away from a heart attack. I've been fantasising about killing him for the past two weeks. The final act of retribution for what happened to me, for the old life that was taken away from me, before a new life can begin, and I'll—

The wind goes from me as I hit the deck, my forehead slapping the ground. It's like a sack of rocks has been dropped on my back from above and, a second later, I realise it's him.

Lockhart is here already, before me, behind me, above the exit door, and he's got the step on me now. How in fuck's name did he?… But there's no time to think about that. There's only time to fight.

He's wrapped his arms around me, pinning me down, but I half-roll and manage to throw a headbutt backwards. I hear it connect with his face and know I've done some damage. I try another but it misses. Then I feel an arm snake around my neck, like he's trying to choke me out, so I open my mouth and bite him. Hard.

He growls and the arm goes slack a second, so I fling an elbow behind me. It hits him, but he keeps moving, shifting his weight. For a second, I can feel the pain in my head where it met the concrete and, as I struggle to get free, a fist collides with my face. My vision explodes into a shower of white dots on black and, before I can recover, he's on top of me.

I hear him yelling at his mum to get downstairs. To go. And he punches me again.

I can taste my own blood. Or maybe it's his, from where I bit him.

I put up my hands in defence. But it doesn't work.

He's in the zone, just like me when I kill.

And the punches keep raining down.

Then a thought pops into my head: *it wasn't meant to end like this.*

*

Lexi looked out through the windshield at the pouring rain, and wondered what was happening up there. Dan had told her to stay here. He was probably right. Blaze Logan was a violent serial murderer with zero empathy who'd kill anyone that tried to stop her. Dan was tough; he was an ex-soldier with training in how to handle this kind of situation. It was his mom who was in danger. And what could Lexi do with a busted ankle? She was best off waiting until the help arrived from Max Smith and the others. Yeah, that'd be the sensible thing to do. Stay right here.

She unbuckled her belt and opened the door, levering herself out and into the storm.

Putting as much weight as she could on her good leg, she hobbled over to the stairwell closest to the car. It wasn't where Dan had gone, but it looked as though it led to the roof. The pain of that short distance was almost too much to bear, needles jabbing her ankle every time it flexed. She was relieved to see an elevator just inside the door.

Then mad as hell to find it broken. She swore aloud.

Supporting herself on the wall, she followed the stair signs around the corner. It was eight floors to the roof. She gripped the handrail and, one step at a time, began to half-hop, half-drag herself up.

*

Smith was in the back seat of a patrol car, racing along the road she imagined Lockhart had taken a few minutes earlier. Riding up front were the uniformed officers they had roped in to help search the park where the Braddock suspect had attacked Green. They'd had to let that bastard go, for now, if he wasn't already long gone. The call Green had just made from the guvnor's phone trumped any other emergency.

Smith briefly wondered what the two lids in front of her had bargained for when they started their shifts earlier this evening. They probably hadn't anticipated going after a serial rapist, let alone a serial murderer. But the woman driving knew what she was doing, taking the other side of the road to bypass lines of traffic while the guy beside her used the blues and twos to clear a path when needed. Both of them looked calmer than Smith felt, her pulse going like the clappers in anticipation of catching this killer, a woman like no other she'd encountered.

The challenge was going to be keeping low profile when they got nearer the location. Lockhart had told her about the potential risk to his mum, and Smith already knew how volatile Logan could be.

Smith had an Airwave radio in one hand, her mobile in the other, and was working both furiously to co-ordinate the arrival of the MIT surveillance cars from Chelsea as well as more local units. Khan had changed direction and was on his way, too.

Whatever happened, there was no chance of Logan getting away this time.

✳

Lockhart felt as though someone else was in control of his body. The sides of his vision had whited-out, and all he could see were his fists pounding Logan, crunching against the bones of her face, drawing blood. It was as if watching Logan hurt his mum had flipped a switch and he'd gone beyond the fight-or-flight Green always talked about, beyond survival instinct, and into some other state.

Revenge mode.

Then the image came to him. That house in Afghanistan.

Suddenly, he was on top of the Taliban sniper, striking his head over and over.

For a few seconds, Lockhart didn't know where he was.

And he froze.

CHAPTER NINETY-ONE

I knew it wouldn't end like this. That it wasn't *supposed* to finish this way. And, sure enough, Lockhart is bottling it. He's stopped hitting me, his eyes are wide and unfocused, like he's seen a ghost, and I feel some of the tension leave his body. I don't need any further invitation.

I take my chance.

Grabbing his wrists, I pull one forwards and push the other back. Then I throw my legs over his shoulders, locking my right ankle under my left knee behind his back. I squeeze my thighs and I can feel them tighten around his neck in the *triangle* choke. There's nothing he can do, now.

No escape.

In Mixed Martial Arts, this is the point where your opponent taps out, the referee steps in and the fight is yours. But there's no referee here, and no rules. One of us is getting thrown off this roof. And it's not going to be me.

So I show him no mercy.

I squeeze until his body goes limp, and I know he's passed out. I unlock my legs and slide away on the wet ground, getting out from under his dead weight and standing. I take a moment to breathe. Then I kick him, hard, in the ribs, and again, harder. He's unconscious, but it's still satisfying. I can picture the detective in LA who screwed me over. Who 'failed' to find any criminal negligence by the film company for my accident. And I kick and stamp some more. I hear something crack.

Now, it's time to finish this.

I grab Lockhart's feet and begin dragging his body towards the edge of the roof. He's heavier than he looks.

I smile to myself, thinking about the mess he'll make when he hits the ground.

It's a long way down.

*

Smith had made sure that the uniformed officers she was with killed the lights and sirens at least two minutes before they arrived, then parked the patrol car out of sight behind the adjacent housing block. She told one officer to stay in the vehicle with the radio, ready to direct the backup when they arrived, and took the other officer with her.

Against the driving rain, they advanced cautiously towards the location they'd been given by Lockhart, a junction of two roads with high-rise flats on one side, and an empty, closed industrial park on the other. The right-hand block was the address Lockhart had given for his mum's place. Assuming Lockhart was right about Logan targeting his mum, that was the most likely spot to find them. But the building was enormous, eight storeys tall and spanning an entire block.

At the far end, she noticed the guvnor's Defender, half up on the pavement. It was empty. It made sense that he was someplace inside the block, but where was Green? She'd been with him in the vehicle as he drove here, because she'd made the phone call. Smith dismissed the question for now; the priority this minute was working out where to go.

She knew that half a dozen others from her team were on the way, plus more uniforms, and she'd need to deploy them once they arrived. If Logan was in the building, then covering each exit they could find was the most logical course of action.

Lockhart's mum's flat was number eighty-two, four floors up, but they'd have to be very careful about how they approached it, given the threat Logan posed. Maybe a walk past by a plainclothes detective, once everyone else was in place, to get eyes on—

Smith's planning was interrupted by a sight that immediately looked wrong.

An older woman, small and frail, had limped out of the nearest stairwell at the bottom of the building. She wore a nightdress and was soaking wet, her thin white hair plastered to her head. She was clutching one arm to her chest, and appeared to be in pain. Smith had never met Lockhart's mother, but it was a fair guess that's who this was. She ran over.

'I'm DS Max Smith. I work with Dan Lockhart.'

'I'm his m-mum, Iris.' The poor woman was shivering. She raised a bony finger. 'Daniel's up there,' she gasped. 'On the roof.'

'The roof?'

'Yeah.'

'Shit.' That made it more complex than if they were inside an apartment. Smith needed a moment to think. She took off her down jacket. 'Here you go.' She wrapped it around Iris Lockhart's shoulders.

'Thanks,' she stammered, her teeth chattering.

'Is he with Blaze Logan?' she asked. 'That's the woman who's been on the news about—'

'Yes. She's up there, too. They were fighting.'

'Was there another woman with your son?' asked Smith, gesturing towards the block. 'Late twenties, about the same height as me, long dark hair?'

'Nope. Didn't see no one else.'

Where the hell was Green?

'Can you get to the roof another way?'

'Yeah, there's a stairwell at each end. And a fire escape on the side.'

Now Smith knew where Green was. And her threat assessment had just gone up a notch. There was an unarmed, untrained civilian up there in the company of a serial murderer.

She heard an engine and turned. The first car had arrived. Khan was behind the wheel. And he had his game face on.

*

After what felt like a lifetime hauling herself up hundreds of steps, climbing half of them on her hands and knees, teeth gritted against the pain in her ankle, Lexi emerged onto the roof. Wind and rain battered her face as her eyes adjusted to the darkness. Her brain took a moment to process what she was seeing. Then the dread began to seep into her stomach.

A hundred feet away, Blaze Logan was bent over, dragging Dan towards one side of the roof. He was on his back, legs together and arms spread wide like a crucifixion, his body offering no resistance. Was he dead? Was she going to throw him over? They were almost at the edge.

There was no time to think. Lexi had to act.

'Hey!' she yelled.

The woman stopped, and slowly turned her face up sideways towards the sound. An image came to Lexi from a wildlife documentary she'd seen, where a lioness had dragged its kill into the bush. Just like the lioness, Blaze had blood on her cheeks and around her mouth, her eyes so dark they appeared dead. A predator with her prey.

Then she smiled, a slow, wicked, malevolent grin. She let go of Dan's ankles, his legs slapping against the concrete. For a moment, Blaze stood over him, like she was checking for signs of life. Then she stamped on his face. Lexi winced at the sickening sound it made, involuntarily shutting her eyes.

When she opened them a second later, Blaze Logan was walking towards her.

CHAPTER NINETY-TWO

All Lexi wanted to do was run over to Dan, to make sure he was still alive, to get him help. But all she *could* do was stand still, rooted to the spot by fear. She was the prey, powerless to move as the lioness approached. As if playing dead was the best way to survive. Blaze Logan made the briefest stumble, but kept her balance and was now just a few yards away from Lexi.

'You a cop?' she demanded.

'No,' replied Lexi, hoping Blaze couldn't see the tremble she felt in her legs. 'I'm Dan's therapist.'

Blaze snorted a laugh. 'His *therapist*?'

'And I'm his… friend.' She wasn't sure where that line had come from. She knew it would achieve nothing with Blaze, except maybe increasing the risk of something bad happening.

'What are you doing here?'

'I was with him in the car.'

'I told him no backup.'

'I'm not backup.'

'No shit. You can't even stand up straight.'

Lexi tried to hold her nerve. Her heart was hammering in her chest, her pulse thumping in her neck. She had no doubt this woman would kill her, given half a chance, if it suited her.

Blaze looked past her into the doorway from which Lexi had just emerged. 'There any more of you?'

'No.'

Blaze narrowed her eyes and sniffed, as if trying to smell the lie.

'I swear,' Lexi added. 'It's just me.'

'So, what the fuck do you want?' Blaze almost seemed amused by Lexi's presence, as if it didn't even register as a challenge, merely a distraction.

Lexi hesitated. Flexed her hands. 'I want to tell you,' she began, her mouth dry despite the rain now drenching her, 'that I know what you've been through.'

'You *what?*'

'Yeah.' She had to hold firm, to give Smith and the others longer to get here. To buy Dan some time... if he was still... *Come on, Lexi.*

'I-I know about the accident on set,' Lexi continued. 'I know it wasn't your fault, and you want someone to take the blame. That's why you've chosen these people, for what – or who – they represent. They become the figures of your hatred. And every time you beat one of them to death, it's like it restores you, somehow.'

Blaze took a couple steps forwards. 'How do you know this?'

'I'm a psychologist,' Lexi replied. 'I researched the accident, put it all together.' She paused, searching Blaze's expression for any hint of understanding, of empathy, of mercy. There was nothing. Lexi had to appeal to the psychopath. *What motivates a psychopath?* 'I know you want payback.'

Blaze said nothing. She looked as though she was working out her next move. But Lexi had her attention, at least.

'I can help you get revenge,' said Lexi.

'What, by helping me drop Dan Lockhart off the side of this building?'

'No. I'm talking about the man who assaulted you at the bus stop. He's done it to a whole bunch of women, me included. You were strong enough to fight him. And you were the only one who saw his face. Tell me what you remember about him. Something distinctive about his appearance. Anything at all could help catch him. You'll want to get the hell away after tonight, I'll bet. But we can look for him in London. Stop him hurting anyone else.'

'I don't give a shit about anyone else.'

'I know.' Lexi held up her palms. 'But you do want revenge for him stabbing you, right? He'd get a long time in jail. And you know what happens to rapists inside. He'll pay for his crimes, believe me.'

Blaze took one deep breath. Lexi knew she could flip back into attack mode in a second, if she said the wrong thing. Made the wrong move. Stopped playing dead.

'Let me get him back for you,' said Lexi. 'I want him to pay too, whoever he is.'

Blaze seemed to be considering the offer. It seemed like a whole minute before she spoke again, though it was probably just a few seconds.

'OK,' she said. Then she described a detail about the rapist's face.

A chill ran through Lexi's body, because she recognised it. And she knew who he was. She felt sick, unsteady even on her good foot.

Eight floors below, an engine revved, and a siren whooped.

Blaze half-turned towards it. 'You lied about the backup,' she stated.

'I didn't.' Lexi swallowed. 'I promise.'

'Stay right where you are. I'm going to finish this, now. And if you try and stop me,' she said calmly, 'you're going over the edge. Understand?'

Lexi nodded silently.

Blaze began walking away from her. She pitched a little to one side before regaining her balance. 'I hope someone's filming this,' she said over her shoulder. 'It's showtime.'

*

Smith had thought she was getting things under control. Where the others had hesitated, Khan had volunteered to go up the stairwell. His objective was to help Lockhart detain Logan. Failing that, he was simply to protect Green and get her out of there. It was a brave thing to do.

There were paramedics on the way, too. Smith needed one to look after Iris Lockhart, who appeared to be slipping into early-stage hypothermia, and others for... well, it all depended what happened on the roof. She had been thinking about heading up herself to give the guvnor some backup when the unthinkable had happened.

A patrol car had swung into the road at top speed, sirens blaring, lights flashing.

The vehicle skidded to a hard stop beside them. Porter got out.

'Where are they?' he cried.

Before she could respond, there was a scream from high up on the building.

Smith tipped her head back to locate the sound, just in time to see a body in the air at the side of the block. It seemed suspended for a second.

Then she realised it was falling to the ground.

DAY EIGHTEEN

CHAPTER NINETY-THREE

Smith knocked on the front door and took a step back. It was 11 p.m. and they'd chosen this time to make the arrest for two reasons. One, it'd taken most of the day to piece together enough circumstantial evidence for a sympathetic magistrate to issue the arrest and search warrants. Two, you were always more likely to find people in their homes at night, especially if they weren't expecting a visit from the cops. This scumbag probably thought he was in the clear. Well, he had another thing coming.

There was no response from inside. Smith threw a glance behind her at Eddie Stagg, who shrugged, craning his neck to check the upstairs windows. She knocked again, harder this time, and heard some movement from within. Maybe the occupants had already gone to bed, and it was a case of waking them up. Whatever needed to be done, she wasn't going home empty-handed. They had assembled a small team of detectives from Wandsworth CID to search the house. It was just a question of how they got over the threshold.

Twenty-four hours had elapsed since the crazy events of last night and Smith was still trying to make sense of it all. According to Lexi Green, one of Blaze Logan's final acts before throwing herself off the building was to pass on a crucial detail about the rapist's appearance that had enabled the psychologist to identify him.

Green's theory was that Logan was concussed from her fight with Lockhart and, when combined with the wet roof, had missed her footing during an attempt to escape the police by jumping between two of the blocks. If she'd made it, it might've worked. They only had the exits of one building covered, so in theory she could've got away. Smith wondered if it was Porter's arrival which had prompted her action. The timings fit, certainly.

Ultimately, though, they'd never know exactly what was going through Logan's mind before she fell eight storeys to her death. Or, perhaps, at any point before that. Green had her theories, of course. And Smith might give them a bit more credit in future. Had the guvnor been right, that Green's mind-reading wasn't so different to her own instincts?

On the subject of coppers' noses, Lockhart was lucky to get away with a broken one, plus a fractured cheek, several missing teeth and a couple of cracked ribs. If Green's account was accurate, Logan had been seconds away from chucking the guvnor off the roof when she'd intervened. Khan – who'd arrived moments after Logan's jump – had been able to help Green stop him bleeding and use his radio to direct the paramedics straight to the roof. Lockhart was recovering in hospital now, and Smith already knew his facial injuries would be as much the source of good-natured teasing as respect for taking on a violent killer barehanded. They all understood that gallows humour was one way to get through the trauma.

But Smith reckoned it'd be a while before she could forget the image of that body falling, the second one she'd seen in the past year.

The memory of it was interrupted by the sound of footsteps behind the door.

'Who's there?' It was a woman's voice.

'This is the police,' Smith announced.

A pause was followed by the sound of a lock turning and chain being taken off. The door opened. The woman looked half-scared, half-confused. Behind her, at the bottom of the stairs, stood the man they were after. Smith registered the detail that Logan had given them: two raised, dark moles, a centimetre apart just on his left cheek.

'Xander O'Neill,' said Smith, 'I'm arresting you on suspicion of the attempted murder of Blaze Logan, also known as Millicent Dimmock, the sexual penetration of Emma Harrison, and the attempted sexual assault of Alexis Green.' There were more offences, but this was a solid start.

As Smith read out the full caution and explained the warrant, Stagg stepped through the doorway, past O'Neill's horrified housemate, and cuffed him. He seemed so taken aback by their arrival that he didn't resist. He didn't even speak. The young actor appeared to have lost all the bravado Smith had seen when she'd met him in Jemima Stott-Peters's house in Wimbledon nearly three weeks ago.

Stagg marched him out to their car, while Smith led the other detectives inside to begin the search. This wasn't the only location they were hitting. From his hospital bed, Lockhart had told her about O'Neill's locker at the climbing wall in Parsons Green. Roland Wilkins, to his credit, had volunteered to go there with another officer and bag up anything of relevance inside. And they still had a whole load of O'Neill's clothing that hadn't been returned to him following his recent arrest. Now, that could be properly tested for forensic evidence of his crimes.

Smith took out her phone to text Lockhart about the arrest. On her home screen, she saw several messages from Wilkins: a text and three photos. The text said they'd already bagged and tagged the contents of O'Neill's locker. She was impressed; the young DC seemed to be getting his act together, and she made a mental note to thank him, help build his confidence a bit.

Then she opened the pictures one by one and gave a sharp intake of breath, followed by a fist pump and an audible whoop.

The images showed a black jacket, a balaclava, and a knife.

TEN DAYS LATER

CHAPTER NINETY-FOUR

'Here you go,' Lockhart said, as he put the plates down on his dining table. 'Sorry it's nothing fancy.'

He'd used the excuse of getting back late after dealing with a shedload of paperwork, but the real reason he was serving a simple meal of sausage and mash was because he didn't know how to make anything more complicated. And he needed a tried-and-tested recipe, since this was the first time that he'd hosted anyone other than his mum to dinner at his flat. His *and Jess's* flat.

'This looks awesome,' said Green. 'Beats the hospital canteen any day.'

'Oh, cheers.'

'It's a compliment, love,' said his mum. 'Wasn't it, Dr Green?'

'Sure it was.' She grinned. 'And please, Mrs Lockhart, call me Lexi.'

'All right then.' Mum picked up the fork in her crooked, swollen fingers, jabbed a piece of the sausage Lockhart had already cut up for her and raised it towards Green. 'As long as you call me Iris.'

'Deal.'

They set about eating and Lockhart was relieved to find that his culinary efforts were halfway edible. He listened as Green described her and Sarah's plan to find a new housemate after getting rid of Rhys, the weird guy Lockhart had run into at her place. Apparently, he'd refused to part company with the 'collector's' knife Green had found in his room, so she and Sarah had decided to kick him out.

He half-thought of suggesting Khan as a potential replacement for Rhys... He'd told Lockhart this week that he was on the lookout for a new place to live, having finally decided to move out of his family home. There'd been a bust-up, apparently, after Khan had refused an arranged marriage that his parents wanted. It must've been tough, but Lockhart was confident the lad would find his feet and enjoy his independence. Maybe he'd mention it to Green later. But he'd understand if she wanted to get some distance from the MIT, after these past few weeks, rather than live with one of them.

Lockhart took a swig of Stella from the can and looked from his mum to Green and back. They were each making progress recovering from their injuries.

Mum had fractured the ulna bone in her forearm, and it was in a cast and sling, now. But it would heal soon enough, and she was showing no lasting effects of the mild hypothermia she'd experienced after being soaked on the roof that night. Green's ankle was badly sprained from her chase with Xander O'Neill, and she still used a crutch on stairs, but it didn't need surgery. Green had even said she'd be back to CrossFit in a few more weeks.

As for Lockhart, his face was a mess, but there was nothing new about that. Doctors had said the swelling and bruising would go, eventually. It was the stuff left behind in his memory that worried him. That was why he'd resolved to see the other therapist Green had recommended to him three months ago. Better late than never, he told himself.

'That nice woman you work with, Daniel – what's her name again?'

'Dunno, Mum. Was it Max? DS Smith.'

'That's the one. Smith. She told me you saved Daniel's life, Lexi.'

'Uh, I don't know about that.' Green was blushing. 'Honestly, I wasn't even thinking. It was just instinct.'

Mum laid her free hand on Lockhart's forearm. 'Well, whatever it was, it worked. He's the only one I've got now, since his dad died, and…' she cleared her throat, 'he's very precious to me. So, thank you.'

'You're welcome.' Green paused a beat. 'I owed you one anyway, right, Dan?'

Lockhart laughed and a stab of pain went through his ribs. He bent forwards, clasping a hand to his side. 'Don't do that to me. No more jokes, OK?'

'It wasn't a joke.'

Their eyes met briefly, and Dan suddenly thought how beautiful she was. He immediately felt guilty and looked down at his plate, busying himself by piling mash onto his fork.

'Liz Jennings is out of a coma,' he said through a mouthful of potato, shifting topic slightly. 'I spoke to her nurse today. She's already making progress on the rehab. They're hoping there's not going to be any lasting damage.'

'Thank God,' said Green.

'Poor thing.' Mum shook her head. 'She must've been completely mental, that Logan woman. Barking mad.'

Green swallowed before speaking. 'In some ways, she was. But she'd had some awful things happen to her, and her brain was wired a little differently to ours.'

'Hang on,' said Lockhart. 'Are you saying it wasn't her fault she tried to lob me off a roof?'

'No way. I'm not excusing what she did for one second.'

'OK. Good.' He drank some Stella.

'All I'm saying,' continued Green, 'is that everyone does stuff for a reason. Including serial murderers. Killing four innocent people is totally unacceptable in every sense, but to catch her, we needed to get why she was doing it. The rage she felt and wanted to vent against surrogates.'

Lockhart's attention wandered for a second, then he brought it back.

'Yeah, I think I get that,' he said.

'There you go.' Green inclined her head. 'And despite all the terrible stuff she did, two good things have come out of it.'

'What are they?' asked his mum.

'OK, so, you arrested the guy who'd been raping women at bus stops. God knows how many more attacks he'd have done before he was caught. Logan made that happen.'

'She helped on Op Braddock, I'll give her that.'

'Come on, Dan. She cracked that case.'

He grunted. 'Only cos she wanted revenge.'

'Does it matter?'

'Same as she wanted publicity by tipping the press off about her own murders.' He and Smith had both wondered if it was Khan, but the DC was in the clear after Logan's PAYG phone record showed several calls to an ambitious but sloppy journalist who hadn't bothered verifying the 'Met source' feeding him details of the case. Apparently, he'd done his own work digging up the allegations of sexual assault.

'Oi, let her finish what she was saying, Daniel. What's the second good thing, love?'

'So, after all the media coverage here, they're supposedly opening an inquiry into what happened on the Hollywood movie set that caused Logan's injury, and how it wasn't properly investigated. It could be pretty big time. The *Washington Post* was talking about how it might change the whole stunt industry in the US. Doesn't justify the violence she used, obviously, but it could protect a bunch more people in future.'

'Serious?' Lockhart stopped chewing a moment.

'Yeah.'

He reached for his can of Stella. 'Well, some not-so-good things came out of it, too.'

'Like what?'

'Porter made Detective Superintendent.'

Green took a sip of beer. 'Isn't that good, though?'

'Good? The guy nearly wrecked the whole operation to catch Logan. Multiple times. And they gave him a fucking promotion!'

'Daniel!'

'Sorry, Mum. Apparently, he even used Operation Thorncross as one of his case studies in the process. *Demonstrating leadership under pressure*, or something.'

'Smart.' Green's brow creased. 'But… if they promote him, doesn't that mean he won't be your boss anymore?'

'That is a possibility.'

'All right, then. Quit complaining.'

'I'm not—' Lockhart began, but stopped himself when he saw Green's smile. 'Oh, piss off.'

'Gotcha.'

'He does appear to have dropped the idea of passing my disciplinary case to the DPS for now, at least. The unauthorised entry of Dobbin's flat.'

'And has he forgotten about your hacker friend, too?' asked Green.

'Jock prefers the term "independent security researcher".'

'Fine. Didn't you have to explain how you'd got to the roof before Logan?'

'Oh, that's simple,' Mum replied. 'He happened to be on his way to see me, didn't you, love?' She winked.

'Just like you happened to be waiting alone for a bus all night, Lexi,' he added. 'Not a textbook investigative technique, but it got a result.'

'Point taken.' Green glared at him, then dug into her food.

The doorbell rang.

Mum turned towards the sound. 'You expecting anyone?'

'Nope.' Lockhart stood. 'Lemme see who it is.'

CHAPTER NINETY-FIVE

Lexi watched Dan get up and move towards the door. She slid her chair back a little so she could look down the hallway. Dan peered through the spyhole, straightened up, swore under his breath, then opened the door.

'What do you want?' he said, his voice gruff.

'Christ! You all right, mate? What happened to your face?'

'What do you want?' repeated Dan. 'I'm in the middle of dinner.'

'I just came to—'

'How'd you get in, anyway?'

'Someone was on their way out, and the front door was open…'

The guy standing in front of Dan was good-looking, with short blond hair and bright blue eyes. Lexi guessed he was about forty. She turned her head to the wall in the living room where Dan had posted up all the leads on his wife. Lexi immediately noticed a strong likeness between the photograph of Jess and the man. Their mouths and eyes were almost identical.

'Who is that?' she whispered, even though she had a good idea.

'It's Nick,' said Iris. 'Jess's brother. He and Daniel don't exactly get on.'

'Oh, right.'

In the hallway, Dan said something that Lexi didn't catch. He sounded mad. She knew it wasn't her business, but she couldn't help leaning back across and listening anyway.

'The solicitor says you're going to appeal,' Nick said. 'About Jess.'

'Yeah.'

'So… Mum and Dad and I wanted to see if you'd like to sort it out before the hearing? You know, between us.'

'No chance.'

'It'd save us all a lot of money. Legal fees and that.' Nick spread his hands. 'We don't want this, either.'

'Really? That why you brought the claim, is it?'

'Come on, Dan, don't be like that.'

'Like *what*?'

Nick sighed. 'We all need to face up to it. Jess ain't coming back. The sooner we admit that, the better. I think about her every single day. But we've got to move on.'

'I'm not moving on,' growled Dan.

Nick looked past him and briefly met Lexi's eyes. 'No?'

'No.'

The word felt like a punch to Lexi's heart.

'Just think about it, OK? We can talk, without lawyers. Work something out.'

Dan didn't reply.

'Right.' Nick rocked back on his heels. 'Maybe another time, then. You've obviously got company, so…'

'Fuck off and don't come back.'

'Well, that might not be up to you, mate. Depending on what the magistrate says.'

'I'm not your mate.'

'All right, chill.'

Lexi could see Dan's shoulders tense up, his right fist balled. This wasn't going to end well. 'Should we do something?' she asked Iris.

Beside her, Dan's mom was silent for a second, then she spoke loudly. 'Daniel!'

'Yes, Mum?'

'I need your help in here.'

'Coming.' There was a pause. 'I meant it,' Dan said, quietly but clearly. 'Don't come to this flat again.'

Nick sniffed. 'We'll see about that.'

'Daniel!' Iris called out again.

The door slammed and Dan stomped back into the living room, seething. 'What is it, Mum?'

'Nothing, love.'

'Eh?'

'I just didn't want you getting in another fight.' Iris waved her fork towards the hallway. 'Your face is smashed up enough as it is.'

'Thanks.'

'Forget about him,' said Iris. 'Now, sit down, and finish your dinner.'

TWO MONTHS LATER

CHAPTER NINETY-SIX

It was one of those late spring afternoons that seemed to stretch out indefinitely. But, despite having a day off work, Lockhart wasn't enjoying the sunshine. He didn't mind, though. The long daylight hours gave him more time to search. This was his seventh trip to Whitstable since the end of Operations Thorncross and Braddock. He'd shown Jess's photo to a hundred more people in that time, but no one here had recognised her.

Of course, it was possible that the woman from the missing persons website who thought she'd seen Jess had been mistaken. But Lockhart reckoned he'd have to speak to every single person here before he seriously entertained that possibility.

Up ahead, he saw a fishing boat moored in the harbour. A man was on deck, stacking plastic crates, his boat bobbing gently in the water. Lockhart approached the quayside and unfolded the photo of Jess.

'Excuse me,' he said, 'I'm looking for this woman.'

The fisherman shunted the stack of crates to one side and crossed the deck.

'She's my wife.' Lockhart stooped to pass the picture over the sea wall. The man wiped his hands on his cargo shorts before reaching up and taking the sheet of paper. He studied the image in silence.

This was the moment Lockhart had experienced dozens, maybe hundreds of times. The tiny flutter of hope before the shake of the head.

'Have you seen her?'

The fisherman looked up at Lockhart, as if appraising him, and back to the photograph. Then he nodded slowly.

'Yeah, I might've done.'

He closed his eyes a moment.

Lockhart could feel his palms getting sweaty. The guy seemed lost in thought.

'Couple a years ago,' he said, eventually. 'She was down here. I didn't speak to her. But I remember, cos she's pretty, for one – if you don't mind me saying – and second, she wasn't dressed for the weather.'

There were about a thousand follow-up questions that popped into Lockhart's head. But he settled on the most obvious one.

'What did she do?'

'She was hanging around for a bit, like she was waiting for someone. Then some fella arrived, and they got on a boat together.'

'What did the guy look like?'

The fisherman wiped sweat from his forehead and nodded at the picture of Jess.

'He looked so much like her, they could've been brother and sister.'

A LETTER FROM CHRIS

Dear Reader,

I hope you enjoyed *Who's Next?*, the second book in the Lockhart and Green series. If you did, please do give it a rating, and leave a review if you have time.

If you'd like to know more about my books, please join my mailing list. Your email address will never be shared, and you can unsubscribe from the updates at any time.

www.bookouture.com/chris-merritt

This book is, first and foremost, a work of fiction and entertainment. But there are a number of real-world issues which inspired the subject matter – spoiler alert if you are reading this first! Most notably, gender stereotyping around violence. The psychological research on this is fascinating, and the theories and examples that Green gives are all genuine. Despite the growing culture of strong women in literature, film and TV, as well as in sports, many people still tend not to believe that women can be capable of physical feats they associate with men. And, yet, the evidence to the contrary is compelling.

In addition to this, several sources inspired me to include the 'Operation Braddock' sexual assault sub-plot. The Netflix series *Unbelievable*, which Lexi watches in the book, is an exceptional dramatisation of a real-life serial rape investigation in the US.

There have been cases of serial sex attackers in the UK recently, too, which remind us how vulnerable many of us are to this kind of predator. Sadly, the statistics quoted on prosecutions for these crimes are real, and must improve. I feel great admiration for anyone who could report the experience of being assaulted, or stand up to an attacker any other way.

Thanks again for your support. If you'd like to get in touch, please drop me a line on Twitter, Facebook, or via my website. The next book in the series, also featuring Dan Lockhart and Lexi Green, is scheduled for release in early 2021 – so keep an eye out for that!

Best wishes,
Chris

@DrCJMerritt

@chrismerrittauthor

www.cjmerritt.co.uk

ACKNOWLEDGEMENTS

I'd like to give a huge thanks to the Bookouture team for continuing to do such an incredible job turning my novels from rough manuscripts into the finished product you've just read. They've given unrelenting support and inspiration, despite simultaneously coping with an office move, significant growth, and the impact of a certain pandemic. Particular thanks go to my editor Helen Jenner for making this book so much better, Kathryn Taussig and Jenny Geras for their strategic input, Kim Nash and Noelle Holten for their fantastic publicity work, Alex Crow for turning masses of data into great marketing, Alex Holmes for overseeing audiobook production, and Kelsie Marsden and Martina Arzu for making sure that everything from proof copies to printing happened on time. I also want to thank my agent, Charlie Viney, for his constant guidance and morale-boosting, even if he has now moved to the wrong side of the river.

In terms of content, this book couldn't have been written without the contributions of several experts in their fields. Though many of them have chosen to remain anonymous for professional reasons, they know who they are and will spot their influence on the story. The stunt performers I spoke to were kind enough to give me a glimpse into their extraordinary world of daredevil action, with all its highs and lows. This helped provide the background to Blaze Logan's character. The Major, once again, was generous with his time, explaining the finer points of military culture and operations to me, which enabled Dan Lockhart to have a more authentic personal history. DC Ellie Lawrence kindly answered my strange and seemingly random questions about detective work, while former police analyst Amy Gorman and another two contacts in the Met provided answers about how things are done there. Dr Becky Dudill was, again, on call as my consultant for medical details and procedures. Any mistakes are mine entirely.

Finally, I want to thank everyone who has helped to promote my books, especially the bloggers, reviewers and festival and event curators. It's a wonderful community and over the past year you've all made me feel a part of it. There are too many folk to mention, but I would just like to give a shout to Zoé O'Farrell, Sarah Hardy, Vic Watson and Simon Bewick, Tom Fisher and Ben Cooper-Muir, Bob McDevitt and Lizzie Curle.

Printed by Amazon Italia Logistica S.r.l.
Torrazza Piemonte (TO), Italy

19644654R00246